Soul of the Age

SOUL OF THE AGE

SELECTED LETTERS

OF HERMANN HESSE

1891—1962

EDITED WITH AN INTRODUCTION

BY THEODORE ZIOLKOWSKI

TRANSLATED BY MARK HARMAN

Farrar, Straus and Giroux

NEW YORK

Library of Congress Cataloging-in-Publication Data
Hesse, Hermann, 1877–1962.
[Correspondence. Selections. English]
Soul of the age : the selected letters of Hermann Hesse, 1891–1962
edited and with an introduction by Theodore Ziolkowski ;
translated by Mark Harman. — 1st ed.
1. Hesse, Hermann, 1877–1962—Correspondence. 2. Authors,
German—20th century—Correspondence. I. Title.
PT2617.E85Z48 1991 838'.91209—dc20 [B] 90-27854CIP

Photograph Credits

Following page 10: Hesse at four *H. Fuchs, Calw* / Hesse family *H. Fuchs,
Calw*. *Following page 18:* Calw *Fritz Eschen, Berlin–Wilmersdorf* / Mission school
Aus Privatbesitz / Maulbronn *Sammlung Eleonore Vondenhoff, Frankfurt am
Main*. *Following page 42:* Hesse at 21 *Schiller–Nationalmuseum, Marbach* / The
Petit cénacle Schiller–Nationalmuseum, Marbach / Fiesole, 1906 *Aus Privatbesitz*.
Following page 68: Hesse around 1909 *Martin Hesse, Bern* / Hesse with Maria
and son *Martin Hesse, Bern* / Hesse and Hans Sturzenegger *Aus Privatbesitz*. *Fol-
lowing page 112:* Hesse before outbreak of WWI *Martin Hesse, Bern* / Maria
Hesse *Schiller–Nationalmuseum, Marbach* / Hesse and Ruth Wenger *Schiller–
Nationalmuseum, Marbach*. *Following page 162:* Hesse with Thomas Mann
Sammlung Eleonore Vondenhoff, Frankfurt am Main / Hesse, 1927 *Martin Hesse,
Bern*. *Following page 232:* Am Erlenloh *Schiller–Nationalmuseum, Marbach* /
House on Melchenbühlweg *Schiller–Nationalmuseum, Marbach* / Casa Camuzzi
Schiller–Nationalmuseum, Marbach / House in Montagnola *Martin Hesse, Bern*.
Following page 298: Ninon Dolbin *Aus Privatbesitz* / Hesse with Ninon *Aus Pri-
vatbesitz* / Hesse in Garden *Martin Hesse, Bern* / Hesse, about 1951 *Martin
Hesse, Bern*.

Title page art: watercolor sketch by Hermann Hesse

CONTENTS

INTRODUCTION

Hermann Hesse was an inveterate letter writer. In the eighty years between a note that the four-year-old dictated to his mother in 1881 and the thank-you note that he mailed to a colleague shortly following his eighty-fifth birthday in 1962, he wrote over thirty thousand letters and cards to hundreds of correspondents. Hesse was seemingly incapable of leaving a communication unanswered. In 1934 he observed that "for many years approximately half of my work has consisted in reading and answering the letters that I receive from Germany"—a responsibility that, until 1950, he carried out personally. And although later—especially following the award of the Nobel Prize in 1946, when he received more than seven thousand letters—he often responded with circular letters or acknowledgments printed for special occasions, he took it as a moral commitment to reply to every communication.

This epistolary impulse merits our attention not just, or mainly, because of the impressive output it engendered. When Hesse was still in his teens, his father noted this compulsion in a letter to Hesse's sister Adele. "He writes remarkably many letters. His correspondence evidently compensates for something else." In this sense the letters suggest a compulsive need for communication. But the fact that so much of his intellectual and spiritual energy went into letters rather than literary works suggests yet another dimension of meaning.

Hesse refused to establish a firm line between his life and his literary works. "If you regard literature as confession—and that's the only way I can regard it at present," Hesse confided in his "Diary of 1920," then art amounts to the effort to express as fully as possible the personality of the artistic ego. "I gave up all aesthetic ambition years ago," Hesse confessed in the same spirit to a correspondent in 1926, "and no longer write poetry but simply confession."

Given this pronounced confessional tendency, it is surprising that Hesse undertook no real autobiography—especially since he was a fan of literary biography and developed detailed (though ultimately unrealized) plans to edit a series of classic German autobiographies. However, writings of a generally autobiographical nature occupy an increasingly important place in his oeuvre. During the twenties Hesse produced a number of brilliant autobiographical essays, including "A Guest at the Spa" and "The Journey to Nuremberg." During the two decades between the publication of *The Glass Bead Game* (1943) and his death in 1962 Hesse wrote no further "fiction" as such, but he turned out a steady stream of autobiographical accounts ranging from reminiscences of childhood ("For Marulla") to notes on a summer vacation ("Events in the Engadine"). (Many of these pieces have been collected in the volume *Autobiographical Writings*.)

Hesse's obsession with autobiography was motivated by the symbolic view he held of his life. When Hugo Ball was commissioned by the publisher S. Fischer to write a biography to commemorate Hesse's fiftieth birthday, Hesse wrote to him (October 13, 1926): "If a biography of me makes any sense, it is probably because the private, incurable, but necessarily controlled neurosis of an intellectual person is also a symptom of the soul of the age [*Zeitseele*]." The letters represent not only an act of communication with others but also a continuing record of Hesse's own life—the raw materials underlying both his fiction and the artistically shaped autobiographical writings. In his letters we have the best account of the process of individuation that he attempted to portray symbolically in his novels—the integration of identity that leads, through disillusionment and crisis, by way of analysis, to a sense of unity and cosmopolitanism. In his letters, which are characterized by a relentless honesty, we have the best access to Hesse's intellectual and spiritual world as well as a lively account of the social world in which he lived and the European history that he witnessed.

Hesse came by his confessional epistolary impulse naturally. The preoccupation with incessant self-scrutiny and confession is one of the hallmarks of the Pietism that dominated the spiritual life of that section of Europe in which he spent the first thirty-five years of his life: essentially, that corner of Germany and Switzerland between Basel and Stuttgart where people speak the Alemannic dialect that characterized Hesse's own speech. Hesse's maternal grandfather, Dr. Hermann Gundert (1814–1893), was a Swabian Pietist who spent twenty-four years in the service of the Basel Missionary Society on the Malabar Coast of India. Soon after his return to Europe in 1859 he became director of the Calw Missionary Press, one of the leading German publishers for the dissemination of theological writings. Gradually recognized as one of the leading European authorities on India, he continued his missionary efforts through such publications as a standard Malayalam grammar and a Malayalam–English dictionary as well as translations of the New Testament and parts of the Old Testament into Malayalam. His daughter Marie (1842–1902) married the missionary Charles Isenberg (1840–1870) and bore two sons, Theo and Karl, before she returned to her father's house in Calw following her husband's early death. Hesse's father, Johannes Hesse (1847–1916), was a Baltic German from Estonia who spent four years as a missionary on the Malabar Coast before he was compelled for reasons of health to return to Europe. There he was reassigned by the Basel Missionary Society to assist Dr. Gundert in Calw, where he met Gundert's widowed daughter, whom he soon married.

Marie, like her father, was a tireless writer who, in addition to letters and diaries, also turned out four popular books—including a biography, *David Livingstone, the Friend of Africa*—for the series "The Calw Family Library." Johannes published fifteen books on edifying subjects, ranging from stories based on his experiences in India to training tracts for missionaries and admonitions to "slaves of masturbation." It was into this family of incessantly writing Pietists, who filled their letters, journals, and books with ceaseless self-scrutiny, that Hermann Hesse was born in Calw on July 2, 1877, the second of four siblings: Adele, Hermann, Hans, and Marulla. Because the family never discarded any of the paper that they filled so compulsively with their perceptions and accounts, we have an unusually detailed record of Hesse's early years.

As early as 1881, when his father adopted Swiss citizenship and moved to Basel to teach at a school run by the Basel Missionary Society, Hermann's "violent temperament" was causing his parents great distress, as his mother noted worriedly in her diary. In June of 1883, Grandfather Gundert wrote to Johannes and Marie that "you must have a great deal of patience with Hermann," consoling them with the thought that "it comes from God that our children give us puzzles that make us stand still in perplexity." But only five months later Johannes wrote that Hermann, though a model of virtue at school, was often incorrigible at home. "As humiliating as it would be for us, I sometimes think very seriously that we ought to turn him over to an institution or to someone else's care." Matters improved in 1886 when the family returned to Calw, where his father soon took over the Missionary Press from Grandfather Gundert, who remained until his death a powerful presence in young Hermann's life.

When he was twelve, Hesse was packed off to Rector Bauer's Latin School in Göppingen to prepare himself for the regional examinations that constituted the entry barrier to the famous Württemberg school system in which generations of Swabian intellectuals, including the poets Hölderlin and Mörike and the philosophers Schelling and Hegel, had been educated. As a prerequisite for this free education, Hesse, alone among the members of his family, had to renounce his Swiss citizenship and become a citizen of Württemberg—a move that was to cause considerable difficulty for Hesse during and after World War I.

During the year and a half at Göppingen, later portrayed in his novel *Beneath the Wheel*, Hesse applied himself so diligently that he was among the privileged few who passed the examinations in the summer of 1891. He entered the seminary at Maulbronn, a beautifully preserved Cistercian monastery that was later to provide the setting for his medieval novel *Narcissus and Goldmund*. At first he responded enthusiastically to new friends and the excellent classical education offered to the aspiring young theologians and academicians. But within a few months the hyperactivity that had traumatized his parents reasserted itself. In March 1892 he ran away from school and had to be brought back by officers of the local constabulary. This episode was the prelude to such a severe fit of depression that in May his distraught parents withdrew him from Maulbronn.

For the next year and a half the future Nobel Prize winner was sent from one institution to another. First his parents turned him over to Christoph Blumhardt, a noted exorciser in Bad Boll, who tried to pray him back to health, with the perhaps not surprising result that the troubled youth tried to commit suicide—the first of several attempts. Next he was sent to a home for weak-minded children in Stettin where, as part of his treatment for "moral insanity," he worked in the garden and tutored less able classmates. Following a third abortive attempt, at a school in Basel, Hesse attended the Gymnasium in Cannstatt, where he managed to obtain a certificate of educational proficiency in July 1893. At that point Hesse, insisting that his only wish was to become a writer, persuaded his weary parents to take him out of school, and thus at age sixteen he ended his formal education along with all hope of following the traditional family footsteps into a theological or missionary career.

Initially Hesse signed on as a bookdealer's apprentice in Esslingen, but after three days ran away again and returned to Calw, where for half a year he scandalized the neighbors by his presence and his wild plans to emigrate to Brazil. From June 1894 to September of the following year Hesse settled down to the job of filing gears as an apprentice in Heinrich Perrot's tower-clock workshop in Calw, an experience that gave him a sympathetic insight into the mentality of the town and country folk who populate his early stories.

Finally Hesse seemed to find himself. Signing on as an apprentice in Heckenhauer's bookstore in the university town of Tübingen, he remained in the position for the four years necessary to receive his apprentice's letter. Moreover, his dream of becoming a writer began to materialize. His first poem was published in 1896; he found a coterie of compatible friends who styled themselves the *petit cénacle*—Ludwig

Finckh, Otto Erich Faber, C. Hammelehle, and others mentioned from time to time in his letters; he devoted himself intensively to the study of German literature, especially Goethe and other writers of the Romantic age; and his first volume of poetry appeared late in 1898 under the revealing title *Romantic Songs*. Hesse's correspondence with the writer Helene Voigt, the fiancée of the young publisher Eugen Diederichs, paved the way for the publication of his prose sketches *An Hour beyond Midnight* (1899). In September 1899, with his letter of apprenticeship in hand, Hesse moved to Basel, where he worked in Reich's bookstore until January 1901 and then, until 1903, in Wattenwyl's antiquarian bookstore. In this city dominated by the memory of the philosopher Nietzsche and the cultural historian Jacob Burckhardt, Hesse was introduced to a sophisticated circle of artists and intellectuals in the home of city archivist Rudolf Wackernagel. Meanwhile, he began to establish his own literary reputation with articles and reviews in Swiss newspapers and journals. Although his mother had disapproved of his *Romantic Songs*, which she considered immoral, Hesse hoped to win her approval with the volume *Poems*, which he dedicated to her in 1902. Unfortunately, she died shortly before their publication, yet Hesse—in the curious ambivalence that characterized so many of his family relations—did not even make the short trip to attend her funeral.

With the distance afforded by his new surroundings, he came to grips ironically with the years of his Tübingen *bohème* in *The Posthumous Writings and Poems of Hermann Lauscher* (1901). The work, though published at his own expense, was impressive enough to interest Samuel Fischer, the enterprising publisher who was building up one of Germany's most exciting presses. Hesse's next novel, *Peter Camenzind*, which S. Fischer published in 1904, was an immediate success that brought Hesse international recognition, prizes, and his first financial independence.

In the course of a trip to Italy in 1903 Hesse had met Marie Bernoulli (1869–1963), a professional photographer from the distinguished family of Swiss mathematicians. Over the objections of her father, Hesse married the talented but moody young woman who went by the name of Mia and, nine years older than Hesse, already betrayed the melancholy that was to lead within a few years to severe emotional disturbances. (It is worth noting that both his grandfather Gundert and his father had married older women; Hesse was following an established family pattern. And it is probably no accident that, a year following his mother's death, he was attracted to an older woman who bore her name.) Mia found an old peasant house without gas, electricity, or plumbing in the village of

Gaienhofen on the shore of Lake Constance—a community so isolated that Hesse had to row across the lake even to buy household necessities. Here, in the course of the next eight years, the new couple built a larger and more comfortable house to accommodate the three sons—Bruno (1905), Heiner (1909), and Martin (1911)—who gradually enlarged the family. Less and less secluded in the village that was rapidly transforming itself into an artists' colony, they received frequent visits from writers and especially the musicians—Othmar Schoeck, Fritz Brun, Ilona Durigo, Alfred Schlenker, and others—whom Hesse had met through the mediation of his musically gifted wife.

Meanwhile, Hesse's literary career thrived. He finished his schoolboy novel *Beneath the Wheel* (1906), and his musicians' novel *Gertrude* (1910), while turning out the dozens of popular stories and poems that were incorporated into commercially successful volumes with such titles as *In This World* (1907), *Neighbors* (1908), *On the Road* (1911), and *By-Ways* (1912). Stimulated by frequent trips to Italy, Hesse wrote biographies of Boccaccio and St. Francis of Assisi (both 1904). He began a busy career as a book reviewer, which eventually produced over three thousand reviews during his lifetime. He contributed to the satirical weekly *Simplicissimus*, whose editor, Reinhold Geheeb, had become his friend in 1906. With Ludwig Thoma, Hesse was a founding editor of the liberal-oppositional weekly *März* (1907–1912).

Yet for all these external signs of success—or perhaps precisely because of them—Hesse was chafing inwardly at the thought that he had become simply another member of the bourgeois society of imperial Germany that he detested. At first his dissatisfaction manifested itself in the increasingly frequent trips that took him away from Gaienhofen for weeks at a time—to the alternative community of "nature healers" at Monte Verità near Ascona (1907), for "nude rock climbing" on the Walensee (1910), on lecture trips through Germany and Austria, and annual tours to Italy with various friends. His nomadic urge was not satisfied by these relatively short excursions. In September 1911—barely a month after the birth of his third son—Hesse embarked on the North German Lloyd steamer *Prinz Eitel Friedrich* on a three-month voyage to the East with the painter Hans Sturzenegger. Hesse imagined this trip as an archetypal return to family origins and to the mysteries of the Orient represented by his "Grosspapa" Gundert. In fact, though he climbed the highest mountain in Ceylon (present-day Sri Lanka), explored Singapore, and visited Sumatra, Hesse never set foot on the subcontinent itself or the Malabar Coast where his grandfather and both his parents had been active. And, as he admitted in a letter to his friend

Conrad Haussmann (November 1911), he did not find a people of paradise but only "the poor remnants of an ancient paradisiacal people, whom the West is corrupting and devouring." Only the Chinese won his admiration.

Immediately after his return to Europe, Hesse gave up the house and his life in Gaienhofen and moved his family back to Switzerland, where they lived until April 1919 on the outskirts of Bern. Their house, owned until his death by the painter Albert Welti, provided the setting for Hesse's next work, the artist-novel *Rosshalde* (1914), which eerily foreshadowed the circumstances of the disintegration of Hesse's own marriage. The other major work emerging from these years before World War I comprised the three stories featuring *Knulp* (1915), whose light-hearted surface masks the underlying quandary of Hesse's early heroes, who long for freedom while they are constrained by the bonds of society and its responsibilities.

World War I shattered the last vestiges of the Gaienhofen idyll. Unlike many of his contemporaries in Germany and France, Hesse was appalled by the war and the militaristic mentality that had permeated Europe. At the same time, his loyalty to the country of his birth produced a conspicuous ambivalence in the widely circulated essays (collected in the volume *If the War Goes On . . .*) in which he exhorted his countrymen to pacifism and to a cosmopolitan humanism transcending all crude nationalistic fervor—most conspicuously in an essay of November 1914 that borrowed as its title the famous words from Beethoven's Ninth Symphony, *"O Freunde, nicht diese Töne!"* (*"O Friends, not these sounds!"*). Although his efforts attracted the attention of a few like-minded Europeans—notably Romain Rolland in France—his essays antagonized many former friends and readers, who denounced him as "a viper nourished at the breast" of an unsuspecting audience. The most vivid example was the "Cologne Calumny" of 1915, in which Hesse was attacked as a draft-dodger hiding out in Switzerland to avoid his patriotic duty. (See the letter "Pro Domo" of November 1, 1915.) In fact, Hesse dedicated himself selflessly to German affairs. Turned down for active service for medical reasons (poor eyesight), Hesse put himself at the disposal of the German Embassy in Bern, where he worked for a relief agency for German prisoners of war, editing two newspapers as well as a series of twenty-two volumes for German prisoners of war in France, England, Russia, and Italy.

Then in 1916, while Hesse was under the strain of his relief work as well as the attacks in the German press, his father died, and Mia succumbed to a gradually worsening schizophrenia that eventually necessitated her institutionalization. As a result of these pressures Hesse decided, toward the end of that year, to put himself in the care of Dr. Josef B. Lang, a young disciple of C. G. Jung, in a sanatorium near Lucerne. The experience of psychoanalysis, which extended through some sixty sessions into 1917 and led to Hesse's acquaintance with Jung himself, struck Hesse less as a revelation than as a systematized confirmation of insights he had gleaned from the great works of literature. (He analyzed his attitude carefully in several essays collected in the volume *My Belief: Essays on Life and Art.*) Above all, Hesse learned through psychoanalysis to rise above the conventional notions of right and wrong that had oppressed him ever since his Pietist childhood and to acknowledge the legitimacy of all human impulses. Instead of forcing his thoughts and emotions into patterns prescribed by society, he learned to accept what he called the "chaos" of his own consciousness, where the boundary between good and evil did not seem so clearly defined as in Judeo-Christian ethics. The immediate product of this psychic release was the novel *Demian*, which Hesse wrote in a few weeks late in 1917. The radical ethical ideas of the novel were formulated more systematically in his two essays on Dostoevsky included in the volume *In Sight of Chaos* (1920). Lang remained Hesse's friend until his death in 1945 and crops up in Hesse's letters and narratives under the pseudonyms "Longus" and "Pistorius."

Demian (1919) was published shortly after the war under the pseudonym of its narrator-hero, Emil Sinclair, because Hesse did not wish to be identified with what he now called his "sentimental-bourgeois" works. The deception was so effective that the book received the Fontane Prize for first novels. When the deception was exposed Hesse returned the prize—but not before he had succeeded in winning a new audience with his new authorial persona. By the time the novel appeared Hesse had made a radical break with his own past. In October 1918, just two weeks before the end of the war, he was finally forced to put Mia in a mental hospital. The following April, having wound up his affairs in Bern, he left his sons in the care of friends and moved to southern Switzerland—in order, as he wrote a correspondent that summer, "to survive and heal my private collapse and to attempt on a small scale what Germany must accomplish on a large scale: to accept what has happened, not to shove the guilt onto others, but to swallow it and say yes to destiny." Here in the Casa Camuzzi, a Baroque hunting lodge in the village of Montagnola, above Lugano, where Hesse was to spend the rest of his life, he experienced what he later regarded as the happiest and most productive year of his life. In a surge of activity he wrote several important essays, including "Zarathustra's Return" (an appeal to German youth, calling for spiritual rebirth and published under the pseudonym of Emil Sinclair), two of his finest novellas—*Klingsor's Last Summer* and *Klein and Wagner*—and began the novel *Siddhartha*. In the company of the artists who now constituted his main society—Louis Moilliet, Karl Hofer, Hans Purrmann, Cuno Amiet, and others—he even toyed with the idea of becoming a painter. In any case, watercolor painting became an increasingly important avocation and, indeed, a significant source of income in the twenties (see the letter to Cuno Amiet of January 5, 1919), when the inflation of the German mark forced Hesse for several years, despite the success of his writings, to live from hand to mouth.

The year that followed the liberating euphoria of 1919 was "probably the most unproductive of my life, and thus the saddest," Hesse noted in his "Diary of 1920." In the lull that followed the frenzy of creativity he filled his time with other and more routine activities. With the monthly journal *Vivos Voco*, which he founded and coedited with Richard Woltereck from 1919 until 1921, Hesse continued the cultural criticism that had occupied him during the war, attacking among other things the resurgent anti-Semitism that, to his dismay, he noted in postwar Germany. The creative lull that interrupted the progress of his novel *Siddhartha* was finally overcome in 1921 by two new factors: his growing attachment to the singer Ruth Wenger, and a series of therapeutic interviews with C. G. Jung, whom Hesse visited in Küsnacht. In 1922 *Siddhartha* was completed and published. In early 1924 Hesse was awarded the Swiss citizenship for which he had applied the preceding summer (see his letter of July 26, 1923)—technically, for a restoration of citizenship he had given up as a child—on the grounds that his three sons were Swiss and that the experience of the recent war had taught him that his loyalties lay with his elective country. His divorce from his first wife was granted in the summer of 1923, freeing him for marriage to Ruth Wenger, which took place—despite a growing reluctance evident in the letters of 1922 and 1923—in January of 1924.

While Ruth had been the muse of such works as *Klingsor's Last Summer*, *Siddhartha*, and the charming fantasy *Pictor's Metamorphoses*, Hesse's marriage to the much younger woman seemed misbegotten from the start. Although Hesse was content to spend his winters in Basel and then in Zurich, where Ruth pursued her career and her social activities, his regular return to Montagnola meant long periods of separation, leading in 1927 to a second divorce. During this period, despite all the complaints in his letters about his life of hermitlike solitude, Hesse was actually engaged in a frenzy of activity. His annual trips (since 1923) to the spa at Baden for the treatment of his sciatica (where he always stayed at the hotel Verenahof) and a lecture tour to Germany generated two of his most brilliantly ironic autobiographical accounts, *At the Spa* (1925) and *The Journey to Nuremberg* (1927). He wrote a number of essays, edited works of his favorite writers—Jean Paul, Novalis, Hölderlin, and others—and translated medieval Latin tales into German. In 1926, in another of his characteristic bursts of creative activity, he completed *Steppenwolf*, which appeared the following year simultaneously with a biography by his friend Hugo Ball that had been commissioned for his fiftieth birthday. Yet the mood of despondence that characterized those years was blatantly evident in the bitter poems published in 1928 under the title *Crisis: Pages from a Diary*.

In 1927 Hesse immediately set to work on his next novel. That same year he met an admirer with whom he had been corresponding since her teens, the art historian Ninon Dolbin, née Ausländer (1895–1966). *Narcissus and Goldmund* (1930) became Hesse's most successful work during his own lifetime. And in 1931 Hesse married Ninon and moved with her into a new house in Montagnola, built for them by his friend and patron Hans C. Bodmer, where they were to spend the remainder of their lives. The fruit of Hesse's new happiness and security was the story *The Journey to the East* (1932), in which he paid cheerful tribute to his friends ("Ninon, known as 'the foreigner' " [her maiden name: Ausländer], "Louis the Terrible" [Louis Moilliet], "Longus" [J. B. Lang], and others), to his cultural icons, and even to figures from his own works.

Hesse's last novel, *The Glass Bead Game*, was originally to have been the story of "a person who lives through the great epochs of human history in several reincarnations," as he put it in a letter to Rudolf Pannwitz (January 1955)—a series of parallel lives beginning in prehistoric times, running through the Golden Age of India, the patristic period of early Christianity and eighteenth-century Pietism in Germany, and ending in a pedagogical province in the future. But in the course of its eleven-year genesis, from 1931 until the novel's publication in 1943, Hesse's intentions gradually shifted under the impact of current events. Barely had Hesse and Ninon become established in their new house in Montagnola when, in the spring of 1933, the first wave of emigrants fleeing Hitler's Germany reached their threshold. Hesse had resigned from the Prussian Academy of Arts two years before Hitler's rise to power, for reasons that he explained in his letter of November 1930 to Wilhelm Schäfer. From that moment on Hesse was involved, as he had been during the first world war, in the support of those overrun by political events. In 1934 he joined the Swiss Writers' Union so that he would be in a better position to provide assistance and to intervene on behalf of needy émigrés. Again, however, as had been the case twenty years earlier, he experienced abuse from voices in Germany, as well as from other countries, who were dissatisfied by the efforts of the Swiss citizen to maintain the politically neutral position that he justified in his letter to Arthur Stoll of September 17, 1933.

Unlike many opponents of the Nazis, Hesse was permitted for a good many years to continue publishing his works in Germany. Indeed, when Hesse's publisher, S. Fischer, moved abroad with many of the firm's authors, the National Socialists did not permit Hesse's copyrights to leave Germany. (The rights remained with the "Aryan" branch of S. Fischer, which was managed in Berlin by Peter Suhrkamp until his arrest by the Gestapo in 1944.) For those reasons Hesse came in for abuse from various émigré writers who felt that he had not spoken out publicly against Hitler and that he should have refused to allow his works to appear in Nazi Germany. It was Hesse's position, however, that he could do more good by continuing to make his voice heard within Germany since he was one of the few writers not co-opted by the Nazis who could still be published there. And that circumstance continued until 1939, when the Nazis finally declared his works undesirable and denied their publication by the indirect method of refusing paper for their printing.

During the same period, Hesse began in 1935 to review German books for the Swedish literary journal *Bonniers Litterära Magasin*—an opportunity he exploited in order to make known abroad a host of works, including notably those of Kafka and other Jewish writers, that were ignored by official German propaganda organs. It was this activity that drew upon Hesse the disapproval of Will Vesper, a Nazi spokesman who was piqued in part, no doubt, by the fact that Hesse had replaced him at *Bonniers Litterära Magasin*. (See Hesse's letter of January 1936 to Wilhelm Schäfer.) That same year brought the death of his brother, Hans, through suicide (as detailed in the letter of December 1935 to his cousin Fritz Gundert). In 1943, finally, the Nazis denied publication rights to *The Glass Bead Game*, and Hesse published the novel in Switzerland. This circumstance not only deprived Hesse of the basis for his income, it also cut him off from his principal readership and, hence, the opportunity to make his voice heard in Nazi Germany.

Hesse's home in Montagnola, where he found solace tending his garden, became the place of first refuge for many émigrés—including

Thomas Mann, the socialist publicist Heinrich Wiegand, and the writer Peter Weiss. And Hesse gave financial and personal support to dozens of others. Montagnola represented for scores of Germans a reservoir of traditional German values that were being trampled underfoot by the Nazis. For this reason it is doubly ironic that, immediately after the war, Hesse again, for a brief time, had to experience political attacks by the democratic forces of liberation—this time in the person of Hans Habe, a German émigré serving in the U.S. Army. With the help of such supporters as Thomas Mann and Theodor Heuss, Hesse rapidly set matters aright. But for the third time since the "Cologne Calumny" in 1915, Hesse came to grief for his efforts to maintain his intellectual and ethical independence, as he explained in his letter of October 23, 1945, to Fritz Gundert.

His public vindication came rapidly. In 1946 he received the Nobel Prize for literature for his representation of the classical ideal of humanity and his lofty stylistic values. That same year he was awarded the Goethe Prize of the City of Frankfurt am Main. The remaining years of Hesse's life were as tranquil as his early years had been tumultuous. To be sure, his correspondence steadily increased: in 1948, he noted, between one hundred and five hundred pages of correspondence arrived daily—letters that he increasingly answered with circular letters that he had privately printed for the purpose (see his 1947 "Response to Letters Requesting Help") or with personally initialed postcards bearing a watercolor from his brush. For the last twelve years of his life, to escape the importunities of visitors who ignored the sign politely requesting no visitors, he and Ninon spent July and August in Nietzsche's Sils Maria, where he could meditate and converse quietly with such old friends as Theodor Heuss.

In 1950 Hesse encouraged Peter Suhrkamp, who had courageously maintained the German branch of S. Fischer under the Nazis, to set up his own publishing company, and during the early years Hesse's works provided the main financial basis for that enterprise. (His *Collected Works* were published in six thin-paper volumes for his seventy-fifth birthday in 1952, and the seven-volume *Collected Works* were brought out in 1957 for his eightieth birthday.) In these final years, although he continued to write letters, poems, and personal essays at an astonishing rate despite increasingly poor eyesight, Hesse wrote no further major literary pieces. He lived quietly with Ninon, surrounded by family and friends. He died peacefully in his sleep on August 9, 1962.

Hesse, like the rest of his family an inveterate paper hoarder, saved some thirty-five thousand letters written to him over the years. However, of the estimated thirty thousand letters that he wrote during his lifetime, only about half have survived. (Until he met Ninon in 1927 he did not routinely keep copies of the letters he wrote.) Most letters from the years up to 1900 are extant because they were sent to his parents and sisters, who threw nothing away. The most important of these have been published in a volume that Ninon Hesse edited in the year of her death, *Childhood and Youth before Nineteen Hundred: Hermann Hesse in Letters and Documents 1877–1895 (Kindheit und Jugend vor Neunzehnhundert: Hermann Hesse in Briefen und Lebenszeugnissen 1877–1895* [Frankfurt am Main: Suhrkamp, 1966]). However, little remains from the Gaienhofen years, and the entire correspondence with his first wife, Mia, was lost in a fire. The letters to his second wife were sealed until 1987 and were not available for inclusion in the *Collected Letters*; while the letters to Ninon remain under seal until the year 2017.

Fortunately, several entire correspondences have been preserved and published separately: the engaging exchange with Thomas Mann, extending from 1910 until Mann's death in 1955; the correspondence with Romain Rolland, which documents the pacifistic and cosmopolitan efforts of these two men brought together by their opposition to World War I; the disappointingly trivial correspondence with Karl Kerényi and the frank and revealing one with Hesse's friend, the socialist publicist Heinrich Wiegand; the businesslike communications concerning copyrights, royalties, and details of publication with Peter Suhrkamp; and others. During his own lifetime Hesse published a volume (*Briefe*, 3rd ed. [Frankfurt am Main: Suhrkamp, 1964]) containing letters of general interest. The four-volume edition of his *Collected Letters* (*Gesammelte Briefe*, edited by Volker Michels [Frankfurt am Main: Suhrkamp, 1973–1986]) contains 1,762 letters from the years 1895 to 1962. Altogether, about three thousand, or one tenth, of Hesse's letters are currently available in German. (Most of Hesse's manuscripts are housed in the Hesse collections of the Deutsches Literaturarchiv in Marbach and the Schweizerische Landesbibliothek in Bern.)

The present selection, which comprises some three hundred letters taken from the various collections listed above, seeks to be representative. It includes letters from every period, indeed from virtually every year, of Hesse's life from 1891 to his death in 1962. And it reveals Hesse in every facet of his personality as well as in every modulation of his voice—from the pious posings of the early letters to parents and siblings and the self-dramatizing aestheticism with which he presented himself to school friends, through the increasingly relentless self-exposure of his missives from Gaienhofen, to the often startling frankness of his communications to his psychoanalysts and physicians, the growing circle of writers, musicians, and painters who became the friends of his maturity, the public figures who approached the famous man of letters, and finally the many readers who turned to Hesse over the years for advice and consolation. The unmediated tone of the man emerges from the very haste of the letters, which—at least in the years until 1930— were never intended for publication and which assume that the reader can fill in the examples for the frequent "etc." that punctuate these lines. The ellipses indicated by brackets occur in the German edition and mark omissions to avoid unnecessary repetitions from letter to letter. The notes, which are based on the notes in the German edition, have been revised and supplemented for the needs of readers in the United States.

These letters contain the raw material for the literary works that have drawn millions of readers to Hesse. They reveal the patterns of the writer's daily life, his reading, his health problems, the expression of his beliefs, his habits of composition. But they also echo the relentlessly honest voice of a man striving for his personal individuation, seeking to maintain a position of integrity in a world grown problematic, and hoping through the miracle of communication to demonstrate his commitment to another human being. We see here the aestheticism of the rebellious youth, the dissatisfactions of the young paterfamilias, the moral ambivalence of the war years, the spiritual awakening that followed, the crisis of *Steppenwolf*, the withdrawal into the supratemporal realm of *The Glass Bead Game*, and the ethical tranquillity of the aging Hesse. The life exposed through these letters exemplifies in a very real sense the "soul of the age."

Theodore Ziolkowski

Soul of the Age

TO JOHANNES AND MARIE HESSE

[Maulbronn, after September 15, 1891]

You would probably most like to hear about my life at the seminary. Incidentally, the teachers and I are getting along fine; Klaiber is in the infirmary with a swollen foot, they're taking good care of him there, he's looking quite rosy.

Well, all winter we rise at 6:30, have to be ready by 6:50. Things can get quite hectic in the bathroom; almost all of us wash thoroughly.

At 6:50 we have precatio (prayers). (NB: There are many more of those Latin words from the monastic era—e.g., dormitorium, precatio, recreatio, etc.) During the service, we sing one verse of a hymn first, accompanied on the piano by one of the seminarians. Then the tutor reads aloud the meditation on a passage from the Bible, then comes a prayer, and then more singing. Here's how the singing works: If we sing the first verse of "God Is Faithful" on Monday morning, we sing the second verse after recollection. In the evening we sing the first or second verse of "Command Thy Ways." Then, on Tuesday morning, we sing the 3rd and 4th verse of "God Is Faithful" and in the evening the 3rd and 4th verse of "Command" and so on, until the chorale is over. After prayers comes breakfast—a rather skimpy amount of milk, not that we get enough coffee to give anybody a stomachache either. In addition, each person gets 1½ rolls. My money is running out fast; had to pay 30 pfennigs for the famulus and bursar; 64 pfennigs for fire insurance at the seminary. Then one needs an enormous quantity of copy books, including three for Ovid alone! We have 41 hours of lessons a week, and that's not counting the hours set aside for disputation and homework. But we also get opportunities to go outside—e.g., from 12:30 to 2 o'clock.

I'd appreciate it a lot if at some point you could send me a batch of ordinary scratch pads. There are lots of things I cannot get my hands on here. I don't have much money left, only spent 11 pfennigs on myself for beer once. Many things are very expensive here, and the famulus occasionally adds a surcharge to make up for his trouble. I can eat my fill at lunch and dinner, then there's afternoon snack. Please do remember to send me as many scratch pads as possible, when convenient, of course. I can put the holes in them.

I wasn't exactly displeased to hear we shall not be having French for a while. There will be Hebrew lessons during the French periods. The teachers, particularly the tutors, are mostly very responsive when we have any questions or requests. In my next letter, if it amuses me,

I shall describe for you our daily routine (not the timetable) at the seminary. Yesterday evening I had to draw on my supply of marmalade, and, lo and behold, almost everybody has one to three caches of preserves. They hadn't yet dared own up to them. We're getting better used to one another. I'm in the largest room (Hellas). In our room, we have the top student in the class, the second as well, also the treasurer, the librarian, and this week I am the "censor," i.e., guardian of the honor code (until Saturday evening).

Greetings and a kiss

February 14, 1892

Many thanks for the package. I was feeling well when it arrived, and treated myself to those delicious items right away—not all by myself, a friend came to my aid (cf. *Odyssey*, beta 16).

I think often of noble Polly, such a charming child. I'm glad to hear he's well. Let's hope he won't be on the warpath come Easter. A special thanks to Hans and Marulla for the waffles; Mother should give each of them a special kiss from me!

I'm feeling glad, cheerful, content! I find the atmosphere at the seminary very appealing. Especially the close, open relationship between pupil and teacher, but also the way the pupils relate to one another. Fights rarely last for very long. The other day I couldn't understand some passages in Klopstock, so I went immediately to the tutor and asked him. Nothing much is at stake usually, but contacts like that forge a wonderfully solid bond; there's no sense of constraint whatsoever. While in Göppingen, I was frequently ill-humored and incommunicative for days on end; there was certainly no common bond like that there, apart from the sheer drudgery. There was also considerable mockery of decency, willpower, ideals, etc.; here there's none of that. Nobody dares make fun of art, science, etc. And what a splendid monastery! There is something rather special about discussing linguistic, religious, or artistic matters in one of those majestic cloisters. And it's no longer just a case of two boys chattering: we really delve into the facts, generally ask the teachers questions, and read some relevant literature. I'd like to describe my fellow boarders; I'm sure you'd be interested in hearing about the kind of people I spend my time with.

Well, first my neighbor Hartmann.* He's a hardworking youth; he likes things to be neat and tidy, and hasn't lost the indolent dignity of

* Studied law; later served as mayor of Göppingen, but was deposed by the National Socialists in 1933.

the inhabitant of the capital. He has a very elegant, graceful way of pocketing his pince-nez, and occasionally ventures a witticism. But he can't be made to change his mind, once he has made it up.

Then there's my other neighbor, Hinderer,* a tiny man with the tiny eyes of a mouse. He's light as a butterfly, laughs often but thinks little, also good-natured, musical. He recently ran a few little rubber bands across a small board, and then tuned them; he can play folk tunes, harmonies, and even dance music on it. He's old Holzbog's pet; he's *notatus* in the class book. He goes out walking a lot, is moderate by nature, and has been reading E. Tegnér's *Fritjof Saga* for quite some time.

Of course, I spend most of my time with my friend Wilhelm Lang.† He's a hard worker, his desk is inscribed with the motto "Ora et labora!" He is extraordinarily practical, can make all sorts of things out of a little piece of wood, some twine, paper, etc. He sketches very nicely, especially ornaments, reads Schiller a lot, is a model schoolboy. He's a little smaller than I am, dresses like me, has a nice, cheerful face, and wears chokers. He's always well supplied with apples and butter, which are consumed with considerable help from me. He has a beautiful handwriting, acts as treasurer of the senior class, and on Saturday leaves half his bratwurst uneaten. He's a bit reserved, loves peace and quiet, rarely gets into fights.

Then there is Franz Schall.‡ He's about my height, a serious and industrious fellow. Some call him a philistine, but he's thoughtful, has a finely developed sense of justice. To him duty is all. He's fond of aesthetic things, Schiller's prose, etc.

I should also mention Zeller.§ He's big, broad, frightfully strong. He's an enthusiast, likes philosophy, is crazy about Herder. He knows Christ as "the friend" rather than the Son of God, and is skeptical about the existence of the devil and evil forces of that nature. Moreover, he's talented, has a good prose style, writes occasional poetry infrequently, and has a very good feeling for music. He evidently feels superior on account of his penchant for philosophy, etc. When asked to prove his ideas, he says with a mixture of condescension and annoyance, "That's still quite over your head!" He's clever, not at all sly. He's not interested in intrigue, and is rather intense, has a strange, comical sort of dignity,

---

* Pastor in Stuttgart, later became a professor in Berlin.

† Studied botany in Tübingen; eventually became a professor of botany in Hohenheim.

‡ Teacher of classics at the *Realgymnasium* in Altenburg. In 1930, he began a lively correspondence with Hesse. It was he who translated the motto of *The Glass Bead Game* into Latin.

§ Teacher in Hamburg.

founded a "literary association," which has lots of external paraphernalia, statutes, etc. Zeller is a good judge of people, especially men; he despises childishness in any form, and perhaps all that is childlike as well, and that's no good.

Häcker,* a sharp-witted preacher's son, is talented, funny, likes nibbling, grimaces a lot, and tells lots of very witty jokes in a most solemn and stoical manner. He often regales us with funny historical scenes, and can transform Homer into a street minstrel. He is kind-hearted, not particularly industrious, dignified, given to pathos. He can declaim philosophical essays on omelettes or herring salad; he never reads the classics.

I'm not close to Robert Gabriel† and mention him only because he has such talent for drawing. He can sketch landscapes, buildings, and many biblical scenes, also expressive portraits of Christ's face, etc.

Rümelin‡ may be the most talented of all: a cheerful day scholar, mathematician, musician, quite practical, too.

Saturday, March 12, 1892

It's nearly five o'clock. I'm sitting out my sentence,§ on bread and water; the detention began at half past twelve and will continue until eight-thirty. I'm on bread and water, but can do as I wish otherwise. I've been buried in Homer, the splendid passage in the *Odyssey*, epsilon 200ff. I'm doing all right, i.e., am terribly weak and tired, physically and mentally, but improving gradually. The detention room is so big I can walk about quite easily; before me I have a table, a desk, two chairs, a warm stove, books, pen, ink, paper, and a lamp.

The first part of the written final exam was held this morning. The Latin thesis was difficult; the Latin passage was taken from Livy V, II, and the Hebrew was easy. Next Wednesday it'll be French (!) and mathematics (!).

I'm being treated very gently and considerately by Professor Paulus and, especially, the two tutors. It was such a relief to be able to drop the violin lessons—permission came right away. I believe I should like to keep up music by taking private lessons. Anyhow, my idea is to accept

* Studied ancient philology in Tübingen; subsequently taught at the seminaries of Maulbronn and Blaubeuren. Hesse describes a meeting with Häcker in his autobiographical sketch "Journey to Nürnberg."

† Became an agriculturalist.

‡ Studied theology in Tübingen; served as an officer in the military and eventually became an engineer.

§ For having run away from school.

the abilities I have and make the most of them. I'm not musical, that I realize; I don't have what it takes to be a good violinist. I have also written Theo today.

I'm going to visit Herr Mährlen tomorrow and shall give him your regards. Unfortunately, they're moving to Stuttgart on St. George's; Herr Mährlen hopes it will be easier for him to find a position there. They always treated me in a very loving, friendly manner, and I'm grateful to them for those many wonderful hours.

Please give my regards to Grandfather, Aunt Jettle, Herr Claassen, and particularly Uncle Friedrich, whom you should also thank on my behalf for his visit here, which I greatly enjoyed. I've had a headache since two o'clock; it's so hot here, my head is on fire, goodbye.

With a kiss

I just read this on the wall of the detention room: "Karl Isenberg, May 28, 1885."

I would be pleased if you could send me a little money by and by. I spent a bit in those twenty-three hours, and have also had a few other larger expenses. I don't see how my funds can possibly last until April.

March 20, 1892

Thanks for the letter and money. My vacation starts in three or four weeks; I don't know exactly for how long. From one to four yesterday we were out on one of those field trips that always leave my feet and head crippled for a few days. I didn't have much of a headache during the actual excursion, but now it's even worse. I'm so tired, so lacking in energy and willpower. I'm merely preparing the assignments, not doing anything of my own. I'm so glad when I get a moment's peace and quiet, and don't have to think at all. But there are few such moments. I'm not so much ill as pinned down by some rather uncharacteristic weakness. I hardly even get annoyed anymore, and I cannot enjoy things either, not even the golden sunlight or the approaching vacation. But I love to sit atop the vine-covered hill for a quarter of an hour or so, when the east wind is blowing. There are no houses or people around, and I have nothing on my mind, am totally passive, just enjoy the gale, which cools my eyes and temples. Klopstock's divine *Messiah* and even Homer's immortal song no longer hold me in thrall; I have left my Schiller all alone, and rarely read the mammoth dirge in Klopstock's odes.

My feet are always like ice, whereas there is a fire blazing deep within my head somewhere. Although I seldom have anything much on my mind during my free time, I occasionally think of Herwegh's* beautiful poem:

> *I wish to leave like the sunset*
> *Like the final embers of day* . . .

The hardest part came yesterday, having to say goodbye to my Wilhelm, the person who really grew to know and understand me completely, who still loved me after my fall and kept on sharing my joys and my sorrows, even though everybody else had nothing but contempt for me. Yesterday, he showed me a letter from his pious, upright father, which demonstrated clearly that his parents despise me, too. The letter was a virtual order calling for immediate separation. It was a beautiful evening; the moon was shining into the ancient hall, as we strolled along, sunk in conversation. I have lost the person I loved most of all; it was to him that I devoted my free time, songs, thoughts. Leaving the oratory after this prolonged farewell, I could hear the soft chimes of Rümelin's wonderful voice coming from the music room: "God forbid, that would've been simply too good to be true."

You will perhaps smile as you read these lines, but believe me, it's hard to stand by the coffin of a friend, and ten times harder to lose a friend who is still alive.

Bad Boll, May 23, 1892

Thanks for the parcel, especially the clothes and the book about games.†

Theo has probably told you a little about my life here. I haven't been feeling all that well lately. Lack of sleep at night has become a real problem. My head feels so hot; I feel an indeterminate, constricting pain most of the time, especially in my chest and forehead, and I haven't made many contacts here. Oh, I'd so love to tell you that I'm doing fine, that I'm singing and leaping about merrily, cheerfully, energetically, but even writing this is difficult. Things are better here than at Maulbronn.

Even though I was in terrible shape in the seminary, I liked to imagine that the principal items—that is, instruction, room, and board—were provided by others, like wages almost. But here I feel oppressed by the thought that you are having to pay for this pleasant, convalescent life. Oh, if that weren't the case, I would so love to remain here forever.

---

* German revolutionary poet (1817–75).

† Johannes Hesse, *Das Spiel im häuslichen Kreise: Ein Ratgeber für die Familie* (*Games in the Family Circle: A Guide*).

I love the splendid air, beautiful region, good company, and free and easy atmosphere.

It's so pleasant to be able to think things over before taking the next step. It's healthy rather than enervating or harmful. Here one can live one's own life amidst society. That's much the way I imagine life to be in the Orient. Clothes are all one needs, everything else is provided for. The bell tends to ring just when we've worked up an appetite. It's we who decide when to go to bed, rise, etc., etc.

Please give my greetings to all present, and to Theo, too, if he's already there.

Stetten, July 29, 1892

Thanks for Papa's letter! I can't think of anything much to say. Of course, I wouldn't be content with a life like this in the long run. To have to work, just so as not to be bored, teaching little children how to read, count, etc. I'm glad I'm here and also like working, but look forward to returning to my usual work, education, school life. My work here isn't particularly well coordinated. I'm in the printing shop, gluing something together, when somebody tells me to go to the school, or takes me away from Livy and sends me into the garden, and so on. The appropriate gentlemen say I could probably start high school in the fall (mid-September). Mightn't I pick up some important things for the future? I would prefer to attend high school in Cannstatt, where I could be in touch with the Kolbs, who are now as mother and sister to me.

I cannot think of anything else to say; besides, I have a lesson to give five minutes from now.

Please give my regards to the others in the family.

Stetten, September [1] 1892

Theo and Karl visited me today. Theo said you were depressed because of me. There's no reason to think that I'm particularly cheerful either. There is nothing I wouldn't be prepared to give up in exchange for death, for Lethe!

Theo said I should beg forgiveness from you. But I shan't do so under present circumstances, and certainly not while I'm still here in Stetten. My situation is miserable, the future is dismal, the past is dismal, and the present is diabolical! Oh, if only that unfortunate bullet had traversed my tormented brain!*

An ill-fated year, 1892! It began gloomily in the seminary, followed

---

* At Bad Boll, in June, Hesse had bought a revolver and tried to shoot himself.

by some blissful weeks in Boll, disappointment in love, then the abrupt conclusion! And now I've lost everything: home, parents, love, faith, hope, myself even. Quite frankly, I can see and admire the sacrifices you're making, but actual love? No —! For me Stetten is like hell. If life were worth throwing away, if life weren't a delusion, sometimes merry, sometimes somber—I'd like to bash my skull against these walls, which divide me from myself. And then a dismal fall and a virtually black winter. Yes, yes, fall is here, fall in nature and fall in the heart: the blossoms are dropping off, ah, and beauty flees, leaving only an icy chill. There are several hundred dehumanized lunatics here, but I'm the only one with this emotion. I almost wish I were mad. How utterly sweet it must be, a drowsy forgetfulness about absolutely everything, all the joy and the sorrow, the life and the pain, the love and the hatred!

However, I've been chatting for too long. Miserable, no, cold is what I want to be, ice-cold toward everybody, absolutely everybody. But you are my jailors, so I cannot address these complaints to you. Farewell, farewell. I wish to be alone; I'm in dread of these people. Don't tell anybody how deathly tired I am, how unhappy! Either let me croak here, a rabid dog, or behave like parents! I cannot possibly be a son right now; I'm having to battle and defy my own misfortune; again, behave like parents but—why not kill me off more quickly instead?

I cannot write any more. I would have to cry, and what I most want is to be dead and cold. Adieu!

Stetten, September 11, 1892

I was about to play something on the violin. I took up the instrument, looked out on the sunny day, when all of a sudden, and quite involuntarily, Schumann's "Reverie" began gliding along the strings. I felt a mixture of well-being, sadness, and languor. The soft, undulating notes matched my mood. Listening to the chords, I got lost in dreams of distant, better times, those beautiful, happy days I spent in Boll. Then—all of a sudden there was a bang, a shrill discordant note: a string had snapped. I woke up from the dream and was back—in Stetten. Only one of the strings had broken, but the others were out of tune.

That's how things stand with me. I have left behind me in Boll all my best qualities, love, faith, and hope. And there's such a contrast between the two places:

In Boll, I used to play billiards in a beautiful salon with my dear, kind friends. The ivory balls roll softly, one can hear the squeaking of chalk, laughter, jokes. Or I'm sitting on a comfortable sofa, playing a game of checkers while the majestic chords of a Beethoven sonata rustle past.

Hesse at four

The Hesse family in 1889. Left to right: Hermann, his father, Marulla, his mother, Adele, and Hans

And here: I'm sitting in the room, the organ close by is producing a drowsy sound, and downstairs some retarded people are singing a children's song in their nasal voices.

But the most crucial difference lies within. In Boll there was a calm happiness or trembling passion; here only a dead, desolate void. I could escape from here, manage to get expelled, quietly hang myself, or get up to something else, but why bother? Fortune is clearly not on my side. Anyhow, Papa is even more enraged than he was when he threw me out of the house. And the doctor either makes unfavorable comments or says nothing at all. Well, to hell with that kind of thing, what good can come of it? If fatally ill, I would be utterly calm. It's quite clear to me that I cannot stay here in Stetten, and if people are trying to make a pessimist of me by dint of force and sacrifices, then I must say that nobody needs to intervene to ensure that I am that way and remain so. If there can be no change in my condition, then there's no point transferring me to another place like Stetten. I don't need a doctor or parents to drive me to despair, criminal behavior. If Papa has no use for me at home as a son, then he hardly has all that much use for a son confined to a lunatic asylum. The world is big, very big, and a single being isn't all that significant.

By the way, I'm expecting an answer. If you don't have anything to say, then the issue is quite straightforward. I still hope, what's that?— nonsense!

Listen, Theo wrote recently: "Just put that girl out of your mind; there are thousands of better, more beautiful girls!" One could write to you in the same vein: "Just put the boy out of your minds," etc., etc.

TO JOHANNES HESSE

Stetten, September 14, 1892

Dear Sir,

Since you're so conspicuously eager to make sacrifices, may I ask you for 7 marks or a revolver right away? You have caused me such despair that you should now be prepared to help me dispose of it, and rid yourself of me in the process. I should've croaked last June.

You write: We haven't "really reproached" you for complaining about Stetten. That attitude would seem totally incomprehensible to me: nobody ought to deprive a pessimist of the right to complain, which is his only, and, indeed, his ultimate, right.

"Father" is a strange word, which I cannot quite fathom. It ought to mean a person one can love with all one's heart. How I yearn for that kind of person! Could you ever give me some advice? In the old days, it was easy to make one's way in life, but that's more difficult nowadays, if one hasn't got the right grades, identification papers, etc. I'm an energetic fifteen-year-old, maybe I could find a niche in the theater somewhere?

I don't want to have any dealings with Herr Schall; he's a heartless, black-suited creature. I hate him, and I could stick a knife in him. He won't admit that I have a family, just like you and the others in that respect.

Your attitude toward me is becoming more and more tense. If I were a Pietist and not a human being, if I could turn all my attributes and inclinations into their exact opposite, then I might coexist harmoniously with you. But I cannot and shall not live like that; I would be responsible for any crimes I committed, but so would you, too, Herr Hesse, since you have made it impossible for me to enjoy life. Your "dear Hermann" has turned into somebody else, a misanthrope, an orphan with "parents" still living.

You should never again write "Dear H.," etc.; that's a dirty lie.

On two occasions today the inspector caught me not following his orders. I hope catastrophe strikes soon. If only there were some anarchists around!

> H. Hesse,
> a captive in
> Stetten prison,

where he "isn't being punished." I'm beginning to wonder *who* precisely is the idiot in this affair.

By the way, it would be agreeable to me if you were to pay an occasional visit here.

TO MARIE HESSE

[Basel, October 20, 1892]

My poor, dear mother,

Things cannot go on this way; I finally have to come out with it. Poor Mother, forgive me, forgive your fallen son; forgive me, if you love me, if you believe that there's a divine spark in me yet.

These roads and meadows, where I once played as a child, seem to be reproaching me, now that I'm no longer a child or even a son. I'm just a miserable being who rails against man and fate and cannot and will not ever love himself.

Please, Mother, don't mention the letter to anybody, especially not Grandfather, or the people in Basel. You alone may forgive me.

Walking along the great, flowing Rhine, I have often imagined how wonderful it would be to perish in these dear, familiar waves. My life and my sins would vanish into oblivion. But best of mothers, I can still find some respite, a haven, in your heart. If anybody understands me, it is you. You are the only person who knows that I, too, am capable of love. I hope these lines persuade you that I also want to be loving. I often think that I shall never, never regain my health; I realize now (only now?) how sick I am, not just physically, but in the core of my being, in my very heart. I've been suffering for a long time from this condition. I felt initially that my first love would soon take care of that, but that passion of mine for a beautiful, warmhearted creature, the sight of those beautiful eyes, the sound of her dear voice actually worsened my sufferings; I wanted to end that anguish by killing myself.

Then there was the time when Father and Theo said to me: "You can defy us for as long as you want." So I did. But I now realize how ill I am. I feel so weak, I'm anxious about the future. Even though I usually greatly enjoy being here, this time I'm aware of my illness, since I'm surrounded by really hale and hearty boys, including Heinz Pfisterer, who is the same age as me. When somebody asks me to play a game outside, I feel sad having to say: "I can't jump," or when somebody asks me why my vacation is so long.

So forgive me! Neither of us will be able to forget the past, but we should be able to forgive. When you're well again, could you ever write, simply as a mother writing to her son, could you?

PS: Please say hello to the others! Fräulein Häfelinger feels sorry for you and sends all her best.

[*Cannstatt, January 15/16, 1893*]

Thanks for the packet! I'm now living in the adjoining room, where I immediately set up my things. Today (Sunday), I was out on the frozen lake, where I ran into Metzger von Altburg, Bühner, and some other people I know . . .

But why talk about all that nonsense! I might just as well be reeling off the names of the cheese stores and factories in Cannstatt. Well, it's just that my head is filled with memories and I want to stay with these thoughts as I write.

Turgenev talks about how pleasurably painful it is to reopen wounds that have already healed. That's just how I feel. I like thinking about last year, especially in Boll, the last place where I felt well for a time. I'm still virtually a child, yet feel I have aged a lot since last spring. I have had many different experiences—some you already know about. There was just too much going on in such a short stretch of time; then, after all the terrible excitement, which lasted right up to Stetten and Basel, came a lull; for months my nerves were in continuous, feverish excitement. Now the worst of the storm is over; the tree has lost its blossoms, and the branches are tired, drooping. You can probably more or less sense what I mean. As a man, scholar, etc., etc., Papa will no doubt dismiss these lines as useless, fantastical palaver. I myself relish opening these wounds, and, anyhow, you don't have to read this.

I've spent many happy hours here. For a time I was enthralled with the school and the teacher, tried to find friends, sought contact with people my own age; then there was a time when I hovered about in an unreal world, where everything seemed bathed in a more beautiful light. The whole experience culminates in the bittersweet feeling of love, in songs and wooing—then the abrupt end, despair, madness, and then deep, dark, sultry night.

Yes, it's so nice to be watching all of this again, one picture after another, as in a peep show. I would like to laugh out loud at the whole thing now, all that purely imaginary happiness, all that unnecessary fervor, the madcap illusion of love and suffering, ideals and friendship; I would like to laugh about this, but it's finished and . . . will it happen again or is it all over? When I recall how interested I was in interpretations of the Bible, etymology, history, etc., the way I made friends, the way I loved—idolizing the flowers "she" had once held in her hand— I find this whole experience so strange and odd and yet as natural as a colorful dream of love. There were some mementos of that time, flowers, poems, etc., but I threw them into the fire—wherefore this abyss, this delusion of the heart, wherefore indeed this silly, miserable heart? And even these lines have a rather silly, "Romantic" flavor to them, which isn't what I had in mind. So I prefer to hold my peace!

TO JOHANNES HESSE

[*Cannstatt, March 14, 1893*]

Thank you for the last letter. I'm a bit worried about Easter. I have a sense that once again things aren't going to work out.

You always seem to think I'm "burdened" by "the woes of mankind." That's just not so. If I'm tiresome and disgruntled, it's partly because the professions that seem open to me aren't in the least bit appealing to me. These days I think about Boll a lot. I have only been there once, but felt whole and content during my stay. Of course, everything came to a rather silly end, but my time there was so wonderful, apart from those final eight to ten days. Decent company, freedom, music, singing, and conversation—all that was beautiful. I used take pleasure in nature then. But now it has become merely a shabby refuge on occasions when the boredom is simply too great; the magic is gone. I probably did poorly on the exam, but I don't care about that, as long as I get my intermediate certificate in the summer.

All would be fine and good if the world were not so beautiful—if only it were open to me. But, as things are, I'm entirely dependent on my own energy, which is being exhausted. Yes, if energy and money weren't so scarce, then —! Sometimes I win a drink from some inept companion over, usually, a game of skittles or billiards—but I don't want to complain, since I have something to eat and a place to sleep, and should be absolutely happy, at least according to you and some other people. You say so often that thousands of people are a lot worse off. That's certainly true, but there's no connection between those other people and me, and I couldn't care less about them.

I shall probably be coming to Calw soon, and shall probably find other people boring and annoying, and they will feel much the same way about my company.

NB: I would be very pleased if Karl happens to have a small pipe from his student days, doesn't need it, and passes it on to me.

Wilhelm Dreiss did brilliantly in his exams.

PS: I may send the important Easter things by mail; I may walk part of the way if the weather is good.

TO JOHANNES AND MARIE HESSE

[Before March 24, 1893]

I'm very anxious about Easter. If I could stay here or elsewhere, but as for going home!? I can tolerate just about everything but love. This cannot go on for much longer; I'm completely bedraggled, and my misery doesn't belong in a house such as yours where love and friendship are at home. It's easier for me to tell people like Geiger what I think! I consider that man a blockhead of the first order . . .

I have to come on Saturday! Don't be startled and—please!—leave me alone at Easter! I cannot tolerate love, and Christian love least of all. If Christ only knew what he has wrought! He'd be turning over in the grave.

I have gone to the dogs in both body and soul; my heart has blackened, as has my life . . .

You're the people who ought to be pitied; I have been such a burden. A pity about that good money!!

The thought of Easter seems more and more terrible, and fills me with revulsion (only if I come?). I'm about to fall silent, without actually shooting myself. That's fine, the best course for us all.

I pity you! Such devout, honorable, upright people; their filius, however, happens to be a scoundrel who despises morality and all that is "sacred" and "venerable." That's almost a pity! I would have been able to make something of myself in life had I been a bit more stupid and allowed myself to be deluded by religion, etc.

PS: Today I met some nice, jolly people, a German-Italian by the name of Ottilio Pedotti and a rich Russian, Duke Fritz von Cantacuszène.

[*Cannstatt, June 13, 1893*]

Well, that's how it is! I spent Pentecost with you: walks, meals, joking around, Bible readings, music—but then a fight, boredom, and so I left a whole day earlier. And now Mother writes saying that my stay at Pentecost was "so brief," and also that I should talk "openly" about whatever is "affecting me emotionally"!

Poor Parents! You think that you're dealing with an eccentric dreamer with crazy ideals, who is driven by his delusion to stir up mischief, but is actually pining away with grief because of the state of the world and also on account of some personal sorrows. That's how you view your son.

You Christians blend optimism and pessimism in strange ways! At the same time as you're pitying me for being such a dreamer, so nostalgic, I'm trying to while away the time here in Cannstatt, am bored, have debts, etc.!

You call me "beloved child," and write of my "struggles," etc.; you imagine that my dearest wish is to spend my life amidst beautiful, good, dear souls who believe in an idealistic philosophy; you think I'm concerned about such things as a Weltanschauung, love, hatred. And as for the reality? What would I actually wish for myself? Well, if you really want to know the whole truth, my ideal would be to have (1) a millionaire father and also several well-endowed uncles, (2) more talent in practical matters, (3) the opportunity to live and travel wherever I please.

I couldn't care less about the aristocracy, yet would love to be an aristocrat, because of the prestige attached to the rank. I think money is absurd, but would really love to be very rich, because of the good life of which it forms part.

And what's the point of all this?

Man lives on bread rather than love; if I had a chance to trade in my exalted ideals, still almost brand-new, for those good Württemberg coupons—ah!

Farewell now! I shall have to think about what you said about the final exam in high school. I'm quite fearful about life at school and possibly also at university.

Write again soon, if you wish and can find the time.

[On enclosed page] Dear Papa! Congratulations on your birthday, and the best of health to you! Have a really enjoyable time on June 14, and fond regards to the others.

[On the reverse side] PS: I have no idea what I would like for my birthday. I shall let you know, if I think of anything. The awful part is that what you have in mind mightn't appeal to me, and vice versa.

By the way, I would ask you not to send books.

[*Cannstatt, October 8 or 9, 1893*]

I don't know whether the Principal has written to you or not. I hope so.

I probably cannot go on like this for much longer. While I don't have ordinary headaches, I always feel an awfully dull, uniform pressure in my head which develops into a headache when I have to concentrate. I can't cope with the assignments, which aren't excessive at all. I have to spend three or four times the usual amount of time on them, and my inattentiveness in class is downright embarrassing by now. I'm not able to follow properly, especially if asked questions, etc., and so I'm continually receiving reprimands, having to copy out lines, etc.

I'm terribly sorry to have to cause you such problems again, and so soon, too, but I had to tell you that I can no longer put up with this. Couldn't somebody come over here to see what might be done?

I wasn't able to recuperate sufficiently during the summer vacation because of the toothaches, pains in my eyes, and the heat. I'm again finding it difficult to walk, especially uphill.

If I could only come home, didn't have to be with strangers, and work a bit in the garden, not too much activity, but just enough! I'm terribly afraid, have many worries, and then school, work, angry words.

TO JOHANNES HESSE*

[no initial greeting]

I decided to communicate with you in writing, so as to avoid unnecessary excitement. Unfortunately, it has become more than evident that we are incapable of having a conversation, because both of us easily become irritated and also have divergent opinions and principles. But to get to the point!

I didn't like it at the seminary, and felt no better at Cannstatt and Esslingen.† You thought my running away like that was pathological. Of course, it wasn't right of me, but I didn't feel the least bit eager, energetic, or courageous when thinking about the future you wanted to impose on me. A feeling of revulsion often overcame me at work or while studying.

I have always employed my free time to further my own education. You used speak of my idle pursuits, but that is how I hope to earn my living. I could never summon the courage to tell you about my intentions and wishes, since I knew they didn't agree with yours, and so we drifted ever further apart. I tried the book trade, and was determined to work very hard, if I could detect a single positive aspect, but the whole affair was quite nauseating. Now a decision has to be reached. I know that you were, or are, thinking of such places as Stetten and Chrischona, and so I really have to say this: Your plans, which I went along with, have come to nought. Couldn't I have a final chance to try out my plans before having to enter a lunatic asylum or become a gardener or carpenter? That's more or less what I'm requesting. But knowing that you appreciate precision in such matters: I would like to try to earn a living by drawing on my private studies. I would start off in a place where I have a foothold already, Cannstatt, Esslingen, Stuttgart. Furthermore, I would need certain papers, because of the police, and some money at

* This letter was probably written before June 5, 1894, when Hesse decided to enter Perrot's workshop in Calw.

†Hesse had run away from this apprentice position sometime between October 29 and November 4, 1893.

(*Above*) Calw in the Black Forest, Hesse's birthplace, where he spent the first three years of his life (until 1881), and to which he returned to attend school for three years (1886—89)

(*Below*) The Mission School in Basel, where the Hesse family lived from 1881 to 1886. Hesse spent his first school years here

Maulbronn, the background for many stories

the outset. If I didn't have a few marks, I wouldn't get as far as Esslingen. If I happened to arrive there on the wrong day, I wouldn't have a bite to eat. Obviously, I have to rely on somebody's help at first. I hope to earn something later, in the foreseeable future.

You have spent a lot of money trying to implement your plans for my future. Wouldn't you be interested in investing a little of that in my attempt to determine whether my plans are viable. To put the matter bluntly:

I would ask you to allow me freedom (rather than the 1,000 marks at the very minimum needed to prepare me for a career as a merchant or something similar), and this means helping me acquire the necessary papers, giving me money so I can get started, and permitting me to keep on turning to you in the immediate future for such things as laundry and shoe repair. If things go well for me, then so much the better! If they don't, then my hopes will have proven worthless, and I shall never again lay claim to a will of my own—i.e., avoiding being confined to a lunatic asylum.

TO JOHANNES AND MARIE HESSE

Tübingen, October 18 to 20, 1895
Friday evening

I intended to write again on Sunday, still do, but who knows whether that'll be possible? I shall be tired, have to wait in any case until Sunday before setting up my books, etc., since there simply isn't enough time, and I've been invited to Aunt Elisabeth's* for Sunday afternoon. So I'm starting to write today, though I may not get very far.

I'm kind of fond of the town, especially since I live on the periphery and not in town. It is narrow, full of little nooks, medieval romanticism, with little Richter†-like scenes, yet it's also rather malodorous and dirty. The castle is wonderful, especially the view from atop the castle mountain, and the avenues are truly splendid.

I can see the castle from my room. The widow of the Deacon is busy mothering me, always bringing butter, rolls, sausages, etc.; she must think I'm a spoiled glutton. It's hard for me to get away from the table after lunch, since she so loves to talk. She knows everybody, people from Calw, Basel, Lapland, missionaries, and can talk about thousands of interesting deaths, engagements, illnesses, trips, and as-

---

* Wife of Samuel Gundert, the second-eldest son of Hesse's grandfather.
† German Romantic painter (1803–84).

sorted pleasures of that ilk. I already know in great detail all about her husband's death and shall soon be just as familiar with her childhood, engagement, marriage, life with her husband, all her joys and sorrows. She seems like a character from a Dickens novel: agile, merry, cheerful, solicitous, always bursting with stories old and new, as well as extremely kindhearted and loving. Today she implored my forgiveness for leaving a bottle of fresh cider in my room. She just had to, the cider was so good, although she had used more apples than usual, costing 6.50 a measure. She asked whether I would like to have a sausage or something in the evening, and I said I would prefer to have a cup of tea with some bread or rolls, if that wasn't any bother. Well, she gives me tea and rolls for supper, and even puts out some butter, too. When I have eaten my fill, she clears the table. I'm just about to get up when a warm sausage with salad appears on the table. The widow of the Deacon bears a slight resemblance to Frieda Montigel, although she's a far finer person than the latter. While she loves to talk, she would never dream of grilling me like an inquisitor. So I sit there enjoying the meal, listening to her talk, and feeling very cozy—through her lively exhortations she ensures that I eat enough and, what's more, stay awake.

Saturday night

Marulla* wants to enclose my letter tomorrow, so I'll have to finish this by then.

The pace at work is like this too, hour by hour. I can imagine the sheer variety of tasks eventually sowing confusion in my mind. I already have the following regular duties: I sort all incoming packages, recount the money in the store's cash register (between twenty and thirty marks) each morning, mail the magazines and keep a record of the books. Besides, I have to examine the secondhand books to ensure they're complete (collation), also possibly go on errands, etc. It's a very large enterprise; the main category is theology, also law and philology, not much medicine, art and music only as a sideline. Students may open their own accounts, and there are some unpaid bills that were incurred by gentlemen who have since vanished into thin air. That sort of thing seems to happen quite frequently. I respect all the gentlemen in the store for their education and knowledge, particularly the two eldest, Herr Hermes and Herr Straubing. Herr Sonnewald wears his hat and coat in the heated office, but takes them off when he goes out. He doesn't talk, he murmurs. I have enormous respect for him.

* Hesse's younger sister.

We have our own well-equipped bindery, large rooms, a store, offices, a warehouse, a cellar (known as Hades), two conveyor belts (caterpillars).

There are some framed pictures on the wall, one of which is actually quite pretty (Columbus). There's a large, colored picture of King Charles above the bed, and a holy picture hangs over the high desk. I'm fully equipped, only need some towels, which we apparently have to supply ourselves. I have two or three; please send me the others whenever you can. I would be delighted if you could include a few sheets of cheap blotting paper or something along those lines, since I don't have a desk pad here.

Daily schedule
Rise: 6:40 a.m.
Coffee: after 7 o'clock
Bookstore opens: 7:30
Lunch: 12 or 12:15 p.m.
Back in bookstore: 1:15 or 1:30
Arrive home: 7:30 to 7:45
Bedtime: between 9:45 and 10:15
We have afternoon tea at work.

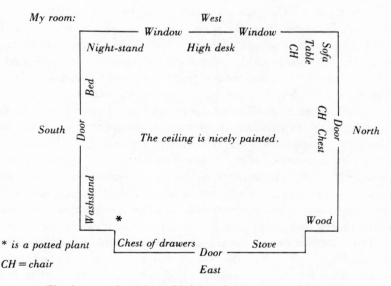

My room:

The doors on the right and left are always closed and have curtains.

NB: The furniture should appear much larger in relation to the rest of the room.

(As I'm drawing this, the maid interrupts me to ask whether I like herring salad.)

TO KARL ISENBERG*

Tübingen [December 10, 1895]

Many thanks for your kind letter! I want to try to finish these lines, and that won't be easy, since I don't get home until 8 or 8:15, and have to go to bed early if I want to be in a moderately good mood the following morning.† You're right, we have to steal the time to write letters, but there is no way we can steal the freshness and concentration that writing also requires.[. . .]

I don't spend much time thinking about matters of great import, my phase as a genius has evaporated, and I'm becoming a philistine; I'm actually becoming quite respectable, since I never go near the pub, and spend my few free hours gazing at the garden of my poetic ideals— it has become a lot narrower—and occasionally I come up with some other earth-shattering things. There is no lack of reading material, and my Sundays too are quiet and go by quickly. When I feel tired and have had more than my fill of new books, Father Goethe drops by to keep me company; I really enjoy him, a bit uncritically actually, since I focus on specific, beautifully carved pillars or arabesques in his marblelike prose rather than on things of his that don't affect me much.

I see no point in boring you with all the details about my profession. There is certainly no shortage of irritation, headaches, and other such delights, but I had certain goals in mind in becoming a bookseller, and nobody is going to talk me out of it. I'm glad to see that my knowledge of literature, including modern, is not nearly as defective as I had feared, and also that my little system for studying the subject was not mistaken. I'm beginning to understand the implications of the underlying factors, and am still hoping to achieve an understanding, insofar as this is at all possible, of the essence and history of European literature. I realize that I'm quite reactionary when it comes to literature; indeed, if one didn't have strong principles and a radical disposition, it would scarcely be possible to profit from a study of the new literature, including the most recent publications. One symptom of the rickety current situation is that, even in satire, the one area that could yield something of lasting value, nothing of any real value has surfaced. I view things aesthetically, and so I'm disturbed to see that this is an era in which even those with talent and genius come into the world equipped with sick, twitching nerves and then destroy themselves, especially the poets. And in the

* Hesse's half brother.
† In October 1895, after his period as an apprentice in Perrot's clock-repair shop in Calw, Hesse began a three-year apprenticeship in Heckenhauer's bookstore in Tübingen (at first as a volunteer and after finishing his apprenticeship as a second assistant for inventory).

theater, which has become the center of artistic creation, these twitching nerves have to entertain a populace that has declined both morally and aesthetically. The sick way those "psychological" dramas and novels wallow in the dirt and dissect everything often horrifies me. This summer in Calw, in our good old Schilda,* a group of traveling players put on plays by Sudermann! And Sudermann is one of the best of them.†

If these are the buds of the promised spring, the first glimmerings of an expected era of "new art," then woe to the age when there will be no champions of the "old school" left, and the "new art" will unfurl itself and take power. I cannot detect in these dusky red lights any signs of a coming morning; all I see are the torches lighting up the wanton orgies of an age that has sunk low artistically. And, when all is said and done, none of the moderns has advanced any further in his very own genre than Goethe did in *Werther* and the *Elective Affinities.* Maybe the historians who see *Faust* as the finest blossom of the present age and of the coming era are right after all, even though I still find it hard to believe that the epigrammatic curse in *Faust* cannot be averted.‡ Or are we approaching an era in which art and poetry will lose their special status and end up as equal or perhaps even inferior "branches" of the book trade? That almost seems likely, and the only way we literary people shall prevail is by keeping our faith against all odds and clinging to our idealistic tenets, no matter how bad the situation gets. If ordinary people would only remain pure, if the good old customs and songs were not being forgotten, were not being killed off by the air in the factories and the nonpoetry of the writers in Grünewald.§

You're probably laughing at my excessive zeal; well, I have just reached the one area that really matters to me. No offense intended!

I hope to be able to write again when things are quieter and I would be delighted to hear from you. And now, God be with you, dear brother!

TO JOHANNES AND MARIE HESSE

[*Written between January 28 and February 2, 1896*]

My dears,

My sincere thanks for the laundry, which was eagerly awaited, for Theodor's balm, and, above all, for the kind letter from Mother.

---

* Proverbial name for a small town with petit bourgeois values.
† Celebrated writer of German naturalism.
‡ Goethe, *Faust.*
§ Berlin suburb favored by writers of German naturalism.

You already know I was at a concert.* I was given a free ticket by a clerk in Osiander's bookstore. The chorus and orchestra were quite remarkable. "Fall" and "Winter" were virtually perfect. The singer was also fine, especially in "Winter," and the chorus was most impressive there, too. Unfortunately, I was very tired from having to be on my feet continuously from one-thirty until 11 o'clock, first at my desk, then in the concert hall.

I had already become acquainted with several of the Tübingen Olympians by the time I called on the idol of the Law Faculty, the famous teacher of criminal law, Professor Hugo von Meyer, to discuss a business matter. A tall, splendid person with a wonderful, long beard and hand-some features, an idealized version of Jakob Staudenmaier. He was utterly charming, honored me with a handshake, and even got absorbed in a conversation about the durability of a certain type of paper. It's fun getting such a close-up view of these gods; a few manage to retain their luster. Meyer, for instance. Yesterday, I spent some time with a person from Transylvania, and heard about the condition of secondary schools in his homeland; tomorrow, I'm going to the Wingolf fraternity house on a delicate mission (debts). At least I shall get to see it that way. I hope to visit some other houses—e.g., the dueling fraternities. Today, I ran into Hermann Nestle,† who addressed me very formally, and didn't seem to have any use for me. He looks good, nice, very clever—I occasionally see Herr Bucher, the Ephor;‡ he now knows me by name, but I don't know how he found out. He's the very soul of amiability, when he has time; he's awfully busy.

I haven't yet paid any social calls; I usually spend Sunday afternoon at my dear aunt's, so I can listen to the piano. I've been suffering for weeks from a shyness bordering on anxiety whenever I have to face people, including social gatherings, and though there is probably some-thing to be said for that, it also messes things up quite a bit. I don't ever feel timid, I just dislike the parties at Häring's,§ especially talk, so I just listen, quiet as a mouse. I don't know why I'm so smitten with melancholia. I just feel despondent and utterly miserable at the thought of having to do any socializing at all. I'm actually happiest when I'm alone, looking at some piece by Goethe‖; those marbled sunrays and

---

* Probably Haydn's oratorio *The Seasons* (1801).

† Public prosecutor in Stuttgart, married to Marie Oehler, a lifelong friend of Marie Hesse's.

‡ Professor of theology in Tübingen and Ephor (Superintendent) at the Evangelical Foundation there.

§ Professor of theology, author of various theological treatises, member of the board of the Calw Publishing Association, and a friend of Hesse's parents.

‖ Cf. J. P. Eckermann, "Conversations with Goethe," Part III, January 2, 1824.

that sunraylike marble edify me. What makes Goethe so unique, the greatest of all, is his contribution to the solution of the puzzle confronting the modern age; fire and water have come together, by which I mean the Classical and Romantic elements in thought and poetry, Yes and No, Plato and Aristotle, thought and irony, Homer and Dante. For everybody other than Goethe, a yawning chasm exists between Iphigenia and Faust. He alone, among millions of thoughtful people born over the last hundred years, was completely unaffected by the French Revolution, because his vantage point was even loftier than that afforded by the great red sun of the modern era.

Forgive these literary and aesthetic excursions, but since my private studies overlap almost entirely with my profession (I'm currently poring over Gottschall,* catalogues and journals), all of this thought and work is no longer sinful, mere skylarking, and has earned the right—also on external grounds—to lend fulfillment to my life. And there's still room enough in my heart to think of you with love and gratitude, to feel glad for Mother on each warm day, and to meditate for a little while in the study as I'm preparing to mail the Calw papers.†

Friday

Another week will soon be over. On Sundays, I'd really prefer to stay at home altogether, and indeed I never do go out until afternoon. Yet, despite my weak appetite, it's too long from 1 to 6:30 or 7, and if I'm not at Auntie's, or, and this happens rarely enough, get to down some seminary coffee, I drink a glass of beer or wine. When away from Calw, what I always miss most of all is the afternoon coffee.

Kübel's brand-new work *Christian Ethics* (two volumes) appeared today, and I've already mailed off more than ten copies. Tomorrow, I'm going to the theological foundation to put a poster on the door, so that students get to hear about it too. Dozens of copies of Kübel's *Sermons* have been sold, some to poor, humble tradesmen.

Sunday

I should actually write some more today, since I don't know when I can get to it next week, with all the work. But it's not possible. I'm absolutely exhausted, even though we're still at the very beginning. So this will have to do, kisses from your

---

* Author of *Die deutsche Nationalliteratur im 19. Jahrhundert* (1855), a popular and frequently reprinted literary history.

† Various missionary periodicals published in Calw.

TO ERNST KAPFF*

Tübingen, February 7, 1896

Beatus ille, qui procul negotiis—!† My work load is almost excessive
this week, and that will remain the case until the Easter fair. The work
is interesting, but quite strenuous! During the inventory, hundreds of
books, all new titles published in 1895, pass through my hands and, if
I want to derive any real literary benefit from them, I have to make
inordinate demands on my memory.[. . .]

I'm producing very little, except for some poetic knickknacks and
a few heartfelt sighs. I have mainly read Gottschall's *Nationalliteratur*,
which has left me little the wiser. He is best on Berlin Romanticism,
Hegel, and perhaps Freytag as well, but I couldn't get myself to read
everything he says about Gutzkow, Prutz, and Jordan. In general, Gottschall drenches the epigones of Young Germany with his vinegar-and-
oil dressing, and, oddly enough, he is serious when he says by way of
farewell: "Cheers, enjoy the meal!" I don't know Gottschall's own writings. If I dabbled in literary history, I'd certainly approach it with a bit
more cheekiness and boldness; I would, for instance, trace the malady
of our literature, its paralyzed backbone, straight back to its only source,
the Romantic element, Tieck and Brentano; that would certainly provide
a regular framework, even though some things would get clipped at the
edges. If I had time on my hands, if I were a person of independent
means, and had no literary ambitions of my own, I would spend the day
lying in the grass or playing billiards, wouldn't give a damn about all
those wee deities in between Varnhagen and Hauptmann, and would fill
the evening hours with *A Thousand and One Nights*, Boccaccio, Cer-
vantes, Fielding, and other idle fancies; I would cull passages from
Heine's poems and always save a bit of Goethe for dessert. I would
maintain an orchestra and keep horses, but would banish bicycles and
lending libraries from my realm, perhaps theatrical performances as
well; I would favor love in the open over free love; my poems would be
printed on vellum, etc., etc., etc. Although I would hardly support
literature at all, I would provide funds each year so that some families
could emigrate and thus improve the quality of the air.

Please excuse these idiocies; my work has left me mentally exhausted, and so the old saying applies:

Reason becomes folly, good deeds a calamity, etc.‡

---

* Author of historical fiction and Hesse's teacher and mentor at Cannstatt.
† "Happy he who (lives) far from all duties," Horace, *Epodes.*
‡ Goethe, *Faust.*

[. . .]I never cease longing for a healthy existence, for a simple culture and an authentic life, in other words for Brazil. I would love to escape from several things: X rays, the dubious science that tries to open buds by force, literature without rules, art without aesthetics. Like the sun weary after the day, I'm drawn westward, and like the sun, I would acquire a new red hue, once the ocean had washed the veneer and dust from my soul. Even souls that are intensely alive will soon age and grow weary of this bustling, frenetic, satiated life. "Give me a great idea so that I can come alive!" As far as those hothouse blossoms in our literature and historical writing, all that stargazing and digging for treasure, they are entirely appropriate as emblems for an age that considers itself unsatisfactory, for a life that is untrue, inflated, shadowy; our entire civilization is addicted to morphine. And I don't want to live like a fleeting shadow, a consumptive, no, I want to live genuinely, with the true warmth and in full bloom. I want to be a gay worshipper in the temple of the Muses rather than a mere hunted prey. Each day I ask in my prayers for the ability to preserve my own inner world rather than become stifled, so that the sweet poison, which I see thousands of people sipping, may not consume me as well. I know of no verse of Heine's more full of anguish and despair—of a kind I have no wish to experience myself—than the following:

> *My songs are filled with poison—*
> *Why shouldn't that be true?*
> *Into my budding manhood*
> *You poured your poison through.**

Everybody has to bury his childhood ideals someday, but I try to keep intact the things I have learned and fought for, and I often withdraw into myself, as I strive to preserve those values from the prevailing atmosphere of decay and homogenization. I want foundations on which I can build a life of my own, without fear or need for support. To transform one's life into a work of art, one needs to have a grounding in nature and in truth; in our society that is beyond the reach of rich and workers alike. What is needed for life to become a work of art, in the larger sense of the term, is a simple and appropriate form of culture. I don't really believe that life can be improved, that social conditions in Germany and in Europe can be transformed; I believe that the rotten leaf will have to fall of its own accord to make way for the new. There is no point in building dams to hold back this "progress," this fever of the nerves, which will eventually outlive its appeal. I don't believe that anybody living in Germany today will be around to witness the new

* From Hal Draper's translation of *The Complete Poems of Heinrich Heine* (1982).

epoch. I think that there will be a long interlude of desolation and barbarism between the breakdown of our way of life and the advent of the new spring. A spring that may come from the periphery, perhaps even from Brazil. A spring that will not be perturbed by social questions. I would like to preserve for that new era the Apollo of Belvedere and the image of Goethe rather than the products of our aged civilization. I'm certain that there will be no Bellamy state* anywhere in the twenty-first century. Won't people in later ages regard our epoch as the mythical age of titanic machines, and then confuse it later on with the legend of the tower of Babel—won't the historians and anthropologists of those later centuries view our era as a pathological curiosity? As you can see, I don't have the time or energy to present my ideas logically and develop them with any consistency. But you can sense that I'm tired of living under present conditions and am trying to head with fluttering wings toward a better spot, some place with sunshine and mountain air, far away from the valleys with their club meetings, factories, agricultural crises, Zola novels, encyclopedias, rhyme dictionaries, as well as all the pettiness and nastiness. Although there is now a plethora of ambitious plans and ideas for the future, the people themselves have actually diminished in stature; they're stuffed to the gills with emancipatory ideals, popularized philosophies, and de luxe edition or paperback literature; it's fashionable to dabble in fortune telling and to serve up the greatest thoughts as after-dinner treats; everything is debased: art, knowledge, all human achievements, especially language, and the corruption of the latter is always a symptom of decay. Words like "beautiful," "good," "luminous," "pure," "bad," "ugly," etc., have virtually disappeared, and it isn't easy for the phrasemongering feuilletons to satisfy the jaded tastes of the masses. Everything has to be "demonic," "phenomenal," "striking," "exhibiting great genius," "wildly beautiful," "madly in love," "magically beautiful," "awful," "fairylike," "delightful," "wildly painful," etc. They are busy coining massive quantities of new compounds, the most amazing tragelaphs†; they torture the deflowered language from one bridal bed to the next, and even expressions that seem strikingly original in Gaudy and Heine come across as absurd and silly in Voss, Jensen, and all those other epigones. How far removed they are from the blithely straightforward and naïvely authentic inventions of Goethe, the Master—for instance, his description of the farmer plowing up the treasure:

---

* Edward Bellamy's utopian welfare state, in his novel *Looking Backward* (1888).
† Fabulous creatures in ancient Greek lore.

> *and finds a golden roll*
> *frightened, delighted in a wretched hand.**

(As always in letters, I'm quoting from memory.)

I'm sure you understand what I mean. I think Germanists should be engaged in something more productive than chasing around anxiously after "foreign words" with a spear and a knife; that is hardly what our modern literati really need. And besides, those older foreign words are not Greek, or Latin, or French, they are international. While I don't use words like *"Korridoren," "Palais," "Souterrains," "Fauteuils,"* etc., I deliberately use words like "classical," "antique," "Renaissance," "Germanicism," "epigone," etc., etc., and it takes a person with Latin to describe certain things in such a fine, clear, and pregnant manner, with such ingenious simplicity, as, e.g., *tertius gaudens,*† etc.

Well, I have touched upon all sorts of things, but don't have the time to develop anything properly. Please take my stammering to heart and write me another delightful letter soon! With the very best wishes!

TO JOHANNES AND MARIE HESSE

Tübingen, March 7, 1896

Papa's note about Mother's trip came as a complete surprise to me. I'm really eager to hear how it went. But I fear it may be quite a strain on her. Don't keep me in this uncertainty!

Last Sunday I spent a few hours at Fräulein von Reutern's.‡ We had an interesting conversation about Russian and French literature, and the young people present seemed rather taken aback by this. Next Sunday, I want to go and see Frau Kieser§ (formerly of Göppingen). I haven't mustered sufficient courage to call on her, but she's now sent word that I should come by. I saw Professor Häring the day before yesterday; we're selling his work concerning δικαιοσύνη Θεοῦ‖ on a commission basis. He says he has already sent Papa a copy. He was as friendly as the last time. I usually spend Sunday evenings at Aunt Elisabeth's. We play music together, and also some board games; I occasionally have a game of cards with my cousin,** but, of course, never

---

* Goethe, *Faust*.
† A third party who benefits from the disagreement or action of two others.
‡ Head of a girls' boarding school in Tübingen attended by Adele and Marulla Hesse.
§ Mother of Hermann Kieser, a roommate of Hesse's at Maulbronn.
‖ Theodor Häring, "δικαιοσύνη Θεοῦ bei Paulus" (1896).
** Hermann Gundert, cousin and brother-in-law of Hesse's. He married Adele Hesse in 1906.

for money or profit. Even though I loathe having to socialize, I find it difficult to spend an entire Sunday all on my own. I'm very grateful to Auntie for her hospitality, particularly now that I'm no longer so dependent on her coffee. The widow of the Deacon has started serving me coffee on Sundays. I'd be very happy to get to know the Kiesers better, and feel somewhat more at home with them. They're nice, fine people. Frau Kieser has three theologians in the family: two sons and a nephew.

I have finished Virgil, and feel I now have the courage to tackle Homer right away, both poems. It will take me quite a while, but what harm? I keep putting off Sophocles in a rather cowardly fashion. I'd like to ask Papa whether he knows of a really good metrical translation of Horace, and also whether he has read Virgil's "pastoral poems" and would recommend them. In any case, I'm going ahead with Ovid. The material is piling up, but I can eliminate some things, since I'm already sufficiently well acquainted with a few Greeks (Xenophon, Isocrates, etc.). I'm not in a great rush and I'd gladly reckon on spending two, three months on Homer, for instance, if this mood holds, since I read slowly, reread some passages, and engage in reflection. I'd definitely like to develop a comprehensive plan for reading the Ancients, as soon as possible. I'd never have foreseen ever embracing the Ancients again, with such enthusiasm. I have become the very thing I used to mock, a gold digger in avid pursuit of the dazzling veins of gold to be found in the books of the ancient world. If I hadn't set myself the task of reaching Goethe, I probably couldn't be enticed away so soon from these Trojan plains, stony Ithaca, the Attic bustle, the microcosm of the Forum Romanum. Before starting Homer, I have to revisit the manifold labyrinths of Greek mythology, and also straighten out my ideas again about such things as the nature of the nymphs and the genealogy of the Titans, so that I can then enjoy the meaningful, captivating intrigues of Homer's gods, which appealed to me even in Virgil's rather discreet version. This colorful world, from Olympus all the way down, seems rather strange and confusing to me, and yet, for anybody who wants to understand the cheerful, clever Greek way, those endless gradations of fauns, nymphs, dryads, and demigods are more important than all the old books. I'm thinking of perusing some abridged guide to the gods while familiarizing myself with the *Iliad*. While I occasionally read some Latin, rarely any Greek, I realize I couldn't possibly read the Ancients, particularly the Greeks, in the original. It would take endless time and effort, and I would have to learn more Greek than I already know. Of course, I regret not being able to go to the source, but, fortunately, I do have access to some excellent translations.

Fond kisses from your grateful

TO ERNST KAPFF

Tübingen, April 1896

Many thanks for your interesting letter! I'm almost tempted to don Romantic armor so as to ward off your sharp attacks against melancholic, sentimental poetry; yet I myself have to admit that I regard most of my lyrical sighs as a sort of bridge, which should lead me toward a place up on high, near the sun, where I can finally become a poet. Yet you're wrong if you think it's impossible to "write away" one's pain; a goodly amount of poison is left behind in the verses, and in any case poetry makes fluid the pain, which often oozes considerately out of the most awkward trochees. I would ask you to think of my lyrics as essays that employ images and meters. Moreover, although I want to be many things, I have no wish to become a Romantic. In my best lyrics I sing about a country, the land of my dreams, that lies beyond the point where almost all of us are stuck—digging our spurs in vain into those old nags, philosophy and poetry—and that is perhaps "beyond Good and Evil." But I still hope that the time will come when I shan't have to fiddle around with rhymes, either because Pegasus himself has taken a leap or because that barrier has disappeared. By then, I think I shall indeed be a poet. But I shan't be satisfied with merely being a singer until I have reached the frontier—my growing wings should carry the songs that far—from whence they can set forth in new but natural forms and go their own way, effortlessly, displaying all of their original force. Only then will the singer have managed to become a creator.

I feel as if the murmurs of the sea and the jungle ought to make the covering that has me enveloped in such darkness burst and thus allow me to blossom and extend myself and compose a redeeming lyric. Then I would no longer care whether Cotta or Brockhaus* published my lyrics, since our dear old literary world today would seem like Golgotha when contrasted with my ideal of what poetry should be. One of my lyrics goes

> *—You leave me alone—*
> *The wind is driving the roses away*
> *And solitude I need not shun,*
> *For I am ever the hot sun.*

Strange, ever since my school days I have been condemned to solitude, and have only come to terms with it recently. I cannot make friends, maybe because I'm too proud and am not interested in wooing anybody, and for the last three years I have been doing everything alone,

---

* Two of the most distinguished German publishers.

thinking, singing; when I'm having a drink, out walking, or at home, I feel as though there were a circle drawn around me which moves as I do and cannot be crossed. I have been alone now for two, three months every single evening and all day Sunday. I'm not turning into a hypochondriac, since I work strenuously every day, but that shadow or "nightmare" which you criticize in my lyrics may stem partly from my odd life. My letters are probably sufficient evidence that I can be communicative, empathic, cheerful, even chatty, and this correspondence with you is just about my only active relationship.[. . .]

I'm glad that you keep a place for my letters alongside those of your dear bride, and I regard this with delight as a sign that my rough edges won't deter you from being my closest friend and counsel—thank you! As for my rough edges, think of the beautiful verse:

> *The earth is round, and that is neat,*
> *For had it corners and peaks*
> *Where would we rest our feet?*
> *But since it's round and we are tall,*
> *For fear there is no call at all;*
> *Were we of similar stature,*
> *We'd be hurtling through nature.*

God preserve us from that! Amen. Yours, from your currently rather whimsical

TO HIS SISTER ADELE

[*May 1896*]

But sleep did not rest on the king: he rose in the midst of his arms, and slowly ascended the hill, to behold the flame of Starno's tower. The flame was dim and distant; the moon hid her red face in the east. A blast came from the mountain, on its wings was the spirit of Loda.*

I'm reading some of the Ossian poems. They're an odd mixture of robust humanity and sentimental pathos, and taste like a delicate pancake garnished with raw chives. Malwina sits on a craggy outlook perched above a brownish-black moor; the black wind ruffling her curls carries snatches of a song from a battle raging in the distance. But she lifts up her white hands; the storm entices songs from her harp, and her soul is

---

* From Macpherson's famous forgery of a "Celtic" saga; quotation here is from the original English version, *The Poems of Ossian*, trans. James Macpherson.

mournful. Her hero and beloved has fallen; the shimmering moonlight lingers over his torn shield, and his last, incomplete song has been cut off and is now a mere plaything of the dark winds. Malwina surrenders her curls to the storm, and sings a lament for her nobly fallen beloved. His spirit is a whitish mist hovering above his grave.

It goes on like this for pages, and often sounds ridiculous, but there are some felicitous, even gripping passages, as for instance when Ossian, the blind bard, sings of his blind old age: "Why does Ossian still sing? He will soon be lying in the narrow house."

A reading of Ossian will convert anybody who knows a little Homer and isn't an overly sentimental oddball into a lifelong lover of antiquity. Ossian is not one for smiles or jokes, and he cannot describe any battle in which men are killed; the moist and desolate autumn mists of the gloomy north of Scotland and Ireland waft around everywhere; there is no light, warmth, color, shape, and above all, no sun. This image could be quite captivating: the ancient bard sits on a mossy hill above the foaming waters, his blind head is sunk as he contemplates past deeds, and he holds a crude, three-stringed harp. However, we have Homer too, who not only smiles and even laughs but also sings in a more serious, genuine vein about a man's steadfast love for his wife and country, the solemn mystery of death, and the dark world of the shades. Moreover, Homer knows all about the sun, which he loves with a passion; it's a warm, southern sun and a golden-blue sky; artfully but unobtrusively, he conjures up colorful, sunny images before our eyes: we see towering, shimmering cities and solid, well-constructed ships sailing on the gleaming sea; we also see gods doling out advice and inflamed men rushing into battle, their shields clanking. And when he describes a character, let's say Helen, she appears before us as flesh and blood, a powerful and radiant figure, a source of joy even to the old men in the assembly. It's impossible to imagine what Ossian's women are like: they have white hands, are expert harpists, and have windswept curls; the only other thing we know about them is that they are delicate creatures, whose inner woes cause them to die off remarkably quickly, preferably on the graves of their fallen sweethearts. Well, that can certainly suit individual heroes very well—even Shakespeare had his Hamlet—but if entire peoples turn moist-eyed and are enveloped in mist, the overall impression will be of a giant tear-jerking enterprise, so vast that it can afford to dismiss lachrymose heroes like Werther and Siegwart* as mere school-

* The sentimental heroes of Goethe's *The Sorrows of Young Werther* (1774) and J. M. Müller's *Siegwart: A Monastic Tale* (1776).

boys. These Ossianic heroes weep so copiously that, if their tears didn't flow all the way downhill into the roaring stream—and fortunately they do—they would drown in them. And their tears flow like little brooks in the meadows—that line of verse often comes to mind. Maybe the youths are always weeping "encores" to stave off that great flood.

Enough of that! The only reason I'm writing this down is to prove that I haven't allowed myself to get totally absorbed in Goethe. I read some Sudermann recently to keep up with the times, and found more than I had expected. *Dame Care* is no masterpiece, but the *At Twilight* novellas impressed me; they are well constructed and as elegantly linked as Persian fairy tales, virtually all of them are technically perfect. Sudermann writes very fine German when he really wants to, but often he just couldn't be bothered. [. . .]

TO JOHANNES AND MARIE HESSE

[September 13–19, 1896]

[. . .] I'm always running into the Sunday God of churchgoing Christians and cannot help noticing that he doesn't help out much on weekdays. There are some Christians like that among our own acquaintances. I must admit that my gods—my ideals in life, my poetry, even my little cult of Goethe—are better and more faithful than that Sunday God. They support me fully when things seem altogether dismal and hopeless, but there's the rub: they suffer and complain along with me, but since they are creations of mine, they don't have the requisite strength to pull me up and rescue me. And what will happen when the evil hour arrives that I have long dreaded, when all my work and dreams are finished, when the hand with which I work, write, and play around is all cold and shriveled, and these eyes, so avid for light, cloud over and go blind. None of my gods or my lyrics will accompany me then.

While out on a walk with the Reverend Strauss and dear Mr. Huppenbauer on my last evening in Freudenstadt, I felt as if a door were opening in front of me; I heard the person I'm looking for pass by, and I lay awake the whole night, praying that he would stay with me, take everything I had in exchange for an assurance that he would help me. And I had nights like that again and again; and now often feel as empty as a dried-up well, and poorer than heretofore.

I'm scanning the heavens again for the stars that represent my previous ideals, and am again trying through a form of poetic pantheism to uncover the secret to peace and health. Once again I feel that I can read the revelations of the poets better than those of the Bible. But I now know, even though no revelation has been vouchsafed me, that the Christian faith is not just a form or parable, it has a palpable, living presence; there exists no other power capable of creating and preserving such a holy sense of community and love.

Forgive me! But why not be open about the only things that really matter? I haven't found a God yet, but I'm grateful that I was able to find some revelation. You may regard the world of my ideas as nothing but a little kindergarten, but since I haven't found anything better, I want to remain faithful to an aesthetic world whose ultimate boundaries are invisible to our eyes. I realize that even the highest achievements of our poets are just patchwork, and I sometimes feel that our entire literature is quite puny and impoverished; but the "world of poetry" that I have in mind is utterly magnificent, and when compared to its splendor, all existing works, even the *Iliad* and *Hamlet* and *Faust*, seem but a shabbily designed forecourt. [. . .]

TO KARL ISENBERG

Tübingen, June 12, 1897

Thanks for your kind and clever letter. I have a free hour right now, so I can pick up the thread again.

I have founded my "center" on a belief in beauty, which is virtually the same thing as a belief in art. You are a pedagogue, so you're professionally more or less hostile to art, since whenever the concept of art crops up in the classroom, you have to start thinking about that ugly essay question on "Art and Morality."

I certainly have no desire for a morality based on aesthetics, since art ("the beautiful") would only suffer because it is too good for 90 out of 100 people. Aesthetics as an educator—legislation without criminal law. This "center" of mine has developed from a passing fancy, a mere plaything, into a religion. As a university graduate and teacher, you may dismiss this religion as a kind of unscientific aestheticism. But it is rich in consolation, rich in the diversity of lived experience, rich in secrets and revelations. I have discovered for the first time what religion is, and since then treat every "belief" unbelievably gently, for I believe firmly that I'm now at a higher stage of existence.

For me, Beauty in Nature and Beauty in Art (also literature) are of approximately equal value, although I'm perhaps a bit more sensitive to the latter. I don't regard Nature as the mother of all Art and the primary mode of being for all Beauty, but rather, just like Art, as an image, a symbol, an attempt to represent ideal Beauty. No work of art or scene from nature ever encompasses within itself all the laws and possibilities of aesthetics that may be valid within its frame. So, e.g., I consider many landscapes to be to some extent subjective creations, marked with the stamp of an artistic personality.

You may think my love for Chopin is characteristic of my taste—but that's only the case in music. Although I admire rhythm and euphony, when it comes to literature I love the beat produced by individual words and the meaningful individual sounds more than the perfect, complex tonal technique that impresses me in Chopin.

TO JOHANNES AND MARIE HESSE

Tübingen, September 25, 1897

[. . .] God help art now that the Swiss are discovering female folk poets. That is a flourishing industry. Not to mention religious poetry! That is the most ticklish and, on the whole, least artful genre I have ever come across. The more lyrical, the less pious—and vice versa! It was the Moravians who really slit the genre's throat.

Do forgive me! It's just that there is something tragicomical from the outset about the religious and, more specifically, nonliturgical verse of Protestant Pietism—and the gems by Gerhardt and Claudius don't necessarily gainsay this.[. . .]

I understand why my Chopin lyric didn't appeal to you.* It's not great. But what Wagner was to Nietzsche, Chopin is to me—perhaps even more so. There is a relationship between the very essence of my intellectual and spiritual life and the warm, lively melodies, the piquant, lascivious, nervous harmony, and all the other qualities of Chopin's remarkably intimate music.

And I frequently marvel at the elegance, reserve, and accomplished sovereignity of Chopin as a person. Everything about him is noble, although he can be degenerate.

One other thing! Over the past few weeks I have written a couple of little essays, which are not intended for publication but for use in personal letters, etc. These are more or less ready now; they were intended for Mother's birthday—as a substitute for my unsatisfactory

---

* "Chopin" (1897), poem with sections entitled "Grande Valse" and "Berceuse" (*Gedichte*, pp. 13–14).

correspondence. All are quite personal and written for you alone. But now I hesitate once again and don't know whether I should send them to you. They certainly won't be any great success—no doubt we shall always be going around in circles searching for mutual understanding.[. . .]

Much love and many kisses, gratefully yours

TO HELENE VOIGT-DIEDERICHS*

Tübingen, August 27, 1898

I'm putting aside Mundt's *Literary History*, Schlegel's *Reviews*, and Novalis's *Hymns*† in order to visit you for a few moments.

As you can see, I'm making steady progress with the Romantics. I'm studying a lot, and am gradually acquiring an overview plus some firm opinions. Romanticism! It has all the mystery and youthfulness of the German heart, all its excess energy as well as its sickness, and above all that longing for intellectual heights, that gift for youthful, ingeniously speculative thought, which our age absolutely lacks. The religion of art: to me that is the essence and goal of Romanticism at its most naïve and refined. I find the amateurish, halfhearted cult of Nietzsche in our recent literature sad and ridiculous. How few understand him, how gloomy and pitiful they seem in comparison to him, and how little there is to show for all the adulation and quotation! The dark, feverish verses of Dehmel‡ have the most life. The era of the Schlegels, Hardenberg, Steffens, Schelling, and Schleiermacher was far richer! If Novalis had been a bit more prolific—a not uncommon talent—if he had been better at putting books together, he would have surpassed all the literati of his time and those of subsequent eras. Anyhow, I love him the way he is. He is one of the few who know more than they say, who are richer than their poems, bigger than their words.

But forgive me for lecturing. That's what happens to people who don't keep a diary. It's not easy for me to find the right conversational tone, since I'm wearing my work clothes and the study lamp is on. I would like to be with you today, asking you all sorts of things, and listening to your answers, which I already know. I would like to hear you speak or discuss one of our favorites together.

* Writer; married to publisher Eugen Diederichs.
† Friedrich Schlegel (1772–1829), the Romantic critic; and Novalis's (Friedrich von Hardenberg, 1772–1801) *Hymns to Night* (1800), a major text of German Romanticism.
‡ Rhetorically powerful social poet.

Some time ago I heard little Pauer playing Chopin's Scherzo in B Minor. It was my first chance since Sarasate* to hear a brilliantly virtuoso performance, and it did me a world of good. I've never heard Chopin played so finely, elegantly and fleetingly, with all the charm of his mysteries and twilights. The shrill high point of the scherzo, which few performers succeed in doing well, sounded pure and captivating.

A few weeks ago I spent an enjoyable day here with my two sisters. I brought them and some friends up the Lichtenstein—it was a beautiful, happy day, full of good cheer, lively conversations, forest fragrances, and mountain light. Since then we have had a succession of hot summer days and humid, sleepless nights; a daily swim in the Neckar was the only way to cool off, and there was a lot of work too, so in the evenings I was glad to get to bed at last, and yet I would start off the next day feeling impatient and not in the least bit refreshed. Then, finally, the day before yesterday, we had some rain and a storm. I lay at the window listening half the night. Now I can use the evenings again to work and read. Besides theoretical works, Novalis and also Tieck, his friend and counterpart. Am reading some things by Tieck for the first time, and understanding others better now. I often find his sense of color delightful; it's interesting to watch his cheerful and often quite daring games with both theme and form; besides, there are some marvelous pieces in his fairy tales and novellas.

Tübingen, October 2, 1898

Thank you for your greetings from Nürnberg. I'm glad that you didn't force yourself to write a more formal letter, and just to prove that I don't want to be the kind of correspondent who simply tots up credits and debits, or questions and answers, I'm getting back to you unbidden.

This is a long, lonely Sunday; I find it impossible to spend the entire day doing intellectual work, and during the past two months all my friends have been away on their travels. I have just come back from a walk. I sat along the splendid path lined with linden trees, and watched the leaves falling and the children playing. An aging, independent scholar disturbed my musings—a desiccated, lonely, and embittered bachelor known as "skullhead." For years now he has been living all alone. He injected his bitter mockery into the elegy I had just begun, and walked around those paths with me for a whole hour, talking and grumbling. It was a strange thing to watch: he couldn't help making bitter and angry jokes, yet he needed so badly to talk about himself and

---

* Spanish violin virtuoso.

be sociable that he thrust himself upon me in a manner I found almost moving.

I'm in my room now, alternating between writing and reading. Schleiermacher's letters are propped open in front of me, and I'm reading them eagerly and with great pleasure. Alongside them is the copybook full of memories that I once mentioned. I'd love to show it to you. The uncovered past is here beside this fresh page, and I'm comparing my active life now to my phlegmatic dreams back then. And that brings to mind my only decent, worthwhile friendship during these years, and I think gratefully of you. I have often been poor, hard-bitten, embittered, but when I examine my life now, I realize that your concern has invigorated and encouraged me, and that I'm on my way uphill.

Just imagine! I have bought myself a violin again, and love fooling around with it, since I enjoy this harmless mode of introspection and meditation.

I don't have any opportunity here to socialize with women, and this makes me feel even closer to you. I always found my relations with women especially meaningful, and miss them even more than family life; I have always profited greatly from the experience of having female company. Especially now, for since I stopped going to social gatherings and ceased drinking beer and wine in the pubs—out of a sense of revulsion and also for health reasons—my friends here have increasingly failed to meet my needs.

Once I get used to the idea of ditching my independent studies for a bit, I may go off wandering—who knows?—maybe next year. It is my inner isolation that makes me long for lots of conversations and activities with people, whom I could really love and learn something from.

An indirect result of this empty life devoid of social contacts is that my mind doubles its expectations of my solitary pursuits. My mind lusts after studies that I simply don't have the free time to pursue; it squints at Plato and chides me every day for not having read the works of Kant and Hegel. I feel those summits are beyond the scope of my studies in literary aesthetics, and if I were leading a more active life, they would certainly lose much of their appeal. Actually, I'm not historically or philosophically minded, although I do have a critical bent; I find life the best test for my heartbeat, works of beauty for my eye, and euphonious song for my ear. My muse cherishes above all else the play of light, feverish colors, the quivering of delicate sounds, music rather than sculpture.

So you see, I was serious when I said I would tell you something about myself. The twilight is interrupting me, and I shall finish now, so I can devote the lamplight to my books.

Where are you now? And were you able to find what you're looking for? In exchange for this glimpse of my solitary retreat, just send me a little whiff of the wide world and all those treasures you are seeing.

TO MARIE HESSE

Tübingen, December 2, 1898

There is no way I would ever refuse to listen attentively to what you have to say. I can see that you read the poems carefully* and kept an eye out for the genuine article. What should I say about your opinion? I believe you are absolutely right in some cases, in others it's a matter of insignificant differences of interpretation, and in others still you touch upon things that to me have the force of law. But what's the point? I wish to thank you for reading all the lyrics so lovingly, and also for going beyond them and thinking of me with such heartfelt solicitude.

Just two things by way of justification! First of all, the very title *Romantic Lyrics* suggests a confession that is aesthetic as well as personal. I believe that they mark the end of a phase and that it just isn't right to draw conclusions from them about my future work. The manuscript has been finished since spring—I have been lonelier, quieter, and more clearheaded ever since. Second, after a lot of reflection, I felt that, in putting it together and deciding which songs to include or omit, I couldn't let myself be swayed by anything personal. The little book was not intended as a miscellany, but rather as a unified whole, a series of modulations and variations on one basic Romantic motif.

Believe me, Mother, your verdict was more important to me than any of the reviews; I'm much in awe of your judgment and sensitivity. Besides, our hearts are not at such a remove that I would find your motherly admonitions and worries incomprehensible and unworthy of respect. You have no idea how many of them seem true to me, even though, despite my best intentions, I'm unable at present to make them my own. When I think of my difficult years, how can there be any part of me left that is ungrateful and doesn't want to submit to you!

I have been having headaches since the day before yesterday and am using phenacetin with good results. I was healthy for so long that I

* Hesse's first volume of poetry, *Romantische Lieder*, appeared that autumn (dated Dresden, 1899).

now feel a bit subdued and dispirited. You will always have to make plenty of allowances for me and my letters!

TO HELENE VOIGT-DIEDERICHS

Tübingen, February 19, 1899

Your kind letter reached me unexpectedly early this time. Your inner eye must be unusually clear-sighted and you must have a remarkable sensitivity in personal matters, since you can read my entire being in a way nobody else can. The nighttime pages that you're holding in your hands originated during countless midnight walks on sleepless nights along streets, bridges, and avenues. These solitary hours under the swaying chestnut and plane trees have become an invaluable and purifying source of memory and reflection; my days have been refreshed and deepened by the cold breath of those nights. During that period I must have reviewed the memories of my entire life some hundred times; I had much cause for self-accusation and regret, since I discovered many extinguished stars in my firmament. But I felt that the remaining ones deserved to survive, and I made friends with my past. My wishes reflect the day and the hour; perhaps I shall never again be able to spend months in humble reflection discovering inner strengths the way I have since last summer. Often, when I had finished contemplating some memory and stood gazing into the dark Neckar, I would see standing beside me in a vision a friend, who was inwardly at one with me. Occasionally I had to smile and stretch out my hand, as if you were coming toward me and knew everything I had gone through and contemplated here in the dark.

On these strolls I'm often approached by the shadowy forms of future works, which have arisen from the depths, those large misty shapes. I used to greet them, and certainly recognized them emotionally, and yearned for a time when I could finish molding them. So I'm expecting two treasures, and wish one of them could be present to share my peace and happiness.

Nighttime sounds heard during one of those late walks—the branches creaking, the river murmuring, the sound of someone's footsteps one night—there is nothing more to those artlessly written pages in my copybook. I had intended to add a wreath in honor of my dear Chopin, but haven't found anything good enough yet.

On Shrove Tuesday a harlequin put his arm around me and asked: "Are you the ghost of the avenues?" I said yes and freed myself; he then called out after me: "If it's poetry you want, you'll have to come up with something more forceful than your 'silken' Romantic verse."

Today (Sunday) I had a most uncommonly pleasant experience. I was at one of the splendid Schapitz matinees and heard two Beethoven quartets, op. 59 III and op. 131. The minuet and allegro molto in the first piece are wonderfully elegant. In all of Germany one couldn't hear anything that would surpass the noble, exceptionally well-rehearsed and tightly disciplined Beethoven quartets of those four chamber musicians from Stuttgart. The audience is very small and just about every connoisseur is there. I really enjoy the whole thing. It takes some courage to give a public concert in that sober hall, in the morning light, standing there with just four stands, the instruments, and those virtually unknown Beethoven quartets. I find this Schapitz music unutterably refreshing. Just imagine: a string quartet on Sunday morning, without the lighting, jewelry, and pomp of the virtuosos, in front of barely a hundred listeners, with no gossipy intermissions and sparkling dresses, so that the audience is extremely attentive and has to do its best to fill the hall with applause. The four performers, on the other hand, are hardworking artists, who are superbly trained and work together cordially, without any trace of virtuoso egotism, to bring pure versions of these masterly old quartets to light. It's a great test for the audience: most drift away; limitations in intellect and education become quite clear. The opera fans are the first to leave; one senses with some embarrassment that the music and orchestra in the theaters have dulled even good ears and made it impossible for them to appreciate these elegant, but by no means pompous works of art. If you had heard today's andante ma non troppo, there would be no need for me to resort to words: the four violinists sitting on their little chairs, painfully misunderstood.

Now it has got very late, so *addio*! I'm eager to hear whether your husband has any use for my manuscript. My thanks for your letter, and also for your friendship. You know, the trust and understanding you have shown have created an echo in me, indeed more than an echo. With an expression of friendship

TO EUGEN DIEDERICHS

Tübingen, April 6, 1899

I was delighted to get your friendly letter. I fully agree with your plan to publish 600 copies;* please let me know if you have any other suggestions. I fully realize that we cannot expect any great demand given

* *Eine Stunde hinter Mitternacht (An Hour beyond Midnight)*, a collection of prose poems (Leipzig, 1899).

The twenty-one-year-old bookdealer's apprentice in Tübingen: "There I struggled through the three-year apprenticeship, which was anything but easy, and remained another year as the youngest employee in the store, with a salary of eighty marks monthly"

(*Above*) The *Petit Cénacle*. Left to right: Otto Erich Faber, Oskar Rupp, Ludwig Finckh, Carlo Hammelehle, Hesse

> *We were considered decadent and modern*
> *And we believed it complacently.*
> *In reality we were young gentlemen*
> *Of extremely modest demeanor.*
> —*"To the Petit Cénacle"*

(*Below*) Drinking Chianti in Fiesole, 1906

> *People warn you against the profession of poet,*
> *Also against playing the flute, the drums, the violin,*
> *Because riffraff of this sort*
> *So often tend toward drinking and frivolity.*
> —*From Hesse's unpublished light verse*

the specific and perhaps all too personal nature of my little book. The very thought of those 600 customers makes me want to burst out laughing.

In accepting my book for your press, you are fulfilling an ardent wish of mine and I shall always appreciate and be grateful for what you have done. I would also like to thank you for giving such an honest account of your impression of me. I hope we can get to know each other at some point by discussing, e.g., the Proteus of "Romanticism." Today I can only give you a hint: I was rather ill when I wrote most of my previous work and had to steal the time and mental energy from a busy professional life. For the time being I have shelved my larger plans. But I'm sure that you will eventually discover those qualities that you find lacking in me. All I can claim by way of literary assets is my painstaking reverence for language, and especially for its musical qualities. That is the keystone of *my* Romanticism: loving care of the language, which I envision as a rare old violin; many qualities are required for such a violin to last and continue sounding beautiful: history, training, careful maintenance by expert hands. Of course, what is language without the mind! Yet "morality is self-explanatory," according to Vischer's *Auch Einer.** Have you noticed also how sloppy, crude, and rather stilted the ordinary language of our contemporary literati is, even of poets, as if they intended to caricature Heine today, Nietzsche tomorrow.

But enough of that! I cordially reciprocate your greetings and those of your spouse. May the time come soon when the give-and-take between our two houses will be more equitable and less embarrassing for me than hitherto.

TO KARL ISENBERG

Basel, January 16, 1900

So you're in Tübingen once again, and I'm not there to greet you. And this time I would very much like to be there since you might well find my presence more agreeable and useful than usual! I think of you a lot and can more or less put myself in your situation. I always hated the thought of having to rest and not being able to move, and yet, when suffering from nervous problems, I've often longed for some rest, hoping to have nothing on my mind but my own condition and ways to get better. Maybe you're going through something similar, in spite of all your misfortune; what's more, you do have your bride and thus you have other

---

* A whimsical novel (1879).

positive things to think about. All of us siblings are with you in spirit, but you already know that. I can't think of anything better than various bits and pieces about myself, some news from Basel, but you may find this more entertaining than a real exchange of ideas.

I like it here—you already know that. And you also know that Basel, even if it has no style of its own, has its own peculiar atmosphere. The city and its people possess a real treasure trove of solid traditions— in the form of money, outward appearance, and, above all, education. Moreover, I'm realizing that there is a decent amount of artistic soil amid these pious, almost puritanical people. In the interiors of these bourgeois homes, one gets to see objects that one only sees in museums or castles elsewhere. One of the most valuable things about the museum, as far as I can judge, is that it has been assembled through private donations and includes several large private collections. What one sees is not so much an assortment of individual pieces as a series of complete collections, and though the museum as a whole is one-sided, it's also more unified than other medium-sized museums. The great cult of Böcklin during the last ten years or so is very much in evidence. The most recent acquisitions are two sculptures by Stauffer-Bern and a splendid picture by Thoma, first-rate things, in other words. As for older objects, with the exception of Holbein, there is more in private houses than in the museum, very many Italians, among them a Leonardo, some Cranachs, etc. There is a quite charming little Böcklin in the house of Wackernagel, the archivist. That house has almost become my home. I read books there with the archivist, look at pictures with his son, discuss everything freely with his wife, play games with his older daughter, and entertain these wonderful children, who are less inhibited by the niceties of a good upbringing than most Basel children and get up to pranks occasionally. I was also there for Christmas Eve.

Besides, I'm sharing quarters with an artist, the architect Jennen, but we seldom chat about art, since he hates talking as much as he hates writing, hardly ever reads a book, and gazes at the world through charming, bright childlike eyes; I have never seen the likes of them. We have rented three rooms together for a few months. But I don't often see him at home; in the evenings he is always gallivanting about with company or else doing sketches. He is working on the new Gothic town hall.

When I walk through those very familiar streets in the Spalen district, I sometimes think of the way you used to stroll along there as a high school student, while I was still a cheeky kid in kindergarten. And you have now reached quite a ripe old age! [. . .]

TO JOHANNES AND MARIE HESSE

Basel, July 10, 1900

My dearly beloved,

[. . .] My ultimate goal is beauty, or "art," if you like; I don't believe my path is any different from yours until one gets to the decisive turning point toward a specifically Protestant form of Christianity. I can probably now accept some kind of belief in God—i.e., a belief that there is positive order in the world—but from then on the form and purpose of religion seems to be either too murky or too ignoble. I cannot believe that Luther, say, lived more nobly and died in a more blessed state than, e.g., the pagan Titian. Whereas Luther had a marvelous, hot-tempered but unpolished mind, Titian attained the kind of harmony and perfection of which the not so gentle reformer could scarcely dream.

But we don't want our words going round and round in circles again; we're actually closer to one another than we realize [. . .]

[Vitznau, mid-September 1900]

Thanks a lot for Mama's letter, which arrived yesterday! I have some free time to write today since I need a whole day's rest, and cannot go hiking, etc. Yesterday, I treated myself to a ten-hour boat trip (8 to 6 o'clock) from here to Gersau, Treib, Brunnen, Rütli, Sisikon, and back again. Apart from a half-hour walk on the Rütli, I spent the entire ten hours all by myself in my boat, and so I could see the lake in every kind of light, etc. After rowing in the fog for the first half hour, the mountains started coming into view, first the beautiful Oberbauen, which I really love, then Bürgenstock, Stanser, and Buochser Horn, then Frohn-alpstock and shortly beyond Gersau the Mythen, from Brunnen past Urirotstock, the Gais Mountains, etc., between them in the distance Glärnisch, at the rear to the left Hohfluh, Vitznauer Stock, and Rigi. I took along a pair of extra oars, a small bottle of wine, and three breakfast rolls, and never left the boat all day. Everything went beautifully until Rütli, then (about 11:30 o'clock) one of the famous storms on Lake Urn caught me off guard. At first I thought it was fun, but got worried when my boat started bouncing about and confusing right side up with upside down. After the storm had seemingly reached its peak—by then I had lost an oar—I took a cue from Epicurus: Let us eat and drink, for tomorrow we shall die. I used the last sip of wine to wash down the last half of a roll, then after vain attempts with countless matches, I finally lit a cigar and took my boots off so I could swim, if worse came to worst. Although that proved unnecessary, I drifted for about two and a half hours until I finally took a few risks battling high waves and came ashore at Sisikon. So, unfortunately, I never got as far as Flüelen. In Sisikon, I waited for a half hour (in the boat), then fought my way slowly to Brunnen, and from there things went smoothly again. Aside from these emergencies, the trip was indescribably beautiful: I rowed into every attractive inlet that struck my fancy; sometimes the sun was beating down on me in the middle of the lake; at times I was shaded by oaks and beech trees beside the shore. I'd never have thought I could keep rowing for ten hours. Of course, I could hardly move a limb yesterday evening, but the only trace I feel today is a certain heaviness in my shoulders and hands. I'm off to Basel the day after tomorrow.

The dining-room bell is ringing—an agreeable sound in hotels—and after the meal I shall be too tired to write—so adieu. I'm gazing out the window again; the lake is sunny, dark green with blue edges, and the mountains are all clear. I have to wash the blue ink from my fingers and go eat.

TO RUDOLF WACKERNAGEL-BURCKHARDT*

Calw, October 19, 1902

This is the first time in months that I have been allowed to write a letter and am up to it. My eyes have been giving me trouble since June, and I've been hanging around in Calw since late August, and have only recently been allowed to read and write a bit. Even though the fall was beautiful and I was quite active as a fisherman, I spent most of the time thinking things over. Illness and involuntary leisure are more conducive to thought than many a doctoral thesis.

I also reviewed those years that I more or less squandered in Basel, and often thought of you. For your house was the only one in Basel that was something of a home away from home for me, where I enjoyed myself and felt stimulated. Forgive me for not showing up at all last year; it wasn't just that I felt moody—most of the time I really was ill. Also, I was nervous once again at the thought of all the insufferable chattering that goes on at large evening parties, and those feelings grew so pronounced that all social occasions seemed threatening to me.

I have been working on a novel for almost a year now, and if I keep going at the current pace, it should be ready ten to twelve years

* Archivist and author of *A History of the City of Basel*.

from now.* In the meantime I have chosen a new selection of my poems, which will appear shortly.† I felt strange when it was being printed, since the proofs were lying around, yet I wasn't allowed to read a single line! I still find reading hard, and writing even more so. It's strange and also sad how dependent one is on one's body—I had wanted to let you know some of my thoughts and future plans, and I now find it so difficult to write that my attitude changes and my mood goes to the dogs whenever I'm actually confronted with the physical effort. So all I can do is give you my regards and assure you of my friendship and gratitude! Besides, I hope to see you soon since I want to try returning to Basel and my work at the beginning of November.

The first weeks of my convalescence were idyllic, very peaceful, I spent a lot of time down by my dearly beloved water (*sor acqua*). Our river, with its old bridges and green banks, is quite beautiful, and it's also well stocked with fish; I stood for days at the waterside, rod in hand, absorbed in the reflected colors à la Lauscher.‡ If it weren't for those nasty customs officials, etc., I'd have gladly sent you a basket of fish.

For the moment, you'll have to make do with these laborious scribbles. They're only meant to prove I'm still among the living. Goodbye!

TO STEFAN ZWEIG§

Basel, February 5, 1903

Thanks for your nice, friendly letter. I'm absolutely delighted that I'm going to receive your book.‖

Being a rather unsteady sort of person, I find it impossible to agree to pacts or commitments of any kind. And I don't have what it takes to keep up a literary correspondence. Besides, at the moment my eyes, which are usually bright and restless, are very weak (I couldn't read or write for months last year). Yet it's not as if we were proposing marriage! So, even though I'm not a letter writer, you'll find I'm grateful for any greetings you send or any interest you show in me, and I shall be glad

---

* *Peter Camenzind*, which first appeared in *Die Neue Rundschau* in 1903 and was then published by S. Fischer (Berlin, 1904).

† *Neue deutsche Lyriker: Gedichte von Hermann Hesse*, the third volume in a series edited by Carl Busse and published by G. Grotesch (Berlin, 1902).

‡ A reference to Hesse's early novel, *The Posthumous Writings and Poems of Hermann Lauscher* (Basel, 1901).

§ Austrian writer noted for early Neoromantic poetry, Freudian fiction, and popular biographical essays.

‖ Possibly Zweig's first book, *Silberne Saiten: Gedichte* (1901).

to let you participate occasionally in what I'm experiencing, whether the tidings be sorrowful or joyful. But on an irregular basis and without stipulations! You know what I mean?

There's little enough to be said about me. Apart from a couple of love affairs, my heart has been touched more by nature and by books than by people. I love the old Italian novellas and the German Romantics, even more the cities of Italy, and most of all the mountains, streams, and ravines, sea, sky and clouds, flowers, trees, and animals. Hiking, rowing, swimming, fly-fishing are what I like best. Except that I don't pursue them as a sportsman, but seem more a lazybones, an oddball lost in his dreams. If money ever falls into my lap, I shall probably withdraw without any farewells to an Italian village in the mountains or by the sea.

Actually, I'm not at all antisocial. I like hanging around with children, farmers, sailors, etc., and can always be counted on to go for a few drinks in sailors' pubs, etc. But I hate the thought of places where it's necessary to wear gloves and choose one's words carefully, and I've been strictly avoiding all such social gatherings for the last two years. During the week I work in a small secondhand bookstore; in the evenings I read or play billiards, and on Sundays I rove around in the mountains and valleys, always on my own. I picked up my literary pretensions along the way.

I did acquire some expertise in a few favorite subjects of mine: the history of German Romanticism, Tuscan decorative painting of the fifteenth century, and a few others. I also have considerable firsthand knowledge about the wines of Baden, Alsace, and Switzerland. I studied philosophy for several years, without coming up with any great insights and so I eventually gave it up.

I haven't been afflicted with literary success of any kind. My little volumes are stacked in neat bundles at the publishers. This has annoyed me at times, but hasn't ever made me feel dejected, since I realize I'm an oddball and thus rather irrelevant. I don't have what it takes to be a literary journalist, being too clumsy, proud, and lazy for that. I write because I enjoy writing, never just because I have to work. However, I do resort to journalism occasionally, for the dreary reason that I need some income.

I'm not sure whether I have given you a clear enough picture of myself. We don't really know ourselves—and I'm not used to talking, especially about myself. This will have to do!

One thing I forgot to mention is that, even though I'm usually unsociable, I make special allowances for visual artists (painters and architects). I'm always happy in studios smelling of paint and creative work, where there are architects' plans hanging on the walls and portfolios lying around. But I have little time for literati, actors, and musicians. Whereas painters are always talking about nature, the others are always going on about their work or fellow artists, whom they envy.

That's all I can think of today. I think I shall put aside my self-portrait (unreadable) for now, and shall be glad to talk to you some other time about more agreeable things, such as rambles, plans for the future, and so on [. . .]

TO ALFONS PAQUET*

Basel, March 20, 1903

Many thanks for your letter, which impressed me doubly, since I had to cough up a postal surcharge of 25 centimes. I hope we shall meet sometime in April; at this point I cannot propose anything more precise than that either. Finckh† is coming to Berlin in mid or late April, and I'm planning an Italian trip for the beginning of May. Well, let's just wait and see.

Unfortunately, you were wrong to assume that I am or have been a student. I have never been a student and have never felt at all attracted to student life. I usually abominate both the academically minded students and the boisterous set; I thought the whole university setup was ridiculous, and feel it's a pity so many young people think studying is the only decent career open to them. During my stay in Tübingen—I was there for a full four years and often lived with students—I got fed up with the whole thing. I've always loathed having to consort with students, professors, musicians, actors, and literati, but am fond of visual artists, especially painters, and tend to socialize almost exclusively with the latter. But I'm certainly no authority on the matter, since even though I believe I'm fairly unprejudiced in all matters of the intellect, I'm certainly a real oddball when it comes to my day-to-day relations with others. If the slightest formality attaches to any social occasion, I avoid it like the plague. I'm deathly afraid of everything that seems obligatory or compulsory, no matter whether it's a party, club, family visit, or friendship. Finckh is the only friend I have, and I've always been frightened of him.

---

* A pacifist writer best known for Expressionist poems and plays.
† Ludwig Finckh, Hesse's boyhood friend, a physician and writer.

As for my profession, I'm a secondhand bookseller—i.e., my job, for about 100 francs a month, is to buy, catalogue, and, if possible, resell the books of bygone eras. I spend my spare time outdoors, in wine bars or writing a novel; I've been playing around for more than a year with the novel, which at present seems little more than a mass of corrections, cuts, and variants. My goal is to have so much money someday that I can drop out of literary and social circles and enjoy the life of a peaceful wanderer, strolling all alone through the beautiful countryside. My paper has run out, and I enclose most cordial greetings, yours

TO HIS FAMILY IN CALW

Florence, April 8, 1903

My dear loved ones,

Now that I have a bit of peace at last, I can fill you in a bit. Here's why I'm in Florence.

An artist friend of mine, Fräulein Gundrun, was about to leave Basel recently to go to Italy for good, and she invited all sorts of acquaintances and friends to travel with her to Florence for Easter. I wasn't thinking of going, until the very last day, when another artist, Fräulein Bernoulli,* got very excited about the idea and persuaded me to go along. I had barely enough time to change, pack some clothes, and leave with them. That was eight days ago today: 6 o'clock on Wednesday evening. The trip to Milan lasted the whole night. Since none of the three of us has any money and we're all traveling third-class, we were rather worn out when we arrived, yet spent all of Thursday running around Milan, viewing things like the Certosa di Pavia, which I'd already seen two years ago. We were on a nonstop train to Florence (via Bologna) from 7 o'clock on Friday morning to 6 o'clock in the evening. Now we're sitting around—i.e., running about energetically—in these beautiful surroundings. It was very strange how much at home I again felt, from the very first moment. I know every nook and cranny here, and had the feeling I was just returning after a short absence. We found a splendid old chamber for the two girls in a large sixteenth-century palace, ridiculously cheap. Since I don't want to strain my eyes, I hardly ever go to the galleries, and hang around instead in the alleys, squares, markets,

* Maria Bernoulli, subsequently Hesse's wife, ran a portrait studio with her sister in the Bäumleingasse in Basel, where meetings of artists were often held.

taverns, and eating houses. I love watching the townspeople, and am also taking advantage of the inexpensive, fine cuisine. Unfortunately, Fräulein Bernoulli has to leave early on Sunday.

So much for today, my time is up. We wish to go to San Lorenzo and later on to a divine service with music in the Annunziata.

TO STEFAN ZWEIG

Calw, October 11, 1903

Strange! Yesterday I thought of you, decided I would write to you soon, then your nice card arrives today. Thanks very much! I fear a second reading of my *Rundschau* novel (it will appear later on as a book)* won't give you as much pleasure as the first, because it's unfortunately rather ponderous and crude.

It was just as well you didn't look me up in Basel. I left the city and have been back for a short while in my old home in the Black Forest, where I intend to remain for the entire winter at least. My little old room, which looks out on the setting of my childhood pranks, is all set up, and it makes quite a diligent and scholarly impression with its desk and books, and already smells of tobacco. Hanging on the wall are my fishing rod, pictures of my mother and my sweetheart, who is still in Basel, a couple of pipes, and a map of Italy, which I sometimes pore over. How far away that all seems now!

Here I have found what I was looking for—real peace and solitude. Nobody around here reads books and writes verse, drinks tea and smokes cigarettes and knows everything, has been to Italy and Paris and speaks several languages, and I'm glad about that.

I hope to accomplish a lot of work this winter—at least a novel or something like that. At the moment I'm still spending most of my time preparing for winter—i.e., every day I carry home two small sacks full of fir cones, which I shall use later on for heating. I already have a large boxful, but need a lot more. So I get to see some wonderful things in the woods. The day before yesterday I eavesdropped on a large flock of partridges, today it was a hare, etc. It's altogether interesting, far more entertaining than city life.

But, unfortunately, I'm far away from my sweetheart and need a lot of stamps. I had hoped to get married this winter, but her father refused in a very rude manner, and we have no money, which is why I

---

* *Peter Camenzind.*

now have to work and earn something.* Once I have scraped together what we need, there will be no more asking that thickhead for permission.

In the spring, at a time when these worries were still far away, I spent a month in Italy and in Venice, and guzzled quite a lot of inexpensive sweet Cypriot wine, also caught crabs, got into some quarrels, and visited a number of old palaces I had never seen before. Now it seems like a dream.

Literature affords me as little satisfaction as ever. I got another beautiful review of my poems recently, but not a soul is willing to buy them, and if the new novel doesn't work out, I shall get fed up with the whole thing, and try something else. [. . .]

Gaienhofen, September 11, 1904

So I can write again, now that you're back. I really enjoyed your wonderful, kind letter and all those cards from your travels. As for your last letter, there was a passage in it I found less pleasing. The affair about the pictures! Of course, I don't want to make a fuss, if nothing can be done about it. But I'd be incredibly happy if it were possible to prevent that newspaper from publishing that picture of me. Please!

Aside from that, I enjoyed hearing everything you said. I found it interesting you didn't like "Amstein."† I'm not a good judge of my own scribbles, and perhaps often value the breeziest stuff highest. I find literary criticism absolutely worthless, but am always glad when a friend tells me what he does and doesn't like. I wrote "Amstein" a year and a half ago, and haven't read it again since. The "Marble Works" was written last winter and spring.

So, since the beginning of August I have been living here, married, on Lake Constance, and I very much hope you will come and visit me sooner or later. Vienna seems more remote and less accessible now that I'm living in the country. Gaienhofen is a very small, beautiful village; it has no railway, no store, no industry, not even a pastor of its own, so this morning I had to spend half an hour wading through fields in the most awful rain to get to the funeral of a neighbor. There is no running water, so I fetch all the water from the well; no tradesmen, so I have to do all the necessary repairs in the house myself; and no butcher, so I have to fetch the meat, sausages, etc., from the closest town in the

---

* In spite of the opposition of Maria Bernoulli's father, Hesse became engaged to her at Pentecost 1903. He gave up his job in the Wattenwyl secondhand bookstore and from October 5 on, he was in Calw again, where he started writing his story, *Unterm Rad* (*Beneath the Wheel*) (1906).

† "Hans Amstein," a novella; first published in *Die Neue Rundschau* (1904).

Thurgau. But the place offers tranquillity, clean air and water, beautiful cattle, fabulous fruit, decent people. Apart from my wife and our cat, I don't have any company. I'm living in a little rented farmhouse, for which I pay a yearly rent of 150 marks.

Long live Peter Camenzind! Were it not for him, I wouldn't have been able to marry and move here. He earned me 2,500 marks, and if I stay here, I can survive on that for at least two years.

I used to look forward to being "famous," but it's less fun than I had expected. Schoolteachers and clubs write to me in a businesslike style, asking for free copies of my book, etc. A journalist said he wanted to interview me for a book about "contemporaries." I wrote back saying he should seek out a hydropathic establishment. All of that took place back in Calw; nobody comes over here to Gaienhofen; it's quite remote. In any case, the letters, etc., have subsided, and peace has returned to the countryside.

We rushed through with the wedding. My father-in-law is opposed to it, and refuses to have anything to do with me; so I turned up in Basel while he was out of town; then we hurried off *subitissimo* to the registry office. We can still hear the old man grumbling in the distance, but he seems to be calming down gradually.

So I'm now a married man; my gypsylike existence is over, for the time being. But my little wife is nice and quite reasonable. Of course, she hasn't found out yet that I've just ordered a small barrel of white wine. The wine here is scandalously sour.

You're going to Paris for the winter, and your collection of novellas* is coming out in February? You now want to begin a larger work? My dear sir, dear friend, would you please accept my best wishes! And do come to Lake Constance at some point! There won't be as many new things for you to see as there would be for me in Vienna, but I'd love to spend the afternoon out on the lake with you; and then in the evening we could sit on the bench by the oven in my farmhouse. I'll make sure the wine doesn't run out.

And, if at all possible, you'll leave my picture out of it, won't you? I've made fun of writer's portraits so often that I can't possibly do the same thing myself now. Of course, you're perfectly free to mention me by name in the text. Also, please think of me, and let me know how you and your work are faring. For instance, I would like to know the title of your dissertation.† Yours faithfully and gratefully

---

* *Die Liebe der Erika Ewald* (1904).

† *Die Philosophie des Hippolyte Taine* (1904).

TO LUDWIG THOMA*

Gaienhofen, January 30, 1907

It's certainly high time for me to thank you for your greetings. I was extremely impressed to learn that you're now forty; I have another ten years' worth of experience to digest before then.

I enjoyed the first two issues of *März*, the second in particular. What's more, I have since acquired another good piece: a novella by our dear friend W. Fischer in Graz.† I sent it to Aram today, and we should definitely accept it.

I had the idea I'd publish a nice selection of old, unknown treasures at some later point, and so I've decided to translate some pieces from the splendid medieval Latin of old Caesarius of Heisterbach‡—that is, if I've enough time left over after the construction and other work.

The lake here has been mostly frozen, and we've been out ice-skating a lot. The alpine wind is blowing once again, there's a leak in the roof, and the ovens won't draw.

Finckh got married recently and he's still in the Black Forest. His animals (two donkeys, two St. Bernards, one cat, some trout) may be getting more company: some hens, ducks, and a nanny goat.

The page with Olaf's§ drawings gave us a good laugh.

A little while ago, when the ice was still here, we made a sail, went out on the lake in a sled, and raced about like a locomotive, causing numerous catastrophes. Our friend Bucherer‖ is inventive, and it's handy having him around. We're busy building a large snowman to commemorate the return of Finckh.

TO JAKOB SCHAFFNER**

February 1908

We ought to learn from each other, and this time I learned something from you. Well, our Weltanschauungen are often at loggerheads, and I understand why you can't make heads or tails of mine, which is not in

---

* Writer and co-editor of the journal *März*.

† *Der Mediceer* (1907).

‡ On July 3, 1908, Hesse published a longish essay, "Cäsarius von Heisterbach," in *März* as an introduction to his translations from the *Dialogus miraculorum*, which appeared in the subsequent three issues of *März*. Hesse published a more extensive selection of his Caesarius translations in 1925 under the title *Geschichten aus dem Mittelalter*.

§ Olaf Gulbransson, caricaturist and graphic artist.

‖ Max Bucherer, painter and graphic artist.

** Published in *März*, February 18, 1908.

the least bit evolutionary. I'm pious in the old-fashioned sense, and thus not prepared to concede that there is any development—i.e., progress— in our lives and intellectual pursuits. Otherwise why would the world have needed a Hegel when it had already had a Plato, and if there is progress, how come the so-called land of thinkers is falling for those Jena world puzzles?*

But there is one form of progress I gladly concede: Today's bicycle is certainly better than the one manufactured in 1880, and a locomotive can certainly travel faster than a handcart. I like that change, but not nearly as much as you do, for the following reasons: Opportunities like this allow us to speed up a little, but don't allow us to conquer time. We're usually just as impatient in the express train as we were in the mail coach, assuming, of course, that we're in a hurry, and nowadays aren't we always in a hurry? People in the Orient also know how to live, and according to the elegant account given us recently by Professor Mez, the native population there has no qualms about letting the Europeans do all the railway construction.

But to the point! I wanted to tell you about my typewriter. My dear sir, you're to blame, since I bought it upon your recommendation and example. But I must say I'm really enjoying this tidy little machine, and I want to recite some of its advantages. Especially for one's wrist! After a hard day's work my hand used to ache all over. The pain may well have served as a warning: Don't overdo it! But after all, writing is our trade, and we should let our heads rather than our wrists protest against any excesses.

Moreover, speaking just for myself, when I wrote by hand, I put a great deal of effort, love, art, and sundry flourishes into the penning of individual letters and lines. I always regretted those wasted efforts when I saw the contrast between the sober printed version and the elaborate, delicate product of my fingers. No call for that anymore.

And then there's another difference, the main thing, really. There used to be a huge difference between the manuscript and the printed page; pieces often looked a lot longer or shorter than they were. And, unfortunately, they didn't object to the flattery! Skimming through the familiar handwriting in that sort of manuscript, one would judge it in a rather flattering light, seeing it the way the mirror sees the bride, and everything would seem very well done, or at least tolerably so, even if there were terrible flaws in the piece. Whereas the cold, printlike type almost seems like galley proof; it looks at you critically and severely, in an ironic and almost hostile manner; it's no longer familiar and can

* A reference to the pantheistic work *Welträtsel* (1899) by the Jena professor Ernst Haeckel.

be properly evaluated. It's always refreshing to see dyed-in-the-wool habits being discarded, and this is temporarily true of typing. The shift from hoe to plow or pen to typewriter is really stimulating. And I'm not at all bothered by the clatter that I had dreaded.

So progress exists after all! You may laugh if you wish. But it's only a modest, technical advance, and perhaps it'll soon be superseded by other, more significant developments. Ten years from now I shan't be quite so proud of this 1908 machine. I have a few relics that I really cherish even though they're also a source of amusement; among them is a heavily worn goose-feather quill, which the late Eduard Mörike* sharpened and split with his clever, light hands before sitting down to write. Now, he is a person who never would have bought a typewriter, even if he had been able to afford one. It's impossible to calculate exactly how much of his potential he wasted in the course of his long and idle life; he spent ages cutting quills, doing calligraphy, painting Easter eggs, and if he had only focused a minuscule portion of his energy, he could easily have written three times as much, and we would all be pleased. But the lazybones did nothing of the sort. Those knick-knacks were just as important to him as the future of German literature.

I think life behaves in much the same way. It doesn't ask itself how things will turn out later on; it has no interest in goals or prospects, and likes to hover aimlessly in the present. Only thus can the present aspire to eternity.

TO HIS FAMILY IN CALW

Gaienhofen, February 29, 1908

[. . .] I'm looking forward to Father's new book† and was wondering whether I could have an inscribed copy. I like browsing around in *The Pagans and Us*;‡ I like listening to Papa, and pick up a lot.

Having recently renovated and fortified the foundations of my philosophy of life, I'm more receptive to religious writings of all kinds. There is one point on which all serious, critical philosophies agree: our minds, and even logic itself, are incapable of resolving the issues most crucial for our spiritual well-being. I'm very fond of the teachings of Jesus and find them indispensable as a source of consolation and as a

---

* A pastor and one of the finest poets of the nineteenth century.

† Johannes Hesse, *Frühlingswehen in der Völkerwelt* (1908).

‡ Johannes Hesse, *Die Heiden und wir* (1901/1906).

guide for practical ethics. The notion that life on this earth is brief and heavenly existence eternal is a bit too skimpy in mythological terms; it completely fails to address the issue of previous existences. I need a mythology, an explanation of the universe, that is more complex and graphic, and often borrow material from Buddha and the Vedic legends. Perhaps this issue of previous existences is ethically insignificant, but I have always felt it was attractive, mysterious, and not in the least bit oppressive. In our heart of hearts, when we think of immortality, we think of the individual, since immortality of a nonindividual nature is quite inconceivable; we then ask ourselves repeatedly what that personal soul might have looked like prior to our present existence. At that point the Indian doctrine of reincarnation affords me some satisfaction—even though I don't actually "believe" in it—insofar as it conveys nonconceptual truths in a splendidly graphic manner. However, aside from that, the Indians aren't of much use to me since they rank knowledge above faith. They accept as beyond doubt an almost modern form of determinism, except that for reasons of dogma, they create a loophole for free will on the way to nirvana. But that's enough, I cannot do justice to the subject in a letter. [. . .]

TO RECTOR OTTO KIMMIG

Gaienhofen, March 10, 1908

Many thanks for your friendly note. I liked what you wrote, and not just because I'm looking forward to the arrival of the Zosimus volume. Now, I don't wish to make you feel you ought to write again; I myself cannot write forced letters, and today I'm just replying out of gratitude, since I sensed from your card that we really understand each other, and that's not exactly an everyday occurrence.

I'm glad to hear that you're planning a visit, even if it's later on. You know that you're welcome. I tell everybody that I hate having visitors, but that is meant to scare off the apes who invade the house just out of curiosity, and to benefit the welcome visitors.

Much could be said about the "tragic novel." Perhaps many such novels have already been written. In reading some good, but hardly optimistic writers, I have felt that the story they tell is no more powerful and sad than any extremely straightforward depiction of life—a narrative that doesn't rely on any preordained scheme or doctrine and in which the laughing and crying, dying and marrying occur in the same tempo, with all events being equally funny or unfunny. I find this pattern in, e.g., several of the Russians.

Yet, on the other hand, the "tragic novel" may well be an impossible feat. Tragic drama consciously portrays a truly exceptional life and fate; it's probably also possible to achieve something similar in the novella (in the older sense of the term). But it seems to me that the novel can best express the ordinary, essentially unchanging things in life that are universal.

I don't believe that literary genres exist purely for the sake of the aestheticians or poets (if that were so, there would surely be more of them); the material simply demands them so that everything human can find its own means of expression. And then there is the novel, which is a patiently formless entity, an all-purpose receptacle for everything that doesn't require a genre of its own, for the common, undistinguished, threadbare human things. And as for the attempts to narrate all of this using broad brushstrokes, without illuminating the woeful material in any way or lending a minor art form any lighthearted personal touches such as humor, etc., they were almost unbelievably depressing. The impression left by "pure" naturalism or verism is thus often unartistic, because art should turn sadness into beauty and portray terrible events in a pleasing manner. Otherwise one might just as well read biology, world history, or critical philosophy, which also leave one, ultimately, with the dark impression of a dark chain of events, whose goal and meaning remain unfathomable.

Art, also in the novel, will probably always rely on—and be inspired by—the only apparition in this arbitrary and monstrously wasteful process whose form is pleasing to us—i.e., life as form. The reason being that each form and each individual—not just the beautiful ones—is a source of wonder, the only object in the flow of events that truly exists, or is at least perceptible. In short, the artist will always find that, even though he has no problem believing in the earth's motion and basing his *thought* on that assumption, to live and be creative he has to stand like a savage on secure ground and see the sun going around in a circle. Anybody who believes fervently that objects do not exist or even subscribes to a determinist point of view—which, of course, logically implies absolute predetermination—would not write novels, or anything else, for that matter.

This has remained very fragmentary, but there is a ratio in rebus, also in the fact that I'm running out of paper. More orally at some point!

OPEN LETTER*

Badenau,† July 9, 1909

My dear friend,

I'm a little ashamed to confess my whereabouts and present condition, but I have owed you a letter for a long time, and besides, there's so little to do here—I haven't felt like this since the long Sundays during my vacations as a youth. I have learned how terrible boredom can be, even thinking about it can give me the shudders; it's worse than all the other illnesses, even seasickness.

The situation is as follows: I've been a guest here at the spa in Badenau for the past two weeks! You'll be astonished and may even laugh, which is what I do whenever I get a chance to reflect on my situation. I shall be released in three weeks' time; till then there is no escape. A clever, sensitive physician has taken charge of my nerves, and a well-to-do friend—you can guess his identity—is paying the héfty hotel bill; I wouldn't be here otherwise. This is how my day goes: After getting up, I take a thermal bath, have breakfast, and must then go on a so-called promenade until one o'clock. Lunch is at one, then I'm supposed to rest until four; from then until early in the night I'm permitted to read and write, and thus engage in what my physician politely calls work. Then, at half past nine, a young attendant in white linen comes to my room; he soaks a large linen towel in cold water, wraps me in it, and then beats it with his flattened hands until he is exhausted. It's quite amusing, and the fellow must have no trouble sleeping soundly afterward, but I certainly can't.

As you know, I'm a native of the Black Forest; when I was a small boy, I used to feel a mixture of amazement and contempt at the sight of the numerous spa visitors, or "air grabbers" as we called them, who came to our region in the summer. Now I myself am an air grabber. My days are spent climbing the clean forest paths, cautiously and in decent attire, lying for hours on the wicker chaise longue in the hotel garden, staring in a bored and envious manner at the farmers working in the fields, exhibiting on my face perhaps a faint, somewhat helpless expression, which I interpreted in my youth as a sign that all air grabbers were idiots.

During my first few days here everything irritated me. A spa such as this can destroy the magic and ravish the beauty of the most beautiful

---

* "Kurgast" ("Guest at the Spa"), an open letter in the review *Jugend*.

† Badenweiler, a well-known spa at the western foot of the Black Forest.

valley in the Black Forest. The buildings are outrageously large and garish; there are hundreds of completely unnecessary signposts painted in all sorts of colors; tiny artificial ponds with decrepit swans and idiotic goldfish, and equally tiny artificial waterfalls with tin gnomes or deer, and little walls with water trickling down. Moreover, a gang of musicians fills the peaceful valley with the sound of an absolutely diabolical brass band, for an hour and a half, three times a day, from which there is no escape. Although the audience here is large, elegant, and cosmopolitan, it not only puts up with this stuff but actually seems to enjoy it. It's enough to make one weep.

Those first few days, I was so tired and the weather was so wet that all I got to see of Badenau was those splendid spa monuments. But, of course, I soon noticed that this elegant spa is tiny and rather laughable; it's a ridiculous little kindergarten in which the guests disport themselves in a very odd, apelike manner. The spa is surrounded by a dark, mighty hundred-year-old forest and soft blue-black mountains, which seem to smile wryly at the colorful and quite childish antics occurring at their feet. These are the fir-tree groves, forests of silver fir, fast, transparent, trout-filled streams, and the old, forsaken mills and sawmills of my youth; they greet me again, and in spite of all that has since transpired, I can hear the old, familiar sounds in my ears and in my heart. Something emerges from deep within my soul, the muffled clamor of my youth, the remnants in my heart of my childhood sensibility; the waves may have submerged that part of me, but they have left it unscathed.

During the four or five hours I spend outside each day, this entire world belongs to me alone, with all its mountains and wide, high plateaus, its wild spots covered with ferns, its strawberries and lizards, its ravines and quiet, sleepy, brown-gold water wagtails amid the alders.

For, strange as this may seem, the guests aren't in the least bit interested in nature. They know nothing about it, and just reject it out of hand. They traipse around aimlessly on a few level paths at the spa, and then sit around on one of the many benches, looking either satiated and happy or yellow and out of sorts, and not one of them ever ventures more than a thousand meters from the pump room. Lots of shimmering white dresses can be seen in this restricted area; costly ladies' hats and hairdresses flit about; all sorts of flowers and perfumes release their fragrance; mouths buzz with the sounds of ten languages—but beyond the perimeter there isn't a trace of a single guest, even though that's where there is a real forest and genuine mountain air. They're paying the high spa fees for all those swans, tiny ponds, tin gnomes, signposts, and concerts. One encounters only a few fat gentlemen outside this Holy of Holies, and they run panting along the forest paths, trying to lose weight. It's not as if the thousand-odd spa guests were weak or ill, and thus incapable of going on hikes—whenever there are evening dances, they all seem astonishingly healthy and agile. But they're all afraid of nature, and can tolerate only the extremely adulterated form of nature they see during their "promenades." They're dimly aware that their narrow, self-imposed regulations no longer apply in the woods, and also that their vain demands and petty worries and ailments would seem just as ridiculous there. If they were somewhere in the mountains a couple of hours away, old Pan might suddenly sneak up on them, gaze into their unliberated eyes, and give them a well-deserved shock. The ravines and wolves are not what frightens people "out there"; it's the solitude, and that's something which none of the guests at the spa can tolerate. So they stay down below in their narrow little garden and, on the rare occasions when they venture out into the very enticing countryside, they venture forth only on group outings in carriages full of merrymakers. On the other hand, some are so stir-crazy that they show up for the morning concert in the park, wearing sports clothes and loden hats, which they take off as quickly as possible afterward. If somebody is known to head off occasionally for distant summits, even if he has only been away for one day on a serious hike, he is treated with diffident awe, partly as a hero, partly as a madman.

At the dinner table I have to sit with my fellow patients for an hour a day, listening to their exhaustive discussions of their ailments. One of them has again slept poorly; it took another four weeks to lose a single pound. A fat man, who is still quite young, spent four hours yesterday running around in the woods, going back and forth the whole time along the same path, only to deprive himself subsequently of the benefits of this activity: that evening he couldn't resist the tempting pudding (which he is not allowed). So once again he didn't lose any weight, and it's the fourth time that this has happened. He goes on a diet and doesn't exercise or vice versa.

Having to contend with such foolish and ridiculous ailments is so aggravating that one feels a sense of relief on encountering genuine illness. One can certainly find examples of the latter here; all these spas and guesthouses were built for seriously ill patients, but one hardly ever sees them now, since the jaded splendor and aimless bustle of life at the resort have pushed them into the background. But there are some places, along a few of the more modest forest paths or in the lying-in room of one of the guesthouses, where one comes across the pale face of real misery and genuine suffering and feels moved and quite shocked, yet oddly enough, the experience also makes one feel good. It's not just that one begins to laugh at the self-important airs of this comical and useless little world; one can see one's own complaints in perspective and doesn't take them quite so seriously. And on a rare occasion one finds oneself gazing quietly and with brotherly fellow feeling at a white, suffering, and very human face, responding to a glance which suggests seriousness rather than curiosity, or a silent greeting.

That's what my life here as a patient at the Badenau spa is like. I roam about the quiet forest paths in the morning, spend the afternoons resting and dozing off, occasionally read a bit of Walther von der Vogelweide or Mörike in the evening until the fellow in the white linen arrives with his water bucket. There are times when I don't have anything at all on my mind, and I just listen to the rustling treetops and murmuring brooks. I sometimes spend hours thinking about the intense suffering marking the anxious, pale faces that greeted me. And I sometimes get a kick out of the guests, the little ponds, the whole fraud. One gets to see some beautiful people here, just like everywhere else. There are few really beautiful English people around since they are either at a higher altitude or at the seaside. But one can certainly find racial features that are characteristically Slavic, German, and Latin, well-dressed children, and some interesting women's faces. I'm pleased to discover that our good Schwarzwald folk have nothing to be ashamed of when set among all these ethnic types; the Alemannic features can stand comparison with the firm, finely chiseled features of all these foreigners.

That's quite enough! You'll be hearing from me soon again.

TO JOHANNES HESSE

Gaienhofen, March 6, 1910

Many thanks for the printed matter, which I read with interest. I'm really sorry that you have become so preoccupied with this idol business, because it's not clear to me why anybody could attach any significance to it.* Everybody knows that Europe produces all sorts of goods in the hope of making a profit, and liquor, gunpowder, and obscene pictures, etc., are, of course, far worse than idols. I don't doubt that manufacturers here are producing idols, but surely they intend to sell these items primarily to European travelers rather than to the natives; those factories churning out idols are, after all, a branch of the arts-and-crafts industry. Every day we mass-produce reproductions of the famous Apollo and

---

* "A new product for export," a note in the first number of *März* (April 1908).

Minerva, and even install them in our schools—so why not reproduce
Krishnas or Buddhas or the like? There are establishments in Munich,
Berlin, and elsewhere where one can buy extremely beautiful, sophisticated Japanese and Oriental objects, and everybody knows that most
of them are forgeries—i.e., sensitively crafted artifacts made in Europe
according to designs from Japan and elsewhere. But no manufacturer is
honest enough to put his own label on items like that, as you saw yourself
in the case of those Indian pictures.

Your investigations will thus be useless, since the most dangerous
manufacturers, those who fear publicity, are never going to give themselves away. There's a lot of factual information available, much of it
widely known, and occasionally a daring journalist will publicize the
matter without being able to prove it. There are trials daily in which
severe penalties are imposed on the journalist or whoever did the in-
sulting, even though everybody in the courtroom from the plaintiff to
the judge realizes that this ugly business does go on, although it cannot
be proven. It's not sufficient to have the right intention when pursuing
such cases of forged curios; one really needs to work like a detective.
In any case, I don't see anything wrong with European "ladies" (why
not "gentlemen" as well?) wanting to buy idols and amulets on their
Oriental travels. You liked having that glass cabinet with Indian curi-
osities in your room in Calw; why shouldn't others be allowed to bring
similar items back from their travels and display them at home? Even
in Italy, I bought rosary beads, etc., merely as souvenirs. The fact that
some Europeans are producing items like this for profit is not in itself
a violation of conventional European business ethics. I have heard from
travelers to India, and I know quite a few, that they consider a "genuine
Buddha"—i.e., a sculpture of Buddha made in India—a rare find.

That's enough; you know all this already. But I would like to stress
the difficulty of proving the allegations in the press. A case in point is
the commentary in *März*, which, incidentally, I didn't find any more
intolerant or fanatical in terms of tone and substance than those articles
in the church paper. I'm sure the author knew for certain that idols are
being produced in Idar (I don't consider it inexcusable that he wasn't
as well informed about the numbers of pagan Maoris as an expert on
the missions), but was unable to prove it conclusively. Perhaps an
employee or business associate of the factory told him about it, but
requested that he never disclose the name of the firm. That happens
every day in the press. All I wanted to say is that a news item or allegation
in the press is not null and void just because it cannot be proven in a
court of law.

Moreover, as I have said before, I don't agree with the point of view of the commentator in *März*; I have become more tolerant, indeed quite impartial in religious matters, and in any case I can no longer believe in the exclusive validity of the religious outlook that I grew up with. I don't think it's right that the natural sciences, the rules of logic, and a sense of equity should determine how we think about everything from nature to history, except for religion, an area which could certainly use that. The only reason I retain my reverence for genuine, deep-seated piety, no matter how worldly the life I lead, is that I have witnessed genuine piety ever since childhood. I would be the last person to oppose any attempt to get everybody on earth to share this particular belief, should that ever be conceivable! But as the years went by, I realized increasingly that there are very few truly pious people and that instances of this genuine, pure, self-effacing piety are to be found in all higher religions. As for the decadent official version of Christianity that is predominant here, I find its attitude toward culture utterly hostile. And that is the only reason why I'm participating, albeit in a secondary role, in an important, serious-minded cultural project that is aimed partly against the Church (not against the faith). This sums up my relationship to *März* as regards that matter. As you well know, my religious needs cannot be satisfied by such activities, so I listen to everything from the Bible and ancient legends to the Koran, and eavesdrop at several gates to paradise.

I'm off to Strassburg tomorrow. If you haven't heard again from Hans, I could ask my Frankfurt physician to make some inquiries and find out how he is doing and which hospital he is in. But since he is an overworked physician, I don't want to burden him until I hear it's necessary. [. . .]

We're surviving somehow, and feel delighted that there is a bit more spring in the air. My nerves long for the sun, summer, and freedom; I often work like mad, so I can travel or just spend time ambling about.

TO FRITZ BRUN*

[*ca. May/June 1911*]

[. . .] All the best wishes to you in your new quarters! It's always fun to settle in, add one's personal touch to a few rooms, and bask in the wonderful illusion of being in complete possession and control, whereas actually those objects possess and control us rather than vice versa. I would give an arm and a leg to be a poor, merry bachelor again,

---

* Composer and for thirty-eight years director of the Bern symphony orchestra.

with nothing to my name except twenty books, a couple of extra boots, and a box with secret poems. But I am now a paterfamilias, a house owner, and an all too popular writer, and since I have little faith in pathos and even less talent for it, I'm trying to take things lightly, so I can at least wind up as a humorist.

TO CONRAD HAUSSMANN*

Gaienhofen, July 9, 1911

Dear Friend,

[. . .] My wife is expecting† about the end of this month, and if all goes well, I shall disappear for some time and there will be no way to get hold of me. I have booked a ticket to Singapore; a friend is coming along;‡ we want to travel around Sumatra, and then I want to spend some time catching butterflies in the jungle near Kuala Lumpur, a mostly Chinese city of 160,000 people; I was invited by a Swiss technician who lives alone there. On the way back, I shall visit Ceylon and, if circumstances prove favorable, maybe a bit of southern India too.

But, please, not a word about any of this yet, since it might not work out at all. At the moment, I'm busy learning English and making preparations, and I get a clearer idea each day of the amount of stuff necessary for a journey like this, not just shirts and clothes, other things as well. I shall look quite elegant since, funnily enough, it's impossible to get into the tropical jungle without first making an appearance on board ship or in the English ports wearing a nice dinner jacket.

While I'm gone, you will have to fill in for me occasionally on *März*, by which I mean you should just keep on trying to influence things in the direction we want. I shall not write anything about the journey for *März*, but hope to return with some worthwhile inner acquisitions.

TO JOHANNES HESSE

Gaienhofen, July 28, 1911
[Original in English]

My dear father!

As I have written on a postcard, we have got a little boy the day before yesterday. The little fellow is in good health and likewise the

---

* Politician, lawyer, and contributor to *März*.
† Martin, Hesse's third son, was born on July 26, 1911.
‡ The painter Hans Sturzenegger.

mother. Butzi and Heinerli have a great pleasure in the new brother. Maria has a nurse that is very good and kind, and we find it better that she has remained here instead of going to Basel or Zurich.

Last sunday I was at Friedrichshafen, following to an invitation of the Zeppelin society, and I took a drive in the new airship "Schwaben."* I was two hours in the air, over Lindau and Bregenz till up to Feldkirch, by the finest weather, and I was very astonished to see how comfortably the drive was effected. One has no uneasiness neither other sensations and it seemed to me the best manner of traveling. I would like to drive in this way to India!

Now my english acquerements are exhausted.

TO CONRAD HAUSSMANN

Steamer York [*end of November 1911*]

I'm again sailing across the bluish-black seas, for days and weeks on end, am living in a cramped little cabin, and trying meanwhile to cure the injuries that the outside world has inflicted on me. Since I shan't be able to write letters for some time after my return (Christmas), I'm sending you a few more lines from on board.

The news about the changes at *März*† reached me just as we were about to leave Colombo. I'm writing to Langen, to say I'm resigning from any further editorial responsibilities. I would find it impossible to keep doing the same type of editorial work (reading manuscripts, dealing with authors, reviews, lots of correspondence) without decent renumeration; being without independent means, I just scrape by, with my three youngsters. It wouldn't be right for me to appear on the masthead as an editor if I'm not actually doing the work. For you and Thoma, the situation is quite different: *März* is an organ that allows you to express your strong political temperaments and your hopes for the future, whereas politics has always felt like alien territory to me. I'm sad to be losing the foothold in the practical world that *März* afforded me, and I shall have to keep an eye out later on for something similar. My departure from *März*—I

* Hesse described his first flight in a Zeppelin airship in "Spazierfahrt in der Luft," which appeared in the *Basler Nachrichten*.

† The founding of a "März Publishing Corporation." Beginning with the first January issue of 1912, the name of the new company replaces the former title: "Albert Langen, Publishers of Literature and Art, Munich." There is a new, separate entry on the masthead, printed in semibold letters: "Editor-in-Chief, Otto Wolters, Munich."

shall, of course, remain a contributor—won't alter our relationship one whit.

I had to abandon lower India—in any case I had only planned to travel in the South—partly because the cost of living and traveling here is far greater than I had expected and greatly exceeds my resources, partly because my stomach, bowels, and kidneys have gone on strike. But I did get a good look at the Straits Settlements and the Malay States, and southeastern Sumatra as well, then spent my final fourteen days in the mountains of Ceylon, but I was, unfortunately, sick most of the time, and it rained a lot. On the whole, I was not all that impressed with the Indians; like the Malaysians, they're weak and have no future. The only ones who really look strong and have a future ahead of them are the Chinese and the English, not the Dutch, etc.

The tropical nature I saw was mostly jungle, but there were also the rivers of Sumatra, the Malaysian seas with their numerous islands, and the fabulously fertile island of Ceylon. As for cities, Singapore and Palembang were particularly interesting. I saw the following peoples: Malays and Javanese, Tamils, Singhalese, Japanese, and Chinese. Nothing but wonderful things to report about the latter: an impressive people! As for most of the others, they are in a sorry condition, the poor remnants of an ancient paradisiacal people, whom the West is corrupting and devouring; by nature these so-called primitive peoples are affectionate, good-humored, clever, and talented, but our culture is finishing them off. If the whites could withstand the climate and could raise their children here, there would be no Indians left.

I also encountered and talked to a lot of salesmen, technicians, etc., from all over the world, and noticed a considerable amount of large-scale commerce. A lot of high-quality local products are exported, whereas the imports from Europe and America are mostly junk. The Malaysians and Indians fall for this; the Chinese don't. The Japanese are generally disliked, even hated, especially as trading partners.

Before my departure, as a farewell gesture to India, I climbed the highest mountain in Ceylon, and gazed down through puffs of clouds at the beautiful and fabulously vast mountain landscape extending all the way down to the sea.

It's a question of being patient for more than two weeks and putting up with the rocking ship, but by now I'm a bit tougher, since I have spent the greater part of the last three months on water, sailing on all kinds of ships. I hope we get to see each other soon.

Please convey my greetings to everybody in your house, also to Thoma and the Munich people.

TO LUDWIG THOMA

Bern, December 17, 1912

You haven't heard from me for a long time, and now that I'm living in Bern,* I can no longer keep a telescope trained on Munich. I haven't heard a word from Haussmann for some time, and only found out through Geheeb† that *März* is receiving a further period of probation. Not that Wolters with his twaddle or indeed you yourself with your long silence were any great help of late. I cannot contribute very much, since there is so little space now for stories—thanks again to Wolters. *Requiescat.* I think I shall continue doing reviews, for the time being.

Won't we ever get to see you in Bern? I would be as pleased as Punch. I'm living with my large family in an old manor house outside the city, with a view of the mountains, surrounded by old trees. I only need a few nice friends, good music, a vibrantly beautiful landscape, a sturdy old city, and a railway station, so I can get away occasionally.

You should come over sometime for a visit. I would like to show you the garden and my three lads, who are picking up the Bern dialect; the oldest is going to school already.

I'm going skiing on the Gotthard over the New Year, and am looking forward tremendously to that.

If only I could drop by your hunter's den some evenings and spend time with you, chatting and smoking a pipe. We're too far apart, and letters are not much use. That window seat of yours under the arched window by the wall is beautiful. We have to get along here without such winter comforts; our old shack is nice enough, but it was only built for summer use and is really run-down. Come out here sometime in the summer; we have good wine, beautiful farmsteads, and there are also other things reminiscent of the late Pastor Gotthelf.‡

TO ALFRED SCHLENKER§

Bern, November 12, 1913

[. . .] You're wrong about my attitude toward Cohen;‖ philosophy is not nearly as important to me as it is to you, and I only need that kind of intense intellectual stimulation every couple of years or so. Yes,

---

* In September 1912, Hesse moved from Gaienhofen to Bern.
† Reinhold Geheeb, editor of *Simplicissimus.*
‡ Pseudonym of Albert Bitzius, pastor and novelist of Swiss peasant life.
§ Composer and dentist in Constance.
‖ Hermann Cohen, philosopher, founder of Neo-Kantianism.

Hesse in Gaienhofen around 1909

(*Above*) Hesse in the garden of the house in Bern, with his wife and his second son, Heiner

(*Below*) On Hesse's right, his friend and traveling companion, the painter Hans Sturzenegger

I would indeed like to "get well," insofar as that seems feasible and necessary, but even the cleverest book isn't much help in that respect, and in spite of my admiration for Cohen, I have absolutely no intention of transforming him again into a minor deity. I have always liked putting gunpowder under the pedestals of the gods [. . .]

TO VOLKMAR ANDREÄ*

Bern, December 29, 1913

[. . .] It's quite a boon having you as a friend. I have always sensed that we are polar opposites by nature (whereas I feel I share some highly unfortunate affinities with Brun†). Your most edifying qualities, aside from the warmth and strength of your personality, are your sparkle and competence, and I can fortunately admire them without any tinge of jealousy.

By the way, I have outgrown my pessimistic philosophy of life; the practical consequences have become obvious during the last few, rather hellish months. I'm not a stable person, and often I encounter great difficulties in life, which often seems quite unbearable. There's nothing I can do about that. But I love the world and life itself, and, even when in pain, I still have the pleasure of feeling part of a cosmic movement. I cannot express all of this philosophically, nor have I any great need to do so. But that may be my task as a poet (am only gradually realizing this myself): the vindication and transfiguration of life by somebody who finds life very difficult, but as a result loves it all the more passionately. During the last few years, I often felt humor was the best solution. A bad stretch recently has induced me to become sentimental and lyrical again. But I'm beginning to get a sense of the general meaning of my existence, and my writing—some novellas, etc., had become excessively playful—may well take me in entirely new directions.

In any case, the only melancholia I acknowledge is that of Dürer, and I'm extremely conscious of belonging to a guild of artists—a guild that takes seriously all forms of art which stem from genuine experience and endeavors to construct a reality of a higher order.

That in itself is a bond between us. I often visited you in Zurich looking for consolation and an opportunity to hear music again and to see somebody who responds positively and appreciates my better traits;

---

* Composer and conductor; one of Hesse's earliest musical friends.

† Through Alfred Schlenker, Hesse had got to know Andreä, Fritz Brun, and the young composer Othmar Schoeck.

my visits were never in vain. I find this sort of friendship invaluable, and not only feel cheerful and stimulated for hours, even days afterward, but also far more clearheaded and eager when I return to my work. And I don't convey hopelessness or pessimism in my verse for its own sake, I have to pass through that stage; I sense somewhere in those dark stirrings a force akin to life itself. My letter is probably not all that clear, but it's not really a matter of spelling everything out. The better things usually get left out. I shake your hand fondly

TO JOHANNES HESSE

Bern, September 9, 1914

[. . .] So all three youngsters are back home now, and it's fun and invigorating, although Mia has her hands full, since we have only one maid. Butzi and Martinli are quite well again, and we hope they will remain in good health for the winter. I'm teaching Butzi writing and arithmetic for an hour each day until September 19, when he goes back to school. We also work together in the garden, collecting wood, harvesting apples, etc.

The only sign of war here is a chronic shortage of cash. Although there is no hope of my earning anything in the immediate future, that wouldn't be an insuperable problem because I do have some savings. However, the banks are hardly allowing any withdrawals, so we keep saving and worrying. Admittedly, those are trifling concerns compared with the large issues on the agenda.

I was recently mustered for the militia at the consulate, then I volunteered to serve, but they don't want me.* I won't come up again for a while, and by then I may be in Germany so I can help out and be close at hand. Intellectual work, etc., is out of the question; literary activities, like so much else, have come to a halt. Most of my friends in Bern, Basel, and Zurich have reported for duty with the Swiss Army; some are officers. Many of my best friends in Germany are on the battlefield; I also have friends who are Austrian officers. As for our poor Gaienhofeners, most of them fell at Mühlhausen.†

If one could only foresee the course of this war and its outcome! The alliances and vested interests are so entangled that nothing seems

---

* Hesse was rejected on August 29, 1914, because of his "severe shortsightedness."

† Battle at Mühlhausen on August 9–10, 1914. The 7th German Army drove the French out of Upper Alsace.

certain; all of Europe will have to suffer the consequences, except perhaps for England, which is watching closely in the hope of making a profit. Although I love many English people dearly and respect others highly, I think that, morally speaking, they're in a downright miserable predicament as a people. But it's consoling to see so many well-intentioned Englishmen speaking out against those despicable policies. In the meantime, half of Germany is bleeding to death, and France is being ruined; the English certainly won't pay any damages. Since things are so desperate, one can only hope for news of a rebellion breaking out in India, or some terrible misfortune befalling the English fleet. If that were to happen, and if Austria can somehow keep on going, then Germany could play the leading role at the peace negotiations, and in that case there would still be some hope for life and culture in the immediate future. Otherwise, England would end up on top, and Europe would then be in the hands of those moneybags and the illiterate Russians, and if we wanted to safeguard our most cherished values, we would have to initiate a kind of secret cult. But, personally, I have a lot of faith in Germany, and even if the other dreams never come true, this enormous moral upheaval will eventually prove beneficial for us, in spite of the victims. A stronger Russia and a seriously weakened France would be terrible news for everybody. It is awful to think that this big war will probably victimize those who least deserve that fate. I like both the Russians and the English, and feel close to them as people, but have political and cultural reasons for hoping they don't grow more powerful.

Adele wrote to tell me that Heinrich Gundert* has been wounded; I found a Hopfauer listed among those missing in action, no other acquaintances.

People here talk sensibly about the war and have a lot of sympathy for Germany; they say French-speaking Switzerland identifies totally with France. This division could be dangerous if Switzerland were dragged into the conflict (perhaps through Italian involvement). At the moment the situation here is peaceful and quiet, although there have been serious repercussions for trade and commerce, and the country is having difficulty absorbing the costs of the mobilization. It's not safe anywhere now, except perhaps in America! I think a lot about Tsingtao and often try to imagine the predicament of the Germans who were in India, Singapore, etc., when the war broke out. England is always bragging about shipping colored troops to Europe, but I don't think that would

---

* Hesse's cousin.

make much difference. The Japanese will not get all that deeply involved, their ground forces would certainly take a beating, and the Indian and Australian troops would not be able to withstand a European winter. Moreover, the elite English troops in Belgium failed to show their mettle.

We are fearful about the Russian offensive in Galicia* and the outcome of what is probably the final German battle against the half-encircled French Army.† If the Germans finally emerge from that as victors, they will have to have a go at Paris, and if France remains loyal to its allies, there will be a lot of bloodshed in Paris. That would really be terrible, and France would probably never recover completely from the shock. Such a shame that the growing cultural ties between Germany and France didn't affect their political relations!

Please send me a card to let me know how you're doing, etc. The little mail I receive from Germany generally takes quite a while to get here. The main thing in the mail now is the newspaper. We get *Der Bund*;‡ I don't normally see eye to eye with it, but its coverage of the war is very good, and now I find it useful. [. . .]

TO ALFRED SCHLENKER

Bern, November 10, 1914

My dear friend,

Your good letter was really delightful. I had been meaning to write to you for ages, but felt a little inhibited because of that silly quarrel of ours in Constance. What upset me was not so much the incident itself as what it made me realize: Since I'm a high-strung, rather defenseless person, I have always expected individuals who are healthier than me to treat me very considerately, whereas I should have shown more consideration when my friends were suffering from equally frayed nerves. Well, let's leave it at that.

I'm delighted that the book of verse§ has found such an appreciative reader. It's never possible to make that kind of book seem entirely

---

* The Russians had penetrated deeply into German and Austrian territory in East Prussia and Galicia. This led to the battle at Tannenberg. In the South, the Austrians were struggling to defend the Carpathian mountain passes.

† The German battle plan sought to achieve a decisive victory in the West through a large encircling movement while continuing to wage war in the East. The plan failed due to the Battle of the Marne, and the "probably final German battle" turned into trench warfare, which lasted until 1918.

‡ A Bern newspaper.

§ Hermann Hesse, ed., *Lieder deutscher Dichter* (Munich: Langen, 1914).

unobjectionable, but I think it's good; at least it represents what I find best in poetry. There are only a very few instances of less than profound tones, which I included out of a sense of fairness.

The war has put me in a somewhat awkward position. Although I feel that I'm on Germany's side and can understand the all-consuming nationalistic fervor that has taken hold there, I'm not a completely enthusiastic participant in this development. I live abroad, and thus at some remove from the origins of the acute psychosis; I cannot quite get over what happened to Belgium;* my family origins have shaped my outlook, and my own experience has become so cosmopolitan that I would seem somewhat suspect in the eyes of a pure patriot. My father was a Russian of German origin, a Balt, and my grandmother came from Neuchâtel; ever since childhood, I have regarded Switzerland as my second homeland, although only the German part. I also feel like traveling and getting to know the literatures of foreign countries. Germany now sees little point in behaving decently and exercising restraint; war calls for a severe state of psychosis or even mania. I fail to see anything delightful or splendid in this war, and don't anticipate a rosy future afterward. As soon as the war is over, we shall have to become better friends with England and France than we were in prewar days; I feel that will prove indispensable in the future, and would have come about more easily without the war. Now we shall have to pay for the miserable policies of France, the envy of the English, and our own political mistakes; Austria, Belgium, and France are also bleeding. There is no point trying to identify the "guilty" party; each side needs to believe that it is in the right. So the whole thing is just a pathetic scrap about values that are far from clear-cut. The war has created a wonderful spirit of unity and self-sacrifice in Germany, but the same applies to the enemy. It's easy enough for those of us who have stayed at home to say that a war which has created that sort of atmosphere is worthwhile. But those who are rotting in the woods, those whose cities, villages, fields, and aspirations have been ravaged and destroyed do not agree, and I cannot think about the war without hearing those voices.

We're having our first symphony concert this evening, a splendid program, just Beethoven, beginning with *Coriolanus* and ending with the *Eroica*. A few weeks ago, I wouldn't have enjoyed that very much; now I can again enjoy music or a good book, and allow myself to get carried away. Otherwise things are the same as ever; I would love to work a lot, but usually cannot, since my eyes are always sore.

* The movement of German troops through neutral Belgium in August 1914.

There are moments when I too sense the harmony of the universe. Since I cannot find any real corroboration for these intuitions in my physical and instinctual life, I try to detect it in the intellectual sphere. And to be consistent, a person has to rely entirely on the intellect, the only organ of ours that identifies strongly with the natural ʹorder and defends it to the hilt, even where there is a conflict with our instinctual urges. But much remains unexplained, since the rational intellect doesn't control phenomena such as war, the life of nations, and also the most valuable forms of art.

I have just noticed that it's high time to get dressed for the concert, and since I shan't get around to writing any more tomorrow, I shall end here and try to dig up a fresh collar.

TO VOLKMAR ANDREÄ

Bern, December 26, 1914

My dear friend Andreä,
[. . .] I know what you're going through—the awful depression that you evaded or lessened by serving as an officer in the early days of the war. The rest of us have more or less come to terms with it. I have so many friends in the various armies, have lost so many too, that I am still deeply concerned. I haven't been able to do any real work of my own since August, and have taken refuge instead in projects of a historical-mechanical sort. It is still quite possible that I may have to enlist in the German militia—I don't relish the prospect at all. As a result of universal conscription, we seem to be witnessing one of those historic crises in modern statecraft in the course of which meaningful statements degenerate rapidly into murderous gibberish. Even though I feel very German, I have always considered nationalism an elementary form of education, an introductory course in ideal humanity. I have never relished the thought of nationalism as a goal in itself.

I find that, on the whole, the moral impact of the war has been very positive. For many people, it was good to be shaken up out of that silly capitalist peace, and also for Germany. I think genuine artists will value a nation more highly if its menfolk have confronted death and experienced life in the POW camps. I don't expect much else of the war, and we probably won't be spared a new outbreak of jingoism.

I simply don't believe that the war is annihilating any genuine form of culture. While it's true that beautiful individual works of art and, of course, valuable people too are being destroyed, the experience of war will strengthen the notion of culture, which can only thrive in a select intellectual environment. Even if the war induced only a fraction of enlisted youths to feel more deeply about life, and to pay more attention to indestructible values, and become less taken with silly nonsense, that gain would outweigh the loss of a few cities and cathedrals.

This war is utterly extraordinary; I like the fact that it doesn't make "sense," isn't about some trifling issue, and constitutes the upheaval signaling a major atmospheric change. Since the atmosphere used to be quite putrid, the change might even be a good thing. It's not for to us to decide whether the price was high, perhaps excessive. Nature is always profligate; she places little value on individual lives. As for us artists or intellectuals, we have always kept apart and lived in a rather timeless world, so the only losses we have to fear are material ones, and that can always be endured. People with a profound understanding of Bach, or Plato, or Goethe's *Faust* know in their heart of hearts that there is only one realm where peace and lasting meaning can be found. That realm is indestructible; it's possible for each one of us to live there, and feel at home, and help expand it. But there are people who feel that they lost everything along with their material comforts, and so their suffering is greater than ours. They could, of course, also learn a lot from the experience. It may be good for them to realize that such things as stock-market indexes and menus, clubs, etc., no longer govern their lives, but rather such basic natural urges as hunger and the fear of death.

That sounds fine, you may think, but what's the point when thousands are shedding their blood each day? It's certainly appalling. But life in the raw is always appalling, except that we're now being reminded of this more savagely than usual. In peacetime, we denizens of the intellectual realm know little about the despair rampant everywhere, about the abominable practices in business and the rat race in general, the miserable conditions in the factories, coal mines, etc. I don't find the ordinary life of the common herd much more preferable to war, and many of them now realize this themselves; they return from the front with a yearning for a life that is more rational, more beautiful, and better, in every respect, than their previous existence. If this is so, then the war will ultimately bring about some good. I view everything else much more skeptically, the frenzied patriotism, the spirit of sacrifice, etc. Like the war itself, that is transitory, and I don't devote much attention in the top compartments of my mind to such transitory issues. I have seen in the eyes of hundreds of injured German soldiers the expression, either tired or excited, but always calm and superior, of men who have come face to face with death and no longer take anything else very seriously.

The ordinary citizen would never be exposed otherwise to that attitude toward life. And a fine attitude it is.

Carissimo, I have started preaching. I'm merely repeating some of my recent thoughts about the war. Culture, in our sense of the term, may indeed spell happiness. But at least until the first of August, official attitudes in Europe were of a different order: happiness was considered virtually synonymous with material comfort. People were preoccupied with the latter and had little time and resources left for real culture; then they went crazy and started killing one another. The only good thing about it is that the killing and slaughtering are no more meaningless than the previous state of supposed happiness.

I was miserable again. But that is transitory. Long live Shakespeare!

Greetings to your dear wife! The children are doing their best to wreck their new toys. That's life.

TO ROMAIN ROLLAND*

Bern, February 28, 1915

I was really delighted to receive your kind note. I'm answering in German, since I have enough French for comprehension and reading, but not for writing.

I don't know whether you have heard about the plans to start an international review in Switzerland. The journal would offer a neutral forum for dialogue and debate among intellectuals in the belligerent countries. French contributors are needed; there are already enough Germans. I was asked to manage the journal and people were also hoping to rope you in. I'm a retiring poet, and lack the necessary stamina. And, as a result, the review is being set up by a Swiss-German† and a Genevan. I'm letting you know just in case. Herr G. de Reynold is the Genevan editor.

I don't have any personal connections with *Die Weissen Blätter*,‡ but I wrote to the publisher saying you would like to get to know them. Although there are quite a few crude youngsters among them, many are decent and well intentioned.

You already know how deeply I regret the silly hatred that is creating

---

* French novelist, historian, and critic. Hesse's extensive correspondence with Rolland has been separately published in German (1954); French (1972), and English (1978).

† Professor Paul Haeberlin. The project never materialized.

‡ A monthly periodical published in Leipzig by Kurt Wolff's Verlag der Weissen Bücher (1913–21).

such strife concerning supranational issues among thinking people. I have become convinced in the meantime that more and more people will begin to recognize the absolute necessity of your "*union de l'esprit européen.*" At the moment, I'm refraining from all political-sounding pronouncements; there seems to be a magic wand transforming every burst of applause into an expression of hostility. There is still a lot of hatred, but that will eventually wear off. I was glad to discover that you're acquainted with a few of my books. So you can imagine why I especially cherish the childhood story of Jean Christophe.

TO ALFRED SCHLENKER

[*ca. March/April 1915*]

My dear Fredi,

[. . .] People with reasonable ideas about the war are talking increasingly about the future of Europe, and not just of Germany. Although that pleases me, I see the unification of Europe merely as an early stage in the history of mankind. The methodical mentality of Europe will rule the world for some time to come, but in matters of spirituality and religious values, the Russians and Asians have a greater depth, which we shall eventually need again. Now that the morality, self-discipline, and rational capacities of our leading intellectuals have sunk to such depths, we can finally acknowledge that nationalism isn't all that ideal. I like to consider myself a patriot, but first a human being, and whenever a conflict arises, I side with the human being. As Goethe said to Eckermann: "The most fervent expression of nationalistic hatred occurs at the lowest cultural levels."

By the way, there are now quite a few good, clear voices to be heard preaching reason, and many soldiers in the field no longer accept the notion that entire peoples are at war; they regard their adversaries as brothers, with whom there has been a quarrel over some blunder or misunderstanding, and they will soon be brothers again. And before long the people who wrote those venomous articles and hate-filled songs about England, Russia, etc., will have to hang their heads in shame. Then there are the jaded hacks who suddenly "saw the light" about the war and started contradicting their previous convictions, only to reverse themselves again with equal flexibility.

I have nothing but admiration for the vitality and unity characteristic of the current mood in Germany, but my love for the country is such that I cannot abide any outbursts of jingoistic patriotism. We cannot go

on blaming everything on England, Russia, etc.: if we don't start ex-
amining ourselves critically and rooting out our flaws, things will only
get worse.

I'm expecting some good news in the near future. The truce, which
I also consider sacrosanct, shouldn't restrict our freedom, and it won't.
Many patriots are sick of the phrasemongering; the very best of them
are still in the trenches, and when they finally get back, they will help
with the cleaning-up. That will do some good. The soldiers are bravely
proving their mettle, whereas the literati and many of the scholars are
showing their cowardice by hastily joining the chorus of philistines, even
if they happened to have been leading liberals at a time when that didn't
require much courage.

Well, things will work out eventually, although not necessarily right
away. There will be some setbacks, but I think some progress will be
made and that a sense of responsibility will develop. It's a good sign
that there was a remarkable consensus along these lines among the
younger literati. If you can lay hands on a copy of *Das Forum** or *Die
Weissen Blätter*, you will see how true this is.

Would have really liked to come and see you at some point, both
to show you my teeth, which have not been checked for ages, and to
find out what's up and how you people are doing. But I cannot get away
now; crossing the border is both difficult and expensive, and I must wait
till I see what my military future is.

Let's hear from you again! [. . .]

TO MATHILDE SCHWARZENBACH†

Bern [end of September 1915]
Having just returned from Germany, I would like to let you know
right away that I'm back; my leave lasts until the middle of November,
and will then be renewed, I hope. But I fear that the war will eventually
devour all of us. Last week, a cousin of mine in Stuttgart was pronounced
fit for duty, even though he is small and frail and used to be considered
unfit for military service; compared to me, he is a real dwarf. The Balkans
will soon be devouring lives,‡ and there are also the tens of thousands
thrown away during the silly mass offensive of the French.§

* A journal with revolutionary leanings (1914–29), published by Kiepenheuer Verlag, Berlin.
† Friend of Hesse's from Zurich; she contributed money to his war relief efforts.
‡ Attack against Serbia by German and Bulgarian troops (November 1915).
§ Battle of Champagne (September–October 1915).

Well, I'm still here for now; this new kind of work is keeping me busy. I have just been asked to supervise the POW libraries, which are being sent to France via Bern. I have examined the holdings in Stuttgart; they have quite a lot of books there, but don't have sufficient funds to expand our collection systematically.

I realize that the POW libraries—along with the prisoners' newspaper, which I'm producing single-handedly—offer a unique opportunity for some adult education work, and I have accepted the position. I shall do everything I can to expand the service. We have already used up all the money and books that I was able to donate, and I'm trying to raise some more money; a few hundred francs would allow me to implement most of my plan. I'm trying to enlarge all the small POW libraries so that each one carries a selection of the best German literary works in cheap editions. Everything is set to go: I have scoured the relevant publishers' catalogues, and as soon as we get enough funds, which I'm trying to raise discreetly, we can send off the orders. Of course, an appeal to the German public would produce quick results, but I have no right to compete with the Red Cross collections, and must save whatever funds I have left over for the larger project, the POW paper.

I was wondering whether you might not like to help, since it's a good cause and those POWs need our compassion. I never expect large sums nowadays. If, in addition to the amount I'm donating, a small number of my friends contribute 50 to 100 francs or marks per person, my plans will be salvaged. These new duties have turned my study into an office. I have become an office worker; it's not bad for a short while, but I couldn't stand it for very long, not to speak of forever! I would prefer to join a German battalion and vanish into oblivion. But I do hope to accomplish some worthwhile things. At some stage, I should like to escape to Zurich for a bit of rest, but it's still not altogether clear whether that will be possible. For now, I would like to ask you to contribute to my project, if you can. If you cannot give anything or don't feel so inclined, I trust you will forgive me for asking. Now that I have taken over this project, I feel I have to promote it by every means at my disposal. The misery crying out for attention all over the world is such that I want to do whatever I can in my little patch.

TO COLONEL BOREL

Bern, October 12, 1915

I heard from Professor Woltereck some time ago that you had expressed interest in our plan to set up a special weekly paper for German prisoners in France.* Shortly afterward, I found out that Herr Ador† of Geneva had promised to try to persuade the French government to allow us to distribute the paper in France.

This was quite a few weeks ago, and we have not heard anything yet.

Dear Sir, could I take the liberty of asking you whether you are interested in my plans? I'm convinced that the project is very worthwhile, and my approach is humanitarian rather than patriotic. I see the paper as a unique forum for educating the public. The prisoners, especially those who are uneducated or only half educated, face spiritual and intellectual dangers that are certainly far greater than those confronting the soldiers at the front. And we now have a chance to supply tens of thousands of them each week with reading matter that really caters to their needs. This presents us with an altogether unusual opportunity to comfort tens of thousands of poor suffering souls in a discreet and undidactic manner. We hope to have a positive influence on their thinking, but I want to make sure that we exclude all denominational biases as much as possible.

Dear Colonel, I'm very keen on this plan and consider it extremely important. If you are interested, and wish to help us carry it out—your role might consist merely of getting in touch occasionally with the French Embassy or with Herr Ador—I would ask to meet you for ten minutes at your convenience, so that I can give you some idea of the sort of paper we have in mind. I have the plan all worked out, and much of it could be implemented straightway. I become anxious when I feel this issue is being put on the back burner and might be shelved.

I'm also trying to enlarge the POW libraries, which were sent here from Stuttgart and are destined for a hundred camps in France, with the idea of providing adult education in literature. After inspecting the selection of books in Stuttgart, I took charge of the project, with some financial help from friends. The necessary arrangements are being made

* *Der Sonntagsbote für die deutschen Kriegsgefangenen* started appearing in January 1916; on January 7, 1916, it was expanded to include the *Deutsche Internierten-Zeitung*.

† Gustav Ador, member of the National Council in Geneva and president of the International Committee of the Red Cross.

very quickly indeed, and I expect that the office headed by Herr von Tavel* will soon be able to get to work. I'm in touch with Herr von Tavel. With sincere and respectful greetings, yours

TO THE EDITORS OF DER KUNSTWART, MUNICH†

Bern, October 23, 1915

While working at home and elsewhere on behalf of our prisoners in France, I was subjected to some vociferous and occasionally coarse attacks by a small segment of the northern German press. I only found out later about these aspersions. The reason for these attacks is a "letter" of mine, which is supposed to have appeared in a Danish newspaper. I have never seen the Danish newspaper in question, and none of the papers engaging in these polemics had the decency to inform me of their accusations. Hence the delay in responding.

That "letter" consists of a short note that I wrote to Sven Lange, thanking him for a kindly favor. Although I never expected that this purely private communication would ever appear in print, I would willingly reiterate and reaffirm every word of it before a court of law.

There were two sentences that got people excited: "I haven't been able to tailor my literary output to the war" (meant somewhat ironically) and "It is my hope that Germany shall continue to impress the world not just through its weaponry but, more importantly, through its mastery of the art of peace and its endeavors to further a genuinely supranational humanism."

What really agitated my antagonists, I'm sure, was the word "supranational." Well, it's up to each individual to decide whether to accept that there are broader, human responsibilities which transcend all national obligations. It seems to me that a person who assumes that a given people is fully conscious of those broader obligations is bestowing a signal honor on that nation.

I now realize that this view is not shared by everybody. So I would like to emphasize my conviction that all peoples have "supranational" obligations, especially the major nations. I need hardly cite chapter and verse for this in Goethe, Kant, and indeed all serious German thinkers, with the exception of a certain section of the press.

* Dr. Rudolf von Tavel, managing editor of the *Berner Tagblatt*, the *Berner Heim*, and the journal *Die Garbe*, was, from 1915 to 1919, head of *Pro Captivis*, which exercised censorship over the *Deutsche Internierten-Zeitung* and *Der Sonntagsbote für die deutschen Kriegsgefangenen*.

† A bimonthly review of literature, drama, music, and visual and applied arts.

I find it almost harder to understand how anybody can think ill of a writer merely because he refuses to churn out war novellas and battle songs. Surely, all of us should not feel compelled to do so, just because some editor has asked us, or because we're having difficulty making ends meet, but only because we feel an inner need? I don't think so. In my case, I have long since abandoned literary life in order to volunteer my services on behalf of the prisoners. Moreover, each time a group of fanatic German militarists annoys the neutral countries with their provocative statements, I try to smooth things over the best I can. Many people here think the recent attacks against me and my Weltanschauung are part of the same phenomenon; I have had some difficulty explaining that this misguided fanaticism isn't at all prevalent in Germany, and that aside from a few journalists, nobody in our Germany believes a writer ought to be punished merely because he cherishes the art of peacemaking.

A section of the press is acting according to the Kaiser's wonderful aphorism, since it only heeds the parties and subjects any opinions deviating from the party program to merciless attack. That section of the press ought to be reminded that it is merely providing the enemy with material for propaganda leaflets, making it harder for Germans living abroad to do their work, and creating obstacles for German diplomacy. Here in Switzerland, for instance, we have many hundreds of volunteers from neutral countries working with us, people who were deeply affected by the plight of those injured in the war, and are now helping to track down the soldiers missing in action, assisting our prisoners and internees, and performing many other errands of mercy. In the Swiss welfare offices, I have seen dozens, indeed hundreds, of pleading letters written by German mothers about missing sons or daughters who disappeared inside enemy territory. How does that small section of our press respond to these volunteer efforts? By bad-mouthing neutral countries! Their tactics are foolish and run counter to our official diplomacy. I don't wish to question the good faith of these journalists, but I would urge them to think about the damage they are inflicting! I hereby invite each of these gentlemen to spend a week in Bern, so that they can examine our work in a neutral country, especially the labor of love on behalf of the prisoners. This might change their attitude toward the neutral countries and those of us who live abroad; they might think twice in the future before subjecting us to such destructive attacks.

PRO DOMO*

Bern, November 1, 1915

The *Kölner Tageblatt*, a newspaper I have never heard of, published an editorial on October 24 attacking me for an essay of mine, "Germany Revisited," which appeared recently in the *Neue Zürcher Zeitung*. The writer lets fly a wild barrage of angry accusations about my "cowardice" and "draft-dodging."

Even though I have no idea yet whether this curious piece has influenced German public opinion—a self-respecting newspaper would scarcely publish it verbatim—I would like to state the following: The Cologne article is a crude piece of libel and lacks all foundation.

He accuses me of "draft-dodging" (the vocabulary to which we have to resort nowadays!); after all, I myself have admitted that I stayed away from Germany for fear I wouldn't be allowed back across the frontier. Unless they are exceptionally malicious, people with any knowledge of the situation at the frontier will understand why I did so. If I had entered Germany so close to my mobilization deadline, I might not have been allowed out again, and would have been cut off from my family and my work for weeks, and possibly even months. But the gentleman in Cologne interprets those words of mine as an admission that I tried to dodge military service in a cowardly fashion.

Then my kind enemy refers grandiloquently to poets such as Dehmel, Löns, etc.: even though some were even older than I, all of them volunteered and saw active service, whereas unpatriotic specimens such as myself (his words!) were just sitting around at home. I find it absurd and demeaning to have to respond to this sort of thing. But since there is no way around it, I would like to state for the benefit of the gentleman in Cologne that I did attempt to enlist in the late summer of 1914, just like Dehmel and the others, but was turned down. Moreover, because of the energetic work on the prisoners' behalf in which I have been engaged for some time, I am now provisionally exempt from German military service.

I hereby wish to reiterate and reaffirm the sentence in my Zurich article that seems to have provoked our Cologne Hotspur like a red rag: I value peace more highly than war, and believe it is far more noble to work for peace than for war. Didn't the Kaiser describe his decision to reach for the sword in rather similar terms, as one taken reluctantly and under duress? Why not let those journalists in their snug little studies

* Appeared in the *Neue Zürcher Zeitung*.

in Cologne and elsewhere go on praising war and ridiculing anybody who favors peace as a coward? After all, they are just cranking out words, words written for a fee or in the hope of creating a sensation. I stand behind what I wrote. At the moment, it isn't so easy to be a German with decent political views—i.e., a person who really loves his people and wants to see them developing deeper and more amicable relationships with the neutral nations. By the time this war is over, I think I shall have aged more than ten years. But I'm not about to walk off and allow those loudmouths free rein. One hopes their shouting will soon be irrelevant. We shall then have to ensure that this terrible war creates a valuable and enduring legacy of peace and culture, for our country and compatriots. The shouting and sword waving of the homebound literati will never accomplish anything; what is needed is a lot of selfless work. I realize that, in Germany, thousands of people, hundreds of thousands even, are determined to pursue this course, and they shall prevail over those noisy hotheads. Don't assume that those loud voices are in any way representative of Germany.

As regards the personal allegations, I should just like to state once again that the libelous article in that Cologne paper was written by somebody who knew nothing about me or the facts. The author may have imagined he was acting as a patriot, but that doesn't make his allegations any less libelous.

TO FRAU HELENE WELTI*

Sonnmatt Sanatorium, Lucerne, May 18, 1916
[. . .] I too may be approaching a crisis, although the physical symptoms are of secondary, if symbolic, significance.† I'm having electrotherapy; the electricity warms me up inside, then I get massaged, scrubbed, and put out in the sun; yet despite all our efforts, we haven't managed to keep my feet warm for longer than a quarter of an hour at a time. They have also been giving me small doses of bromide, and for the last few nights I have been getting a decent amount of sleep, for the first time in weeks.

---

* American-born wife of legal historian Friedrich Emil Welti. The Weltis were old friends of Hesse.

† From April until the end of May 1916: electrotherapy in the Sonnmatt Sanatorium near Lucerne, where Hesse had his first twelve analytic sessions with Dr. Josef B. Lang, a young follower of C. G. Jung. Hesse subsequently traveled once a week to Lucerne for treatment.

But these physical ailments are not very significant, since most of them are merely symptoms of an inner malaise, a process of dissolution, which has been going on inside me for years, and has now reached a stage where it will erupt, and a solution has to be found, otherwise it would be pointless continuing. I have no idea where this path is heading—it will either lead me back to the "world" or make me even more isolated and withdrawn. At the moment, I feel that my once lively instincts and thought processes are shriveling; something new is germinating, it's still indistinct, and I feel greater anxiety than joy. The painful pressures exerted by that awful war have actually quickened this growth.

I'm really looking forward to hearing all the news from my wife. I often think of you as a friend, and wish you well.

TO HANS STURZENEGGER

Bern, December 25, 1916

[. . .] Those ranting barbarians we have to listen to nowadays allege that our prewar lives were absolutely sybaritic and emotionally vapid, whereas now we are again faced with real life and genuine emotions. How stupid and deceitful! I now know from experience that it's not only more attractive to write a poem or sing a song, it's infinitely cleverer and also more valuable than winning a battle or giving a million to the Red Cross. The highly "organized" world inhabited by politicians and generals is absolutely worthless, and the craziest dream of an artist is of greater value. Take the word of this poor wretch of a poet who has been preoccupied over the past fourteen months with nothing but business, politics, management and organization.

So I was doubly happy and grateful to receive that wonderful picture from you; it makes me think even more fondly of you. Ah, the beach at Penang, with the archipelagoes in the distance and the numerous bays! If we didn't carry the best of it around with us, the nostalgia could make us ill.

Come to Bern sometime! And if peace ever returns, I shall arrive on your doorstep and frighten you with an exhibition of my own pastel paintings; I no longer have any time to write and think, so I have started painting in my free moments, and have taken up charcoal and paint for the first time in nearly forty years. I'm no competition for you, since my subject isn't nature, only dreams.

Bern, January 3, 1917

I would like to thank you for your kind letter, even though it isn't easy to answer.

When the preacher says: "Heed the voice within you," he is often asked: "Well, what does the voice say? Can't you explain it to us?" The preacher cannot do so, since he is evoking a very different voice; the obligations he is talking about have nothing to do with marks and pfennigs; he is asking each of us to listen to our inner voice and reflect on what it says.

Quite a few other people have written asking the same question: "What should we do now?" My response has always been: "There's no way I can tell you that! I don't know what your conscience is saying and how much energy you can draw on. I'm not in a position to ask anything of you, but you yourself certainly can!" And if you focus on that voice, you will eventually find your own path, just as I've been finding it again or searching for it anew, day by day and week by week, for two and a half years now. One person will content himself with occasional good works, some will get together with their friends, others will refuse to do military service, yet another will try to do more and make a laudable attempt to knock off Sonnino* in Italy or Tirpitz† in Berlin. That's a matter for each individual to decide. If I shot Sonnino, I would be committing a crime, because the act would violate a deep-seated conviction of mine. But there are individuals who would be perfectly free to carry out such deeds. They would, of course, have to be prepared to face the consequences. I have realized for a long time that my position on these issues (also with regard to my official duties) may eventually cause me to sever my links to my country of origin, my official position, my family, my previous reputation, etc., and, if necessary, I'm determined to go ahead and do just that.

All I can say at the moment about my position on the issue is this: I feel that writers, artists, etc., such as myself, act as the antennae or early-warning posts of mankind and are the first to sniff any new developments. The artists then describe that new world, even though nobody is willing to believe in it yet, and they themselves cannot implement it. A letter from Romain Rolland arrived at the same time as yours, and in it he simply says: *"Notre espoir même et notre foi sont un des piliers*

---

* Sidney Sonnino, Italian statesman. On April 26, 1915, he signed the London Treaty with the Entente, which resulted in Italy's entry into the war.

† Alfred von Tirpitz, German admiral and statesman, the advocate of the unrestricted submarine warfare that led President Woodrow Wilson to break off diplomatic relations with the German Reich and declare war on Germany on April 6, 1917.

de l'avenir."* I have confidence in the power of an idea, since I feel ideas aren't just crazy notions, but intuitions about what lies in store for mankind.

So maybe you won't ever have to ask me "for forgiveness for having been so petty." Your attitude is plausible, and certainly cleverer and more reasonable than mine; it may well prevail during our lifetime. But regardless of when that new world comes about, every great new idea of mankind, every big change in the world will be introduced, in the manner I suggested, by people brave enough to trust their own hopes and premonitions rather than by shrewd operators who rely on all the usual political tactics, etc.

One example should suffice: Everybody is making fun of conscientious objectors! I consider this phenomenon one of the promising symptoms of our age, even though some individuals come up with odd justifications for their decision. And now, finally, a motion is being introduced which would allow those who reject military service on moral grounds to perform alternative civilian duties. It may not pass today, but will at some point. A time may come when there will only be three soldiers for every ten doing civilian duties, and war, insofar as it still exists, will be waged solely by rowdies and bullies. But none of this would have happened had certain individuals not felt so strongly about the issue and staged a brave protest against the status quo through their refusal to serve.

And the same thing will be repeated everywhere. Those causes for which people are prepared to risk their lives will ultimately prevail. Thousands volunteered to fight in 1914, but not a soul will in 1918!

Well, enough said for now, I've lots of work on my hands. My dear Sturz, you're a civilian and have read a lot about the war, but you have no firsthand experience of it. Nor have I; I haven't suffered any injuries, my house hasn't been destroyed, but I have spent two and a half years of my life trying to help some victims of war, the prisoners, and my experience with this small aspect of warfare has given me some insight into the meaningless abomination that is war.

I'm not bothered by the enthusiasm for the war that ordinary people in several countries have been displaying. The populace has always behaved stupidly. When given a choice between Jesus and the murderer, they immediately chose Barabbas. Perhaps they will always choose Barabbas. But I do not have to follow their example.

All the best for the New Year! I'm overwhelmed with work, but there are plenty of interruptions since I'm, unfortunately, not particularly

---

* "Hope and faith are two of the very pillars on which our future rests."

healthy and occasionally have splitting headaches all day long. Let's remain friends, even though we don't see eye to eye on such matters. You'll always be a kind, decent fellow, no matter how hard you try to act like a cautious Swiss citizen with an eye on a seat in the National Council. I'm willing to go along with that as far as I can, and in any case I'm not making moral demands on anybody other than myself.

TO WALTER SCHÄDELIN*

Minusio, April 21, 1917

[. . .] I am spending entire days painting and drawing; in good weather I'm outdoors from 9 or 10 till 5 or 6, painting a watercolor a day, sometimes two; the results are still rather pathetic, but I'm not in the least bit discouraged.

Painting is so wonderful. I used to think that I had eyes in my head and could see the world as I strolled by. But that's just a start. To escape from the accursed world of the will, you just have to sit down in a valley surrounded by cliffs, clear your mind of absolutely everything, and absorb the magic of the physical world. Although it's impossible to capture all of that in paint, you can watch the marvelous surface of life as the lights grow dim and the shadows begin to dance! In the evenings, you're dizzy from tiredness and you may fall asleep after looking critically at your unsuccessful sketch in the lamplight, but in any case you remember a piece of moss on a rock, a thin web of shadows under the blackberry bush, and realize that you will have to paint again tomorrow.

Then the mail arrives, a somewhat outdated newspaper with news of war, avalanches, and starvation. Surely painting is preferable?

TO FELIX BRAUN†

Bern, June 7, 1917

I was delighted by your kind greetings, which arrived just about on my fortieth birthday. Thank you very much.

You may well be justified in criticizing *Rosshalde*. Critics are entitled to adopt that attitude. But, speaking for myself at least, I think poets ought to steer clear of it. I only aspire to formal perfection when it's possible to create a closed form, as in poetry. In larger works, which

---

* Professor of forestry in Zurich.

† Austrian writer and man of letters.

reflect the sum of my feelings and experiences over many years, I only set myself a single aesthetic requirement: the emotions must be genuine, the language pure and exact. Our literature may need to stutter before it can speak; the latest literary arrivals suggest something along these lines: their rhapsodies can sound cheeky and maladroit, but by and large I take them quite seriously.

Oddly enough, my former self and past deeds have begun to affect me slowly, in retrospect. I felt entirely isolated, and was actually suffering from a near-fatal illness, even though I only spotted the external symptoms after my recovery. People said I was too prolific at a time when that was no longer the case, since I could barely write anymore. The war has put me in an awful situation, which is fraught with inner turmoil, a situation I can neither describe nor turn into literature, yet by the time my friends and the world at large begin pestering me with questions and reproaches, I shall probably have something to show them.

In the meantime, I have set literature aside; it would be incompatible, in any case, with my wartime duties. I'm also cooped up a lot because of a protracted illness. I found my own way of coping with these woes, which were often unbearable: I have taken up painting and drawing for the first time. I don't care whether my painting has any objective value; for me, it's a way to bathe in the solace that art affords, and which I was no longer finding in literature—devotion without lust, love without expectations.

Although the war has changed the way I—and indeed everybody else—relate to the world, it hasn't made a political animal of me. Quite the opposite. I see the line dividing the inner and outer worlds even more clearly than usual, and am interested solely in the former.

I responded to your letter because I was struck by its warm, affectionate tone. There is, however, a much less personal matter that I thought I would mention. I'm supplying the almost 200,000 German prisoners in France with reading matter. Requests for books pile up each day; they're often quite moving; our limited funds are quite inadequate. So I'm asking some of my friends to help out. As a writer, you probably don't have any money, but you have some connections. Maybe you could send me copies of your own books, and perhaps you could procure some other good books if you raised the matter with your friends. But don't feel any obligation. Only if you really feel like it. We get numerous requests each day for good contemporary literature, but I have to restrict myself to paperbacks from publishers such as Reclam. Some writers, Hauptmann, Wassermann, Thoma, and others, have already responded to my appeal, donating in some cases as many as fifty to one hundred copies, but we would be happy with less. [. . .]

I'm not trying to badger you! If this doesn't strike a chord, just forget about it. On the other hand, if something useful does occur to you, go ahead and do it!

TO ROMAIN ROLLAND

Bern, August 4, 1917

I was deeply pleased to receive your kind greetings. I have been constantly ill and isolated ever since. Life has become difficult and leaves a bitter taste. Whenever possible, I turn from present-day events to timeless issues, and cherish poetry all the more. I have failed in my attempt to introduce love into political matters. I don't consider "Europe" an ideal. While people continue killing one another, under European leadership, I remain suspicious of all such divisions between human beings. I don't believe in Europe, but rather in humanity, in the kingdom of souls on earth, in which every people participates, and I think we are indebted to Asia for its noblest manifestations.

Dear Herr Rolland, you're one of the few people whose names I associate with hope and substance.

TO HIS SISTER MARULLA

Bern, December 10, 1917

[. . .] While celebrating Bruno's twelfth birthday yesterday, I realized I must have forgotten your birthday. Everything has been horribly frantic, and is still. Since the end of August, I have been busy preparing for the POWs' Christmas, also a somewhat sentimental occasion, and yet haven't had time to prepare Christmas surprises for my own children. I shall soon have to give up this silly racket.

I'm even starting my own publishing house:* I spend thousands of

---

* The Publishing House of the Book Depot for German Prisoners of War. Hesse edited twenty-two separate titles with an average run of 1,000 copies, including: *Don Correa* by Gottfried Keller, an anthology of poetry from Novalis to Ernst Stadler; *Dichtergedanken* from Herder to Stifter; *Zeitvertreib*, a collection of anecdotes and jokes; *Schüler und Studenten*, stories by Stifter, A. Zweig, and Alfons Paquet; two anthologies of "strange" and "funny" stories; two novellas by Thomas Mann, *Tonio Kröger* and *The Railway Accident*. Hesse described the project in a letter to Emil Molt of January 8, 1918: "I feel that this attempt to influence the hundreds of thousands of people whose lives have been completely disrupted by the war is assuming ever greater importance for our future. The government has other priorities, and its interventions serve only to exacerbate the patriotic warmongering."

francs buying paper, then print the booklets for the prisoners myself, since we can no longer get them from Germany. I'm also office manager of a branch of the POW welfare organization. I supervise several POW camps, edit *Der Sonntagsbote*, and manage the literary side of the book depot. Moreover, when we run out of money, I'm the one who has to go begging. I have raised more than ten thousand marks. As you can see, we too are sick and tired of the entire mess. There are some prospects for peace again, but I don't have much faith in that. Yesterday was Bruno's twelfth birthday; he has been in bed for ten days with a small wound in the leg, which developed an infection. Things seemed quite serious for several days, there were signs of blood poisoning. There is still a little pus coming out. But he is quite cheerful and has kept busy reading and doing handicrafts. Heiner is in good health. We want the youngest to spend Christmas here. He is always in Kirchdorf; I hardly know him anymore, since I almost never get to see him. Mia visits him from time to time. He is doing reasonably well over there, but gets very irritable and nervous whenever we decide to take him back with us. This has been going on for years now.

It's a pity my news isn't more cheerful. But at least it's not all that terrible, and nowadays that's saying something. There is no point mailing things across the border anymore; either most items are forbidden or the appropriate regulations are so cumbersome that there is no point. I'm sending you a couple of marks for Christmas, and hope you will buy yourself something with it.

If Zündel's life of Blumhardt* is among Father's books, I'd like to borrow it. It used to be in Calw, but was hardly Papa's own.

We're burning our last bit of coal. If the war is still going strong next winter, we shall all freeze. If worse comes to worst, I shall drop everything and head off to Ticino, where at least they have a mild climate and hardly any frost.

That's it for now. I have to go to the office to see my staffers, who have been working overtime up to midnight, almost every evening.

---

* *Johann Christoph Blumhardt* (1880).

TO MAX BUCHERER*

Bern, December 25, 1917

It's so long since I have been able to spend a decent amount of time in Zurich. When I'm there, I have to meet all kinds of people and don't manage to have real conversations with my friends. Actually, I'm now leading a quiet, secluded life, and I try to ensure that the bustle going on outside remains as unintrusive as possible. What I mean by "bustle" is not just the war, my official position, the scandalous conditions in politics and government—I never had much time for that sort of thing—but also most acquaintances, "events," exhibitions, performances, etc. The war exacerbated an inner conflict that has isolated me over the past two years, and although I don't regret that struggle, I haven't yet fully come to terms with it.

I spent an evening with some German politicians last week (Haussmann was there) and was not particularly impressed this time either. We can hope at best that the Prussians don't jeopardize the likely peace treaty with Russia† by coming up with exceedingly cheeky demands, which they could easily do. I have nothing against the people themselves, and have met splendid individual Prussians. Moreover, I don't believe that those who hold power in England or America are any better. However, the principle underlying the form of our government and way of life is more clearly articulated in Prussia than anywhere else. And I have increasingly come to regard that principle as my polar opposite and archenemy, something I need to fight with my entire being. And that's a feeling shared by those supporters of entente who talk about Prussian militarism. A man came to see me today who used to move in the highest circles of German officialdom; he had a top position at Krupp's, and worked for some time with Jagow and the Foreign Office.‡ He was still there during the first year of the war, and was entrusted with important missions in then neutral Romania. He left Germany a

---

* Painter and graphic artist.

† Negotiations were held in Brest Litovsk and lasted from December 22 until March 3, 1918. There was a Russian offer (renunciation of annexations, evacuation of the occupied territories, national self-determination) and burdensome German demands (Russia had to give up its claim to Poland, the Baltic states, Finland, the Ukraine, etc.). Lenin finally surmounted the opposition of many of his comrades and accepted the German conditions.

‡ Dr. Johann Wilhelm Muehlon, a pacifist, served as a diplomat in the German Foreign Office and as a director of Krupp's, retired from that position shortly after the outbreak of the war, then served as a German emissary entrusted with secret diplomatic missions; resigned on February 1, 1917, the day Germany declared unrestricted submarine warfare, subsequently in contact with Germans in exile, whom he tried to unite.

year ago, because he couldn't tolerate the prevailing mentality, and cut off all ties. I see signs like this all around me, almost daily.

I have been absolutely overwhelmed, my office workers have been working overtime for the past three weeks up to midnight almost, but nonetheless our Christmas packages for the prisoners will be late once again. I placed some large orders at the end of August, but they haven't even arrived yet. Good books are becoming as scarce as flour made from real wheat. There hasn't been any Gottfried Keller available for months from any publisher. But there is paper galore for bad propaganda books and pathetic things like that little book by the aviator Richthofen* (ca. 350,000 copies in print). Even though I'm constantly fighting to preserve these efforts on behalf of the prisoners and ensure they remain uncontaminated by patriotic or political tendencies, I nevertheless feel increasingly that I'm fighting a losing battle for a master whom one ought not serve. I would have given up the whole thing long ago if I didn't know and love a Germany that doesn't at all resemble its official incarnation. A certain bashfulness is holding me back, and while I must have some reason for feeling that way, I often think it's just foolishness or cowardice.

We have a couple of official holidays here, so I don't have to be in the office today and tomorrow. I'm in the process of setting up a small publishing house. Since most of the books I need are either hard to procure or unavailable, I want to publish some small, easily produced works myself, here in Bern, as long as I can still get paper, so I can send them to the prisoners as gifts.

During the negotiations about prisoner exchanges, which went on here for weeks, France took such an obstructionist attitude that all the fine plans had to be ditched. The ruthless policies being pursued over there as well leave little room for human considerations. Hundreds of thousands of people are cooped up together; they have been imprisoned for three years now (roughly equivalent to the sentence formerly handed down for second-degree murder!) and are not just being treated badly; they're being systematically destroyed. The other side doesn't want so many useful people ending up in enemy hands; the idea, after all, is to cripple the enemy! I have no interest in politics, otherwise I would have joined the revolutionaries long ago. I really long to get away from the endless abominations being perpetrated on both sides, get back in touch with myself, and pursue some purely intellectual tasks. At present, my official duties permit me to do so for only a few hours at a time [. . .]

* *Der rote Kampfflieger* (1917).

TO SIGMUND FREUD

Bern, September 9, 1918

Dear esteemed Herr Professor,

I was rather embarrassed to receive your letter thanking me,* since I am really indebted to you. I am delighted to have this opportunity to convey my gratitude to you. Unconsciously, artists have always taken your side, and they will become increasingly conscious of this alliance. Most heartfeltly and cordially

TO HIS SISTER ADELE

Bern, October 28, 1918

Dear Adis,

I'm writing today because there is something you should know about, even though there is not much I can say. I have drifted away from the family over the years and am now very much alone, but I am still keenly aware of the bonds between us.

Nobody knows about some of the things that I had to endure during our fourteen years of marriage. The last few months were the most difficult of all, both for Mia and for me: I had thought for some time that I knew the meaning of suffering, and had emptied the chalice. But it's not over yet. A great misfortune (not entirely unexpected of late, but so sudden it exceeded our worst fears) has befallen us. Mia, who was in Ticino with Brüdi† for three weeks, developed a severe psychosis; she was brought to a sanatorium in a confused state, suffering from mood swings. I haven't seen her since. She is now in Küsnacht near Zurich.

I haven't figured out yet how to manage the household and children alone. Some friends have been lending a hand. I shall either try to find a housekeeper, and keep things as they are, or (and this seems more likely) find lodgings for the boys, get a maid, and remain here in the house myself.

There's no need for you to get worried. It's possible, indeed probable, that Mia will get well again, but there is, of course, no way of knowing how long her recovery would last. She is well taken care of,

---

* Freud had thanked Hesse for his essay "Artists and Psychoanalysis" (*Werkausgabe*, 10:47ff) and for his works, which he had been following "with pleasure since *Peter Camenzind*." Hesse expanded these views in reviews of works by Freud in 1919 and 1925 (*WA*, 12:365–68).

† Hesse's youngest son, Martin, who was being cared for at the time by Johanna and Alice Ringier in Kirchdorf near Bern.

and at present there is nothing more one can do for her. The children are fine; they know only that Mama is sick and cannot come home. Brüdi will probably stay in Kirchdorf—we had just decided we wanted him to spend the winter at home. I don't want to describe the actual misfortune, or my attempts to trace the early signs of it, and track down Mia's missing luggage, etc. We have come through the first bout, and shall continue to prevail. You should only mention this to my closest friends.

My dear little sister, I know that you think of me often, and feel sorry for us, and also remember us in your prayers. I share your belief that this is not in vain. I have been reading Mother's letters, and am often with you in spirit.

TO CUNO AMIET*

Bern, January 5, 1919

Today I send you my greetings and I also have a request, but expect a reply only if the idea appeals to you.

The war has really hurt me. I have served as a wartime official for over three years (I'm a German subject), and have had to neglect my own work to attend to these other duties. I still had some income from my books, but that was all in German currency, and you know how much that is worth now. Then along comes the revolution, so I now stand to lose most of my previous savings, which are invested in German State Bonds. But quite apart from that, I'm in a very awkward situation right now, because I cannot get any money at all out of Germany.†

The situation was quite tolerable, and I didn't worry much about it while my health held out and conditions at home seemed reasonable. But my wife is now suffering from a severe nervous illness. She has been institutionalized for the past few months, and I have had to put the children in lodgings. And my financial predicament has worsened as a result. Some of my friends are helping out, but I have to make sure that I earn something in the near future, of necessity in Switzerland, since my German income is virtually worthless.

Hence the following request: I have copied out a number of manuscripts this year and illustrated them with little sketches. Each of these

---

* Painter and graphic artist; became foster father of Hesse's oldest son, Bruno.

† Hesse had written in a similar vein in a letter of September 11, 1917: "I have been short of money for the past two years, haven't bought myself a suit for over two years, and walk around in torn shoes."

manuscripts, which contain twelve poems and a title page—thirteen pages, in other words—could be sold for 200 to 250 francs. They would appeal to connoisseurs and collectors of beautiful books, curios, etc.; some have already been sold. I donated the first few copies to a fund-raiser for the German POWs, but need to use the rest for myself.

The manuscripts have thirteen mostly colored illustrations, and each is one of a kind: no two have identical contents and drawings.

It would certainly be helpful if you could mention this to friends of yours who buy pictures, etc. Of course, only if you feel like it. Please ignore this letter if you don't like my naïve, childlike sketches. They're worthless as art. Whatever value they have has to do with the common origin of the poems and pictures; both were created by the same hand, stem from the same sensibility, and the resulting unity of text and "illustration" is quite unusual.

Enough of that! I hope your New Year has been better than mine. Please keep this to yourself; I don't want compassion from my friends, and have gradually withdrawn from everything. I don't feel devastated, have kept up my work, and know for certain that there are better times ahead. [. . .]

PS: I'm enclosing a few pages, and hope you will accept them as a New Year's greeting from me.

TO FRITZ BRUN

March 9, 1919

I was delighted to get your letter. You're absolutely right. But there is one thing you're mistaken about: I don't feel alienated and isolated just because of the material hardship. It's true that I cannot count on my savings and don't have access to most of my income, but even though that is a cause for concern, it isn't enough to finish me off.

I have been doing a lot of rethinking since the end of the war, and am not yet done. The most pressing issue at the moment is the family situation, but I think that I may have found a provisional solution. You already know that my wife is suffering from a nervous disorder, and that I have been on my own for almost half a year now. I realize now that I have to make certain changes in my life; my marriage is falling apart. I'm trying to find a way to disengage myself from the family and withdraw. That would be easy enough if my wife were in good health, since she has the best will in the world. But I have to make provision for her and the children before I do anything else. I think my wife will first set up a smaller household, and then, if she stays healthy, she can gradually take the children back. I shall look for a hideaway somewhere else, probably in Ticino.

Please don't tell anybody.

Your kind letter shows that I do have friends—not that there was ever any real doubt, but it's nice to see some proof. Many thanks!

I see myself sprouting new leaves for a few more summers, and hope to hear them rustling in the wind; it doesn't matter what age the trunk is. I also intend to keep on playing all sorts of music in my usual fashion, but there are still some clouds obscuring that delightful prospect.

TO EMIL MOLT

Montagnola, June 19, 1919

[. . .] My family is still in the house in Bern. We have given notice for the fall, but it's almost impossible to find another apartment in Bern. The shabbiest city apartment with only half the present space, and without any garden or anything, would cost more than what we now pay. We're trying to stay here. If we succeed, my wife will stay put and rent out a few rooms. It would be a terrible pity if they had to leave Bern, since the boys attend local schools, and the cost of moving has escalated.

My plans are uncertain, but I intend to remain ensconced here as long as possible. The length of my stay will depend on how my wife fares. I'm hard at work, writing and painting, but haven't yet fully recovered, since I'm still coping with the aftereffects of those upheavals. Things are gradually improving.

These last few evil years have made me, and every other serious-minded person, define my personal mission in life and stick to it, regardless of the immediate consequences. My mission has more to do with intellectual matters than with practical or political affairs. I see a relationship between the events taking place in the world now and ideas I had before the war about European intellectual life and the decline of Europe. I still think along those lines. These experiences have certainly deepened the psychological element in my work, but they have also forced me to confront a number of technical challenges. Writing has become a real struggle. But I now have confidence in my goals again, and feel that this is the right path for me. [. . .]

TO LOUIS MOILLIET*

Montagnola, July 24, 1919

Caro amico,

I have bolted the door and the window, there's a bottle of Chianti on the desk, it's chilly and disgusting outside. Life is often quite unbearable.

I just finished the piece I've been working on just about every evening since I got here. It's a long novella,† the best thing I have ever done, a break with my earlier style, and the beginning of something entirely new. The piece is certainly not beautiful or comely, a bit like potassium cyanide, but it's good and needed to be done. I'm drinking wine and starting a new piece,‡ and without the work and the wine, everything would seem intolerable.

You have occasionally seen me when I was sad and ill, since, after all, one cannot always be a *figlio d'un ricco Signore*.§ By the Lord Zebaoth, I hope this doesn't scare you away. I assure you, my dear Moilliet, that your presence in this odd world comforts me no end.

We have had some beautiful, enchanting days; at night the moon chased like mad around the heavens; morning soon dawned, and we crawled home with red wine all over our waistcoats. We were in Carona, saw the cannonballs‖ again and Generoso** all violet. Our elegant Ruth†† ran around in a fiery little red dress, accompanied by a splendid menagerie: an aunt, two dogs, and a piano tuner, who was unfortunately insane. The whole affair finished up in a dark grotto, which was suspended somewhere in the air, lit-up trains roared by below, women were kissed, and also some tree trunks. It was painfully beautiful.

Little pleasures like this cheer up our poor hearts and shorten the lengthy trajectory of life. Unfortunately, my eyes have been out of action for the past few weeks and hurt a lot. At times the going is rough, and unfortunately, these days it's impossible to do any painting outdoors. I often put a blob of geranium lacquer on a sheet of white paper at home, and use it to draw illustrations or something imaginary. In the evenings,

---

* Painter and close friend of Hesse's.
† *Klein and Wagner* (*WA*, 5:204ff).
‡ *Klingsor's Last Summer* (*WA*, 5:293ff).
§ Son of a rich man.
‖ Presumably trees pruned to a round shape.
** Mountain near Lugano.
†† Ruth Wenger, who became Hesse's second wife in 1924.

when I cannot work or my eyes are troubling me, I can always succumb to the lure of a rustic tavern, where I can sing praise to the Lord and see double versions of my stars on the ceiling.

TO WALTER SCHÄDELIN

August 16, 1919

I was delighted to get your letter this morning. Many thanks! You have a strong faith in God, and your life has a center. In my case, the pressures are centrifugal. But I'm also determined to mature fully; you're perfectly free to rename the phenomenon that I call the will to self-destruction. Now that I'm alone and more in touch with myself, I'm gradually coming to terms with the loss of everything that has disintegrated over the past few years. I tend to interpret my own experiences, and those of my people symbolically, viewing them as part of a larger development.

We seem to have misunderstood each other in our letters. You wrote saying that I shouldn't leave the boys with my wife, since you felt she couldn't provide any stability. That fear, the thought that my wife could have another breakdown, is the sword that has been hanging over my head since the fall of 1918. So your letter came as a shock, since I know that if I start worrying about that again, I shall be racked with infernal torments for days and nights on end. My own feeling is that I cannot adopt your suggestion to cut off my wife completely, treat her like an invalid, have her confined, and take away the children. That would deal her a mortal blow. Besides, she still means a lot more to the children than I ever could. Nothing is left of family life except the worries; the rest has receded into the past. At the moment, I'm trying to center my life on my intellectual, creative activity or task, whatever one wants to call it, because I have to, if I want to survive. I'm being crushed by fate, and just have to let the wine in me flow. That isn't always easy. The world has changed and with it my life, and these developments pose intellectual and artistic challenges for me. My previous methods are not equal to that kind of challenge; I now live in a makeshift hut, and each day I have to produce and test some new tools and weapons.

You like to imagine there is a wide disparity between the two of us, and I find that rather sad, since I feel you do so out of habit rather than modesty. My aim in life is no different from yours or anybody else's, but I have had to face up to deeper inner conflicts, and am compelled by my temperament and disposition to create art—i.e., somehow I need to express and shape my inner life. For years (prewar) I was rather complacent about my literary successes and accomplishments, but the war and the catastrophes in my private life have induced me to make drastic changes and, ultimately, start again from scratch. During the war, after the fake German splendor had crumbled, I saw that my intuitive premonitions were accurate, and seeing the young people helped renew my faith. But that was my only positive experience; everything else affected me negatively. I'm ready now to close the books on this matter and begin assuming new tasks. I'm sure very few of my friends will like my current style of writing, and I shall feel as hemmed in and isolated as I did during the war, in both political and human terms.

I shan't budge from here as long as I keep making headway with my work. I haven't been in a railway station or train since April, and haven't bought a newspaper since the first of July. It's possible I shall stay isolated for quite some time; that would be delightful, but I cannot swear it will happen.

Letters are a poor substitute for friendship. On the whole, I must have seemed very passive during our friendship. But when I love somebody I don't let go easily, and as you can see, I'm forcing myself on you again.

Red wine still plays a part in all of this, but my work has the lead role. In any case, dear forester and chum, the chestnut trees in the forest reverberate at night to the sound of your friend's folly.

If Walter Schädelin ever comes through the Gotthard Pass, I shall have lots to show him, and not just wine bars and watercolors, even though my room is full of the latter.

TO GEORG REINHART*

Montagnola, September 8, 1919

Please accept my sincere thanks for your kind letter!

At first, I was tempted to accept your kind offer immediately, since my present troubles are, of course, partly financial. Because of the exchange rate for the mark, my income has sunk to a fourth of what it was previously. I probably stand to lose even more of this income, since I have changed tack, and my old readers may not be quite as eager to sample my latest works.

But, really, the more I think it over, the more I realize that my

---

* Merchant, art collector, and patron of Hesse's.

difficulties extend far beyond those financial concerns, and the prospect of complete financial security wouldn't necessarily make me happy or relieve my main worries. My family is a great cause of concern, because its well-being depends very much on my wife's condition. Since she is moving to Ascona this month, I shall probably visit her soon; I haven't seen her in six months.

So, under present circumstances, I should like to keep on trying to make ends meet on my own. If you wish to do me a favor and be of some help, you could perhaps give me a small electric heater as a present, since I fear I shall have heating problems this winter. The current is 600 volts.

My dear Herr Reinhart, could I possibly accept a modified version of your offer? If the worries keep mounting and the situation becomes oppressive, I shall approach you and ask for help. But for now, and let's hope forever, I feel relieved to have a friend and supporter like you, even if I never need to ask for help. The depression you noticed is largely a reaction against my feverish work habits since last May. I have harnessed that smoldering intensity and manic energy in a short, expressionistic piece, which is full of fantasy. I can show it to you sometime. From October on, I shall be helping to edit a new review in Germany, aimed at young people;* I don't have much faith in it, but we had to make an effort. Financially, I don't stand to gain anything, but since I haven't put any money in it, I cannot lose anything either.

TO HIS SISTER ADELE

October 15, 1919

I got your kind letter yesterday. There was one from Marulla the day before yesterday. I like to sit alone on the grass in the morning sun. I have chosen a sheltered spot by the wall of the small church at Agra, so I can spend an hour here without freezing; I'm gazing at Italy across a stretch of sea and a flat promontory. I come here along woodland paths, which often remind me of Calw, even though there are no pine trees in this region, only a few beeches, and the ground is strewn with chestnuts rather than pinecones.

I shall have to accept eventually that I was never destined to experience home and country, wife and children, etc., as anything other than parables and images, and was never meant to tarry there. Someday even the pain of separation and the more serious torments I had to endure

* Hesse was literary editor of *Vivos Voco* from 1919 to 1922.

during my wife's illness will seem remote, insignificant, and tranquil, just the way Calw, Basel, and Gaienhofen now appear in the picture album of my life.

We shall have to find out soon whether anybody is willing to assume the role of guardian for my wife and children, since that is beyond me. Then we shall see what happens. It would naturally be easier for me if one or two of the children went to live in Germany, but I cannot decide that now. I don't know whether Mia's brothers and sisters will offer their help or show hostility, since there is going to be a divorce;* in any case, I have decided that I'm never going to see Mia again under any circumstances. Terrible things await us, since Mia will start clamoring to have the children back the moment she starts feeling better, and we shall probably have to say no. I feel sorry for her, but she and I no longer belong together, and it was she who rejected me, not the reverse. It's true that this was not the only reason why my marriage failed: I was never a good husband and father, and eventually I arrived at a crossroads where I had to make a decision: I turned my back on bourgeois life, which I had always regarded merely as a mask, and focused instead on the task which I regard as my fate and the very meaning of my life. I shall be venturing onto difficult terrain, but my state of mind will be lighter and freer than heretofore; I never was happy or carefree during the long years of my marriage.

I was delighted to receive the card with Finckh. He is a good fellow, and probably not all that satisfied now with his war poems about the Lord, who always happens to side with the most powerful cannons. I have no faith in his God, and never believed in his cannons, but those were external differences.

TO HELENE WELTI

Montagnola, November 7, 1919

Many thanks for your wonderfully kind letter! I couldn't agree with you more, since I never expected you to be enamored of my painting and of recent artistic style in general! So I'm pleased that you are courageous enough to want to go along with it, even if only a bit of the way. And now to the question you raised: why is nature stylized this way rather than that? I don't consider the question mysterious, although I do find it hard to articulate my ideas on the subject. I believe that the stylistic shifts in art are intimately related to the flux in other areas of

---

* Hesse was not divorced until July 14, 1923.

life, such as in fashion. There is a dark, unconscious instinct underlying those fluctuations, and like the changing fashions in clothes each season, the most recent art acts as a very fine, sensitive barometer of the nervous impulse of our age. I don't believe anybody is obliged to participate in all these changes and fluctuations, or praise them to the heavens, and I for my part refuse to do so. Nevertheless, it seems clear to me that there is a deeper meaning behind all of this and, should the Expressionist tide sweep across Europe from Barcelona to Moscow, then we cannot simply attribute the phenomenon to a strange "coincidence" or to the whims of a few individuals. The entire younger generation has decided that it doesn't like "Impressionism," a word which they pronounce in a hostile manner; I don't share their sudden antipathy and still feel exceedingly fond of Corot and Renoir. But I find their reaction understandable. Impressionism allowed one area of painting to develop fully; the delicacy and subtlety of that art ushered in a sophisticated form of high culture, and young people suddenly began to rebel against it. It was too one-sided for them; they wanted to hear new sounds, having grown tired of a style that wouldn't allow them to convey their own needs and feelings. Of course, none of this impairs the quality of any good work produced by the previous generation; one ought not take the revolutionary antics of a portion of the younger generation too seriously, except in one respect: they have a deep need to find new ways of expressing worries and emotions that are indeed new.

By the way, I feel a certain kinship with Kreidolf.* My watercolors are a sort of poem or dream; the "reality" which they convey is but a distant memory, and subject to the vagaries of one's needs and feelings. Kreidolf does much the same thing. But, of course, I never forget that he is a master of the art of drawing, and also has the gentle, highly trained hands of a consummate craftsman, and I realize that by comparison I'm just a dilettante.

So I'm not tempted to laugh or get angry at you, as you half feared! On the contrary, I'm glad that you at least like my way of combining colors. But I think you will find my new literary works much more accessible (with a few hitches again) than the little pictures.

You have sensed the essence in both cases: you don't necessarily appreciate or condone the means of expression, but you sense that my work is the serious product of a certain inner necessity.

You ask about my wife, who is in the Clinic for Nervous and Emotionally Disturbed Patients in Kilchberg near Zurich. Her sisters want to have her transferred to Meilen, where they think she will be a

* The painter Ernst Kreidolf.

little better off. I haven't heard anything directly from her, and have no intention of reestablishing contact myself, but am sure she would be very happy to hear from you. Please don't pay any attention if she starts asking for money or the like.

I wish you all the best at the start of winter. It saddens me to hear you describing yourselves as old people who live mostly in the past. Compared to my own solitary, burrowlike existence, your lives are lively and varied, especially considering all the wonderful people you know. Of course, I have my life all to myself, and my motor runs smoothly, purring along amid tranquil days of uninterrupted work.

TO LUDWIG FINCKH

Montagnola, January 17, 1920

Dear Ugel,

Your questions about life here are so detailed that I have drawn you a sketch of the palazzo where I live, with its steep mountain garden and protruding conifers and palm trees. It's a very large, ostentatious house.

The family was wealthy at one time, but has come down in the world, and there are quite a few tenants living here. My windows are to the right. Each morning since October, a little old widow from the village has been coming to tidy up the place and do the cooking, mending, and washing. Natalina—that is her name—never disturbs me; she knows that I need peace and quiet and she respects that. But once a month I listen to her talking about Nino, her only son, who died a couple of years ago, at the age of around ten or eleven. She is always going to his grave. Nino behaved like a saint, drew like Michelangelo, sang like a nightingale, and impressed everybody. But he looks very different in the photographs she shows.

So that is what my life is like here, and contrary to your suggestion, I have no need of anybody else to set me laughing, crying, and so on.

You're wrong to think that I have disowned my previous work. It can stay the way it is. But I discovered one day that I couldn't continue in that vein. I have no idea whether my present work is more significant or not; I just know that I have to write like this. Yes, I realize that the language of my earlier efforts was highly cultivated and rather musical. But because of the war and everything else, I now realize that we were just turning ourselves and our potential into the stuff of popular literature.

I find the best consolation in painting. I have quite a few holes in my shoes and socks, the hole in my wallet is to blame for that, and hope I can earn a penny or two through my painting, since there is unfortunately no way one can make any money from literature in Switzerland. I'm having my debut: the art gallery in Basel (where I haven't set foot in fifteen years) is holding a small exhibition of my watercolors, and I shall know by the end of January whether the reviewers can abide me, or just want a good laugh, indeed whether there is any interest at all in my work. Hanging in one corner of my large study is a beautiful fifteenth-century Italian Madonna, which I cherish, having bought it in Brescia in the spring of 1914, that year of grace. My small pictures are the only other things on the wall, so I'm sitting here surrounded by my dreams. That can be quite nice.

We have been having summery weather for the past few days, the sun is extremely warm and there's a lukewarm breeze; I'm going out walking again today, sketchbook in hand, for a few hours. That allows me to wait until evening before lighting a fire, so I can save a lot of wood.

My dear friend, I can sense what you're going through, and there is one thing I would like to say to you: We tend to overemphasize the objects of our love; no matter what we choose, family, fatherland, or whatever, the objects themselves are of secondary importance. We are endowed with love so that we can love and suffer, and I myself feel a much greater, if rather uncomfortable affection for poor, defeated Germany, and feel more personally moved by its suffering, than I did when it was throwing its weight around. After all, I was being told at the time that I wasn't much good, that my previous work was unimpressive. Everybody was saying so, my friends at home, the newspapers, officialdom. I discovered there was no understanding in official circles for the ideals I was trying to uphold, a situation which hasn't changed one bit. But the experience has taught me to cherish those ideals all the more.

TO JOSEF BERNHARD LANG*

Montagnola, January 26, 1920

Dear friend beyond the Gotthard!

I should indeed have written ages ago, and am glad that you were so kind as to think of me. I haven't been ill, but am feeling jaded and

* Psychiatrist and disciple of C. G. Jung; Hesse had some seventy psychoanalytical sessions with Lang in 1916 and 1917.

depleted, and my work on the new review* is rather mechanical. But I have also been doing some painting again—e.g., a picture of a small golden "ichthys," an early Christian fish, which will hang on a wall in my lodgings. As you can see from the enclosure, I had an exhibition in Basel this month. I had vaguely hoped I might sell something, and although I didn't, I shall probably come to Zurich in the late spring for an exhibition.

I should either start another serious artistic project or else go back to analysis, but that is something I, unfortunately, cannot do on my own. For a while, I was behaving like a blockhead, reading like crazy and writing mechanically for the new journal. I feel freer now, although I have frequent attacks of anxiety, and am not nearly as committed as I should be. Art cannot be created halfheartedly; a man who wants to write or paint has to catch fire everywhere. I myself am gradually becoming an old man, with some gray hairs and a constantly dripping, pointy nose—well, to hell with it! I'm still feeling the repercussions of those upheavals that occurred during the last few months. Fortunately, there was a lot of sunshine in January; I spent a lot of time outdoors, and didn't have to start a fire until the evening.

For now, I'm managing to make ends meet: a friend is helping a bit, but the situation is pretty ridiculous. If I work really well for a few days, I earn a hundred marks, for which I get eight francs. But somehow I'm surviving.

I'm hoping you can come to stay with me for a week in the spring. I can pay for the ticket so that you don't have any expenses, and I can probably offer you some fees for analysis. Think about it [. . .] Demian has begun to sink in. There are indications that the identity of the author may not be a secret for much longer. It will come out eventually, and that saddens me, since I would have preferred to remain anonymous. I would prefer to edit each new work under a new pseudonym. After all, I am not Hesse, but in the past have been Sinclair, Klingsor, Klein, etc., and there are others to come. [. . .]

I had a friend make small frames according to my specifications, and now there are paintings of mine hanging all over the apartment. I think I shall start playing my violin again in the evening, for the first time in many years. That will afford me a pleasant half hour, and I feel that I shall keep sending more flares up into the dull heavens of this world, thus affording my friends a little solace and pleasure. [. . .]

* *Vivos Voco.*

My dear friend, I often think of you fondly. Ultimately, both of us regard the entire world as a purely psychogenetic phenomenon and thus don't have to take things too seriously all the time.

TO GEORG REINHART

Montagnola, August 14, 1920

[. . .] Things have been going badly for months. I feel tired and irritable and am up to my neck in trouble.

Literature is thriving! Some people in Germania, including the very young and the revolutionaries, have begun to realize that I'm one of their few leading spirits. Unfortunately, as with all wishes fulfilled in life, this is happening too late for me to feel particularly exhilarated. This has always been true: I got everything in life that I desired and seriously pursued, only to find it losing its value right away, and slipping out of my hand to make way for some new striving. I had the same experience with literature, getting married, having a house and garden, children and marriage, journeys, successes, insights. Someday, art itself may lose the significance which I now attribute to it, so that there will be space for something new to unfold.

I feel no connection with Germany, the literature it produces, or the youth over there; the notes that I hear sound false and strange, even though they are also flattering. There was only one thing I really liked: In his *Travel Diary*,* the cleverest German book in years, Keyserling recommends as an ideal for our future the doctrine of God-within-the-self, which I have been presenting under all sorts of guises for the past three years (*Demian, Zarathustra*, etc.). Keyserling's philosophy derives from India and from Bergson, and reaches conclusions virtually identical to mine. I think that is why books like *Demian* have a strong impact, even though few people understand them. Quite intuitively, progressive people sense the existence of the goal, which those books seek to evoke obliquely through language and other covert means.

I hope to be able to send you something new soon. But my big Indian work† isn't ready yet and may never be. I'm setting it aside for now, because I would have to depict next a phase of development that I have not yet fully experienced myself. [. . .]

I have to travel to Ascona soon to see my wife, who wants to find

---

* *Reisetagebuch eines Philosophen* (1919).
† The first part of *Siddhartha*, which was dedicated to Romain Rolland.

a job working in a household for the winter, and is having a hard time. The divorce didn't come through; all those efforts were in vain, since in order to get one, I would have had to put the children at risk.

TO LISA WENGER*

Montagnola, February 10, 1921

[. . .] Yes, my relationship to India goes back quite far. My mother's father spoke nine or ten Indian languages, lived in India for decades, spoke Sanskrit with the Brahmans, my mother spent part of her life there, spoke three Indian languages, and my father was a missionary in India for a shorter period. As a boy, I started reading books about India, Buddha, etc., in my grandfather's enormous library; I also saw Indian pictures, occasionally some Hindus, and paid a brief visit to India myself.

For years, I believed in Buddhist doctrine, my sole source of consolation at that point, but gradually my attitude changed, and I'm no longer a Buddhist. I now feel far more attracted to the India of the gods and temples, and have just to grasp the deeper meaning of pantheism, etc. To my mind, the relationship between Buddhism and Brahmanism somewhat resembles that between the Reformation and Catholicism. I'm Protestant and, as a child, I believed in the value and meaning of the Reformation, and even heard a Punch-like figure such as King Gustav Adolf being praised as a hero and great mind. I only noticed later on that, while the Reformation was a good thing insofar as the conscientious behavior of the Protestants contrasted nobly with indulgence trading, etc., the Protestant church itself had nothing much to offer, and the various Protestant sects nurtured the cultivation of inferiority complexes. That is also more or less how I view Buddhism, which adopts a rational attitude toward the world without gods, and seeks redemption solely through the intellect. It's a beautiful form of puritanism, but it is also suffocatingly one-sided, and I have become increasingly disenchanted with it.

When Siddhartha dies, he will not wish for Nirvana, but will be content with his reincarnation, and begin the cycle anew.

My fond greetings again to all of you! I feel the true import of your remarks about Herr Wenger, know what this means for Ruth and you, and wish you the best from the bottom of my heart.

* Writer and painter.

I'm glad to be off again on my travels in eight days' time, because I haven't felt at all well since my arrival here. I have been invited to give a lecture at the Psychological (i.e., Psychoanalytic) Club in Zurich. They agreed when I offered to read from my manuscripts instead, and the event will take place on February 19. I hope to meet some friends in Zurich and hear some music, then I have to go and see my boy in the vicinity of Frauenfeld.

Greetings to Ruth, I hope she leaps over her current inhibitions!

Montagnola, May 2, 1921

Thanks for your nice letter, which shows wonderful confidence in me. I want to get this off today, since I shall have to interrupt my usual routine tomorrow. I'm going to Locarno to discuss something with my wife. A few days later my sister is coming for a visit, and I may travel back with her to Zurich about the 20th of May. I shall stay a while in the hope of seeing Jung. If only he could squeeze me in! I haven't figured out yet how I'm going to pay for the analysis; Jung may refuse to accept payment, or perhaps there will be somebody in Zurich willing to help me out. I need some therapy so I can loosen up. I just cannot go on like this. I often feel paralyzed by the thought that our entire literature is worthless. Of course, I can always do some painting, which is peaceful and tranquil. Yet, although painting keeps me alive, it doesn't help me justify my life, either intellectually or materially.

You have your own inhibitions, and the following thought came to me as I was reading your letter. Wouldn't it be wonderful if Frau Wenger were as kind and considerate toward herself as she is toward others? After all, the Gospel doesn't say that you should "love your neighbor instead of yourself," but rather "as you love yourself"!

Even though Herr Wenger is very practical, I consider him an introvert, who has been seeking in his work a substitute for certain unfulfilled spiritual needs. Childhood left him with a religious burden, and he also had a powerful father. I think it's wonderful that he is trying to delve into himself in spite of all his professional and social successes: I don't think he really needs analysis, it wouldn't necessarily do him much good. I think he is finding the right balance all by himself.

It's not easy to practice the Indian-Buddhist form of "meditation," which you also mention in your letter. One cannot expect a sudden flash of insight. It's a discipline, an exercise to be repeated constantly, every day. Given the lives we lead, it's difficult to remember for more than a few seconds at a time that our physical, transitory self is absolutely insignificant; to live according to that knowledge, one would need the concentration of a monk. Christianity is no different: the ordinary rituals of every Christian denomination are emergency solutions, rather superficial adaptations to new circumstances, which can, if necessary, help people conduct their lives. Christianity has access to more serious and intellectual disciplines, practices and modes of redemption, but they have never been practiced in the "real world," just by saints or aspirants to sainthood, monks. The old monasticism of Mount Sinai and Thebes is almost as sophisticated intellectually as Indian monasticism, to which it fundamentally bears a close relation.

We're suffering because we would like to follow that path, but that is no longer possible. We're being held back, not just by the desires and egotistical cravings of the "real world," but also by all the duties and responsibilities we have assumed. We have to transcend those obligations or acknowledge them and live up to them as best we can. Few people, even monks, attain perfection or sainthood, and if that is indeed our goal, we must first try to attain the greatest amount of harmony possible in the present, an objective which we can never reach entirely: it will constantly slip away, but can always be found again. I don't believe that it's possible to hold on to it for long during life on this earth.

TO HANS REINHART*

[*May 1921*]

I should have thanked you long ago for your letter, but I have been undergoing psychoanalysis, which is quite demanding. I would, however, like to respond to your remarks about analysis.

You would like to arrive at some sort of compromise between psychoanalysis and the philosophy of Steiner. But that is altogether impossible, since psychoanalysis is not a creed or philosophy, but an experience. Analysis is only worthwhile when one is prepared to experience it fully, and bring it to bear on one's life. Otherwise, it's nothing but a nice little game.

I'm going through the upheaval induced by psychoanalysis at a time when my life is difficult, intolerable at times.

I have no way of knowing whether you too need analysis. I can only say that Dr. Jung is conducting my analysis with extraordinary assurance, even a touch of genius.

* Brother of Hesse's patron Georg Reinhart.

Zurich [May 1921]

I'm leaving tomorrow. I had really wanted to spend a few more days in Zurich and then visit you again in Winterthur, but I ran out of money, and may have to leave sooner.

I would have liked to continue the analysis with Jung for a little longer. He has a lively personality and a brilliant intellect, a splendid human being; I owe him a lot, and am glad I had the opportunity to spend some time with him.

Please tell your brother Georg that I shall be in Montagnola, after all.

TO THEO WENGER

Montagnola [1921]

Many thanks for your second letter. It arrived while I was thinking about a letter I was going to write to Frau Wenger, but now that is unnecessary.

Your first letter made me feel very worried about the three of you. You can always protect Ruth from the outside, but if you wish to understand what is going on inside her and really help her, it would be important for you to realize why Ruth's affections settled on me. I was afraid that it would be impossible to reach such an understanding if you persisted in seeing only my negative qualities.

Now that I have read your letter, I feel reassured and relieved on that score. And I also feel delighted about the conscientious efforts you're making to assess the situation fairly, without forgetting the bonds of affection and respect that have developed recently between the two of us. I would like to thank you for that; I realize that the recent upheavals have been just as difficult for you as for Ruth and myself.

I believe that Ruth and I shall always remain close friends. We are both sensitive and defenseless by nature, and have a deep need for love and understanding. We discovered that capacity in each other, and know each other so well now that the bond between us may last forever. Never before have I confided so many of my most secret urges, weaknesses, and sufferings. And if it were in my power to transform Ruth's love for me into feelings of pure friendship, I would do so right away. I love her, not just as a friend and soul mate, but as a woman. Yet I have never considered the erotic element the most important aspect of love. I know how easily and often I fall in love, but I have never been able to confide as much of my soul in any person as I have in Ruth, and that is a far stronger bond than any infatuation.

But I'm forty-four and Ruth is twenty years younger. She doesn't really know the difference yet between friendship and love. Only time will tell whether her love for me can turn into friendship, and make her a free woman again. I'm concerned about that. But if there was a time—perhaps even a protracted period—when Ruth missed other marital opportunities because of me, it must also be said that she has gained something from the experience, which should stand her in good stead.

Dear Herr Wenger, I do not believe in chance. The things that occurred to me in your house were fated to happen, and I have even benefited from this gloomy situation, which reflects the will of our stars or gods. I gained a lot from the relationship with Ruth, and also owe much to her mother. I also sense that you too find it hard to believe that our encounter was entirely accidental and futile.

Please do not mention any of this to Ruth. To me, she is not a plaything or conquest, as you once thought, but a soulful, delicate child.

I would be delighted to talk with you as soon as possible. But I can perfectly understand it if you want to hold off on this for the time being. What Ruth needs is not palaver and bustle, but patience and love. I send my grateful greetings to you and your wife.

[1921]

I have just found out that, contrary to my intentions, Ruth has informed you about the content of the recent conversations between the two of us. So now you know about the problems which would arise in the event of a second marriage. I had hoped that Ruth and I would come to a clearer agreement on these matters before bringing them up with you. Something similar happened a few months ago: I held off letting you know that my relationship with Ruth was getting more serious and intimate because I knew that I was not yet in a position to make definite plans or binding promises. You know that I love Ruth and that she loves me. At the moment the legal and economic obstacles to marriage seem quite insuperable. Even if I do manage to get a divorce within the foreseeable future, that will entail a financial burden for years to come, and will make it impossible for me to support a wife. But I do not mean to suggest that these material issues are solely responsible for my predicament. I attach more importance to the inner causes, which are connected to the artistic task or mission with which I feel entrusted. They also reflect some of my own weaknesses and problems. I'm at a stage in life known symbolically to those engaged in intellectual struggles

Hesse shortly before the outbreak of World War I

(*Above*) Maria (called Mia) Hesse, née Bernoulli (1868–1963), mother of Hesse's three sons

(*Below*) With Ruth Wenger (1920), whom Hesse married in 1924

as "forty days in the wilderness," although I have been in the wilderness for three years now, with no end in sight.

But there were two beautiful, really promising signs amid all this turmoil: first of all, my work went through a process of transformation and renewal (from *Demian* to *Klingsor*), and second, I met Ruth. I have known Ruth for almost two years now, and love her with all the love of which I'm capable. I'm not yet sure exactly where our relationship is going. But I feel that omens like that are always meaningful.

Marriage is completely out of the question at the moment. I realize that I am thereby violating a tenet of bourgeois morality, but I cannot behave otherwise, since I'm bound by another form of morality no less sacred to me: my inner voice.

I very much regret that you didn't hear about these reservations directly from me, but I had intended to do things differently. There is little more for me to add, other than what I have just implied. I hope that you will spare Ruth's feelings and not lose faith in me entirely.

As regards my reservations about marriage (that is, conventional marriage), I would ask you to keep in mind that I had a very difficult first marriage, which lasted a long time. I have to admit that I was just as much to blame as my wife for the failure and collapse of the marriage. The wound is still there, but it may eventually heal.

I'm not claiming for myself the alleged prerogative of the artist, as a superior type of human being, to live by looser standards of morality. To the contrary, I'm far more critical of myself than is the average person. Nor do I consider myself a leader or important intellect and thus somehow worthier than others. As I see it, I have an unusual sensitivity that makes me more prone to certain experiences. My mission is to endure them and then articulate them in my work. It's a sensibility which makes marriage rather difficult.

I'm not yet sure how to find a practical solution to this difficult situation. My standards of morality are certainly not bourgeois, since they are based on the belief that fate (e.g., my encounter with Ruth) is never meaningless, and that is why I feel I have to be especially honest with her. I could easily have kept my inner reservations about marriage to myself, since there will be many external obstacles in the years ahead that would automatically rule out a new marriage. But there would be no point in that. Respectful greetings

TO JOSEF BERNHARD LANG

Montagnola, April 17, 1922

My dear friend,

I had just been thinking about you when your letter arrived. I paid a quick visit to Delsberg* the other day, talked to Ruth about you, and also told Mama Wenger that I wished to see you again. She said that it might be possible at some point to have me stay a couple of days in Delsberg as her guest, and have you over for a day or two. In any case, plans are being made. So we were both thinking of each other at the same time.

There are families everywhere now, because of Easter; I'm always running into acquaintances, chiefly from Zurich. Well, that is an established ritual here: Swiss-Germans swarm across Ticino twice a year, always in the wettest weather.

Otherwise, I'm my usual isolated self, and since I don't find painting and writing very meaningful any longer, my life often feels empty. However, I have reached a level of rapport and understanding with Ruth that goes beyond the wildest dreams I used to have. On the other hand, I'm still in a shabby predicament vis-à-vis my wife and family.

The autobiography you mentioned is just a myth. For the past few months, I have been regaling the audience at my public readings with that legend. I do, of course, have something serious in mind, but the only part of it to have seen the light of day is a short introduction plus a sketch of the magical ending, which I have read on several occasions, to the amazement of the audience.†

When are you going to visit us again in Ticino? For the past year, my social life has centered on Ruth. She was living in Zurich, and I tried to get there as often as possible; I succeeded through a stroke of magic. This winter I was asked to give quite a few lectures, but that's over now. Ruth wants to spend the summer in Baden with her sister and only come to Zurich occasionally for lessons (singing with Meschaert). I'm still hoping to get to Delsberg sometime this summer. Then I shall be in touch. On the 10th of May, I went to hear the premiere of Schoeck's *Venus*‡ in Zurich.

Although deep down I feel quite miserable and out of sorts, I have more or less managed to keep my head above water. I'm very pleased

---

* The Wenger family lived in Delsberg (Delémont) in the Swiss Juras.
† *Kurzgefasster Lebenslauf (Life Story Briefly Told)* (1925; *WA*, 6:391ff).
‡ Opera in three acts by Othmar Schoeck.

that you want to keep in touch with me. As you can see, I have been trying to find a way for us to get together again and talk. And now it's really going to happen. Fond greetings

TO ERICH OPPENHEIM

May 13, 1922

Caro Dottore,

Many thanks for your kind letter. I feel sorry for you, now that you are going to have me as a patient, and feel you should be forewarned.

I'm not at all interested in the nomenclature of my various complaints, and as far as I'm concerned, a term such as "gout" might well be based on myth. After all, medicine is not an exact science either.

Well, here is how things stand: I'm not at all the saint, or even the person, you see in me; when I unleash my temperament, I can be a real monster, a Satan. I decided to embark on a radical cure, and your suggestions, especially about sunbathing, are a bit late. I have been sunbathing for many years, whenever the sun was out, this year too; I expose everything thoroughly to the harsh sunlight, not just my stomach and chest, but also my head. I have always bathed in the nude, protecting my eyes either with sunglasses or by keeping them closed, and the treatment seems to agree with me, even though it usually makes me feel rather uncomfortable for several days afterward.

You're quite right about my smoking. But there too, moderation is not one of my strong points. I did stop smoking four days ago, and intend to keep this up for a few more days, and then I'll start up again, not smoking much at first, but things will soon get out of hand, and I'll have to mount another abstention campaign.

There is little danger of my poisoning myself with toxic substances other than tobacco. Alcohol is a possible exception, but I don't really overindulge in it, and I stick to the very light local wine. I eat quite erratically, but I'm not addicted to anything in particular, and favor mild, light food.

I hope we get to see each other soon, so we can continue this sparring match. But I feel all of this is quite ominous. Decay is setting in, Klingsor's skull is tottering.

Dear Dr. Oppenheim, my thanks for now, in the hope that I shall remain in your good esteem.

TO GEORG REINHART

Montagnola, July 8, 1922

I have been wanting to write to you for a long time, but waited for weeks in the hope of sending you a book with some nice, old stories, which I edited.* But it still hasn't arrived from the publishers. So, for now, I'm just sending you fond greetings.

I turned forty-five eight days ago. The best thing I can say about the past year is that last May I finally completed my *Siddhartha*, which will be appearing in book form in the winter. I spent two and a half years on it, and even though I'm not altogether satisfied with the book, I feel that I have reformulated for our era a meditative Indian ideal of how to live one's life.

I was saddened, but not at all surprised to hear about the assassination of Rathenau.† I corresponded a little with him some years ago, when he was beginning to influence public opinion through his writings. I know all too well the mentality, or rather the mindless behavior and boorish pistol waving that led to his murder. It is something I have been trying to combat and bring out into the open for years. The German universities are, unfortunately, one of the main bastions of this nasty and utterly ridiculous anti-intellectualism.

Fond greetings to you and your wife

TO ROMAIN ROLLAND

Montagnola, August 10, 1922

You ask in your kind letter whether I am still "in Lugano." Well, there isn't an easy answer to that question. All I can say is that I'm still living in Montagnola, but haven't set foot in Lugano for more than a year, even though it would only take me an hour to get there. So you can see the kind of life I'm leading: St. Jerome in his little hut.

Many thanks for the helpful information. If the conference‡ is held, I shall try to attend part of it, and would be delighted to get to know your Indian friends.

* Either *Novellino: Novellen und Schwänke der ältesten italienischen Erzähler* or *Geschichten aus Japan*; both were published in 1922 by the Seldwyla Verlag in Bern.

† Walther Rathenau, who took office as German Foreign Minister in February 1922, was murdered in Berlin on June 24, 1922.

‡ Conference of the International Women's League for Freedom and Peace in Lugano, August 18–September 2, 1922.

I have finally finished my *Siddhartha*. It will appear in book form next winter—almost three years after I started work on it—and you shall receive a copy right away. Part One still bears a dedication to you; I have dedicated Part Two to a cousin of mine who has been living in Japan for decades,* and is steeped in Eastern thought; we are especially close.

I'm delighted to hear that you're in Switzerland again. And I hope we shall get to see each other. A few months ago, I lost a dear friend, the German politician Conrad Haussmann.† The intellectual climate in Germany smacks of anarchy and religious fanaticism; it's the climate of an apocalypse or imminent thousand-year Reich.

Cordial greetings from an admirer of yours, who wishes you all the best

TO HELENE WELTI

Montagnola, August 29, 1922

Your kind letter arrived yesterday, and there was a package today with all sorts of things. I would like to thank you ever so much for all this kindness, and I look forward to trying out the lotion. I shall have to be careful with most of the foodstuffs, since I seldom partake of such luxuries, and have not eaten any meat or sausage in a long time. Those things won't keep for long in this heat, without a basement, and somebody will have to help me finish off the sausage. I could only eat a little myself. Actually, I would be much better off with apples, if you ever have any from your garden; they're very scarce here. I eat a bit of macaroni or rice once a day, but apart from that I live almost entirely off milk.

I'm glad that you have read *Siddhartha*. While it doesn't amount to much as literature, it represents the sum of my life and the ideas that I have absorbed over the course of twenty years from Indian and Chinese traditions. The ending of *Siddhartha* is almost closer to Taoism than to Indian thought.

I received a rather odd form of vindication over the past few days. There was an international conference in Lugano, and rather than give

* Professor Wilhelm Gundert, an expert on Japan, translator of the *Bi Yaen Lu* (1912), the "Bible" of Zen Buddhism.
† A member of the Reichstag and a defender of parliamentary democracy, Haussmann was one of the first politicians to become a close friend of Hesse's.

a talk, I read the ending of *Siddhartha*. Naturally enough, there were only a few who understood it. Among the audience was a Hindu, or rather a Bengali, a professor of Asian history in Calcutta, and afterward he got somebody to translate the whole thing verbatim. He turned up the following day in Montagnola, and said he was astonished and quite moved to find a European who had reached the core of Indian philosophy. He spent many hours with me, and soon we were friends. He told me all sorts of things, sang old Indian songs, some more recent ones, etc., etc.

Romain Rolland is coming today, so he can catch the end of the conference. It's quite awkward for me to have to go to Lugano right now, since I always hate going to the city, and would in any case have to worry about the cost of every single telephone call or stamp, since my pockets are virtually empty at present. But I hope to receive some money in the next few days, and then I can invite my Indian friend for a cup of tea in Lugano.

I believe *Siddhartha* recapitulates for our era something that is truly ancient, and hence its significance for a small group of people. The Indian was extremely excited. He said that, while he realized that we Europeans were aware of Buddhist doctrine and were studying it actively, he was amazed that one of us had got so close to the real, inner, nondogmatic Buddha.

I did a lot of painting over the summer. I showed the sketches to my Hindu friend, and asked him to select one for himself. He chose one with trees and a bridge, and said he had selected that one because he feels I know and love trees and understand the language they speak, as he does himself, and because he interpreted the bridge as a bridge between East and West, which people were discovering anew through our efforts.

I very much hope that *Siddhartha* will eventually appear in English,* not for the sake of the English themselves but for those Asians and others whom it would vindicate.

There were other nice, interesting people at the conference (the International Women's League for Freedom and Peace; Rolland's sister is one of the leaders), but I only went down twice. Some of them came here to see me—old Frederik van Eeden,† for instance. You may have

---

* The first English edition did not appear until much later: *Siddhartha*, trans. Hilda Rosner (New York: New Directions, 1951).

† Dutch poet and psychoanalyst who was influenced by socialist and communist ideas. He founded the Walden colony in 1898, but the experiment proved a failure. *Young John* (1886–1906) is an autobiographical, fairy tale-like novel about adolescent development.

read his *Young John*. His background is entirely different from mine. He converted to Catholicism recently, at over sixty, and yet we have become friends; I caught in his voice and eyes a glimpse of a state of mind which is neither Eastern nor Western, a world which exists outside time and space, and yet is more real for all who dwell in it than anything the external world has to offer.

Fortunately, it's still summer, and very hot. I have often thought about the time you were here last year, and would be delighted if we could repeat the experience.

TO BERTHLI KAPPELER

Montagnola, February 5, 1923

There is really nothing left for me to say. You yourself write in your letter that you found *Siddhartha* disturbing, that it turned everything inside you "upside down"—all of which suggests, as you yourself realize, that this book has prodded you to discover new things, challenged your soul. I expect that you too will soon begin to recognize the utter vapidity of your colleagues' questions about the "voguishness" of Indian books and such trifles.

Yet you still felt you needed to raise a question that makes me feel ashamed and also gives me food for thought: Was I serious about *Siddhartha*, do I stand behind it, mean what I say, or was I just having a bit of fun, passing the time, and writing something for its own sake?

I would ask you, before you read any further, whether you have not already answered this question. Your answer was yes. You understood the serious intent of the book and accepted it as a personal challenge. Of course, you have no way of knowing what I put into the book: three years of hard work, many difficult experiences, and ideas drawn from East Asian traditions, which I have been studying intently for the past twenty years. But, actually, you know all of this already, you can sense that I am serious and broach these matters with considerable awe. In any case those kinds of personal considerations and notions about literature seem trivial, since *Siddhartha* raises issues that are truly substantive.

You have also sensed that Siddhartha and I are somehow identical, as is Knulp. Siddhartha is doing the same thing as Knulp (searching for God), but he is much more serious, intense, and, in particular, more conscious about it.

The one thing you find disturbing: why does the backdrop have to be Indian? That is a harder question, but I shall nevertheless try to answer it, since I can feel these questions mean a lot to you.

What follows is a brief credo (intended as a response to your intimate question, not as material for your colleagues' funny parlor games). There is, of course, only one God, one truth, but each people, each age, and each individual perceive it differently, and there are new forms evolving constantly to express that truth. One of the most beautiful and purest such forms is undoubtedly the New Testament—i.e., the Gospels and, to a lesser extent, the Pauline Epistles. There are some proverbs in the New Testament and also in Lao-tse, Buddha, and the Upanishads which rank among the truest, most concise and lively insights that man has ever recognized and articulated. But I could not follow the Christian path to God because of the rigid piety of my upbringing, these ridiculous squabbles in theology, the emptiness and excruciating boredom of the church, etc. So I looked around for other paths to God, and soon discovered the Indian way, which was natural enough in my family, since my grandfather, father, and mother had intimate connections with India, spoke Indian languages, etc. But the most liberating experience of all for me was when I discovered the Chinese way in Lao-tse. Of course, I was also reading Nietzsche, Tolstoy, and Dostoyevsky, who exposed me to modern experiments and problems, but I found the deepest wisdom in the Upanishads, Buddha, Confucius, and Lao-tse, and eventually in the New Testament, once I had overcome my aversion to the specifically Christian form of truth. Yet I remained faithful to the Indian way, even though I do not consider it superior to Christianity: I was simply disgusted by Christianity's attempt to monopolize God and the truth, beginning with Paul and running right through Christian theology, and felt that the Indian methods of finding truth through yoga, etc., are far more practical, astute, and profound.

That is my answer to your question. While I don't feel that Indian wisdom is superior to what Christianity has to offer, I find it somewhat more spiritual, less intolerant, broader, and freer. The Christian truth was forced upon me in my youth in an inadequate form. The Indian Sundar Singh* had quite the opposite experience: having been force-fed with Indian doctrines, he came to believe that the splendid old Indian religion had been corrupted, just as I had felt about Christianity. And so he chose Christianity, or rather didn't choose it but simply became as convinced, captivated, and overwhelmed by Jesus' message of love as I was by the Indian idea of Unity. Other people will find other paths leading to God and the center of the world.

---

* Indian missionary.

But the experience itself is always the same. People who suspect the truth (and, like you, initially feel "completely confused") have a sense of what is important in life and strive after it, inevitably experience—whether in the form of Christianity or otherwise—that God or, if you wish, life is very real. All of us participate in that life; we can resist it or serve it, but nobody who is truly awake could ever live without it.

In the case of those who are deeply intellectual, these experiences may consist partly of thoughts and insights, but they can also take other forms: Thought and awareness are not necessary, life itself can mold us in such a way that we strive increasingly after perfection, value things that are sacred and eternal, and become more and more indifferent to the reality of the other, so-called everyday world.

You know enough now; everything else can be found in *Siddhartha* itself. Please keep these words to yourself. They are intended just for you, but you may share them with one or two others if you feel certain that their interest in the matter goes beyond idle curiosity.

TO ROMAIN ROLLAND

Montagnola, April 6, 1923

My dear friend Rolland,

My friends have never left me as much in the lurch as they have in the case of *Siddhartha*, hardly a single person bothered to drop me a line saying they received the book. Hence the pleasure I derived this morning from reading your kind, wonderful letter.

You're right: I have extremely few colleagues who can appreciate and understand *Siddhartha*. The reviews I have seen convey only a sense of respectful embarrassment.

On the other hand, there are a few people who are completely receptive to *Siddhartha*—to its Indian and human elements as well as to my utterly private mythology—and who breathe it in like air from the homeland. One of the best is the person who shares the dedication of the book with you, my cousin in Japan. He has picked up all sorts of things from his fifteen years living in East Asia and through his long, intimate relationships with Japanese eminences.

Thank you for your kind expression of interest in my book. And also for the idea of recommending a French edition in Paris. I would very much welcome that. Since this book isn't destined for the crowd, I want to ensure that it's available to the small group of individuals for whom it is intended.

I'm a little embarrassed by your question about my book *From*

India. But, of course, I shall give you the information you need. There are no illustrations, only text. It includes a strange little story, taken from the world of British India, which I enjoyed back then (1911) and still consider good.* But, unfortunately, there isn't much worth recommending in the greater part of the book, which consists of notes from my journeys in Malacca, Sumatra, and Ceylon. The book is skimpy, and the journey was actually quite disappointing at the time; it has since produced some utterly beautiful fruit. But back then, having wearied of Europe and fled to India, I found only the lure of the exotic over there. That materialistic exoticism did not lead me toward the spirit of India, which I had already encountered before and was seeking again; it separated me from it.

Well, I have now been able to repay part of my debt to India in *Siddhartha*, and I believe that I may never need to have recourse again to this Eastern guise.

How well off we are basically as writers! Anybody who tries, as an artist, to portray how he feels about this diverse, multifaceted world has so many more alternatives than the person who tries doing so in a purely intellectual manner. Nowadays this can be seen quite clearly in the case of Count Keyserling, whose way of formulating things makes his beautiful, significant ideas banal. It's the same with the journalistic pieces of Tagore.† But Keyserling and Spengler‡—I have been reading both of them—have nonetheless become very important to me. Both have a tendency to exaggerate and sound arrogant, which is common among scholars, the younger ones in particular in Germany. They feel threatened by the very existence of their colleagues and believe that they are ushering in an entirely new era. That is true only on the surface; both of them have an extremely nutritious core, which one can profit greatly from.

Warm regards to your dear sister. I'm counting on your getting nostalgic about Lugano, and then visiting me in Montagnola. I don't feel at home in Lugano; I'm almost as much of a stranger there as in Berlin. I only come alive up here, in my cell, which is in a primitive, peaceful, rural setting, but also has all the sophistication of a hermitage for gourmets.

Best regards, my dear friend, from my heart

---

* "Robert Aghion." Cf. Hesse's *Der Europäer, Gesammelte Erzählungen* (Frankfurt: Suhrkamp, 1977), Vol. 3, p. 160.

† Indian writer, philosopher, and painter.

‡ Philosopher of history. His major work, *Der Untergang des Abendlandes (The Decline of the West)*, appeared during the period 1918–22.

TO GEORG REINHART

Montagnola, April 17, 1923

So I have to send you greetings once again without really knowing where you are. I hope that your surroundings are beautiful, and that you're feeling well and enjoying yourself.

I'm not faring all that well in my private life. Several things make me feel uneasy, including a problem with my girlfriend, which surfaced just when I was beginning to think I might get married again. Well, each one of us has to sort these things out for himself. [. . .]

It's very beautiful here in Ticino at the moment. The woods are just starting to turn green again, and there are flowers everywhere. My son Bruno, who lives with the Amiets, is spending a week with me here; he is outside, painting assiduously.

I paid a visit recently to my reclusive neighbor, Mardersteig.* He has set himself up very nicely in his printshop, and will no doubt produce first-rate work on his press, since he not only has very good taste but is also a most painstaking and conscientious craftsman. His work is always marvelously precise and faithful.

I'm reading the thick volumes of Oswald Spengler's opus—have only acquired a copy now—and am enthralled, even though I rarely agree with his opinions on specific issues. I'm amazed that this clever and occasionally inspired work has been subjected to such vituperative attacks. To some extent, those barbs are probably directed at Spengler himself, who comes across in the introduction and elsewhere as an exceedingly vain person, just like Keyserling. But there is a worthwhile mind behind that vain, self-confident, rather Prussian façade.

Give my greetings to the parrots, crocodiles, and chimpanzees. I would so love to be at your place! And even fonder greetings to your wife and Vrene.

Fondly yours

---

* Hans Mardersteig, co-editor of the review *Genius*, was director of the Officina Bodoni.

TO JOSEF ENGLERT*

Montagnola, July 1, 1923

It's a cloudy and somewhat humid Sunday morning. The birds are chirping away in the trees at Camuzzi,† and besides, it's my birthday tomorrow. I'd like to thank you very much for your kind letter. I have been wanting to write to you for days, if only to apologize for not visiting you in Zug. But, first of all, my personal mail is quite different from yours. There are letters every day, often quite a few, and things have also been quite hectic these past few days: Fräulein Wenger and her mother arrived, and my divorce came through.

I would certainly have liked to visit you on my way back, but I was so exhausted I had to husband my energy. I'm still barely mobile, each step is painful. I did get to the theater in Zurich one evening to hear Handel's *Rodelinda*, which is exceptionally beautiful and fine. It brought Spengler to mind. Whenever I hear that kind of music, or see Gothic or Baroque architecture, I sense clearly that those aesthetic creations belong to a formal universe that has disappeared completely. I have thought like that for a long time, and now Spengler is saying the same thing systematically. I'm still reading the second volume. It contains many mistakes and distortions, but is nonetheless the most significant book to have come out of Germany in the past twenty years.

My dear friend Englert, you foresee a wonderful future for me.‡ Let us hope your predictions come true, before I dry up altogether. I appreciate your friendship and am grateful for it.

I'm sure your inner compass will guide you to a place where your life can take root, and I hope you end up close to me!

The Dr. Lang who dabbles in astrology has just written saying that the signs favoring marriage are so strong this year that I shall hardly escape that fate. I agree with his assessment, but cannot banish my fear of getting married again and the feeling that I should avoid it. But we all have areas in our lives where we behave passively and just follow our stars.

Fond greetings from a grateful friend, who sends best wishes to you both!

---

* Engineer and architect; Hesse's friend since 1919.

† Casa Camuzzi, in which Hesse rented a small apartment from 1919 to 1931.

‡ Englert had composed a horoscope for Hesse.

TO THE SWISS DEPARTMENT OF POLITICAL AFFAIRS

Montagnola near Lugano, July 26, 1923

The undersigned writer, Hermann Hesse, hereby presents a petition to the Swiss Department of Political Affairs requesting reinstatement as a Swiss citizen.

I am Swiss by origin, since my father had been living in Basel for a number of years before I was born, and he acquired citizenship for the entire family. He remained a citizen of Basel for the rest of his life, and my only other brother is still a citizen.

But in my case, in accordance with my parents' wishes, I became a naturalized German citizen in Württemberg at the age of fourteen. They had strong reasons for this step, since I was suited only for an intellectual profession by talent and nature, and I would need to get state foundation scholarships (a free place in the theological academy and in boarding school in Tübingen) if I were to continue my studies in Württemberg, to which my parents had moved. So, in 1891 or 1890, my parents decided that the best way to safeguard my prospects for the future was for me to apply for naturalization as a Württemberger. I was naturalized, and have been a Württemberger ever since. When I came of age, I had to reaffirm in writing that I had renounced my Basel citizenship.

In actual fact, I have been a continuous resident of Switzerland since 1912, living in Bern from 1912 until 1919, and in Montagnola up to now. Prompted by a variety of considerations and feelings, I would very much like to become a citizen of Switzerland and Basel again, and hope your esteemed department will accede to my request, if this is feasible.

I have just discovered that this petition requesting reinstatement of my citizenship should have been submitted within ten years of my return to Switzerland. I was not aware of that regulation, and so in that regard my petition is not altogether immaculate. There are two reasons why it has taken me so long to petition for reinstatement of my citizenship. First of all, I see more clearly than heretofore that my sons, who have grown up in Switzerland, have put down roots here and have no desire to keep in contact with Germany. Second, even though I was more or less compelled to become a German, I couldn't quite manage to desert my adoptive fatherland during the first years of the war. But as far as I'm concerned, those considerations no longer apply.

TO GEORG REINHART

Montagnola, October 29, 1923

I just wrote something today about the Officina Bodoni, which I revisited recently, and I have sent it off to Hans Trog at the *Neue Zürcher Zeitung.** I'm enclosing the carbon copy, which I don't need back.

After spending nine days hunched over the typewriter, with rain pouring down outside, I have finally completed my Baden manuscript. It's entitled *Psychologia Balnearia: Notes from a Baden Spa*, and I think it represents something new and different. The manuscript is very intimate, some parts are purely confessional, and at this point I definitely don't intend it for public consumption. However, I would very much like to have about two hundred copies printed for friends and a small number of devoted readers; I would have to sell enough of them to cover my costs. The pamphlet would not be available in bookstores; people would have to purchase it through me. I have already contacted my Berlin publisher about the project, but don't know yet whether the whole thing is financially feasible or not. If I'm unable to fulfill my wish, I shall at some point read you the *Psychologia Balnearia* (about 100 pages long, the size of this sheet) or see to it that you eventually receive a copy.

I haven't written in such a frenzy since *Klingsor*, a nice experience, but so feverish that I'm now totally exhausted. I'm thinking of going to Basel within the next couple of days, and shall be staying at the Hotel Krafft. Some obstacles to my marriage plans have surfaced, and there has been no progress, even though I have been trying for weeks to make the necessary arrangements. The German authorities are being very bureaucratic. They insist on petty details and keep demanding additional documents and formalities, so much so that I shall probably have to withdraw my application for a marriage certificate. I shall try to become a naturalized Swiss citizen as quickly as possible, and then get married. That is quite disappointing, and it is a real blow to my plans that the German authorities, who have kept me waiting for many weeks, are bringing up new difficulties and complications.

I hope you're in good health and things are going tolerably well for your daughter. With many fond greetings

---

* " 'The Officina Bodoni' in Montagnola," *Neue Zürcher Zeitung*, April 11, 1923.

TO CARL SEELIG

Basel, Hotel Krafft, December 28, 1923

Thanks for your kind letter. I had wanted to wait until my marriage had actually taken place, before notifying you about it. So you found out in advance. I have to pass through a few more bureaucratic hoops before I can get married, but it should take place within the next fourteen days.

There is no contradiction between my remarrying and what I have said in my letters. I have naturally entertained thoughts along such lines—e.g., people like us shouldn't marry—and, in theory, I think that is all very fine and absolutely true. But if you have ever read a book of mine, *Siddhartha* say, you must realize that I regard clever ideas like that as a game, nothing more, since I feel one has to endure whatever happens in life and just submit oneself to one's fate. So I'm getting married because that's how things have turned out. I am as little concerned with free choice or hopes for my future happiness as I was last year when my divorce came through. I'm getting married quite reluctantly, with a lot of reservations, even though I love my bride very much. I haven't taken this decision actively, for compelling inner reasons, but rather as a means of fulfilling my fate.

I would like to thank you for your love, and kind gifts, and encouragement. I wish you all the best for the New Year. Fondly

Basel, Hotel Krafft, February 17, 1924

Your kind letter arrived yesterday and also your present of the beautiful paper. Many thanks.

I have been married now for several weeks, have spent virtually the entire winter in the city, and my life has actually hardly changed at all. I didn't attract any attention walking about in the streets; as usual, I kept to myself more or less. My wife is a singer, still a student, but quite advanced; she has a beautiful high soprano voice, with a special aptitude for Mozart. The problem is that I'm an aging man with a wife who is still very young, and this has led to all sorts of new experiences, both pleasant and difficult, which have required some adaptation and change on my part. We don't always have the same roof over our heads; I shall go to Montagnola again in the spring, and stay there alone, apart from a few brief visits. We hope to discover bit by bit a suitable style and modus operandi for our marriage. [. . .]

My Berlin publisher, Fischer, has been here for the past two days. We haven't met in person for ten years; the last time we were together was on Lake Garda in the spring of 1914 during those balmy prewar days. That period is, I believe, not so much a lost paradise as a form of childhood, which, of course, is irretrievably lost. I wouldn't dream of asking to relive those years, even though my life back then was a lot more agreeable and brighter than it is now.

TO HIS SON HEINER

Montagnola, May 5, 1924

Your letter arrived early yesterday; thank you for writing so quickly.

My last lines were rather moody and cantankerous. I wouldn't have expressed my feelings in that manner if I could have chosen when to write the letter, but I couldn't keep you waiting, because of the permission slip.* I was angry because I had been expecting to see you here during your vacation. I canceled a trip, put off several visits, and even gave up a full day's painting excursion so as not to miss you. But all to no avail. It wasn't my fault that I suddenly had to leave on an important trip.† If, instead of just dropping by at the last minute, you had had the courtesy to let me know of your visit a few days in advance, you would have spared us both a considerable amount of aggravation.

Moreover, I had attempted to make your Confirmation—it was you, after all, who had wanted it—as pleasant an experience as possible, for your sake. Having guessed from a hint in one of your letters that you would like Mama to attend your Confirmation, I scraped money together so she could travel,‡ and sent it to her in time. Yet I only discovered indirectly, through Mama, that you had suddenly decided you didn't want to be confirmed; I didn't hear a word about it from you.

And then there is the small present of money that I sent you recently. It was somewhat discouraging not to get even a word of thanks.

As a father, I not only have a right, but also a duty, to tell you that your inconsiderate behavior has offended me and that you should be a little more civil toward me. If you want to get through life, you will have to learn better manners and show others a bit more consideration. That's all I have ever asked for, and you're not being serious when you imply ill-humoredly that I'm forcing you to undergo religious instruction,

* Permission to refuse Confirmation.
† Hesse traveled to Bern to sign his naturalization papers.
‡ Maria Hesse had been living in Ascona since August; Heiner was attending the Kefikon State Boarding School near Frauenfeld.

attend church, etc., or wish to castigate you for being a freethinker.

Thank you for your letter, which I liked despite those intemperate passages. But look, everything turns out better, especially when people don't get along all that easily, if one tries to be polite and considerate! That's why I'm asking you once again to have the decency to let me know about your various trips and vacations, and visits here, so that I can plan things accordingly, and at least tell me you have received any presents I send. Those are little conventions in life that one has to learn, just like reading and writing. It would be boring if the only thing I did as a father was pay the bills.

Enough said about that. The only other thing I wanted to say is that I certainly don't expect you to mount a hypocritical display of emotions you don't really feel. I would prefer to get an honest letter, even if it is a bit crude, than none at all, or one that says nothing.

I also wish to tell you that I'm fond of you and am interested in everything you do. I'm certain this will mean more and more to you as the years go by. A lot of things came between us, such as the problems with the marriage and separation, and Mama's long and frequent bouts of illness, but you're still my son and, if I were to die tomorrow, you would always remain my son and carry within you a portion of my being and my intellect. I sincerely hope that in the years to come we can develop a better and mutually satisfying relationship.

My dear son, I'm sending you a fond kiss, and shake your hand in the conviction that we shall never lose touch with each other.

With good wishes. Your father

TO GEORG ALTER

Montagnola, July 5, 1924

Thanks for your fine letter. It was nice of you to think of my birthday. It was not my fiftieth yet; I still have quite a few years to go, and hope that by that point I shall have acquired enough wisdom to make the celebration tolerable for me and those around me. My young wife, who lives most of the time in Basel, arrived for my birthday along with her mother, and we bought flowers and a cake; it was nice. Two sons from my first marriage had just visited me. The eldest is already over eighteen; he hasn't a clue about the so-called problems and ailments of our age, wants to become a painter, and was outdoors with me every day, working assiduously on his watercolors.

I'm pleased to hear that you are rereading my fairy tales,* but I don't understand why that requires a background in anthroposophy! I managed to write them without anything of the kind.

I was most pleased to hear you will soon be leaving Berlin and heading for the more tranquil south. That will surely do you some good! I can fully understand why you feel disgusted with the situation in Germany and the current mentality among German youth. But there is a magical solution: we can always shake off our dependence on the external world and nourish the soul with whatever we consider beautiful, alive, and sacred, whether that happens to be Buddha, Jesus, Socrates, Goethe, music, or nature. I admire the fidelity and quiet devotion with which you pursue those ideals, and believe you will find out how to prevent the external world from becoming a serious source of torment.

It's hot; the big, white blossoms of a big, dark magnolia are peeking into my room. There is a vase full of wildflowers beside me. But even though all of this is very beautiful, there are certain things about my external condition that I would wish differently, especially in regard to my health. But, even the way things are, the life here is good and beautiful.

I think about you from time to time, and always wish you well.

TO ALICE LEUTHOLD†

[*December 1924*]

Me oh my, what has come over me! So I forgot to send you my current winter address? Hesse, who is usually so organized and punctual? It's yet another sign of rapid aging. What is coming up in January, my golden or silver anniversary? I feel, in any case, that something like twenty-five years must have passed since we had that festive meal in Basel.‡

On orders from my dear spouse, I'm spending the winter in Basel and have a nice, quiet attic room in the city, near St. Johann's Gate. I am living in my cell, Ruth in hers—i.e., in the Hotel Krafft—and in the daytime we go about our serious activities. I sit at work in the university library all day long, even though the pain in my eyes is quite atrocious. And in the evening I turn up in Frau Hesse's apartment, where I find some dinner ready, and we spend the evening together, along with

---

* *Märchen* (Berlin: S. Fischer, 1919).

† Wife of businessman Fritz Leuthold, who met Hesse on his trip to Southeast Asia in 1911.

‡ On the occasion of the marriage on January 15, 1924.

the cat, dog, and parrot. The latter, Koko, is an especially good friend of mine, and makes me feel very attached to the house. Then in the nighttime fog I head off along the Rhine toward my part of town. Schoeck was telling quite a yarn if he really said I had been to Munich. It's true I visited Stuttgart with Ruth, and performed my party piece there. I always have a nice time in Stuttgart, the only city where I enjoy reading in public, where I can stand in front of an overcrowded room and feel that people understand me, that I am talking to friends. The most important part of the trip occurred after I had acquitted myself of that duty. We went to Ludwigsburg, where I have a brother;* Ruth and I stayed in the royal castle, in gigantic chambers with twenty-foot ceilings, and for two evenings Ruth, along with my brother and his son, sang the entire *Magic Flute*. She has made great strides forward, and I find her singing increasingly impressive.

She also sends greetings, and often dreams of seeing the Leutholds again and even of eating rice with you again.

Should a box of those pleasant cigars, called Ehrenpreis or something like that, fall into the hands of Master Leuthold, the great Tuan,† perhaps he would be so kind as to think of me. And we shall have to see one another again.

TO CARLO ISENBERG‡

Montagnola, May 28, 1925

I'm not having any luck at the moment, and feel I ought to let you know about a part of it that also concerns you. Yesterday I got a rejection slip from the Stuttgart publishing house. In other words, the entire series of books I had planned has been scrapped; so I have to start again from scratch. The publisher pulled out because of an advertisement by the Fischer Verlag for the *Merkwürdige Geschichten* which they had spotted. Stuttgart stupidly insisted that the Fischer books would compete with our projected series for them. Well, more about that when we meet, if we're still interested in the matter by then. Although the Stuttgart publisher had signed a contract agreeing to publish our series, I offered to take back all the unpaid work I had done over the past seven months, and have done so. I shall keep you posted about further developments. The only consequence for you is that I shall have to ask you not to

* His half brother, Karl Isenberg.
† Malaysian, "Mr."
‡ Hesse's nephew; a musician and music historian.

proceed with the other volumes in our series after you have completed *Romanticism* (which I shall certainly get another publisher to do*), but to work first on the Schubert for Fischer, which is absolutely certain. You can imagine how thrilled I feel. However, I shall try to find another publisher and save at least part of the series.

One other piece of news: My wife, Ruth, who had been ill for months, has just had a checkup. She has TB in the lungs, and has been sentenced to a year of complete rest, which means not singing a note or taking a single step. Many of my plans will just have to fall by the wayside, the whole thing is quite crippling.

Addio, and don't let this publisher business get you down! If I cannot salvage the planned series, then *The Romantic Mind* will have to appear on its own; in any case, Fischer has already accepted it. I hope to find a home for some of the volumes at least. But now I have to look forward to the awful bother of negotiating, and finding a publisher. Best regards to you all

TO HIS WIFE, RUTH

[*June 4, 1925*]
Beside a wood above Locarno, Thursday morning
It's hot, and I'm sitting here early in the morning, trying to find a moment of inner peace. I just said goodbye to little Martin† an hour ago at the station. He went off with his little rucksack to friends in Bern; once again he no longer has a home to call his own, since his mother has become mentally ill again and her condition is worse than last time. She has even had awful attacks of epilepsy. I'm witnessing a most terrible tragedy and occasionally feel I'm being dragged into it. Her elder brother took his own life; the other brother went mad as a result, and is now an inmate in Friedmatt;‡ and Mia has driven every one around her half crazy with her condition—her nurse, the boy, the lodgers, etc. Her spirits seemed to improve after I arrived yesterday, and I managed to have a proper talk with her, but then she got frightfully excited again, especially after saying goodbye to the boy, and the nurse is afraid she won't be able to cope with her. I have had to assume total responsibility

---

* Like the other titles in the series, *The Romantic Mind* did not appear during Hesse's lifetime.
† Hesse's youngest son, then fourteen years old.
‡ A mental institution in Basel.

for her and the boy, since her brother is himself ill. If Mia has to be put in an institution, there will be nobody here to look after her house, which is full of lodgers, etc. Even if I had no other worries and were in good health, I would still be consumed by all of this. For the past three weeks, I have been subconsciously exacerbating this whole business, and now I'm in it up to my neck. I'm astonished at the impact conditions like this can have on everybody in the vicinity, and am quite amazed I survived the awful period around 1918–19, and the ensuing dependence on her state of mind, without losing my own sanity. I see that the mere proximity to the situation is infecting some nice, stable people, who aren't directly involved, so much so that they're losing their composure. I shall certainly not lose my sanity this time either, another fate awaits me, but my nerves are quivering.

I shall go home again as soon as possible, maybe even tomorrow. My most important goal was to rescue the boy. Let us hope he has not yet come to any great harm.

Dear Ruth, amid all these worries, I am constantly thinking of you. Your illness has dragged you another hundred miles away from me. I don't see any way around that; we shall have to grin and bear it. I hope I can take a bath today or tomorrow at Dr. Bodmer's* (I haven't had one in two months), and then go back home, where a big void awaits me, along with mail from publishers, etc.

Addio, just lie there quietly in your garden, pluck a little flower, and sniff its fragrance. As you lie there in your convalescent's garden, I walk past on the other side of the wall in the sultry dust, laden with the baggage of life, and we shall both have to accept these burdens. [. . .]

Goodbye. I'm thinking of you as I stand here amid the hot dust from the roadway.

TO ROMAIN ROLLAND

Zurich [January 30, 1926]

Dear Romain Rolland, my dear friend and colleague,

It was very kind of you to send that printed material to Nagi† and to drop me a line as well.

---

* Dr. Hermann Bodmer ran the Kurhaus Victoria in Locarno.
† Indian historian, a friend of Hesse's since 1922.

I didn't know that *Siddhartha* had appeared in French;* I have just found it in a bookstore here and purchased a copy. You're quite right: the dedication has been omitted!† I feel really sorry about this. Fortunately, the translator does at least mention in the introduction that I dedicated the book to you.

I can certainly understand your attitude toward the great majority of Frenchmen; during the war I had a very similar relationship to official Germany. But I was fortunate enough in the sense that my fatherland lost the war. As a result, I'm being read by the very people who would have put me up against the wall and shot me if the outcome had been the other way around.

It's very sad that this is so. But those conditions don't deserve to be taken all that seriously. It isn't characteristic of France, or indeed of our era, it's an age-old phenomenon, and characteristic only in the sense that it is a human trait.

I'm also enclosing a short essay,‡ which will allow you to get acquainted with my present life. I'm going through a rough period and begin the day only with considerable reluctance. But there are times when I can also laugh, moments when I possess some wisdom and humor.

The translator's foreword in *Siddhartha* is well meant, but the data and facts aren't particularly reliable, and much of it was just dreamed up—I wanted to tell you about this anyhow.

TO ANNY BODMER§

[*Zurich, postmarked February 10, 1926*]

I was really delighted to get your kind letter—I mean the bit about me, the rest is quite sad. But I was glad to see the extent of your understanding, empathy, and friendship.

I don't often get to write letters here, am actually seldom at home, spend a lot of time with Lang, also see Tscharner,‖ Schoeck, Hubacher, etc. I usually spend the evening with Lang; we eat in a pub in Niederdorf, then go to his place or mine, talk a lot, and drink cognac, which he downs like a virtuoso. But he has taught me a thing or two—e.g., about

---

* *Siddhartha*, trans. Joseph Delage (Paris: Grasset, 1925).

† "Dedicated to my dear Romain Rolland."

‡ "Ausflug in die Stadt," in *Frankfurter Zeitung*, January 17, 1926, rept. in Hesse, *Die Kunst des Müssiggangs* (Frankfurt, 1973), p. 222.

§ Painter, and wife of Dr. Hermann Bodmer.

‖ Johann von Tscharner, a painter born in Poland, who had lived in Zurich since 1916.

the fox-trot, which I tried out recently at a masked ball, my first ever, until half past seven the next morning. It wasn't exactly my style, but I want to go back again on Saturday anyway. I like observing myself in action, the wise author of *Siddhartha* dancing the fox-trot and pressing his women against him. Progress always comes about in an irrational, dumb, crazy, or childish way, I certainly agree, but the drinking and lack of sleep have made me awfully irritable.

I'm enclosing a few lines I wrote recently for a newspaper. It should interest you, since you know Oppenheimer.*

I shan't go into your problems, except to say that my thoughts are with you and that I can sense your dilemma. If only you could borrow some of Milly's vitality and her frivolity in amorous matters—but then you wouldn't be my dear, sensitive Anny, and that would be a great pity.

TO HIS SISTER ADELE

[*Spring 1926*]

Thanks for your letter and also for the card, which arrived this morning. Yes, it's now already ten years since Father's death—and it will soon be ten years since *our* death—I'm amazed at everything we have to undergo before then. At present I'm in Zurich, and don't feel like returning to Montagnola, have even thought of living in Paris, on a trial basis at least.

In your letter you write the following about the time around Papa's funeral: "There was not just a wonderful atmosphere, but a real force." Now, listen, dear Adisle, I cannot go along with you there, with all those subtle distinctions that remind me a little of our parents. Papa or Mama often spoke very appreciatively about a poem or piece of music, with a rather revealing smile, only to add that all of this was, of course, "only" atmosphere, "only" beauty, "only" art, and, fundamentally, wasn't anywhere near as valuable as morality, character, will, ethics, etc. This doctrine has ruined my life, and I shall not return to it, not even in the kind, gentle form manifested in your letter. No, if there was a wonderful "atmosphere" at the time of Papa's death, I have no wish to add "only" to that description, but want to accept that atmosphere with gratitude. [. . .]

---

* "Gedanken über Lektüre," in the *Berliner Tageblatt* of February 6, 1926. The article recommends an essay by Franz Oppenheimer, "Der Staat und die Sünde."

TO RICHARD WILHELM*

Zurich, June 4, 1926

I received a visit yesterday from the writer Oskar Schmitz,† a versatile and resolute gentleman, who mentioned, among other things, that he was going to spend a few days with you in Zurich. And your card with Goethe, the well-groomed Privy Counselor, arrived this morning. This is the second time you have sent me greetings, and even though I'm not a great correspondent, I would at least like to reciprocate with my best wishes.

You and your work have been dear to me for a long time.‡ Whatever relationship I have to Chinese culture I more or less owe to you. My interest in China increased markedly, whereas I had been more oriented toward India for years.

I have been meaning for a long time to thank you for several of your essays, especially those on Lao-tse, Chuang-tze, etc., etc., and I wish to express my gratitude now. I have often felt glad that my cousin Gundert in Mito is a mutual friend of ours.

I don't know very much about your current work, my life is that of an outsider§ who has turned his back on the contemporary intellectual world (as represented by the likes of Keyserling, etc.). However, I am discovering that China devotees such as Reinhart also have ties to you. I'm not that close to the Zurich psychoanalysts; Jung is an exception, I find all the others likable, but narrow and success-oriented. They're convinced their duty is to affirm life in a bourgeois sense, so they avoid its tragic implications. I have not kept up contact with them either.

I'm attracted by the magical side of your Chinese world, but, being an antisocial creature, I'm inevitably alienated by its splendid system of morality. Unfortunately, the *I Ching* is only partly accessible to me as a result. I occasionally gaze at the deep, luxurious world full of color contained therein, but cannot really relate to the ethics in the commentaries. Unfortunately, I'm sitting on a barren branch, which cannot sustain those flowering political, familial, and social interrelationships.

So I'm all the more grateful for the calm, intellectual love affairs that I have experienced in my life, one of them being China, which I

---

* Pioneer in German sinology and author of authoritative German translations of the works of Confucius, Lao-tse, and Chuang-tze, among others.

† Hesse reviewed Schmitz's *Das dionysische Geheimnis: Erlebnisse und Erkenntnisse eines Fahnenflüchtigen* (1921).

‡ Wilhelm's translation of the *Tao Te Ching* (1921), his study *Lao Tse und der Taoismus* (1925), and also the translation *Dschuang Dsi: Das wahre Buch vom südlichen Blütenland* (1912).

§ Hesse uses the English word "outsider."

got to know through you. Hence my grateful feelings toward you and your work. I'm glad to have this opportunity to convey my thanks.

I shall soon be off again to Montagnola, but shall probably be back in Zurich in late fall and winter, at which point we may run into each other.

TO HUGO BALL*

Baden, October 13, 1926

Thanks for your greetings. I think you will reach an agreement with Fischer quite easily. In any case, you can always count on me as an intermediary. †

My sister's address‡ is Frau Pfarrer Gundert, Höfen an der Enz (Württemberg).

Then we can talk about the illustrations. I don't have any good recent photographs of myself, but shall have one taken in Zurich, if necessary. There is quite a good picture of me as a child; my sister has it.

When we get to see each other, I should like to show you two or three letters from readers whom I have never met, so you can get an idea of the way strangers react to my writings.

If a biography of me makes any sense, it is probably because the private, incurable, but necessarily controlled neurosis of an intellectual person is also a symptom of the soul of the age.

Then, in addition to the questions you want to raise, we shall have to discuss all kinds of biographical issues, also my long-standing ties to India and Asia, and my wartime job. My first marriage has receded far enough so that it can be discussed briefly, if necessary. There should be no discussion yet about my second marriage.

You will probably be disappointed with the chapter on my work as a critic. Does that really deserve an entire chapter? I have always mistrusted the self-confident posture of critics who engage in sweeping critiques of the age and its culture, and so I have never managed to write any genuine criticism. Perhaps an instinct of psychic economy warned me not to express myself intellectually, so as not to dry up the source from which literature springs. You may also include my last

---

* Writer, co-founder of Dadaism, pacifist; Hesse's close friend since 1919.

† Ball was commissioned by S. Fischer to write a biography on the occasion of Hesse's fiftieth birthday.

‡ Adele, who provided Ball with information about the family.

incarnation as Steppenwolf, which is as yet only half realized, since the poems entitled *Steppenwolf** that I wrote last winter will come out before your book. Fond greetings to you and Emmy

TO LISA WENGER

Zurich, December 22, 1926

Dear Mama Wenger,

Yesterday I received my first Christmas greetings of the year—your kind package. And although I am generally quite hostile to Christmas and its trappings, which only makes sense for people with families, I was very pleased indeed to receive your package, especially the letter. [. . .]

You end your note by asking me to stay on friendly terms with you. I was really pleased by that. It's true that I put our friendship in jeopardy and made a big mistake by transforming the friendship into a family relationship. I don't believe the marriage will last forever; Ruth has left me entirely to my own devices for the past year and a half. And my thought, and even hope, is that Ruth is sufficiently young and in good enough health to fall in love with a person whom she would like to live with and devote herself to. I shall certainly not stand in the way of her freedom.

Dear Mama Wenger, we should obviously keep these things to ourselves. I had no wish to pull the wool over your eyes. And I believe seriously that our friendship will prove happier and more enduring than our family ties.

Because of my nature and the sort of life I lead, I don't have much to recommend me as a relative, but I can be a decent and loyal friend. For me, the family has never been a source of happiness or joy, whereas I have gained a lot from my friendships. I have had many good friends over the past few decades, and have not lost any through any fault of my own. I noticed this again during my travels.

And, dear Hüsi, I have always considered you a friend. The shift from a friendship to family ties has also been painful for me, and I'm grateful for those words of yours, since I want to remain friends with you, and also with Ruth, insofar as that is possible.

---

* *Der Steppenwolf: Ein Stück Tagebuch in Versen.* The series of poems appeared in *Die Neue Rundschau* in November 1926, subsequently published under the title *Krisis.* (Berlin: S. Fischer, 1928; *Gedichte.*)

I was already acquainted with portions of your book.* I like it and am looking forward to reading the whole thing.

At present, I am trying to finish my new book;† the first draft is almost ready. I started work on it over two years ago in Basel. It's very daring, full of fantasy, an attempt at something quite new. I have now reached a stage where the book is largely done and could, if necessary, be published in its present form, but I want to revise and rewrite it, which will probably take the rest of the winter.

This book deals with the same problem as my new poems, but creates a much wider circle around those issues. [. . .] I hope that you will accept my thanks, greetings, and friendship.

TO HIS SISTER ADELE

Zurich, January 21, 1927

I have been thinking fondly about you a lot recently—especially while Hugo Ball was here for some discussions. [. . .] But I never told you about that. And yet you went to such trouble digging up all that old stuff for Ball. Dear Adis, I would like to thank you heartfeltly for your help. And don't get angry at me for enclosing whatever German currency I have lying around. You have incurred quite a few expenses.

Unfortunately, Ball didn't bring my boyhood poems with him; they would have interested me. But he did bring the pictures, and I particularly enjoyed the bright, clear portrait of Father with curly hair, which I had forgotten completely. Thank you for your labor of love.

For the past few weeks, I have been working like mad, day in and day out, finishing the prose version of *Steppenwolf*, and now I have just about collapsed, and suddenly noticed the effect of the overexertion, sleeplessness, etc. I'm also sad, since I shall have to forgo the pleasure of creation, which has infused my life with meaning and pleasure, and there is going to be a void. I shall have to wait years before encountering that experience again, if it ever comes my way.

My wife, Ruth, gave me a surprise for New Year's: she suddenly informed me that she wanted a divorce. I told her I can understand her decision very well, and shan't put any obstacles in her path.

So that is how my family will be celebrating my 100th birthday. Ruth's letter arrived at an awfully difficult time, while Heiner was here

* Possibly her memoirs, *Im Spiegel des Alters* (1926).
† *Der Steppenwolf.*

(which she knew), and he is so difficult to talk to and get along with. Having no idea about Ruth's intentions, I mentioned to her that Heiner was coming for a visit, that I was expecting lots of arguments,* and was apprehensive about our few days together. Yet that is precisely when she chose to let me know about her decision. She has already handed over the whole affair to a lawyer. But don't tell anybody about this. If I say anything unflattering about Ruth, it is for your ears only.

If I had had an inkling of what this fiftieth birthday would entail, I would have canceled everything right away, Ball's book too. Something new crops up every couple of days: ten publishers want to exploit the occasion for commercial reasons, composers wish to publish songs of mine, painters want to paint me or do etchings of me, editors want to know the important dates in my life, the mayor of Constance asks for permission to hold a Hesse festival on July 2 and requests my presence, and so on. It's enough to make one throw up. And now I have to spend my time hunched over the typewriter trying to answer all the letters somehow and also take care of the correspondence with Ruth's lawyer.

You must be bored after hearing such a litany. Well, don't take any of it too seriously; I myself only take it seriously when I'm feeling particularly bad. You shouldn't spend any time on *Steppenwolf*, either in verse or in prose, because it would only hurt you. *Addio*, Adis.

TO HUGO BALL

[June 1927]

Hugo, dear friend,

I really owe you an answer today. This morning feels strange after so many rainy days (I cannot wait to start painting, the weather has given me hideous pains all over). Yesterday there was a note on my front door for you, since I was away in Lugano for a few hours, and thought it very likely that you might come by my place, O prophet to the mountain. Well, here I am, bearing a small bouquet of paper flowers† with which to congratulate you on the appearance of your book‡—first of all, because it has arrived; second, because it looks very fine; third, because I have just finished reading it again. Now I can finally say something about it after rereading it without any interruptions.

I have to congratulate you for the book, and myself as well, even

* Concerning Heiner's choice of a profession.
† A bouquet of flowers painted on the letterhead.
‡ Ball's biography of Hesse, published by the S. Fischer Verlag (1927).

though I don't, of course, always agree with you, and even though I'm generally rather bashful, and actually don't like being the focus of attention. Last night, I dreamed about something in connection with your book: I could see myself sitting there, not in a mirror, but as a second living figure, who was more alive than I. I was unable to scrutinize myself, because that would have violated an inner taboo, would have meant a fall from grace, but I was able to squint through the chink for a second, and I saw the living Hesse.

Well, I don't intend this as a quibble, but it has just occurred to me that this is your second-best book (it would be your best if the subject were as dignified as that of the Byzantine volume*). I have also just noticed how well you describe the legend of this life rather than the banal facts; you have discovered the magic formulae. And even when you make a mistake—e.g., incorrect dates—you are nevertheless right and on target. I still have some slight objections to a very few passages, but do not yet have the distance necessary to assess matters of detail correctly. You taught me some new things about myself, not only in the Maulbronn chapter, but especially in the section on the relationship between Lauscher and Camenzind. Maybe I shall eventually get around again to reading *Camenzind*, something I haven't done in at least fifteen years.

Your words occasionally make me feel embarrassed out of modesty. But since you have again shown in this book your mastery of genuine literature, the art of discovering hieroglyphs and ideograms, I can tell you how delighted I am that this essential point has been understood by one of the few people whom I regard as a brother and fellow practitioner.

I hope that you are pleased with the finished book and receive some joy from it.

I bought a few copies and have given one each to my sister, Dr. Lang, Schoeck. I'm telling you this, so you don't send those people another copy.

To celebrate the birthday or launching of your book, I would like to invite you to select a watercolor at my place.

PS: My morning mail has just arrived. A dear friend in Germany† to whom I sent your book writes: *"Librum excellentissimum, quem de Chatti vita, moribus, operibus egregie conscripsit Hugo Ball, hesterno accepi die gratiasque tibi ego vel maximas."‡*

---

* Hugo Ball, *Byzantine Christianity* (1923).

† Franz Schall, a school friend in Göppingen and Maulbronn.

‡ "Yesterday I received the exceptional book in which Hugo Ball provides an excellent account of Hesse's life, being, and work, and thank you very much for it."

TO HERMANN HUBACHER*

Montagnola, June 24, 1927

Caro amico,

You were right to send this pretty girl to live in my house.† Actually, I'm not alone at the moment; Frau Dolbin‡ is here for a while, but I like having beautiful Lilly around.

I understand what you're saying about your piece, which I like a lot. It has a certain lyrical quality, which may have been something of a danger to you in the past. But to this reader the lyrical note sounds wonderfully genuine, melodic, and natural. I'm delighted, and wish to thank you, my dear friend!

I have changed a bit since I vanished. I now have a dark brown tan from sunbathing on my terrace at close to a hundred Celsius, am also thin because of my fasting, and look like a Hindu—which is quite appealing to the ladies, but doesn't impress my wretched gout, which is awfully stubborn. I have also been off cigarettes for the past five weeks.

People are pestering me every day about my birthday, which is eight days away. I'm not going to receive the few things I would really like, whereas I wouldn't mind getting rid of all those birthday wishes. There was a nice one from a Japanese man of letters who said he brought me greetings from my Japanese readers; I am the European writer they know the best, they don't like the others. He is going to send me some Hiroshige reproductions.

I'm almost a hundred years old, have written all my books, and have even had a biography written about me, so it's high time for me to enter the Academy of the Immortals and be buried. You will be notified in due course.

Addio, greetings to Anny and the boys, and let's remain good friends.

---

* Sculptor and graphic artist.
† A small bust of "beautiful Lilly," which Hesse had admired in Hubacher's studio.
‡ Ninon Dolbin, née Ausländer, art historian; Hesse's wife from 1931 to his death.

TO HELENE WELTI

Montagnola, July 25, 1927

Thanks for your kind letter. I'm glad to hear that you're thinking of coming to Ticino and may visit me at some point. Please do!

You would like to hear more about my birthday? Well, my report will have to be rather brief. My girlfriend from Vienna has been here with me all summer, but there hasn't been a complete symbiosis. She lives in the house next door, and eats in the restaurant, but she is around, and I'm no longer leading the life of a hermit. I wanted to celebrate my birthday with her and also Hugo Ball and his family, but that was impossible, because three days beforehand Ball had to be rushed to Zurich for an operation,* which actually took place on my birthday. However, we went ahead with the party. The Wassmers† came by car from Bremgarten. They brought along some wine, and had already reserved lunch in a nearby country inn. Those present apart from me were my friend Ninon, the Wassmers, Hans Moser‡ (who came with the Wassmers), a brother of Louis Moilliet with his beautiful wife, a sister of the painter Cardinaux, a daughter of Frau Ball from her first marriage, and my friend Dr. Lang with his daughter. We ate a chicken, a good vegetable soup, and cake, drank Fendant and Chianti, and eventually repaired to my apartment, where there were dozens of telegrams and batches of letters, which kept piling up for days afterward. It took me three weeks to read them all. We drank tea at my place, sat on the terrace, which has new garden furniture, danced the fox-trot; then the girls had to kiss me, which affected my girlfriend's mood. In the evening we went to a grotto in the wood, where we had some bread, cheese, and local wine. That was the end of the party, and everybody left by car at around ten in the evening.

By the way, not a single official body, university, or institute in Switzerland or Germany has pestered me.

The press, on the other hand, has been yapping away. If quantity were decisive, I would certainly qualify as a great man. I was sent more than eighty newspapers, but the majority of the articles contained silly fabrications. Most of them had only heard of *Camenzind* or, at most, of it and *Rosshalde*. The nationalist papers ignored the entire affair, the

---

* For stomach cancer.

† Max Wassmer and his wife, Mathilde. He was proprietor of Bremgarten Castle near Bern and a patron of Hesse's.

‡ Author of novels and short stories, also a music teacher, whom Hesse visited in 1919. Appears as Hans Resom in Hesse's *The Journey to the East*.

bourgeois publications were polite but superficial, and the socialist press asserts virtually unanimously that I'm a bourgeois author who cannot be taken seriously. [. . .]

They only brought Hugo Ball back yesterday from Zurich, where half his stomach was removed. He is lying in bed, wants to get well, and doesn't yet realize the hopelessness of his condition. I was with him yesterday and today, and shall be very concerned about him in the immediate future. He is happy about the reactions to his book, which have been almost entirely favorable. My elder sister was here for a week since then, and my son Heiner also spent a few days here after walking across the Engadine. [. . .]

TO NINON DOLBIN

Stuttgart, Tuesday evening, April 10 [*1928*]

My dear, clever woman,

My head is still rumbling terribly from the noise of the propellers. I flew in a very large, uncomfortable airplane halfway across Germany, from Berlin to Stuttgart, in just five hours. I wanted to tell you that I saw a lot and really enjoyed myself. The world generally looks wonderful from a height of 600 to 1,200 meters—e.g., the sand-dune colors of the naked earth, empty fields, etc. And we had a delightful flight over the forests and mountains of Thuringia; in some ravines, I could spot the last traces of the snow that we ran into two weeks ago. The nice thing about flying, as opposed to traveling by train, is that you get to see so much forest, sand, fields, and moors, whereas the cities and factories look like relatively insignificant pockmarks.

And now to the most remarkable part: I flew over Würzburg about two or three in the afternoon, in bright sunshine, at about 900 meters, right above the Residenz and the Hofgarten, and within a few minutes I had seen every bridge, street, church again: the chapel, river, St. Burkard, everything! That was the most beautiful experience of all.*
[. . .]

I saw a big Berlin horse race in Karlshorst on Easter Monday, yesterday in other words, but that seems like months ago, and I have forgotten everything.

* Three weeks previously, Hesse had visited Würzburg with Ninon.

TO THEODOR SCHNITTKIN

Montagnola, June 3, 1928

Thanks for your letter. I'm finally at home again after an absence of seven months.

Psychoanalysis is quite problematic. In theory, the method—that is, the simplified categories which Freud uses to depict psychic mechanisms and also the Jungian mythology and typological classifications—ought to help identify psychic phenomena. But in practice the situation is very different. Of the half dozen psychoanalysts I have known, not one would, for example, be capable of noticing any positive or worthwhile qualities in a person such as myself or, let's say, a poet like Rilke, if we hadn't received any public recognition! Suppose a good contemporary psychoanalyst had to evaluate me. He would get to know all the material about my life, and also read my works. But if he didn't know that those works are widely read, and have brought me money and fame, he would no doubt classify me as a gifted, but hopeless neurotic. After all, nowadays the average person (i.e., the standard by which a physician determines normality) has no appreciation for the inherent value of productive work and creativity. To them, figures such as Novalis, Hölderlin, Lenau, Beethoven, Nietzsche would just seem like severely pathological types, since the shallow and absolutely bourgeois-modern attitude of psychoanalysis (including Freud's) precludes any understanding or assessment of creativity. That is why the voluminous psychoanalytic literature about artists hasn't yielded anything worthwhile. They discovered Schiller suffered from repressed patricidal longings, and Goethe had some complexes. If the analyst reading the works of these writers were not aware of their identity and reputation, he might even fail to notice that these men have constructed a world of their own by drawing on their complexes. Analysis, and modern science in general, has no conception of the following: Every cultural achievement is a product of complexes; culture itself arises out of the resistance and tension between instincts and intellect. Achievements do not occur when complexes are "healed," but when extreme tensions can be creatively satisfied. How could it? Medicine, including analysis, doesn't set out to understand genius and the tragic nature of the intellect; it tries to ensure that patient Meyer gets rid of her asthma or psychosomatic stomach problems. The mind has other paths to follow, certainly not those.

Enough, I can rarely afford to write such chatty letters.

TO ANNY BODMER

[End of September 1928]

Thanks a lot! No, I have no use for visitors, and keep my front door tightly bolted. Why should I stand around chatting with people who feel so comfortable in their thick skins? No, let's proceed to Aquarius and Pisces. [. . .]

Ah, a hellish winter is upon us again.* I have to get the big suitcase from the attic and spend the next few days packing. The old rigmarole is starting again next week: Baden, Zurich, the same pointless old cycle. How tired I am of this ritual!

There is a new book about me by a certain Herr Schmid,† who wrote it for his doctorate. I have never seen a person's life and work being plucked to bits in this manner. The world has given me nothing in return for my thirty years of ascetic labor, whereas Schmid is awarded a doctorate for pilfering a book full of quotations from me and then poking fun at my decadence. The world is absolutely delightful. So I'm off soon to Baden, and then on to Zurich. Ninon is going to Vienna; I'm happy about that, since she has been quite moody and depressed of late. Goldmund will keep me company.

Anny, let's keep in touch. One really feels grateful to one's few friends. Fond and heartfelt greetings

TO ERHARD BRUDER

[October 1928]

I received your greetings while traveling, and read your essay about *Krisis* early this morning.‡ Thank you very much for it.

I realize that you needed to distance yourself from the problem by writing this piece and that you just cannot afford to keep mulling over these issues, which are similar to your own problems. By the way, I also have three sons, but am unfortunately only on good terms with one of them. I know all about what it means to support three growing sons financially (the youngest is seventeen already) and also about the moral responsibility one feels for their lives.

I very much liked your essay, which is unusually dense and well

---

* Since there was no heating in Hesse's rented apartment in the Casa Camuzzi in Montagnola, he usually spent the winter months in apartments in the city (Basel, Zurich).

† Hans Rudolf Schmid, *Hermann Hesse* (1928).

‡ The essay was never published.

articulated. You have come up with a wonderful description of the difference between being alone and being lonely in relation to the "crisis," and I now see some things more clearly than heretofore.

Since you have understood so much, I should tell you where I feel you didn't fully understand me. In the first place, everything in my being and thought has its origin in religion, and this is something none of my critics, with the exception of Ball, has ever understood. Regardless of whether we consider this a plus or a minus, my upbringing was intensely and even passionately religious, and this has affected me strongly, even though its religious character has been modified and in my case somewhat perverted. So Harry's* despair is not just about himself, but about the entire age. Nothing could be more symptomatic of the era than people's indifference to their wartime experiences, which they soon forgot entirely. Between 1914 and 1919, there was no way a religious German who had any feeling of personal responsibility for the well-being of humanity and of his own people could avoid experiencing that kind of despair.

Which brings us to the second point. Like all the other critics, you think that Harry keeps mulling over the "old war stories" just because he has some bee in his bonnet. Well, I certainly don't consider those four years of war, all that murder and injustice, the millions of corpses and the splendid cities lying in ruins, an "old story" which thanks be to God every rational person should have long since forgotten. I'm absolutely convinced that the issue is serious, since I can see, feel, and even smell many, many signs all over the place suggesting a certain readiness to repeat that experience.

So those are the things that come to mind after reading your essay. I find it so valuable that I was wondering whether you would like to publish it somewhere. Maybe I could get *Die Neue Rundschau* to run it. But that isn't at all certain. Although they treat me and my "crisis" politely, they haven't a clue what it's all about. But I would try nevertheless.

TO HELENE WELTI

Baden, Verenahof, October 23, 1928

Thanks for your kind letter, which I found very moving. That remarkable funeral journey to Milan reminded me of the funeral of my dear friend Hugo Ball. A tiny and odd group of mourners assembled

---

* Harry Haller, the main protagonist in *Steppenwolf.*

during a downpour; six of us carried long wax candles behind the coffin during the solemnly Catholic funeral rites. One of the candle bearers was a Catholic who had been excommunicated, and three of the others were fanatical freethinkers. The priest, who wore his most ornate vestments and sang the liturgy in a sweet melting voice, had shot down a songbird right beside Ball's balcony, while he was still alive, just three feet away from his deathbed, so close in fact that the dying man was greatly startled by the clattering windowpanes. And that's more or less how the whole thing went. We just stood about, freezing, feeling embarrassed and rather dumb in our grief, and the only person at all superior to the situation was the occupant of the coffin.

I'm glad to hear that you are taken with the *Meditations.** As far as I'm concerned, the only worthwhile thing about it and the *Picture Book†* is that they assemble pieces written over a twenty-five-year period and show that, even though I have weathered a number of crises, my thinking has never undergone any serious rupture. The wartime upheavals, which destroyed my marriage and private life, have certainly left a deep mark on me, but they haven't altered my thinking, my fundamental philosophy of life. However, the experience made me realize the utter isolation and defenselessness of man's noblest aspirations, his humanism and idealism. I saw that I would have to express my convictions more consciously and with greater passion than heretofore.

I'm sitting bolt upright at my typewriter, like an Egyptian god made of basalt, because of a stiffness in my back and neck; they are going to get diathermy and some massage a half hour from now. Frau Ninon is currently in Vienna, and from there she will travel to Cracow to visit relatives; she dropped me off here before she left. She will be back in Zurich sometime in December. It's slow going, but I am getting some work done and am reasonably pleased. The situation is different when I cannot work at all, either because my eyes are strained and filled with tears or because I'm feeling otherwise indisposed. I'm thinking of you and greet you fondly

---

* *Betrachtungen* (Berlin: S. Fischer, 1928).
† *Bilderbuch* (Berlin: S. Fischer, 1926).

TO MARIE-LOUISE DUMONT

[*Arosa, February 1929*]

Your letter reached me in Arosa, where I have come for a short rest. I can only answer briefly; I get several batches of letters a day, and find it hard to get to my own work.

The people in *Demian* are not any more "real" or any less so than the characters in my other books. I have never used real people as characters. A writer can, of course, do just that, and the results can be very beautiful. But, generally, literature doesn't copy life; it condenses it by reducing incidental occurrences to representative types. *Demian* is about a very specific task or crisis in one's youth, which continues beyond that stage, but mostly affects young people: the struggle to forge an identity and develop a personality of one's own.

Not everyone is allotted the chance to become a personality; most remain types, and never experience the rigor of becoming an individual. But those who do so inevitably discover that these struggles bring them into conflict with the normal life of average people and the traditional values and bourgeois conventions that they uphold. A personality is the product of a clash between two opposing forces: the urge to create a life of one's own and the insistence by the world around us that we conform. Nobody can develop a personality unless he undergoes revolutionary experiences. The extent of those experiences differs, of course, from person to person, as does the capacity to lead a life that is truly personal and unique.

Demian portrays an aspect of the struggle to develop a personality that educators find deeply disturbing. The young person who feels called upon to become a strong individual and deviates significantly from the average, ordinary type will get involved in incidents that seem crazy.

So I think you are on the right path, because you are aware of these difficulties. But the issue is not how to force the world to confront one's "craziness" and thus bring about revolutionary change, but how to protect the ideals and dreams one has in one's soul from the world and thereby ensure that they never dry up. The dark inner world nurturing those dreams is always at risk: friends make fun of it, teachers avoid it; as a condition, it's unstable, constantly in flux.

The present age seems to make life especially difficult for the most sensitive young people. There are attempts afoot everywhere to homogenize people and deprive them of their most individual traits. Our souls rightly resist this tendency, hence the experiences of Demian. The form those experiences take is different for each person, but the ultimate meaning is always the same. Anybody who is truly serious will prevail, and if he is strong, he will change from a Sinclair into a Demian.

TO NINON DOLBIN

Stuttgart, early Friday [November 8, 1929]

I'm through with the second reading, which took place yesterday in your favorite hall. Then we went to the restaurant you also know so well. On the face of it, nothing much has changed in the intervening year and a half, but to me everything felt different. Although I had put a lot of work into it, I was disappointed by the outcome. I had great difficulty performing and was trembling from sheer exertion. I didn't enjoy the reading, and began to think it had all been a waste of time. Which it was.

Afterward the "circle of friends" (i.e., the sisters, the Ludwigs-burgers,* Molt, and several classmates, also Hartmann and Hammelehle) went to the inn. I hadn't eaten anything all evening and was also dead tired. They all ordered themselves wine, beer, schnitzel, salad, ham; I just sat there quietly for a half an hour between ravenous eaters (Rosenfeld† was sitting right next to me with an enormous omelette). Nobody even offered me a glass of wine, and since I wasn't very pushy, I never managed to catch hold of the busy waitress. So I just sat there for a half an hour watching them, then slipped out, put on my coat, and went home; nobody even looked up.

It wasn't as bad as Tübingen, if only because I was hardly in any pain. My kidney has been pretty much settled ever since I took the opium. But, come to think of it, Stuttgart was even worse, very disappointing. After you have read your poems with great concentration, somebody claps you on the back, then you sit there like an unwelcome guest and watch everybody else eating schnitzel and sausages; it's a chilling feeling. [. . .]

All the best wishes for your work, for Vienna, and the other matters.

---

* His half brother, Karl Isenberg, and his family.
† Otto Rosenfeld, a friend of Hesse's in Stuttgart.

TO FRITZ MARTI*

Zurich, December 12, 1929

Thanks for the greetings and also for the well-meant verses of that dilettante. Of course, you couldn't publish them.

I'm enclosing a short piece of prose, which you may wish to publish at some point.† I very much missed not seeing you in Bern. There aren't many colleagues in Switzerland worth taking seriously.

I was afraid you wouldn't be able to come, and even though I knew you were ill, I thought I would drop by in any case.

That didn't work out; I was simply too tired and dejected after the reading (that always happens when I have any direct contact with readers and the outside world). It's true that the audience usually responds very warmly, that the halls are full, and that some people are extremely friendly. But no matter how well disposed the public, this kind of encounter can never satisfy intense obsessive types such as ourselves. The response to lectures about taxation or how to bring up children may be positive or negative, but it is always direct and lively. Pianists and singers can reasonably expect audiences to appreciate their abilities, technique, etc., and even offer an informed critique. A poet is convinced that his calling is supremely important, but the world he evokes is strange, and the world to which he speaks is no less so. All he will ever get in return is a number of well-meant pats on the back; he won't find three readers, not even among his best, prepared to allow the impulses they receive from him to affect their lives. Well, this you already know. I just wanted to say I was sorry I couldn't show up, and also explain why.

TO HIS SON HEINER

Chantarella, January 31, 1930

[. . .] I'm sorry that you had a conflict with your employers and feel disappointed by the outcome. But you aren't a socialist; they're a different breed altogether.

I would like to explain what I mean, since this is a matter of principle and since you bring my friend into it.

I have good reasons for being neither "bourgeois" nor socialist,

* Editor of *Der Bund*, Bern.
† From *Geschichten aus dem Mittelalter*, published in *Der Bund* on January 26, 1930.

even though I believe that, politically speaking, socialism is the only decent attitude. Yet I haven't become a socialist, since the intellectual foundations of socialism (i.e., the teachings of Karl Marx) aren't altogether unimpeachable, and besides, the social democrats everywhere rejected their most worthwhile principles long ago. I was particularly disappointed with the German socialists, who joined the chorus of warmongers in 1914 and went on to betray the revolution in 1918.

But it is not the quality of a person's convictions that determines his worth as an individual. I myself judge people by their character rather than their convictions. In any case, most people espouse the beliefs of their caste. Ninety-nine percent of capitalists and socialists would be incapable of justifying their beliefs in intellectual terms.

My friend [. . .] is certainly a capitalist, a businessman; his utterly bourgeois ideals focus on outward success and the accumulation of wealth. His attitude is typical of the majority of businessmen and industrialists in his country, and most lawyers, doctors, etc., also subscribe to these shabby convictions. I couldn't care a dime about the political and commercial credo of Herr [. . .], and I feel the same way about the so-called convictions of the sort of socialist who behaves just like the bourgeoisie and is only looking for better food and greater political clout.

Herr [. . .] is always finding fresh evidence in the newspapers for his "convictions," which have been drummed into him since early childhood, but those ideas have absolutely no bearing on his *personality* and *character*. Although he is a tough-minded businessman, he is as hard on himself as on others and demands an awful lot of himself. I got to know him first in India in 1911, and even though I often felt that his commercial projects and goals were rather ridiculous—and frequently told him so—I always had a lot of respect for his character. He was one of the very few people who came to my aid during the period from 1919 to 1925, when I was virtually starving and crippled by worries about your mother and you children. For my sake, he pretended not to notice some of the things you were up to. He also talked about you in glowing terms, even though he disapproved strongly of your attitude toward work.

I have often learned to respect and admire people who subscribed to convictions that I found strange, repulsive, or silly. Some of the people I got to know during the war who held views similar to mine—i.e., opposition to the war—were extremely untrustworthy, whereas some of my virulent opponents seemed like decent, worthwhile people.

Of course, the issue goes far beyond Herr [. . .]; it's quite fundamental. Moreover, there is one thing I'm quite convinced about: Let's suppose that Herr [. . .] had been born just yesterday rather than fifty years ago. Assuming that his personality remains identical and that he is born into the same, rather impoverished rural milieu in Toggenburg, I'm confident he would adopt socialist ideas before long, and perhaps even join the party eventually. But that wouldn't by any means affect his personality. He would remain as strong, loyal, stubborn, and industrious as ever, with all the same virtues and flaws.

You have never said very much about your own convictions: I would have liked to discuss such matters with you. In any case, I was somewhat astonished to hear what you said about an acquaintance of yours with a keen interest in politics, since his convictions seemed so utterly bourgeois, indeed almost fascist. I had imagined that you might wholeheartedly embrace the socialist ideology, and I certainly wouldn't be upset if, for example, you ended up as a single-minded revolutionary, not just in your words but also in your deeds. However, being a revolutionary requires not only conviction and enthusiasm but also a willingness to make the greatest self-sacrifice imaginable. I would be extremely delighted if each of my sons embraced some "conviction" or ideal and were willing to give up his material comforts and, if necessary, lay down his life for that cause. While the nature of the conviction or party he selected wouldn't be altogether indifferent to me, I wouldn't attach all that much importance to that. I consider a person who is willing to sacrifice himself for the most naïve ideals in the world to be far preferable to somebody who can speak articulately about all kinds of ideals yet isn't prepared to make any sacrifices on their behalf.

You will have to fight your own battles on the job at [. . .], and I understand fully why you don't get on at all with my friend Herr [. . .]. All I can do for you is show my love by following the matter very closely. However, I should like to correct a mistaken assumption in your letter.

You think it's only a question of sticking it out as an apprentice; then the whole situation will change, and you will be your own man. That will never happen. Even as an employee—or perhaps a boss—as opposed to an apprentice, you will still be serving the interests of a class that you basically cannot abide. It would be far better if you tried to get to know the enemy—i.e., capitalist society—by embarking on a serious study of socialism. That should get you out of this rut. I'm not a socialist, and believe that socialism is as open to refutation as any other ideology. But nowadays it's the only creed that openly criticizes the kind of lives we are leading in this inauthentic society. My current studies have rekindled my interest in such questions. I'm reading the memoirs of Trotsky.

Addio, dear Heiner, I wish you all the very best. As regards your job, etc., we were not any better off in the old days. As an apprentice, I had to live for years on a hundred francs a month, and had to work very hard for that. Some of the things you can do weren't possible back then; there was, for instance, no question of moving in with a girlfriend. In some respects life is tougher for you young people, but some things are easier and a lot nicer.

Addio, my dear, we shall be seeing each other again, and there will be time to talk things over; I'm looking forward to that. Fond greetings from your father

TO GEORG REINHART

June/July 1930

Thanks for your letter. I was delighted to hear from the horse's mouth. So somebody has told you about our plans to build a house? Hubacher, I suppose; I mentioned it to him and some others. We haven't started construction yet; indeed the builder-owner and I haven't drawn up the contract, which will give me a legal right to live there. But we have discussed everything and finished the plans. My patron Herr H. C. Bodmer-Stünzi* had originally wanted to give me the house as a gift, but that would have put me in an awkward position in many respects, and so I asked him to let me build the house and live in it, on the understanding that it will remain his property and merely be on loan to me. In the case of my death or if I ever give up the house, it will revert to him. Please don't tell anybody about this. I think I should let you know about it, but there is no reason why other people have to find out about it.

I had a wonderful time talking about Asia while my Japanese cousin (the person to whom I dedicated the second part of *Siddhartha*) was here. He has been living in the Orient for over twenty-five years and was spending a brief vacation in Europe. He has much of the wisdom that I admired in Richard Wilhelm, and their careers were also quite similar. He went there first as a Christian missionary, and is now trying to foster intellectual dialogue and exchange between the two cultures.

Prinzhorn† has written once again after a longish silence; he recently translated some André Gide, has become friends with him, thinks I should get to know him and start a correspondence, which is all right by me, but I'll have to put that on hold for now.

---

* Physician, musician, and collector of Beethoven; Hesse's patron.
† Hans Prinzhorn, author and essayist.

TO HIS SISTER MARULLA

[*ca. mid-November 1930*]

So this is what it means to grow old: a touch of rheumatism in the legs, a stiff back, graying hair. Yet, deep down, I feel I'm not all that old: it doesn't seem so long ago that I was a schoolboy going to Dölker's school and buying fruit, etc., from Frau Haas at the market. That sort of thing would be going through my head, and there was another crazy notion that helped me delude myself about my age: "Even if I'm no longer a spring chicken, my little sister must still be a youngster, since she has only just sat for her teacher's certificate." Then, all of a sudden, I discovered that this little sister of mine has become old on the sly, and is about to celebrate her fiftieth birthday. It's hard to believe. I just shook my head, and sat down to write my little sister a birthday letter.

I only found the short piece entitled "Johannes" by Monika Hunnius* recently, even though the almanac put out by Salzer, the publisher, has been lying around here for over a year. I dislike Salzer† and his devoutly Christian business acumen, and am not particularly fond of Monika as a writer. She believes that having a temperament suffices, and rides roughshod over every nuance. She also seems to believe that the Baltic region is some sort of paradise on earth. But I did read her essay, since I felt that I might find something. I was delighted to discover the nice sketch of Father and the reminiscences about you.

Whenever I think about Father, a funny experience comes to mind. It has to do with certain theories of heredity. I never doubted that I had inherited my artistic talent and temperament more from Mother than from Father. Yet I have always seen myself more as Father's son than as Mother's, and I also feel that my various psychic oddities and assorted nervous complaints stem more from Father than from Mother: sleeplessness, headaches, eye problems, etc.

But on several occasions recently some relatives on the Gundert side have said that we Gunderts have a hard time because we inherited a temperament that makes life difficult for us and predisposes us to conditions such as melancholia, etc., which are difficult to cope with. To put it briefly, those people (not related in any way to Father, of course) attributed all their nervous complaints and psychological problems to the Gundert legacy, whereas I had always felt I had inherited those very problems from my father's side! I learned something from this, and also found it amusing.

---

* Baltic writer, cousin of Hesse's father.
† Eugen Salzer, a publisher in Heilbronn.

And in the course of time my attitude has changed in other respects as well. I can no longer distinguish some traits of Father from those of Grandpa Gundert: a very gentle intellect, a refined diffidence in the making of judgments, a genuine fondness for the customs and intellectual traditions of India, which is quite apparent underneath all his Christian scruples. At times, the two figures almost merge in my mind. Anyhow, I'm discovering that some of my intellectual qualities, the ones I consider anachronistic, non-German or non-European (in other words, the best), were also attributes of our father, or of Grandfather Gundert. [. . .]

I don't yet know what to make of my new house, even though we often have sessions with the architect, which are mostly handled by Ninon. The house already has four walls and a roof, but won't be ready for us to move into until July. At the moment, I can only see the drawbacks: the difficulty getting servants, the big increase in our cost of living. I'm very reluctant to leave the old apartment, which was so beautiful (even if only in the summer), and also my pied-à-terre in Zurich, which I have to give up in the spring. But everything will eventually sort itself out. [. . .]

Farewell, Marulla. I have to say goodbye to my little sister; you were a schoolgirl at old Ansel's not so long ago. I find it difficult to accept that my sister is now an older lady, and that, between the two of us, we have racked up over a hundred years. With fondest wishes

TO WILHELM KUNZE

[*November 1930*]

I haven't been able to work for the past few weeks due to constant pain, but I have read your book with interest.*

I don't really have a newspaper I could review it for. I just wrote a few lines about it, and shall send them off today to the *National-Zeitung* in Basel, which may publish the piece. I'm enclosing a carbon copy.

You won't be very pleased with the piece. But reading your book has reminded me once again of a postwar phenomenon, which I have often noticed before: the indifference of young people to moral issues. I felt that I needed to criticize this attitude, which your book conveys all too clearly, because you yourself have not done so. One feels pity

---

* *Die Angstmühle* (1930). Hesse's review appeared in the *National-Zeitung*, Basel, on November 30, 1930.

for these young people, who are often very likable but have a basic flaw. They have no sense of responsibility, fail to uphold any values of their own, and go around accusing other people of guilt and baseness, which they detect in everybody but themselves. Seducing girls or boys is the only contribution they have to offer. They're annoyed at the mess their fathers, government ministers, etc., have made, but they themselves just sit around twiddling their thumbs. They don't feel any responsibility toward a world they did not create. Yet they're surprised by the lack of change. They're now getting older and are beginning to burden themselves with an ever-increasing sense of guilt, the guilt they used to reserve exclusively for the older generation.

Dear Herr Kunze, please share the following ancient wisdom with your generation: Acting morally is only justified and worthwhile if one is prepared to accept one's own responsibility, not just for the wretched state we call life but also for death and all one's sins, original sin in other words, and this means one can no longer attempt to pin all of the guilt on others. In refusing to admit any guilt and blaming everything on your fathers, you young people are actually imitating their wartime behavior, since they blamed everything on the Russians, the Italians, the Kaiser, or the Jews. You haven't learned anything at all and don't intend to either—Latin, geography, or math would be such a chore.

I had to say this to somebody of your generation. It was in 1914— i.e., the time of my awakening—that I first realized how abominable a state the world was in and how virtually universal the tendency was to pin all responsibility for this state of affairs on other nations, classes, or political parties. I have been preaching the following message ever since: "Before any progress can take place, a person, class, or people must first try to discover its own guilt and put its own house in order." This applies just as much to the youth of the postwar era as it did to previous generations. If young people aren't willing to chip in, if they insist on adopting a superior attitude from the outset and expect others to take care of everything, they are thereby crossing out their own names in the Book of Life. I can no longer blame the decent, if rather stupid soldiers of 1914, or their fathers, for all the problems of our age, and to me the mental and physical lethargy of the younger generation represents a greater evil.

But I have also tried to suggest the beauty of your book.

Please use the piece any way you wish, either the whole thing or just excerpts. You have my permission. As I said, I hope it appears in Basel, but I cannot be sure, and if not, your publisher can quote those lines, if he finds them useful. It would be a pleasure to be of some use to you and your book.

TO WILHELM SCHÄFER*

Zurich, November 1930

Your kind letter arrived too late, since I asked O. Loerke the day before yesterday to go ahead and announce my resignation.†

I have something to add: More than two years ago, I asked the selfsame Loerke (whom I really like, by the way) to suggest a way out of the Academy for me, since I never felt I belonged there. Loerke didn't bother answering. But now that your words have given me sufficient cause to repeat my request,‡ he has replied, although his answer is not yet to my satisfaction. But I hope this entire affair will soon be over. My dear friend, could you bear with me for another two minutes? I have no wish to elaborate on the reasons why I cannot remain in the Academy. What are "reasons" anyhow? Bad air could be enough to drive a person away. For years now, I have been listening in on the chatter of this debating club through the reports. I disliked the majority of the motions, and the few I liked were immediately defeated. I was amused to see Molo§ presiding over this assembly of German writers—i.e., a man who cannot write a decent German sentence. And there were other irritations as well. My life is not easy, and can no longer carry a useless burden, which has begun to torment me. I really have to get out.

After being elected to the Section, I declined the offer of membership on the grounds that I was Swiss. But they refused to accept my reasoning, and since there was a scandalous fight going on in the Academy at that time over Arno Holz, I wanted to be nice and collegial, and tacitly accepted membership. As I mentioned before, about a year later I asked Loerke to help me leave. He never answered. Since then, I haven't been on good terms with the society, and then you, my dear friend, gave me a welcome opportunity to resign.

One more minute, please. I would ask you to reread first the lines you wrote about purely "passive" members and then rethink your most recent argument. You said earlier that those who never speak up and aren't willing to lift a finger don't deserve to be members, and you claim in your letter today that my resignation (i.e., that of a silent and indif-

---

* Nationalistic writer, who became one of fourteen founding members of the new National Socialist Academy of Arts in 1933, when the Prussian Academy of Arts was dissolved.

† From the Prussian Academy of Arts, to which he had been elected four years previously.

‡ In a circular letter of November 4, 1930, Wilhelm Schäfer, who at that point was convenor of the Academy's meetings, had tried to persuade the less active members of the Section for Literature to resign.

§ Walter von Molo, writer, was president of the Prussian Academy of Arts from 1928 to 1930.

ferent member) would "destroy" the organization. I have little faith in
your letter, but have no trouble believing what you said to those of us
who are "passive" members. If the Academy, or Section for Literature,
wants to justify its existence, it will first have to weed out all the lukewarm
members, then focus on the goals it is genuinely committed to, rather
than on the usual blather. Those who question the raison d'être of the
institution and merely consider themselves reluctant appendages will
have to leave. So I'm actually doing the Section a favor, and am glad I
shall soon have severed my first affiliation ever with an "official"
organization.

I wish the Section all the very best, and I cannot claim my reasons
for resigning are particularly rational. I think the atmosphere is bad,
that's all. But I also have some hunches. In the next war, the members
of this Academy will constitute a sizable proportion of the ninety or a
hundred prominent figures who, as in 1914, consent to spread state-
sponsored lies among the people about the critical issues they have to
confront. I'm not laying claim to any particular authority in political and
moral matters, except insofar as I go my own way and obey my own
laws. That is why I'm withdrawing from the Section, as I have done in
the past by dropping several pleasant affiliations. You don't really believe
my resignation will burden the Section with anything more than a slight,
temporary inconvenience. People will say: "Oh yes, Hesse, he was
always damn sensitive and terribly unsociable," and then things will
revert to normal. I think that's more or less what will happen.

I'm really in bad shape, have got a terrible pain in my eyes and
awful headaches, which will scarcely enhance this letter. But I'm sure
you will be able to figure out my position. I preferred your demand that
the Section rid itself of lukewarm members to your subsequent request,
which rescinds the former. Schäfer, let's remain on good terms; this
Academy affair isn't of any great moment. Now that the election has
made the members feel more responsible, I hope they do half as much
for their colleagues and the books they write, especially the younger
ones, as I have been doing for the past twenty-five years.*

---

* In the course of his life, Hesse published over 3,000 reviews drawing attention to new
books and reprints of noteworthy older titles.

TO WILHELM KUNZE

December 17, 1930

Today I received your essay from the *Würzburger General-Anzeiger*. I am glad to have it, and regret that it has arrived at a time when I shall have to disappoint you.

I should like to say a few words about the essay, which I really like. I do not consider "idyllic" a valid term. I feel that the religious impulse has had the most decisive impact on my life and work. To my mind, the individual—regardless of whether he is faced with a world war or a flower garden—should view the outer world as a place where the One or the Divine manifests itself and should try to fit into that framework. Of course, in my case this primary religious experience doesn't assume any of the forms commonly found in the traditional church; I consider it irrelevant whether the circumstances triggering this experience are "idyllic" or not. To my mind the "idyllic" label is an attempt by urban dwellers to reject certain aspects of life that are as strange and unfamiliar to them as they are paramount in the minds of rural folk.

I intend to take another look at your book at some point in the future. It just so happens that it has helped me to crystallize and articulate my fundamental objection against some of the positions that your generation espouses. I have always taken a dim view of all attempts to emphasize or organize youth. The distinction between young and old only holds true for people who are run-of-the-mill; individuals who are truly differentiated and gifted are sometimes old and sometimes young, just as they are sometimes happy and sometimes sad. Enough. Your book just happens to have aroused in me certain feelings and considerations of a more general nature.

But I feel that this lack of balance will eventually redress itself. I realize that these excessively general observations have not done justice to you—but what are words anyhow? And doesn't my generation have as much right as yours to express its views?

I found regrettable one of your phrases: "They can try pulling that off." Had I been able to respond to that orally, I would have left you in little doubt as to where I stand.

TO A YOUNG MAN IN SEARCH OF
SOME KIND OF "LEADER"

Chantarella, Winter 1930

Your letter has reached me in the mountains. I have been overworked and really need to rest. I can only answer briefly.

There is no call for despair. If you are a person born to lead your own individual life rather than an ordinary everyday one, then you will eventually discover that difficult route toward your own personality and a life of your own. If you are not called upon to do so, or if you cannot muster sufficient energy, you will have to give up sooner or later and reconcile yourself to the morality, taste, and customs of the majority.

It's a question of how much energy one has. Or, as I prefer to see things, it's a question of faith. For one often finds very strong people who soon fail and very delicate and weak people who, in spite of their weakness and illness, make their way splendidly through life and impress their stamp upon it, even though they may be merely enduring their lot. Whenever Sinclair has sufficient energy (or faith), Demian is enticed by that energy and approaches him.

It isn't easy to put into words the faith I have in mind. One might describe it as follows: I believe that, regardless of its seemingly nonsensical qualities, life does have meaning. I accept the fact that this ultimate meaning transcends my rational faculties. I am, however, prepared to be at its service, even if this means having to sacrifice myself. Whenever I am truly and fully alive and awake, I hear an inner voice proclaiming that meaning.

I want to try to fulfill the things that life demands of me at such moments, even if that runs counter to conventional fashions or laws.

It's not possible to impose this belief and compel oneself to accept it. One has to experience it, just as a Christian cannot acquire grace through mere effort, force, or wiles, but has to experience it through faith. Those who are unable to do so seek their faith in the church, or science, or patriotism or socialism, or anyplace that furnishes readymade moral codes, programs, and solutions.

It's impossible for me to ascertain whether people are cut out for this rather difficult but beautiful path that leads to a life and a meaning of one's own—even if I were to see them in person. Thousands are called, many go a bit of the way, but few continue beyond the frontiers of youth, and perhaps nobody stays the course until the very end.

TO THOMAS MANN*

Chantarella in the Engadine, February 20, 1931

Many thanks for your greetings and the essay by your brother. Ninon was delighted to hear from your wife. We have often talked fondly about the three of you. † [. . .]

I'm increasingly perturbed by the Academy question, because I'm being lumped in with the others who resigned. Your brother's essay just refers to the "gentlemen" who resigned. ‡

That will be quickly forgotten, and those ultranationalists invoking my name nowadays will soon get another chance to view me as an enemy and treat me as such.

My position on the issue, just between you and me, is more or less as follows:

I'm suspicious of the present state, not because it is new and republican, but because it isn't adequately so. I'm very much aware of the fact that the Prussian state and its Ministry of Culture, which serves as the patron of the Academy, are also responsible for the universities and the terrible anti-intellectualism prevalent there, and I regard any attempt to unite "free" minds in an Academy as an attempt to keep tabs on these often inconvenient critics of the regime.

Moreover, as a Swiss citizen, I cannot play an active role. If I am a member of the Academy, I thereby recognize the Prussian state and its control over cultural life, even though I myself am not a subject of the Reich or Prussia. That was the incongruity I found most disturbing, and the need to remove it was the most important reason for my resignation.

Well, we shall get to see each other again, and with the passage of time, all these things may seem very different.

---

* Nobel Prize-winning German novelist. Hesse's correspondence with Mann, extending from 1910 to 1955, has been published in English under the title *The Hesse/Mann Letters*, trans. Ralph Manheim (New York: Harper & Row, 1975).

† Mann had left Chantarella with his wife and daughter Elisabeth a week earlier.

‡ Heinrich Mann writes in his essay: "The Section fully understands the reasons for the resignation of those gentlemen. . . . Henceforward, it will have to defend intellectual freedom, regardless of the nature of the intellectual position being suppressed."

With Thomas Mann in Chantarella, February 1932

Hesse, 1927

TO R.B.

May 4, 1931

. . . I could not let your letter go unanswered.

This is more or less how I see the matter: It's wrong to say that people couldn't possibly base their lives on the principles I have advocated. I do not advocate a complete, well-articulated doctrine; I am a person who grows and undergoes transformations. So my books also stand for something other than the pronouncement that "each person is alone." All of *Siddhartha*, for instance, is a declaration of love, and one can also find a similar declaration in some of my other books.

You can hardly expect me to show more faith in life than I actually possess. I have often said quite passionately that the mentality prevalent in our era precludes the possibility of our leading a genuine, truly worthwhile life. I'm utterly convinced of that. Of course, I'm still alive, and haven't been crushed by this atmosphere of lies, rapaciousness, fanaticism, and coarseness. I owe this good fortune to two auspicious circumstances: I have inherited a goodly portion of natural vitality, and I am able to be productive as a critic and opponent of this age. Otherwise, I wouldn't be able to survive. But even so, life often seems like hell.

My attitude toward the present is hardly likely to change all that much. I don't believe in our science or politics, thought, faith, or amusements; I don't accept a single ideal of this era. But this does not mean that I don't believe in anything at all. I believe that there are laws binding humanity which have existed for thousands of years, and am convinced that they will outlast the hubbub of our era.

I cannot possibly show anybody a way to abide by those human ideals that I consider eternal while retaining faith in the ideals, goals, and comforts of our age. Besides, I'm not in the least interested in doing so. Throughout my life I have experimented with many ways of transcending time and living in a timeless world (and have frequently portrayed these attempts, both playfully and seriously).

I often encounter young readers who, in the case of *Steppenwolf* let's say, take everything it says about the craziness of our age very seriously, but fail to notice, and don't in any case believe in, those issues that I consider to be of immensely greater significance. It's simply not enough to dismiss out of hand phenomena such as war, technology, rapaciousness, nationalism, etc. One has to replace the false gods of the age with some other faith. I have always done so: Mozart, the Immortals, and the Magic Theater in *Steppenwolf*, the same values appear under other names in *Demian* and *Siddhartha*.

I am sure it's possible to base one's life on the force that Siddhartha calls love and the belief in the Immortals to which Harry subscribes. That faith can make life seem bearable and can also help overcome time.

I know I'm not really conveying what I want to say. I'm always rather discouraged to discover that readers haven't noticed certain things that I consider clearly evident in my books.

Read my letter, and then pick up one of my books again to see whether you cannot discover some articles of faith there that would make life truly possible. If you fail to find anything of that nature, you should discard my books. But if you come up with anything, you might use that as your point of departure.

Recently, a young woman asked me to explain what was meant by the Magic Theater in *Steppenwolf*. She had felt very disappointed to see me poking fun both at myself and at everything else, as if I were in some sort of opium-induced daze. I told her she should reread those pages, bearing in mind that the significance and sacred quality of the Magic Theater outstrips that of everything else I have ever formulated, and that it also serves as an image and mask for issues to which I attach the utmost value and importance. She wrote a little later to say she now understood.

I understand why you ask, Herr B., and it may indeed be true that my books aren't right for you at the moment. You may have to lay them aside and attempt to overcome the things that attracted you to them. Obviously, I cannot advise you on that. I can only reaffirm what I have experienced and written, including all the contradictions, zigzags, and disorder. I don't agree that my task is to produce work that could, in some objective sense, be considered the best. I have to create work of my own in the purest, most honest manner possible, even if the result should merely sound like an expression of suffering, a lamentation.

TO JOSEF ENGLERT

[*ca. May 14, 1931*]

My dear friend Englert,

It's Ascension Thursday today, and we're still in Zurich, where your kind letter reached me. It's definitely our last day here; Ninon has finally got all the curtains, lamps, carpets, and cooking equipment together, and we're leaving tomorrow at noon for Ticino. Things will be hectic for a while. We cannot move in before July, and Ninon has to vacate her present apartment beforehand, then comes the move itself, etc. I hope I shall be doing better by then. My eyes have been giving me a terrible time for weeks, and I also have to contend with a painful sinus condition.

The person who owns the house and had it built has signed a contract giving me the right of occupancy for the duration of my life.

I'm almost envious of your wonderful journey through Italy by car, even though I'm no longer all that curious and haven't traveled "for fun" since the war. Just imagine: I haven't been in Italy since 1914, except for the few occasions when I stepped a few feet across the border near the Ponte Tresa. Up to 1914, I used to visit Italy nearly every year; the last time was in the spring of 1914, at Lake Garda, in Brescia, Bergamo, etc., etc. Then the war broke out, and when it ended, I found out that I not only couldn't afford to travel but had lost much of my previous curiosity about countries and people, along with my belief in a better future. So I'm not very surprised when you say that a new world war is in the offing. I have thought so since 1919, and have seen many signs confirming this. I have confronted the issue frequently, warning about that very prospect not just in *Steppenwolf* but also in numerous essays, which the editors often considered ridiculously "pessimistic."

Yes, there shall be more abominations, but I may never live to see them, which would actually suit me fine. I was very glad to get the two photos of the children. Of course, you know I'm very fond of your children, and these pictures are particularly charming. Regardless of whether the world is about to be destroyed or not, we want to go on enjoying those few great indestructible things in life: Mozart, Goethe, Giotto, also the Savior, St. Francis, etc., etc. They will live as long as there is a human heart who comes alive through them and can dance to their rhythm. If I'm still alive and can hum a bar from Bach or Haydn or Mozart, or recall lines from Hölderlin, then neither Mozart nor Hölderlin has perished yet. It's great, too, that there are such things as friendship, loyalty, some sunshine occasionally, the Engadine, and flowers. My dear friend, I greet all of you fondly, and Ninon also wishes you all the best.

TO THOMAS MANN

Baden, early December 1931

Your kind letter has reached me in Baden. I'm fatigued from the cure, have an eye condition as well, and can hardly keep up with my mail. So please excuse the brevity of this reply. The actual answer to your question will certainly not take up much space—it is no. But I should like to explain as fully as possible why I cannot accept the Academy's invitation, even though I'm receiving it from a man whom I love and respect. The more I think about it, the more complicated and metaphysical the matter becomes. Since I nevertheless have to give you some justification for my no, I shall have to resort to the excessively clear-cut and pointed formulations that such complicated matters often assume when it suddenly becomes necessary to articulate them in words.

Well, then: the ultimate reason why I cannot be part of any official German body is that I deeply mistrust the German Republic. This un-principled and mindless state grew out of a vacuum, the general state of exhaustion at the end of the war. The few men who spearheaded the "revolution," which was never anything of the sort, have been murdered with the approval of ninety-nine percent of the population. The courts are unjust, the civil servants indifferent, the people completely infantile. I was enthusiastic about the revolution in 1918, but my hopes for a German Republic that could be taken seriously were dashed long ago. Germany never managed to create a revolution of its own and develop its own political forms. It will be bolshevized, a prospect which isn't repellent to me but will make it lose its unique national potential. And unfortunately, a bloody wave of white terror will doubtlessly precede that event. I have been thinking along these lines for a long time, and even though I feel a lot of sympathy for the small minority of well-intentioned republicans, I believe they are utterly powerless, with no more future than the appealing ideology of Uhland and his friends in the Paulskirche in Frankfurt. Even today, nine hundred and ninety-nine out of a thousand Germans still refuse to acknowledge any guilt. They didn't wage war, never lost it, and didn't sign the Treaty of Versailles, which they consider a treacherous bolt from the blue.

In short, I am as alienated now from the prevalent German mentality as I was in 1914–18. I find the events I'm seeing absurd, and I have been driven miles to the left since 1914–18, whereas the German people have only taken one meager step in that direction. I cannot read a single German newspaper anymore.

Dear Thomas Mann, I do not expect you to share my convictions and opinions, but I hope you will respect them, out of sympathy for me. As for our plans for the winter, my wife is writing to yours. Please give my kind regards to Frau Mann and Mädi; we have grown fond of them both. And don't think ill of me, even if you are disappointed by my answer. I doubt if it will come as a surprise.

With undiminished affection and admiration

TO F. ABEL

Baden, December 1931

Thanks for your letter, which reached me in Baden; I had finished a cure and was just packing my suitcase. I shall be here in Zurich until the middle of January.

Over the years I have adopted the habit of ignoring the visible impact of my books—i.e., the responses and interpretations of readers and critics. I would characterize my attitude toward my readers more or less as follows: Although I realize that certain issues and experiences of mine are somehow related to those of a large segment of contemporary youth, I feel as if they haven't really understood me at all. Most readers want to find a leader, but they are not in the least bit prepared to submit themselves to intellectual principles and then to make some sacrifices on their behalf.

I would like to leave you to your own devices as much as possible, especially since there are other dissertations being written about me. A lady from Münster in Westphalia wrote to me recently saying she was doing a dissertation on "Hermann Hesse and Swabian Pietism." I couldn't get myself to reply to her, such was the extent of my interest in the matter . . .

But you have made it easier for me to respond to your straightforward questions, which I shall try to answer briefly.

You are right to say that *Demian* introduces a new tone in my work. It's already present in some of the fairy tales. There was one turning point that affected me deeply. It had to do with the world war. Up until the war I had been leading a hermitlike existence, hadn't yet been at loggerheads with fatherland, government, public opinion, academic establishment, etc., even though I considered myself a democrat and was glad to participate in the opposition movement against the Kaiser and the Wilhelmian system. (Served as co-founder of *Simplicissimus*, and also co-founder of the democratic, anti-imperial *März*, etc.) I realized in the course of the war not only that the Kaiser, the Reichstag, the Chancellor, and also the newspapers and the parties did not amount to much, but also that the entire population enthusiastically supported the revolting display of coarse behavior, infractions against the law, etc., and that the professors and sundry other official intellectuals were among the most vociferous advocates of those policies. I also noticed that our modest attempts at opposition, criticism, democracy had amounted to nothing more than journalism, so that, even among us, there were very few people prepared to take matters seriously and give up their lives for the cause. The idols of the fatherland had been destroyed, and the idols of one's own imagination suffered a similar fate. I scrutinized our German intellectual life, our present-day use of language, our newspapers, our schools, our literature, and had to conclude that everything was mostly empty and bogus, and I'm including myself and my earlier work, even though it had been written in good faith.

The war opened my eyes, taught me a lot, and caused a radical change in everything that I wrote from 1915 onward. Afterward, I saw things a bit differently again. After a few years of not being able to abide my books, I began to realize that they contained all future developments in nuce* and I occasionally felt fonder of the earlier works than of the later ones, partly because they reminded me of a more benign period, partly because I realized in retrospect that the moderate tone and evasion of the main problems constituted some kind of premonition, as if one had startled right before a rude awakening.

But I certainly stand behind what I said in my early books, and that applies also to the many mistakes and weaknesses in them.

But I wouldn't mind at all if you relegated the early books to a subordinate role and chose instead to rely on those works that seem to you to grapple most forcefully with the issue, especially *Demian*.

Approach the topic as freely and personally as your method permits, trust your instincts, even when you cannot corroborate those instinctive judgments in a methodical manner.

And since you're no longer dependent on Thiess's contrary viewpoint, please treat my books as art rather than merely as a literary vehicle for expressing opinions. Please heed only that which strikes you as being genuinely artistic. The literati themselves aren't an easy target for criticism. They're always coming up with a multitude of ideas and making them sound wonderfully convincing. However, they look at things rationally, and the world always seems two-dimensional when viewed through the lens of reason. Art cannot promote ideas, no matter how hard it may try, since it only comes alive when it is genuine—in other words, when it creates symbols. I think Demian and his mother are actually symbols. Their range of meaning extends beyond that which is rationally comprehensible; they are magical incantations. You may express this differently, but you should let yourself be guided by the power of the symbols rather than by the program and literary attitudes that you derive rationally from my books.

I don't know whether I have made myself clear or not. I could

* Latin, "in a nutshell."

certainly have expressed these matters better orally. Feel free to make use of those observations in my letter that you consider plausible and appealing, and feel free to discard the rest.

TO HEINRICH WIEGAND*

February 29, 1932

Your kind letter arrived yesterday; we're packing today, and traveling to Zurich tomorrow. We had a going-away party two evenings ago at the house of the magician Jup,† a fellow guest here, and yesterday evening we invited Louis Moilliet (Louis the Cruel, the painter) and his wife. There will be no more of this wonderful mountain life this year, with its mixture of natural beauty, childlike sportiveness, plus the atmosphere and ridiculous luxuries of a racketeers' hotel. I only went on one skiing expedition, and that was last Wednesday with Louis. At Corviglia,‡ we were at an altitude of about 3,100 meters, and had a breathtaking view of the Bernina Mountains and beyond; at midday, the sun was warm and everything was completely calm. The journey back was quite adventurous, since there isn't enough snow on the ground as one approaches the valley, so we had to ski over the alpine roses. Everything was very beautiful, but also very strenuous, and I haven't been feeling well since then, couldn't sleep, etc. Ninon's rather frayed nerves were also partly responsible, but on the whole we're grateful to be feeling in such good shape as we leave the mountains.

Your attitude toward the present-day German parties, etc., is quite right, I think. Since I'm not a politician, I naturally don't have to worry about how to adapt to current conditions, but rather about how to remain in touch intellectually with the future. Unlike the autarkists, etc., I cannot separate the future of Germany from that of the world at large; to me it is a country that has not yet completed its revolution, hasn't fully accepted its new form of government, and is game for all sorts of adventures. It fears rationality as much as the devil. Because of its position between the Soviets and the West, I feel Germany should try to discover new alternatives to capitalism and thus renew its stature and influence.

* Journalist and editor of the socialist workers' paper *Der Kulturwille*.

† Josef Englert, who was Jup the Magician in *Klingsor's Last Summer*. He owned a house near St. Moritz, where Hesse spent some months convalescing in 1931 and 1932.

‡ The highest station on the funicular on the Piz Corvatsch (3,458 meters), a mountain near St. Moritz, Switzerland.

We shall remain in Zurich until the beginning of April, and shall get to hear one or two more Haydn concerts. I shall find it hard to leave this Zurich apartment,* which was my winter refuge for six years. Quite a lot happened there, but now I'm married, and have a house, etc., and must try to keep the house, even though the immediate prospects look less than cheerful. I'm dependent on German money, a currency the rest of the world frowns on, and which is, in any case, subject to ruthless emergency decrees. So, once again, I have my back to the wall, and I wouldn't have done any of these things had I been able to foresee this. Well, I don't regret what I did. Nowadays life is more of an adventure, and a merry one at that, than it was before the war. Nevertheless, I find it embarrassing to be so dependent on the Reich, its currency, the situation there, etc., while living elsewhere and holding a different citizenship. [. . .]

TO FRITZ AND ALICE LEUTHOLD

[*April 17, 1932*]

My dear friends,

I went to *The Magic Flute* with Ninon on our last Sunday afternoon in Zurich. That brought back in a most beautiful, moving way the entire Zurich period, the time of *Steppenwolf*, when I spent a lot of time with Ruth, also with you. This was my way of saying goodbye to a phase in my life; it has faded, I must leave it behind, but still find that difficult, and am actually quite heartbroken.

My stays in Zurich over the last seven years were no doubt just as significant as the time I spent in Montagnola. During those Zurich winters, I wrote more than half of the work I have produced since 1925. If I hadn't been able to work in this hideout here in winter, and hadn't had friends like you, I wouldn't feel so grateful now about the time I spent here.

I have to go over to the Bodmers' in a half an hour. We're leaving at noon tomorrow, and I would like to use this final, peaceful moment to convey my sincere thanks for all your friendship, trust, and generosity during the years when I was your guest here. I shared with you so many of my joys and worries. I couldn't find the right words to say this yesterday, because I was too close to tears.

---

* Hesse's Zurich friends Alice and Fritz Leuthold allowed him to use an apartment at Schanzengraben 31 for winter quarters.

I'm looking at all the nice furnishings that you bought for the Zurich apartment; they made the place seem so cozy. I recall how you used to greet me each time I arrived with flowers, pillows, and all kinds of thoughtful gifts. I also remembered the patience and concern you showed constantly, no matter what was going on in my life: during the times I was ill or unproductive, the good and not so good times with Ruth, the time with Ninon. You showed great empathy, kept your faith in me, and demonstrated your love.

I hope we shall often see one another again and continue sharing our joys and sorrows. But before leaving this Zurich home, where I have been your spoiled guest for so long, I felt that I had to convey these feelings to you again.

I'm heading back again to the country with some ideas for new pieces. I have been contemplating a large, wondrous, complex work.* I have been toying with the idea for some weeks, but I don't know yet whether I shall ever succeed in completing even a portion of it.

Goodbye, my dears [. . .], and think of me from time to time.

TO GEORG WINTER

September 1932

Somebody sent me a copy of the journal in which you published your review of *The Journey to the East*. I should like to thank you for the piece and also respond to it briefly, since people seldom take authors seriously. I have only had this kind of experience a few times over the course of several decades.

Of all the reviews, yours articulated the central issue from a perspective that shed the most light on the paradoxical (or rather bipolar) meaning of my little book. You say that, as soon as the author attempts to write about the League, he ceases to belong to it.

I cannot fully accept your final conclusion, and not just out of a need for self-preservation. But you have certainly hit the nail on the head, and this sense of having been understood felt so wonderful— authors rarely have this experience—that I decided to write to thank you. Having done so, I should like to say a few words about the justification for my work and my existence.

On the whole you're quite right. It's impossible to think or write about the matters of greatest import. Indeed God prohibits us from doing

* *The Glass Bead Game.*

so. I fully agree with you that we ought not consider literature an arbitrary, superfluous intellectual appendage, but one of the strongest functions of the mind.

So it's basically impermissible to write or even think about sacred matters (in this case the League—that is, the feasibility and significance of human community). One can come up with various interpretations of this taboo and of the intellect's frequent transgressions against it, psychologically, morally, developmentally—e.g., the prohibition against using the Lord's name, which separates the magical stage of mankind from the rational one.

Once you start criticizing me for sinning against that original prohibition, you yourself seem to develop a bad conscience of sorts. You even imply that the mistake, for which you criticize the author, may actually be a fault on the part of the critic. Indeed, by reading books to form a judgment about them and then write reviews, you're sinning against what is most sacred. At heart, you no doubt realize that reverence is the principal intellectual virtue; you also realize that intellectual considerations have inspired both the object of your criticism in the review and your own activities and that both have been undertaken in good faith—and yet you feel that you have to commit the sin of criticism by rejecting certain things and perpetrating the sort of injustice always entailed in summary formulations.

I wouldn't have wanted to see you doing anything differently. But I would be glad to see you admit to yourself—as I myself have done in the light of your review—that your actions and judgments are "basically" unnecessary and sinful, and that this transgression against that age-old prohibition is precisely the sort of sin that the mind must necessarily take upon itself. This sin makes the intellect question not only the League but also its own activities and nature; sends it on endless errands of thought and conscience, back and forth between self-reproach and self-justification; prompts it to write books. This sin is ominous, tragic, irresistible, and it certainly exists, it's fate.

My work, the confession of an aging artist, attempts, as you rightly say, to render that which cannot be rendered and to evoke the ineffable. That is certainly a sin. But can you say in all seriousness that you know of any literary work or philosophy that isn't an attempt to make the impossible possible, to counter taboos responsibly?

There is only a single passage in your review that seems rather weak and questionable to me: you suggest the existence of other problems, which are more feasible and appropriate than mine, that could be tackled by thinkers and artists. I don't believe that authors should ever set off on the adventure of writing without feeling somewhat remorseful and having the courage to experience that feeling; the same holds true for the critic who is assessing the author. I felt assured that you would understand me when I noticed your hint along these lines. So I decided to write you a note. Not because I felt any need to justify myself, but because nowadays one so rarely comes across a feeling of community, of comradeship, or sense of collegiality that one is glad to discover a trace of such things.

TO ERHARD BRUDER

Baden, November 1932

It's a pity one has to hurt the other person where there is a clash of ideas and the truth is at stake. But at least we have learned to take the personal sting out of these attacks and not indulge in them for their own sake. [. . .]

You're quite mistaken about the point at issue. I said that I agree with Ball and not with Finckh; we can discuss the many implications of that point of view at some time or other. I don't think you realize yet just how radically I reject fatherland, patriotism, etc. But there are other differences between Finckh and me; for example, I believe Germany bears a large share of guilt for the outbreak of the war. I'm still disgusted that every German knows all about the tyrannical and shameful Treaty of Versailles, but isn't aware of the shameful ultimatum to Serbia in 1914. The latter is one of the most revolting documents in history, and ought to make every German reflective and ashamed. And there are countless other examples.

Whenever I bring up any such charges against Germany, and thus also against myself, I have to listen to the following: Beg your pardon, but what about the Serbs, Russians, etc., who are every bit as guilty as we are. They always lied or managed to deceive us. Why can't you criticize *them* and not be constantly attacking your own people? I still have to listen day after day to that ridiculous old question, which I have always answered in the same way, well over a thousand times by now. I'm not trying to ascertain the enemies' guilt, but rather our own, since I have no cause to feel ashamed of French sins, but I certainly am ashamed of German ones. What I despise above all else is the talent Germans have for forgetting their own sins, and simply lying about them. It's always the same old story. People say: Well, you were living abroad and weren't starving like us. I respond: You can have no idea what I went through from 1914 to the present. I lost my fatherland, had a shared burden of responsibility for the war, and felt that my own people no longer understood me. And like you, I lost all my savings and income twice, first because of the war and then because of the inflation, etc. [. . .] What concerns me now is not so much Germany, or any individual country or people, or the bourgeoisie and Bolsheviks, but endangered humanity as a whole. People are always telling me that such thoughts are a luxury reserved for peacetime. A German needs to support his people through thick and thin, has to go along with its decisions, condone its lies, cowardly acts, and the intoxicated warmongering from 1914 to 1916. I cannot accept those arguments. I know where I stand, and realize that these attitudes have put me out on a limb, but I have no intention of changing my mind; my attitude has been dictated by fate. I exposed myself a lot in my books and essays, partly because of the moral repercussions of the position I had adopted toward my people and fatherland, and even though this openness on my part has been gleefully exploited by some people, I am nevertheless prepared to sacrifice everything. I shall not retreat, not even a single step.

There is a contemporary whose experience resembles mine, even though he hails from a very different background: Romain Rolland.

I have no difficulty understanding your fixation on potatoes. I'm like that too, although my obsession is a little different. Whenever I catch sight of a newspaper, or hear a demagogue—sometimes just reading the word "Germany" is enough—all the wartime despair floods back.

You know what I mean. At the moment I'm at the spa in Baden for a cure and can seldom allow myself the luxury of writing such long letters.

TO OTTO HARTMANN*

November 24, 1932

[. . .] I'm not at all interested in what the critics have to say. I recall them saying more or less the following about *The Journey to the East*: This is certainly not art, although it has some value as a biological function. Its symbols are genuine, but quite pathological. Since it is neither comprehensible nor universal, it lacks the hallmarks of genuine art. I suppose that is well meant, but a similar insistence on universality elevated Theodor Körner into a German classic, whereas Hölderlin was

---

* Boyhood friend of Hesse's; later mayor of Göppingen.

entirely forgotten. [. . .] There isn't much going on in literary criticism, and I haven't paid much attention to it for years. I got to know it during the war. In more than thirty years I have rarely learned anything useful from reviews. Literary journalism has reached a sad pass. But quite apart from this public criticism by professional critics, one often gets to hear very informative criticism in private circles. Readers can be either receptive or hostile, but their judgments are often very lively, an acute consequence no doubt of that "biological function."

The opinions I value most are those of my fellow writers, but one seldom gets to hear them. In the case of my other artistic friends, I am most interested in the opinions of Schoeck, the musician. I was delighted to learn that the writer Kafka, whom I greatly admire, loved my books.*

But readers supply the most honest criticism. And there too, the thing we least want to hear is the most effective. I have never forgotten a little incident which occurred about fifteen years ago. A rather idolizing reader quoted a short poem of mine, which he had read years ago in a literary review. He didn't have a copy, but had learned it by heart, except for one line, which had unfortunately slipped his mind. Would I be so kind as to send him that line? I checked it, and was quite taken aback. The line he had been vainly trying to memorize was the weakest in the poem. For years, I had considered the poem one of my better ones, but had subsequently relegated it to second or third best precisely because of that botched passage. As penance, I had to copy out that dead passage for the reader. But I was happy and a little proud to hear the verdict of a girl of about thirteen, who had been asked to read a piece of mine to her mother: "One of the wonderful things about H. is that there is always a comma or a period when one is running out of breath."

Goodbye and greetings to you and your wife

TO HIS SON HEINER

[*January 1933*]

[. . .] The tax situation in Berlin could have ruined me. They were insisting that my entire income, except for the Swiss earnings, be taxed in Berlin, at very high rates (since the officials in Berlin first have to

---

* Kafka's friend and executor, Max Brod, wrote to Hesse on December 1, 1926: "I don't know whether I have ever told you that Franz Kafka loved your works and, although he usually didn't pay much attention to criticism, the receipt of a review of yours was one of the final pleasures he had as he lay on his deathbed in Kierling."

approve every penny I earn and then issue a permit for transfer abroad). They also threatened that I would have to pay back several years' worth of taxes retroactively. So I have had virtually no income at all for a number of years. They have softened their attitude and postponed the decision for months, but this affair has been eating up a lot of my time. Of course, they may well issue a new emergency decree in Germany tomorrow that will once again render all of this null and void, but for now I can breathe easily.

You're right that we are powerless in the face of institutions as powerful as the state. But I think you're wrong to conclude that we ought to defend ourselves by jettisoning "all scruples." Dear Heiner, we absolutely cannot do that. There is no point complaining about the unscrupulousness of other people if we're going to behave just as unscrupulously ourselves. If we have any claim to nobility, it is because we have certain scruples; we don't think that everything is permissible, we refuse to go along with the heinous killings and other repulsive activities taking place. Therein lies the source of all culture and of every spiritual stirring in life, which is fundamentally quite bestial, also the source of art, religion, indeed all genuine intellectual values. You people weren't the first to come up with the reaction: "To hell with all that crap." Throughout history certain people have responded in a similar vein. One can interpret that kind of response as a rebellion by weak and uneducated people against a cruel and overpowering adversary, but we ought not condone or approve it in any way. You may learn from Els's household what happens when people believe in something, are affectionate and good, and transmit those values to their children.

We had a cheerful Christmas; it was actually my first Christmas at home in twelve years. I received a lot of presents, as did Ninon, but it was all a bit too much for me. The milieu was excessively bourgeois and got a bit on my nerves. Of course, I was the one who decided to come to terms with this milieu by remarrying and accepting the Bodmers' offer of the house. I don't regret the decision and am very glad Ninon has her security and a "decent" household, but nevertheless I'm just a guest, and feel strange there. [. . .]

Your father

TO HERMANN HUBACHER

[*January 1933*]

Caro amico,

So you were mad at me? No harm in that. Somebody once asked me: "What's the point in having friends? They're never there in a real emergency, and the rest of the time we could get on fine without them." I said: "We have friends so that there will be somebody there to get mad at us. Others may like us, and occasionally poke fun at us, but it takes friends to get really mad at us, become peevish, and hold grudges over trifles, and that is what they're for. Getting mad is an expression of male tenderness, a kind of substitute for big words and expansive gestures, and it's no doubt better than nothing."

It's news to me that I was in Zurich over New Year's. My friend Dr. Lang spent a few days with me in Montagnola over New Year's. I was at the spa in Baden for a short while in November, and thought of getting in touch, but never plucked up the courage, because I wasn't well enough to go and visit you (all my Zurich friends seem to believe that an old man having sulphur baths would do wonders for his health by traveling frequently to Zurich, which would, of course, mean standing around in drafty railway stations, etc., etc.), and didn't have the nerve to ask you to visit me in Baden. When I naïvely suggested as much to my friends, I was told that this was out of the question. And yet some people did visit me in Baden, another reason why I didn't write to you. One day Morgenthaler arrived with Sasha,* and I assumed that if he knew I was in Baden, you would too. Yes, that's more or less what happened, and besides, as usual, I had to spend three or four hours a day reading my mail and writing letters, since that has to be done all year round, even during visits to the spa and vacations. I hope I have convinced you that I wasn't being uncivil when I failed to get in touch with you. On the way back, I wanted to hear music again after six months' abstinence, so I spent two nights in Zurich with the Bodmers, but I was too exhausted after the spa and didn't go out. I only got to hear Haydn's *Creation*.

We shall soon be into February, which used to be my favorite month for skiing in the mountains. My days as a skier are numbered, and now it seems as if I shan't even get to use the remainder, since my friend Englert, who used to help pay for the skiing trip, cannot anymore. I

---

* Hesse and Hubacher were both friends of the Swiss painter Ernst Morgenthaler and his wife, Sasha.

haven't published a book for years, apart from *The Journey to the East*, which is not much of a breadwinner. I'm staying at home and saving up my pennies so I can go see my oculist in March. (I don't expect much from him, but am cooperating, since the examination will reassure my wife, who does have some faith in doctors.) [. . .]

Apart from that, it's life as usual here in my feudal house, but I'm beginning to feel fed up with this sort of life, which I find constricting. I have been planning a new literary work for a year and a half now, but haven't managed to write a single line, for several reasons: I'm getting too old, my life here is too comfortable, each day the mail, etc., etc., forces me to assume the role of the overworked famous man. Something similar happened to the elderly Tolstoy, who, just before he died, got up and left, so that as he breathed his last, he could at least feel the presence of country roads, freedom, fresh air, and open spaces.

I shall probably arrange things differently, and may even write the projected book. But the whole thing isn't that much fun anymore. Few people notice the fine points. I would actually prefer to go skiing now. But as soon as it gets warmer, I shall have to start shoveling snow again. So, *tanti saluti!*

TO ANDRÉ GIDE

[*March 20, 1933*]

I was extremely pleased to receive your kind and unexpected letter,* which has arrived on the very day when my guest bed is expecting the first refugee, who is fleeing from the fists and revolvers of those right-wing zealots in Germany.

A student in high school loves and admires a somewhat older peer so much that he wouldn't dream of approaching him. He fears his idol is about to disappear for good, but just then the older student, who is close to graduation, looks at the younger one, smiles at him, and beckons. That is more or less what your greetings mean to me.

So I can respond to your kind words with heartfelt sincerity. I first

---

* André Gide's letter of March 11, 1933, read:

"*Depuis longtemps je désire vous écrire. Cette pensée me tourmente—que l'un de nous deux puisse quitter la terre sans que vous ayez eu ma sympathie profonde pour chacun des livres de vous que j'ai lus. Entre tous,* Demian *et* Knulp *m'ont ravi. Puis ce délicieux et mystérieux* Morgenlandfahrt *et enfin votre* Goldmund, *que je n'ai pas encore achevé—et que je déguste lentement, craignant de l'achever trop vite.*

"*Les admirateurs que vous avez en France (et je vous en récrute sans cesse de nouveaux) ne sont peut-être pas encore très nombreux, mais d'autant plus fervents. Aucun d'eux ne saurait être plus attentif ni plus ému que André Gide.*"

got to know your books when *Strait Is the Gate* and *The Immoralist* appeared in German for the first time, long before the war. Ever since then, you have been the contemporary French author in whom I have been most absorbed and for whom I feel most affection.*

TO ARTHUR STOLL†

Montagnola, March 24, 1933

I only sent a card recently to thank you for your wonderful present; that was the best I could manage at the time. Well, I very much hope that you have recovered from the bout of illness and are now feeling better. The sun often smiles at us here, and even though the warm alpine winds can be oppressive, the spring has been rather agreeable. A refugee from Germany is sleeping in our guest bed. The Berlin newspapers, and the Swiss ones as well, have been cowed amazingly quickly by the threats emanating from Berlin, and are now very mealymouthed. Over in Germany, they are conducting a really vicious pogrom against intellectuals: people are being imprisoned, fired from their jobs, deprived of their livelihoods; there have been rapes, assassinations, and the victims are not loudmouths and troublemakers, but mostly retiring scholars, peace-loving civil servants, diligent artists, etc., etc. I'm expecting Thomas Mann here today. He is number one on the blacklist.

In the midst of these depressing circumstances, which also affect me deeply in many ways, I unexpectedly received a pleasant surprise: a note from André Gide, copy enclosed. Not that it's anything special in itself, but I admire A. Gide a lot; aside from Hamsun, he is perhaps the only world-famous author whom I respect and love. So it was a revelation when this colleague of mine—he is a few years older than I—wrote to me in that vein.

Montagnola, beginning of April 1933

So you have turned up once again like a friendly, helpful magician. Thank you very much for your kind letters and gifts. The gift is very welcome and I shall use it, exactly as you wished, to provide hospitality for the exiles and émigrés.

The first guest, from Leipzig, left for Italy the day before yesterday.

---

* From 1905 to 1933, Hesse wrote fifteen reviews of works by Gide, in which he tried to spark interest in his works (*WA*, 12:417–19).

† Director of the pharmaceutical division of a Basel chemical firm. Hesse met him in 1924 during his first cure at Baden. Stoll supplied Hesse with medicaments in return for books, paintings, and special printings.

These people are all in bad shape financially. The editors of the leftist German press, and all the contributors as well, have suddenly lost their livelihoods. Many were in mortal danger, or might have been imprisoned, so they had to flee—e.g., my guest, whose wife stayed behind to give notice and pack their things, and if possible collect a payment owed them. But the editorial offices of the papers in question have been closed down, the printing works are in chaos, some have even been demolished, all the employees have been sacked and are now unemployed. For the socialist press alone, that amounts to some 80,000 to 100,000 people all over the Reich.

Another of my German acquaintances and colleagues will be here tomorrow. Thomas Mann and his wife have been here quite frequently, and I'm glad to see that he is slowly recovering from an initially severe depression. We have spent half days together on several occasions. He doesn't have any material worries, and is in good shape for now. But he has no idea what will become of his house and children in Munich. His passport is going to expire in the next few days, and no German consulate is willing to grant him even a provisional renewal; so he is going to ask the League of Nations for a passport. Th. Mann's statement of his allegiance to the socially progressive Republic appeared in Berlin just before Hitler came to power (I'm enclosing a reprint, which is somewhat condensed).* Since then he has been number one on the terrorists' blacklist. I have not had any problems so far; I received a couple of letters from worried readers warning me to keep my mouth shut and act cautiously, since there have already been threats to boycott my books and confiscate my German royalties. That may happen, but in such matters there is no such thing as certainty. I'm expecting my publisher here on Monday; he wants to discuss the situation with me on his way through to Italy (to visit Gerhart Hauptmann). The founder and the owners of my publishers are Jews, and so there is also danger lurking there.

But I think the present situation is so unbelievably crazy that it can hardly last very long. Hitler's terrorism will certainly prevail for a long time (until he stumbles into a war and loses it, or the economy goes bankrupt). But aggressive, pathological phenomena such as Minister Göring, who makes those sadistic speeches (he is apparently a morphine addict), will hardly survive that long. Unfortunately, Germany will become increasingly corrupt, and some people with big names will join the bandwagon. I wouldn't be surprised if, for example, Hauptmann

---

* "Statement of Allegiance to Socialism" (letter to Adolf Grimme, Minister for Education), in *Sozialistische Bildung*, Berlin, February 1933.

capitulated and started kowtowing to them. But, ultimately, the crucial element is the minority of people who hold genuine convictions, and they certainly exist. [. . .]

Montagnola, September 17, 1933

Thank you once again for your various kind gifts. The package with Allisatin and calcium, your order for a manuscript, and the wonderful letter. I was delighted with everything, and am sending you the manuscript* today; I tried to do a particularly attractive job on yours. Could you please deposit the money in my account rather than send it by mail (Schweizer Kreditanstalt, Lugano)? And if you get a chance to draw attention to my manuscripts, please do so by all means. A time may come when I shall have virtually no income.

I, too, have often noticed the same phenomenon: those clever, sophisticated Germans who used to laugh at Hitler now take him ever so seriously. Here's my explanation: Since 1918, Germany has been ignoring reality completely, and hasn't recognized or acknowledged in any way its moral responsibility both for starting the war and for the consequences of losing it. Germany hardly participated in its own direly needed revolution, which was carried out by a tiny group of militant left-wing socialists. All of its governments were constituted without popular approval, and the people never had any confidence in them. The only political event in which the people really took part was the election of General Hindenburg (the old corporal who deserves much blame for present conditions). Now, all of a sudden, a party has won favor with the people, and the nation has regained its patriotism or self-confidence. Many Germans who love their own people fear that if this hope is unwarranted and the people are let down, everything will start falling to pieces. That is incorrect, or at most only half right, but it's an understandable reaction, and that may be why so many intellectually prominent people have offered their services to the present regime. If they can restore Germany's fortunes without waging war, and if they manage to stop the disgusting excesses of the current movement, that

---

* Hesse was offering his friends manuscripts of poems illustrated with colored drawings. The following note was attached:

"In the summer of 1933, I wrote a small cycle of poems (eleven in number). Since they cannot be published at present, and since the situation in Germany is such that my income has sunk to the level of the inflation years, I would ask any friends of mine who can afford it to purchase a copy of these poems, either for themselves or as a gift for somebody else. I have copied the text on very fine paper, and illustrated it with colored drawings. No two copies are identical, each is different in some way. Handwritten copies cost from 200 to 250 francs, depending on the particular request; typed copies are 150 francs."

will please me. But I doubt that will happen; the situation is too wild, forced, demagogical, ignoble, also too dumb and anti-intellectual.

I am irritated by the frequent demand of some of my colleagues that I state publicly that I belong to the opposition against Hitler. I refuse to do so; I don't belong to any party, and even though I personally find communism more attractive than fascism, I am not willing to support it, or any other expression of the lust for power. I believe that poets and intellectuals ought to foster peace, not conflict.

I am glad to have my sister* here for a visit. In the evening she reads from the diaries and letters of my mother, who mentions the battles of Solferino and Sedan!

TO HERMANN HUBACHER

[*Baden, December 1, 1933*]

Thank you for your kind greetings. Few people know how to read poetry seriously, and so I'm delighted to hear that kind of comment.

The poem† is by no means a "revelation," the expression of a sudden, irrational insight. Like most of my poems, it came to me during a sleepless night, and it began as a sober and rather disciplined effort to evoke in words those beliefs I have made my own. Of course, the poem doesn't convey all my beliefs (which actually have somewhat more in common with religious, Christian convictions). It suggests their intellectual foundations, particularly in acknowledging the primacy of the intellect and the difference between the creator and his creation. But the "spirit" in my poem is not merely divine, it is God, and is not meant to be pantheistic.

I don't know much about the divisions developing now among Christians in Germany, but I have always felt that the Protestant tendency to conform and capitulate to the demands of the state was awfully repulsive. At first, after Germany silenced the Catholics and put them to sleep with a concordat,‡ I felt the Protestant church movement was merely a brutal regression to barbaric, Teutonic customs. By now it is clear that, in addition to that marvelous Jew Buber, there is quite an impressive Protestant movement, which is waging war on stupidity and decadence

---

* Adele Gundert.

† "Besinnung" ("Contemplation") (*Gedichte*, p. 623).

‡ The concordat between Germany and the Vatican was signed by Vice-Chancellor von Papen and Cardinal Pacelli, the State Secretary, on July 20, 1933.

and has some extremely courageous adherents. I received a letter recently from one of them, a Tübingen professor named Hauer,* whom I have known for a long time. [. . .]

TO GUNTER BÖHMER†

Brief report from the garden, February 20, 1934

Caro amico!

We have been having warm weather for weeks, and except for some small spots near the woods, there is no trace left of the snow. Lorenzo has just finished cutting and binding the vines; there are some new, gleaming white posts, all properly aligned, and below that, amid the arid, almost colorless winter grasses, the cheerful smiles of countless tiny yellow primrose islands.

I have mercilessly weeded out the vines on the flower terrace—it's to the left of the path by the boccie field—where we had dahlias and azaleas last year, because they take sunlight away from the flowers. And I have been burning the leaves and branches continuously for the past ten days on the cleared terrace. Head gardener Vogel‡ carts the stuff over from the paths, beds, etc. There are eighty to a hundred baskets of leaves on the boccie field alone, and I have already disposed of about fifty. At first, the piles of leaves seem very loose and dry. But after lifting the top part off, one can see that lower down they are damp and stick to the ground; to avoid destroying the field, I have to rake up the whole thing again and allow it to dry, then have to peel off the lower layers, virtually one leaf at a time.

Perched on the head gardener's back, the Lion occasionally acts as an assistant. But, like the Tiger,§ he is rather nervous and shy; both are preoccupied with puberty, and have become very thin and gangly. An enemy and rival showed up the other day. Frau Wiegand‖ from Lerici is here. She brought along her splendid Angora tomcat; the two brothers have completely rejected him. They are either afraid or jealous of him, and so the Angora has to keep to itself and must be fed separately.

---

* Jakob Wilhelm Hauer, a scholar in religious studies and an expert on India, who served for some time as head of the German Movement for the Faith.

† Painter and graphic artist, illustrated several of Hesse's books and designed the dust jackets for all his works in the Suhrkamp editions.

‡ "Bird," a nickname for Hesse.

§ The Lion and the Tiger: Hesse's young cats.

‖ The widow of the publicist Heinrich Wiegand.

When I attempted to explain the situation to my wife in psychological terms, she asked: Could the two thin household cats really notice that the new tomcat is a luxury animal with a fine pedigree? She wasn't even sure the tomcat himself realized that's what he was. My response: "Do you really think Gerhart Hauptmann doesn't realize he is an Angora writer?"

We're worried about the large cactus outside the studio, which was outdoors all winter for the first time; an attractive covering provided some shelter. At the moment it's a cause for concern. We're not yet sure whether it will pull through or not; it may be frozen.

Thanks for the greeting and those pretty sheets. I like each individual piece, but find the overall effect, the colors and the gold, somewhat too playful. I greatly enjoyed the sketches in your letter, which always appeal to me.

Bruno wrote me a wonderful, long letter expressing various worries about a love affair, which seems quite serious. I only saw Heiner briefly in Zurich; he was extremely busy. The youngest, Martin, spent half a day with me in Zurich. Herr Bodmer* conveyed his gratitude again for the "Bird."

Frau Emmy Ball has gone to Germany, on what is probably just a short visit; she mainly wants to talk to publishers. I must get to work.

TO JOHANNA GOLD

[*After Easter 1934*]

Your beautiful package arrived on a terribly wet morning. It had been pouring all night and all day for two days, and the low clouds were almost touching the lake. I really needed something to cheer me up. So your gift couldn't have arrived at a more appropriate moment. Only one egg† was broken; the others are in perfect condition, and I'm really delighted with them. Ninon says she had been hoping for years that I would eventually get to see the colors and ornaments on those eggs. Like Oriental carpet design, this ancient peasant art is spectacularly beautiful. Similar objects can be found all over the world, except in places where wars or mechanized civilizations have obliterated them. I believe that if a great flood came about and were followed by a slow

---

* In 1933, Hesse gave the typewritten manuscript of his fairy tale "Vogel," with illustrations by Gunter Böhmer, as a Christmas gift to his patron H. C. Bodmer (*WA*, 6:460ff).

† Painted eggs from Romania.

increase in population, man would create identical beautiful objects from scratch. Those designs are part of a reservoir—or "collective unconscious," as C. G. Jung would say—that every people can draw from.

I understand how you feel about the forcible expropriation of creditors in your country. I also lost a lot due to the war and inflation, and I have to reckon on new losses, since I too am forced to live like a capitalist—i.e., I have to make sure that the savings left over from my fortuitous successes earn interest, so that I have funds to draw on during the frequent lean years. Since I don't have the talent or skills necessary for speculative investment, I have to rely on conventional capitalist procedures, and have been badly swindled several times by certain individuals and also the state.

We're putting something nice together: a small selection of my poems, which will appear as one of those attractive little volumes* in the Insel series. Apart from that, I have been working a lot in the library over the past six months, preparing for a projected story.† [. . .]

TO MANUEL GASSER

[July 1934]

[. . .] It was kind of you not to send over that young boy who wanted to meet me so badly. But at this point, one more wouldn't have made that much difference. I have a visitor of some kind every single day. At times there are several here at the same time; nine-tenths are young people from Germany and German-speaking Switzerland. A high school senior from Hannover, who was here recently, admitted that everything wasn't ideal in the Third Reich. But when I said that I found the complacent response of German youth to news about people being tortured to death in concentration camps absolutely disgraceful—we had just heard of Mühsam's death‡—he said with a superior Germanic smile: Probably none of those imprisoned authors has anything worthwhile to say to the German people. I replied: If, as an eighteen-year-old, he was already so certain about that, and felt it could excuse the utter bestiality of the Third Reich, then he should spare us in Switzerland the pleasure of his visit; so he departed, looking quite crestfallen. [. . .]

* *Vom Baum des Lebens: Ausgewählte Gedichte* (Leipzig, 1934).

† "The Fourth Life of Josef Knecht"; originally intended as part of *The Glass Bead Game*.

‡ Erich Mühsam, poet, dramatist, essayist. In 1919, as a member of the "revolutionary workers' council," he took part in the proclamation of the Bavarian Republic of Soviets. He was tortured to death in the Oranienburg concentration camp.

TO C. G. JUNG

September 1934

I should like to thank you for your letter, which was a pleasure to read. But the "eagle eye" that you mentioned isn't particularly impressive. My tendency is not so much to set up analytic distinctions as to adopt a synthetic perspective, with a view toward harmony.

Your remarks about sublimation go to the heart of the problem, and demonstrate the difference between your view and mine. We're dealing, first of all, with an incidence of the linguistic confusion so prevalent nowadays—so many people use the same term but mean something different. You regard sublimation as a term best employed by chemists; Freud means one thing by it, and I have something else again in mind. Maybe some chemist originally conceived of the word *sublimatio*, I have no idea, but there's nothing esoteric about the word *sublimis* (or even *sublimare*): it's classical Latin.

There would be no difficulty resolving that particular point. But this time there are real issues at stake behind the linguistic quibble. I agree with your interpretation of the Freudian concept of sublimation. I wasn't trying to defend Freud's notion, but rather the actual concept itself. I feel that it's an important concept where cultural issues are concerned. And this is where we part company. As a physician, you regard sublimation as something volitional, the transference of a drive to an alien sphere of activity. In the last resort I, too, regard sublimation as a form of "repression," but I only use that lofty term in cases where it's possible to speak of "successful" repression—i.e., the effects of a drive on a sphere that is no doubt alien, but also extremely significant in the cultural sphere, art. For me, the history of classical music is the history of a technique of expression and discipline, in which entire groups and even generations of masters have—for the most part completely unwittingly—transferred their drives to an area that, by virtue of these genuine sacrifices, achieves a degree of perfection and classicism. I believe that it is worth making every sacrifice to achieve that form of classicism, and if, for instance, classical European music between 1500 and the eighteenth century consumed its maestros, who were more like servants than victims, ever since then it has been emitting light, comfort, courage, joy for thousands of people, and has been, again rather unwittingly, a school of wisdom, courage, and savoir vivre, and will continue as such for a long time to come.

And I have a high regard for any talented individual who devotes a portion of his instinctual drives to such activities, even if he happens to be rather pathological as a human being. Whereas it would seem wrong to me to cling to some form of pseudo-sublimation in analysis, I feel that it is permissible, indeed extremely valuable and desirable, on occasions when that works and the sacrifice bears fruit.

That is why psychoanalysis is such a difficult and dangerous experience for artists. Those who take it seriously might easily have to refrain from all artistic activity for the rest of their lives. That is fine if the person is just a dilettante, but in the case of a Handel or a Bach, I feel we could do without psychoanalysis if we got Bach in return.

In our own sphere, we artists practice a genuine form of *sublimatio*, not out of assertiveness and ambition, but in a purely graceful way. I do not mean the type of artist that the people and the dilettante have in mind, but rather the artist as servant; Don Quixote, a knight even in all his madness, is also a victim.

Well, I want to stop. I'm neither an analyst nor a critic. If you look at the review I sent you, you will see that I only very rarely say anything critical, and then always *en passant*. I never dismiss anything, and if I cannot take a book seriously or find some value in it, I shelve it silently.

I have always sensed that your personal belief is genuine, a mystery. I was glad to find confirmation for this intuition in your letter. You use the analogy of chemistry for your secret, just as I use the analogy of music for mine, and not just any music, classical in particular. Everything that can be said on this subject has been formulated in a remarkably pointed manner in Lü Bu We, chapter two. For years I have been pursuing this musical analogy in a dreamlike fashion, and hope that I can eventually show you a portion of it.

TO HEDWIG FISCHER

[*October 16, 1934*]

My thoughts have been with you and my dear departed friend since hearing of his death earlier today.* We were just talking about him yesterday. Thomas Mann and his wife were here; Ninon is away in Italy on vacation. I shall always treasure fond and grateful memories of my friend Fischer: his friendly manner and reflective nature, his lively interest in others, that wonderful, concerned, fatherly glance of his. And I feel I shall miss him often.

But today I'm thinking mostly about you. Your life with your husband, the collaboration and comradeship you had together, and your constant concern about his well-being—that has always struck me as

---

* Hesse's publisher Samuel Fischer died on October 15, 1934.

beautiful and exemplary. It's hard to believe that this union has been so cruelly terminated! I cannot find the right words to express my condolences and sense of bereavement. I truly hope that you will overcome this painful loss, and that, through the mourning process, you will acquire an image of your union with the deceased which will be with you always, like a benevolent spirit. With condolences from an old friend

TO HIS SON HEINER

January 19, 1935

I was delighted with your letter, even though some of the news was bad. I have had to maintain a rather hectic pace for days on end, but there was one pleasant event in between the gloomy news and constant work. Around Christmas, Annemarie told me that her mother (Frau Ball) would be fifty on January 17 and that we should think of her. That was rather late in the day, and I was extremely busy, but I did everything I could at that late stage. I made sure that as many people as possible were informed about the date; I wrote many letters and cards, and contacted several newspapers, etc. Since Frau Emmy lives in such poverty, I was hoping that some people would send her not only birthday greetings but a few pennies as well. That wasn't easy, since she hates it when people refer to her impoverished state and start behaving like condescending benefactors. Something of that kind must already have taken place by that stage, since after I had already spent several days virtually killing myself organizing this birthday, I received a letter from Emmy (who, of course, didn't know what I was up to) saying: She had to tell me that she was about to turn fifty; people were constantly mentioning her birthday, congratulating her, being condescending, etc.; she just couldn't stand that sort of thing and wanted it to stop. She also asked us to be so kind as to refrain from celebrating her birthday, congratulating her, etc., etc. Well, it seemed as if my foolish preparations had all been in vain, and I was feeling a little sorry that I had taken over the responsibility for the whole affair from Annemarie. But then I said to myself, and Ninon had the same idea, that Emmy might change her mind tomorrow, and so I didn't respond right away. We waited a few days, then wrote to Frau Ball saying that since she was ill and on her own, she shouldn't dream of spending her fiftieth birthday crouching over the fireplace and freezing in her village, but should spend the day with us. We would have a car go to collect her, etc. She agreed right away, and so the 17th was a big day. We had all silently thought about my fiftieth birthday, since that was the very day Hugo Ball was operated on in the hospital, when they ascertained that his condition was untreatable. That was on July 2, 1927. He lived until September. So Emmy came by car, and at our front door received a congratulatory poster drawn by Böhmer. Then we had lunch with wine and coffee, and afterward Emmy was shown the table with her presents. She said later on that it had been her most wonderful birthday ever. From me, she received a small manuscript with pictures, lots of writing paper, books, and cognac; Ninon gave her a suit; Alice Leuthold had sent flowers and some money; and there were also several gifts of money from acquaintances of mine, on whom I had prevailed, about 200 francs, perhaps slightly more. That evening after she left, I felt like keeling over, but I had to stay up for hours trying to catch up with my work.

One seldom gets a chance like that to organize some fun for one's friends, to cheer them up and help them out a little. I know dozens of people who have absolutely no prospects and are in a diabolically convoluted situation. For instance, there is poor Luschnat, whom I would like to help, and I have managed to do something for him. Here is his situation: He is as poor as a beggar, and has been ordered to leave Switzerland, but he has received a short reprieve due to our efforts. His wife and child stayed behind when he fled from Berlin in March 1933; she doesn't want to emigrate. They have filed for divorce, but it won't come through for ages. You can imagine the way the German bureaucrats will deal with the case of a suspicious emigrant. In the meantime, he has fallen very much in love with another woman. She is an impoverished political refugee who cannot earn a living here or elsewhere, or even gain admission to other countries; her passport is valid only for Switzerland. A child is due at the end of May, and her landlords in Ticino are continually evicting her. Luschnat's deadline for leaving Switzerland happens to coincide with her due date. He will not leave without her and the child, and nobody knows what will happen. And I have many such cases to worry about. It's almost enough to destroy a person.

The Basel *National-Zeitung* has managed to highlight a nasty and coarse remark about my publisher S. Fischer: in the new edition of a book by Annette Kolb, the "Jewish publisher" cowardly omitted a positive footnote about the Jews.* Well, I happen to know the prior history

---

* In a column in the cultural section of the *National-Zeitung* of January 13, 1935, the author accuses the S. Fischer Verlag of opportunism vis-à-vis the Nazi leadership because of a deleted footnote in *Die Schaukel*, a novel by Annette Kolb.

of this footnote,* and I'm also well acquainted with Annette Kolb, her book, etc. It's a small episode in the quiet struggle that we are waging to preserve intellectual life in Germany; for example, my pieces in Fischer's *Rundschau* are the only efforts by a German critic to review and occasionally promote Jewish books. I wish to continue this activity, and have just agreed to write a twice-yearly review essay on the state of German literature for the main literary review in Sweden.† Here is the story of the footnote: Nobody even noticed it in the first printing— the publishers courageously permitted its inclusion, which was danger- ous for them. Then, perhaps through a denunciation, a German court discovered the passage in the book, and our publisher was forced to choose between dropping the footnote in future printings or having the book banned and existing supplies immediately confiscated. Even then the publisher didn't agree to this right away, as every other German publisher would have done, but took the time to think the matter over, traveled to Paris for a discussion with Annette Kolb, who naturally agreed that the passage should be dropped. And now the *National-Zeitung*, no less, mocks the publisher for his noble, courageous behavior by calling his firm a cowardly, kowtowing Jewish publishing house! It would nor- mally be possible to defend oneself against such charges by presenting the facts; the newspapers would then be forced to retract their calumny. But in this case the publisher can do nothing of the sort. If this leaks out, a Nazi spy will be sent to the firm, which will even have to pay him, and the publisher may end up in a concentration camp.

I get to see all these cases, or many of them at least, and I have to investigate them, furtively and in private, since my current role some- how is to work for Germany while remaining Swiss and European. I don't expect to have much impact on a large scale. I'm just hoping to preserve a tiny group of thinkers and readers who have kept clean and could transmit a legacy of intellectual honesty beyond the chaos of the present. And it's even difficult to quell the fighting and hatred between people who ostensibly share the same convictions. Take, for example, the man responsible for that disgusting comment in the *National-Zeitung*. I sus- pect that he is a fervent democrat and an enemy of the Nazis who deep down also hates Jews. The filth everywhere! And I'm stuck in the middle

---

* The footnote reads: "Ever since the day when the Jews gained some influence in intellectual life, artists began to sense the presence of certain opportunities, and they no longer had to contend with their former hardship, which often amounted in subjective terms to an absolute standstill. [. . .] These days we are a small band of Christians in Germany who remain conscious of our indebtedness to Judaism."

† *Bonniers Litterära Magasin.*

of it and would like to stay clean. There are some sources of consolation, but one wishes at times that everything was over and done with.

Enough. I shouldn't really allow myself the luxury of such long letters. But I wanted to give you a glimpse of the stuff piling up each day on my desk, and on me, too. *Addio*, heartfelt greetings from your Papa

TO HERMANN HUBACHER

[February 16, 1935]

Caro amico,

Your letter has taught me something new about you: like so many of my friends, you hate writing letters. That's unfortunate, since it upsets the balance in our relationship. People like Schoeck, for instance, who spend hours each week in public houses and have perfectly healthy eyes, wait until I have been writing and sending them letters, poems, books, etc., for over a year before they pull themselves together sufficiently to write a postcard. Yet they can all write marvelously, as posterity will discover when it comes across the rare letters of these seeming illiterates. This is awful for me, since I'm far away and all alone, and even though I try very hard to inform my friends about my current work and thinking, I seldom hear any echoes. In this respect, Switzerland, and the Swiss artistic world, closely resembles the flailing heroics of the German barbarians: Away with pen and ink! To hell with scribblers! Their ideal image is more or less the following: blue eyes and a coarse fist, a throat thirsting for some Neuenburger, perhaps some talent as a card player. Well, I haven't altogether given up hope, and am still expecting a few words conveying your impression of *The Glass Bead Game*.* Your opinion will not influence me, but I look forward to hearing it. The Germany of 1810 or thereabouts, especially the circle around Schlegel and Novalis, would have had less difficulty with this work and understood it better. It's remarkable how vehement the two camps have become! Some people—often they are loyal, old friends of mine—dismiss *The Glass Bead Game* quite adamantly. Some of them also objected rather vociferously to *The Journey to the East*, which they called a mistaken excursion into the intellectual sphere, as if there were a place for everything in literature except the intellect! Then there are others who are so fascinated by the

---

* The introduction to *The Glass Bead Game* (published in *Die Neue Rundschau*, December 1934).

main idea that they more or less swallow the whole thing in one gulp, but they are not well enough educated or sufficiently well read to discern the finer nuances of *The Glass Bead Game*.

Things aren't going particularly well for me. I have been overworked for months, which has been getting me down. Quite a lot of the work was in vain. As a way to make a living, I used to contribute to a journal that ultimately swindled me.* Even if they paid up, my earnings would hardly cover even half my living expenses, and the trickle from Germany is dwindling constantly. I'm eating up my savings, which may tide me over the worst. I occasionally get rather depressed when I think of how difficult it is to earn a living, despite all the hard work. But then again, I like seeing signs that I'm thoroughly dispensable as far as the contemporary world is concerned, and I regard that indifference as a privilege and an honor.

I'm expecting Carossa this evening, for one day only.†

Good luck with your recovery, dear friend, and greetings to your family

TO ALFRED KUBIN‡

[*Early summer 1935*]

I was delighted to receive your kind letter and the beautiful little sketch. Life isn't easy these days, I have lots to worry about, and I suppose you are in much the same situation. So it's great to receive something positive and comforting.

I just got hold of a copy of the new book by Heinrich Zimmer, whose formulations are often brilliant, although he occasionally sounds too much like a virtuoso.§ Nobody writing in German has ever captured so well the aesthetic side of Indian culture, its amoral and entirely playful devotion to spectacle, and the eternal flow of images.

I'm enclosing a new poem from *The Glass Bead Game*. You already have several of them. I wrote this one at Pentecost.‖ Intellectually, I have been living for over three years in the world of *The Glass Bead Game* and the mythical cycle around it. This imaginary world began to crystallize in my mind as a kind of sequel to the saga in *The Journey*

* The *Schweizer Journal* had declared itself insolvent.

† On his way back from Rome, the physician and writer Hans Carossa visited Hesse in Montagnola.

‡ Painter; designed the cover and title page for *Die Morgenlandfahrt (The Journey to the East)*.

§ *Indische Sphären* (1935).

‖ "On Reading the Summa Contra Gentiles."

to the East. I often inhabit that realm, as if the cycle were a genuine saga or even religion rather than something purely imaginary. But even though I live there, I seldom add more words to it; although I certainly haven't lost my appetite for daydreaming, I don't feel the same urge to be productive. At times I only write one or two poems in an entire month. Of course, I'm doing some other literary work on the side, book reviews, but I don't count them, since that sort of work is purely intellectual, not creative.

I'm delighted to hear that you're going to be illustrating *Faust*, and think you're right to focus more on the folk tale than on Goethe.

It's decently hot at long last, and all I do most days is the daily work in the garden. A heavy hailstorm has just destroyed virtually everything; there's quite a lot to do, and when I'm watering tomato plants or loosening the ground around a beautiful flower, I don't have that terrible feeling so familiar to artists: Does any of this make sense at all? Is it a permissible activity nowadays? No, I'm happy to be doing this, and that's always a nice feeling.

My youngest son will be coming to see me soon; I hope that he stays at least two or three days. He is really an architect, but hasn't been able to find any work for two years, so he has taken up photography, works as a newspaper photographer, etc., and barely manages to make ends meet. He's a courageous, decent fellow. Well, that's it for now, and many thanks for the drawing.

TO WOLFRAM KIMMIG

[*Received October 18, 1935*]

Thank you for your kind letter. I'm having no luck at all with the German Reich. The people who owe me money did not pay me when I could have used it, and when some of them eventually started paying, I was denied access to those funds. I have lost virtually all my savings (the earnings from *Steppenwolf* and *Narcissus and Goldmund*); they were in German Gold Bonds, which are absolutely worthless nowadays outside the Reich. The highest I got was a fifth of the value, even less for the rest. I have hardly any income, and am witnessing another "great era" as a mourner.

I would prefer to let you decide how to handle payments to my account.* Even if I cannot buy a crumb of bread with all that money,

---

* The lawyer Dr. Wolfram Kimmig had the power of attorney over Hesse's bank account in Constance, Germany.

I can occasionally use the account to purchase a book for my sisters.
[. . .]

Unfortunately, there are no more copies of *Hours in the Garden*.*
Such luxuries are a thing of the past; otherwise I would certainly not
have forgotten you. This year, I received an honorarium of one hundred
marks for *Hours in the Garden* and a few marks for the latest issue of
Corona, plus roughly the same amount for my book reviews (which eat
up three-quarters of my time). Sales of my books are virtually nil. I lost
the savings that I had sentimentally invested in local German stocks
(Württemberg, the city of Stuttgart, etc.). So we are doing without a few
nice luxuries; food may be next. Fortunately, I can go on living in this
beautiful house, nobody can say a peep, since I don't own it, am just
a guest.

As for *Hours*, it will most probably appear in pamphlet form a
year from now—if it's still possible by that stage to publish anything
poetical.

TO HIS SISTER ADELE

Baden, November 28, 1935

Yesterday was Marulla's birthday, and yesterday you wrote enclosing a little letter for Hanno,† which I still have. I haven't had the
courage to hand it to Frida.‡ Something awful is happening there. Our
dear Hans has long feared losing his job§ and his livelihood, and during
the past few week this anxiety has developed into a fixation. He began
to interpret everything at his workplace in a negative and hostile manner
and became suspicious of everybody. The young office girls would occasionally poke fun at him, and he imagined that they were conspiring
against him and informing on him, so that he would be fired. He felt
each word he overheard was a confirmation of his theory. He had said
much the same thing to me recently; I felt that he was exaggerating a
bit and told him so, and he seemed quite willing to accept this. But he
was in a far worse condition than anybody had suspected; his behavior
in the office occasionally astonished his boss, but he pulled himself
together when he was with Frida. He woke up from a nightmare once

---

* *Stunden im Garten* (Vienna: Bermann-Fischer, 1936).
† Hesse's brother Hans, who lived in Baden (near Zurich).
‡ Hans Hesse's wife.
§ Hans Hesse had worked twenty-four years for the Brown Boveri Corporation.

and screamed. On another occasion, he claimed to have heard a woman on the floor below crying, and he said she was crying because she knew he and his family would soon be penniless.

Well, briefly, Hanno left a little earlier than usual yesterday morning, but failed to arrive at the office. As I write, he has been missing for about thirty hours, and nobody has any idea of his whereabouts. We don't even have any clues; yesterday we called in the police, who are out looking for him. I was at Frida's a few times; she is a wonderful person with lots of courage, but she broke down yesterday. They left the light on the whole night, and somebody was always up, just in case Hans came home. I was last there this morning; unfortunately, it's quite far away. I got in touch with an acquaintance of mine; his wife is going to call on Frida this afternoon and look after her. Her sister from Freienwil has been with her for the past couple of hours.

the 28th, evening

I have just returned from Frida's; her two sisters are there now. Well, they have found poor Hans, and his troubles are over. I have been running around and been so busy all day (I also had a literary visitor today, and Emmy Ball has been here since yesterday) that I have not been able to absorb all of this.

God be with you, dear Adis, be brave, and here's a kiss

TO HIS COUSIN FRITZ GUNDERT*

[*December 1935*]

Hans seemed to be leading a quiet, uneventful, happy life ever since he got married (1918); he no longer suffered from bouts of anxiety and despondency, at least as far as others could tell. Apparently, he was indeed happy, and his friends, also his in-laws, were particularly fond of his sense of humor, his delight in puns, puzzles, occasional verse, etc. Of course, all of this helped mask his tendency to get depressed, and twelve years ago, when his boss tried to get him to accept a somewhat different job, which would have offered better chances for promotion to more responsible positions within the corporation, he rejected the offer. He said that he was having enough trouble coping with his clerical position and his own expectations of himself. His latest and final crisis began when the corporation lost some business and started

* Transcribed from a copy of the letter, without any initial greeting.

cutting back on the work force: he had long been afraid of losing his job and the wherewithal to feed his wife and children. Over the last two to three months this anxiety got out of hand, particularly the crazy notion that his younger fellow workers were trying to get rid of him. He thought that they were talking to the boss behind his back, etc. After losing control of himself, he called the office, and said in a fit of anger that he was fed up with everything (this was six weeks or so before he died). He thought afterward that they would soon be giving him notice. Then he reproached himself for having jeopardized everything. He brought up these matters occasionally, but only piecemeal. It was only thanks to hindsight, after we had pieced together the things he had said, that we realized how severe his mental condition must have been. His work at the office had become somewhat inaccurate and unsatisfactory. But on the day before he disappeared, after consulting his wife he went to see his bosses, who assured him emphatically that they weren't thinking of laying him off. Those comforting words came too late; he was no longer able to believe them. He left for work on November 27, but never turned up at the office. They realized right away that he was missing and started looking for him, and came to my hotel to let me know. We spent a day and a half looking for him. The light was on in the apartment all night, and there was always somebody up, in case he came home. They found him the second day. He had apparently been dead for hours, having slashed his wrist with his penknife. We buried him on Saturday, and if the previous days were horrible, the funeral itself was beautiful. We spent a consoling hour in the rainy cemetery at Wettingen. Many friends were there despite the season and the rain; Hans's little choir sang,* Pastor Preiswerk spoke beautifully and consolingly, and it was quite clear that many people were fond of our Hans.

TO ALFRED KUBIN

Montagnola, Christmas 1935

Your roll arrived the day before yesterday, at a time when I was in need of some friendly sign, so I opened it and peeled out your sketch,† which is now hanging on my wall. Your urge to create this fine homage to our dear Stifter makes me feel even closer to you! What a beautiful, mysterious, intimate sketch! The worthy man is surrounded by the forest

---

* The choir of the choral society, to which Hans Hesse had belonged.

† Possibly an illustration for Adalbert Stifter's stories *Der Hagestolz* (1852) or *Abdias* (1853).

of his life and works, and the two gently lit figures approaching him bear with them the fragrance of strawberries and woodlands. I'm not just pleased with the sketch—I would have been delighted with anything you chose to give me—but regard it as a very special gift, which I shall absorb like a melody.

The year is almost over, and I wish the same could be said for all the problems and worries I have had this year. There are no indications that this is so, even though I have already had to contend with more than enough bad luck, disappointment, and misfortune. My life is rather messy at the moment, and I'm no longer in touch with my own work. In the last two years the new novel hasn't grown an inch, and I cannot even look at it anymore. Of course, I'm still diligent, more so than ever, in fact. I read and review hundreds of books, etc., but that's a substitute, a mere gesture. And then I wasn't feeling well all year, had gout and other ailments, felt no joie de vivre whatsoever. I also had to contend with all sorts of losses, the loss of friends either through death or acts of disloyalty, attacks on me in Germany, professional disappointments, total uncertainty about the continued existence of my publisher and the availability of my works, and finally a special blow: In November, I went to Baden on the Limmat, where I go almost every year, to bathe and, if possible, rest a bit. I didn't have much of an opportunity to rest. I had brought along too much work, and since Baden is so close to Zurich, I often had visitors, etc. I had a brother in Baden; he had been living there for many years, worked as a low-level clerical employee, had a wife and children. He was such a kind, childish person, musical, great friends with children, loved games, but he was unhappy and completely alienated in his awful career. In recent times he very much feared losing his job and seeing his family starve. He complained to me about this, and we spent an evening together: I tried to comfort him, offered some advice, promised to help out in an emergency, suggested that he be patient and keep his sense of humor. His mood eventually improved somewhat. Then I visited him again with two of my sons, who had come to Baden for the day to see me. Four days later, I was told that my brother had left home in the morning, but had failed to appear at the office. He was missing for two days, and we searched for him; he was lying in a field, with a severed artery. I buried him on the last day in November.

Actually, the absence of my brother doesn't mean that there will be a large gap in my life; he had no part in my life. But I was very shaken by the discovery that he, who had seemed so petit bourgeois, childish, and harmless, was even closer to the demons than I, and had slashed himself with his penknife when the situation became intolerable for him.

So instead of thanking you for your Stifter, I have told you all sorts of lugubrious tales. Well, that's all for now; I shall have better news some other time.

All the best for the New Year!

TO WILHELM SCHÄFER

[*January 1936*]

You sent greetings recently through Schmidtbonn,* and so I feel I should let you know about an episode that, to my mind, reflects very badly on the current state of German literature and the manners of the literati.

I mean the vociferous attacks—or rather denunciations—that Will Vesper has been launching against me over the past few months.† The ostensible reason for these attacks is that I occasionally write reviews of German books for a Swedish journal. I realize that Vesper doesn't share my opinions; there was a time when he couldn't lay hands on enough Heine for his *Ernte*,‡ but now he is virulently anti-Semitic, etc. He has started resorting to a despicable tactic: he just floods the German dailies with articles claiming that I am an émigré and have no right to call myself Swiss, etc. What is really intolerable is that his assertions are based on "facts" invented by himself, quite unabashedly so. It is obvious what he has in mind: Vesper wants people in Germany to treat me as an émigré and traitor. I also happen to know the driving force behind all of this.

I am enclosing a copy of a letter that rebuts the assertions he has made about me and corrects his falsified biographical data. Vesper has never sent me copies of his attacks—in order to lessen the likelihood of my refuting his fabrications. But the world of German letters may well feel that an outspoken fellow writer should not be treated that way. In

---

* Wilhelm Schmidtbonn, short-story writer, novelist, and playwright.

† Since November 1935, Hesse had been the target of venomous and slanderous assertions by Lily Birmer and Will Vesper in the journal *Die Neue Literatur*. Vesper criticized Hesse for writing book reviews in *Bonniers Litterära Magasin* "for Jewish money." Vesper himself had been Hesse's predecessor, but was fired for spreading National Socialist propaganda. He went on to say that, while Hesse "praised" books by Jews, Protestants, Catholics, and other authors inimical to the Third Reich, he had only critical things to say about the "new German literature" of the Third Reich.

‡ *Die Ernte aus acht Jahrhunderten deutscher Lyrik* (1906–10), an anthology of poetry in two volumes, edited by Will Vesper.

any case, there are some colleagues whom I respect, and I want to make sure they get to hear about this. Hence this importunity.

Funnily enough, their opponents—the German press in exile— accuse me of exactly the opposite.* But that campaign (using methods similar to Vesper's) is directed, not at me, but at my publisher, Fischer, whom they're out to destroy.

TO OTTO BASLER

[*January 24, 1936*]

I now find myself in a situation that I have long expected and predicted: the press in the German Reich has called me a traitor to the *Volk*, etc., etc. (a hint to officialdom that my books should finally be banned); at the same time the German-Jewish refugees are writing about me in the manner suggested by the enclosed article,† even though I have really done everything I can to help them, and have had to make quite a few sacrifices as a result. The man who wrote that piece probably knows just as well as I do that I am a Swiss citizen, not an émigré, and that it has been over twenty-four years since I last lived in Germany. He probably also knows that I have done a lot for the émigrés, especially their literary output. But, of course, when there is such strife, the facts and even truth itself become irrelevant, and the émigré press, which is determined to get rid of my publisher, has long since adopted the methods of the Nazis: they even persecute imaginary enemies with the utmost brutality, using every means at their disposal, no matter how illicit.

And now they have also gone and destroyed what I was trying to

---

* On January 11, 1936, Leopold Schwarzschild had described the publisher Gottfried Bermann Fischer as the "token Jew in the National Socialist book trade" in a periodical of the German émigrés in France, *Das neue Tage-Buch*. He claimed that there was "considerable suspicion that the Propaganda Ministry in Berlin is a silent partner" behind Fischer's efforts to set up his publishing house in Switzerland or Vienna. Whereupon Thomas Mann, Hesse, and Annette Kolb published a letter of protest in the *Neue Zürcher Zeitung*: "[Gottfried Bermann Fischer] is in the process of securing new quarters for the S. Fischer Verlag abroad, in a German-speaking country. The aforementioned article hinders these efforts by . . . making it seem . . . as if they had already broken down . . . The undersigned hereby declare that to the best of their knowledge the accusations expressed and intimated in the *Tage-Buch* article are both unjustified and harmful to the person involved." In the *Pariser Tageblatt* of January 19, 1936, Georg Bernhard printed the full text of this protest letter and then asserted in his editorial, "The Case of S. Fischer," that the Third Reich was using Thomas Mann, Hesse, and Annette Kolb as window dressing. He asserted that Hesse and Kolb were helping "to deceive the outside world" by contributing to the *Frankfurter Zeitung*, that "fig leaf of the Third Reich," and thus lending support to Dr. Goebbels: "Their position shows that they don't feel morally bound to avoid dealings with the propaganda apparatus of the Third Reich." Hesse also published an immediate rebuttal of this article, in the *Neue Zürcher Zeitung*.

† Georg Bernhard's editorial in the *Pariser Tageblatt*, January 19, 1936.

do for German literature, which is in a sorry state; I had buried myself in that work, but cannot keep it up for much longer.

This isn't particularly interesting, and doesn't surprise me in the least. But I thought I should let you know.

Bernhard's assertion that I am a contributor to the *Frankfurter Zeitung* is an utter fabrication.

Addio.

TO GEORG BERNHARD, EDITOR, "PARISER TAGEBLATT"

Montagnola near Lugano, January 24, 1936

You mentioned me and my work in an article criticizing the Fischer Verlag; you were not just disparaging, but downright nasty, and, unfortunately, your comments also distorted the facts.

I have no wish to dwell here on my work as a critic, which has been acknowledged by the presses of the German émigrés. As a contributor to *Die Neue Rundschau*, the only German journal for which I still write, I am the only critic in the entire German press who is always prepared to discuss books by Jews, etc., in a most sympathetic manner.

Just in case you haven't forgotten your obligation to the truth in the heat of the battle, I would like to point out that your remarks about me bear no relationship to the facts.

First of all, I am a Swiss citizen, not an émigré, and have lived continuously in Switzerland for the past twenty-four years.

Second, contrary to your assertion, I am not a contributor to the *Frankfurter Zeitung*. I don't know where you dug up this lie.

Occasionally, however, German papers, usually smaller ones, have published old feuilleton pieces or poems of mine. Those are reprints, and they got the texts, not from me, but from a licensing agency, which purchased the rights to these old, short pieces years ago. If, contrary to all its traditions, the *Frankfurter Zeitung* published a reprint of something by me, which I very much doubt, I was entirely unaware of the fact.

Fighting is fun, but it can have a negative effect on one's character. The world war has taught us that the communiqués of every army are riddled with lies. It would be beneath the dignity of the German émigrés to adopt those tactics. Otherwise, why keep on fighting?

Your article makes statements about me that bear no relation to the facts. I wanted to draw your attention to this matter.

TO THOMAS MANN

March 12, 1936

Thank you for your letter, which I found enjoyable and comforting. You were right to suspect that I might need something of the sort. We're good friends with J. Maass, and perhaps it was he who told you I'm not feeling well.

My three years of book reviewing have proved very disappointing. All I received for my well-intentioned and, in the end, utterly strenuous labors was a slap in the face from both sides—i.e., Germany and the émigrés. This disappointment has shown me the extent to which my activity as a sympathetic commentator on German literature was also an escape, an escape from having to be a passive onlooker on world events, and an escape from my own work, from which I have been separated over the past two years by an increasing vacuum.

I shall first cut back on my critical activity, reduce it to a minimum, in the hope that I can thus recuperate from the exhaustion and saturation brought on by excessive reading. It will be harder to resume work on my book, which has suffered such prolonged neglect. The idea of writing the book is still there; I have been thinking about it a lot, but have not felt the urge to be productive, to work on the details, and make the spiritual become visible and tangible.

I'm glad to hear that they haven't been bothering you in the Reich. If your works are banned, I shall be distressed by the thought of carrying on my little business all alone over there. But time will tell; it's still conceivable that we shall be banned together, and that would please me, although I ought not provoke that. Our work nowadays is illegal. It is in the service of causes that irritate all fronts and parties.

I think of you rather often and am glad to know that you are spending some hours each day in Egypt.* I, too, am again hoping for a journey to the East. Without that, it would be hard to put up with this soulless world.

---

* Mann was working on the third volume of his Joseph tetrology, *Joseph in Egypt*.

TO THE MARTIN BODMER FOUNDATION

Montagnola, March 29, 1936

Dear Gentlemen,

Today, on this beautiful Sunday morning in spring, I received a kind letter from Herr Martin Bodmer with the surprising news that I have been awarded the Gottfried Keller Prize.*

This unexpected news reaches me at a time when I am sorely tried by the enormous crisis confronting German literature, and I am therefore doubly pleased to receive this award.

Although I tend to view my literary achievement quite skeptically (my character is, on the whole, more moral and religious than artistic), I feel that there is at least one quality of mine that meets the requirements and objectives of your foundation: Ever since childhood, my Swiss identity has been closely linked to my being German in linguistic and cultural terms. Grandson of a Swiss-French woman, son of a Balt who became a citizen in Basel around 1880, I heard, learned, and spoke in my childhood the Baltic German of my father and also the dialects of Basel and Swabia.

Gentlemen, I should like to convey to you my heartfelt thanks for the support, honor, and joy that the award of this prize has brought with it.

With an expression of sincere appreciation, yours

TO ALFRED KUBIN

[September 1936]

Thanks for your letter. I had just arrived back from what I consider a long journey; I was way up in northern Germany, where I consulted my ophthalmologist again and spent fourteen days undergoing treatment. There is nobody else doing these treatments, and he is seventy-five years old and can no longer meet me someplace along the way, as he formerly did.

Officialdom treats me the same way it treats you, with hostility, interference, and suppression. On several occasions they were all set on banning my books, but up to now the head person at my publishers

---

* The Martin Bodmer Foundation in Zurich awarded Hesse the Gottfried Keller Prize (6,000 francs) on March 28, 1936. It was the first literary prize Hesse had received since 1904, when he was awarded the Viennese Bauernfeld Prize for *Peter Camenzind*.

has prevented this from actually happening. The publisher, which was once a leading house in the Reich, has dwindled in size and is now quite impoverished.

I have just sent you a short essay* about Green; I mailed the same essay to you once before, but it must have got lost. Please return it (no big hurry).

My wife has read Green's book *Minuit* and likes it a lot; I no longer read anything in foreign languages and shall wait until a translation appears.

You got my little garden poem;† I wrote it for my sister in the summer of 1935; I gave it to Dr. Bermann, Fischer's son-in-law, to help him out a bit, since he's setting up a new publishing house in Vienna; apart from that, I'm still bound by contract to the old publisher in Berlin.

I want to publish a little volume of new poems‡ there next year. That is all I have by way of new material. After completing *The Journey to the East*, I started fiddling around with a new work, and this has been going on for years now; every now and then I add a short passage. [. . .]

Caro amico, the journey through Germany was less than gay; they are busy rooting out more and more of the things that people like us love and cannot live without. However, some of the values we worked for and upheld in our lives will survive this whole mess, and they will act as a narrow bridge connecting the humanity of tomorrow with the world that preceded us. This is our one task, and it is certainly sufficient.

TO FRIEDRICH EMIL WELTI

[*September 1936*]

A very beautiful book has just come out, which I would like to recommend to you, if you haven't seen it already: *The Letters of Jacob Burckhardt* in a Kröner paperback edition. I have already read the editor's biographical foreword,§ which is affectionate but poorly written, and a good portion of the letters. I had seen some of them before, but when arranged chronologically in this manner, they serve as a substitute for a biography, and what an exquisite substitute it is! As I read, I

---

* About Julien Green's novel *Le Visionnaire*.
† *Stunden im Garten*.
‡ *Neue Gedichte* (Berlin, 1937).
§ With a biographical sketch by Fr. Kaphahn (1935).

realize once again just how pervasive the spirit of Burckhardt was in Basel around 1900, while I was living there; I used to socialize with many of his disciples, Wölfflin, R. Wackernagel, Haller, and others.

Even though I was more strongly influenced by Nietzsche at that stage, I had already read *The Civilization of the Renaissance* with great enthusiasm in Tübingen, and then, gradually, with the appearance of *Meditations* and the cultural history of Greece, I realized how much I had profited from Burckhardt's mind and vision. I have learned more from him than from any other historian.

May things go well for you, despite the evil times!

TO VICTOR WITTKOWSKI

[January 16, 1937]

Thanks for your letter. I enjoyed some of your poems (the "dedications" are the only things I might have advised you to leave out), and I'm sorry I no longer have the opportunity to write a few favorable lines about it anywhere. For years, I have been doing these "summarizing reviews," as you call them, and the young writers used to court me, then boo if I didn't find their books altogether delightful. The years since 1933 have been difficult, and that kind of work has completely ruined my eyes and made me neglect my own writing. On average, I earned around one franc for a full day's work, only to be branded in Germany as a "traitor to the *Volk*" who had accepted "Jewish pay"—not an unexpected charge—and I have also been libeled by the émigrés and the Jews, even though I risked my neck for their authors and publishers. At the top of the list were people like Bernhard in Paris and Schwarzschild in Prague. The experience has taught me a lot, and I don't have any regrets. But it would have been suicidal of me to keep up that activity.

Yes, my experience with German reviews is similar to yours. Previously, when a book of mine appeared, there would be reviews in over a hundred German papers, nowadays only in three or four.

I shall try to devote my remaining energy to *The Glass Bead Game*. It gets a bit longer each year.

For me, the most attractive poems were those in which you conjure up your home territory, the cathedral, Clerics' Pond, etc.

That's enough, Christmas and the New Year have put me hundreds of letters in arrears.

TO OTTO KORRADI

[*December 24, 1937*]

I was glad to get the books,* once again many thanks. The first book we are going to read in the new year is Buchwald's *Schiller*. At the moment we are reading the beautiful volume by Strowski on the "French mind."†

In your recent letter, you inquired about my interest in Chinese culture. That goes back quite far. But before Wilhelm's first Chinese editions started appearing, I was far more interested in India than in China. Since then—i.e., 1911 or 1912—I have often sought out the ancient Chinese (just in translation, of course). You can spot traces of that preoccupation in many of my earlier essays and books—e.g., in "The Way to Art,"‡ the fairy tales, and elsewhere. I am thinking about devising a Chinese "Life," which would appear after the Indian one (I mean the fictional "Lives" of Josef Knecht).§ China enters into *The Glass Bead Game* (*Die Neue Rundschau*, December 1933)‖ through the long quotation from Lü Bu We.** Moreover, there is a remarkably worthwhile and insightful book by a contemporary Chinese woman about the essence and distinctiveness of Chinese culture; the author is Lin Yutang, and it was published by the Deutsche Verlagsanstalt, Stuttgart.

Do you know Ernst Wiechert's moving essay "Building a Wall Around Us"? It has just been published in a limited de luxe edition by the Werkstatt für Buchdruck in Mainz. Wiechert spent a couple of hours with me in the fall, along with the physiognomist Picard, with whom I am on friendly terms. We are having beautiful sunny days, thanks be to God. The only snow to be seen is at around 1,400 meters and above, apart from a few shady slopes. We are celebrating Christmas this evening. A friend from Berlin†† is here with us for a visit. She is very young, and has completed a good dissertation on Novalis this year; some

---

* Hesse had asked Korradi (possibly in exchange for a manuscript of a poem with Hesse's own illustrations) for three books which had just appeared in Germany: Reinhard Buchwald, *Schiller*; Daniel Chodowiecki, *Von Berlin nach Danzig*; and Ernst Hello, *Abglanz*.

† Fortunat Strowski, *Vom Wesen des französischen Geistes* (1937).

‡ The fairy tale "Der Dichter" or "Weg zur Kunst" was written in 1913.

§ The plan was never carried out. In the preliminary sketches for *The Glass Bead Game*, however, there is mention of a learned article by Josef Knecht, "Some Hypotheses about the Pre-Confucian Commentaries on the I Ching," which is said to have appeared in print.

‖ "The Attempt at a Comprehensible Historical Introduction," which had just been published separately.

** *Frühling und Herbst des Lü Bu We*, translated by Richard Wilhelm (1929).

†† The philologist and publicist Anni Carlsson.

time ago she wrote the supplementary pages for the second edition of Ball's book about me. Gunter Böhmer, the artist, is coming tomorrow with his mother; and then, the day after tomorrow, Emmy, the widow of Hugo Ball. With very best wishes for the New Year

TO MARTIN BUBER

[*Early February 1938*]

I have been told you're probably in Jerusalem already, so that is where I shall send best wishes for your sixtieth birthday.* My first wish is that you, and also your wife, have managed to retain the flexibility and energy that I so often admired. My second wish is that you are enjoying your work and that your appetite for life and work is being whetted anew. I imagine that the existence there of a community and the need for hands-on, constructive work must be a source of strength and support, regardless of what you have had to endure. Whereas I often feel that I lack a sense of community and have nothing on which to lavish my efforts, worries, and love. All I have is a vague, far-flung diaspora, consisting of people who, like me, have no fixed abode amid the present upheavals; we have only a dim feeling that we are here to transmit at least some portion of the tradition to a future which is not yet visible.

Although I can only form a very incomplete picture of your present surroundings and current work, my thoughts and wishes are with you; my wife and I often think of you.

TO OTTO BASLER

March 11, 1938

Thanks for your letter. I read about the new attack on Thomas Mann by Krieck† in the newspaper; I am not prepared to read the essay, life is too short for that. I am quite sure that it's awful. Something happened recently which I found far worse: Wilhelm Schäfer, who is now seventy,

---

* Buber, the writer and philosopher of religion, was appointed professor of social philosophy at the Hebrew University in Jerusalem in 1938 and left Germany in March of that year.

† The racist anthropologist Ernst Krieck, professor at the universities of Frankfurt and Heidelberg, who, in an article in his journal *Volk im Werden*, "Death Throes: A Final Word about Thomas Mann," had called Mann a senile, destructive liar who would have to be "cleared out" of Germany.

couldn't resist putting some nasty comments about Mann and the Nobel Prize into a speech of his, which was actually very beautiful otherwise. When one sees a decent writer—a decent and responsible seventy-year-old like Schäfer—making a gaffe like that, one realizes the impact that a diabolical leadership can have on the morality of an entire people.

Robert Walser's* sister wrote to me yesterday. He is really in need of help, since there is a danger he might have to enter the poorhouse. If you happen to know of anybody who might be willing to make a donation, tell them about the situation. We would like to ask the Writers' Club for a donation in his honor. Although Switzerland has, for once, produced a writer who could really write German, we have to send the plate around to help him eke out a very frugal existence, in third-class institutions for the most part! The cost of the bombs dropped by a single plane in one sortie in Spain is probably greater than the sum needed here. [. . .]

You're right about Kassner's† book. He isn't easy to read (which, by the way, is also true of Picard), but he is not at all a professor. He is one of the few sages of this era who write in German. However, he is esoteric, and his language is platonic.

Addio, please consider the enclosure‡ a belated Easter greeting, yours

TO THE COMMISSIONERS OF THE ALIEN POLICE

April 28, 1938

Please permit me to put in a word for my esteemed colleague Albert Ehrenstein.§ He was deported from the canton of Ticino, and his only crime is that he has an Austrian passport.

Although I realize that the Alien Police has the task of protecting

---

* Swiss author, who published three novels, including *Jakob von Gunten* (English translation by Christopher Middleton; New York: Vintage, 1983), and a large number of short prose pieces before entering an asylum in Waldau, near Bern, on January 25, 1929. Three selections from his shorter works have appeared in English: *Selected Stories*, trans. Christopher Middleton (1982), *Robert Walser Rediscovered: Stories, Fairy Tale Plays and Critical Responses*, ed. Mark Harman, trans. Walter Arndt (1985), and *Masquerade and Other Stories*, trans Susan Bernofsky (1990).

† Rudolf Kassner, philosopher and essayist. Hesse had championed his writings in several reviews (the first appeared as early as 1900). Hesse wrote on November 28, 1937, in the Basel newspaper *National-Zeitung* that Max Picard and Kassner, "who often says the exact opposite, but corroborates him just as often, are the two really genuine physiognomists nowadays, at least in the German-speaking world."

‡ A small watercolor by Hesse.

§ An Expressionist poet.

Switzerland against an influx of foreigners, I cannot understand why the lower echelons often take brutal measures against individuals who have earned a reputation in the arts or sciences, devote themselves quietly to their work, and are not a burden to anybody.

Rather than feeling ashamed or threatened, Switzerland ought to feel honored that it is being sought out as a refuge by a highly gifted artist such as Albert Ehrenstein, at a time when the political world has gone berserk. There is absolutely no reason to think that the further presence in Switzerland of a man such as Ehrenstein can cause the country the slightest harm. We Swiss artists and intellectuals are becoming more and more ashamed of the raw force that our authorities and police forces are employing against colleagues whom we greatly admire.

Herr Ehrenstein, who was an Austrian citizen until the invasion of Austria, is seeking to become a Czech citizen, but the formalities will last another couple of months. I would like to lend my most heartfelt support to his request that he at least be allowed to stay in Switzerland until then.

TO GEORG REINHART

Montagnola, May 28 [1938]

Thank you for your letter. I am enclosing Dr. Schäffer's* letter, which I found very sad.

Unfortunately, your assumption that there might be charitable institutions for dealing with such cases is mistaken. There are thousands of similar cases, and I know of some that are just as complicated as your protégé's. But there are simply no organizations capable of providing assistance. Occasionally, in desperate cases, somebody manages to rustle up a Nansen passport for some poor unfortunate by, say, getting the League of Nations involved, that's all.

Dr. Schäffer is afraid he might be arrested by the Gestapo while in Vienna, but that's probably an exaggeration. Nobody is entirely safe, of course, but I do know quite a number of authors living in Austria who have greater reason for such fears yet can move around without hindrance.

But the other complaints of my poor colleague are entirely justified.

---

* Dr. Emil Schäffer, author of *Habsburger schreiben Briefe* and a monograph on Hermann Hubacher, the Swiss sculptor and friend of Hesse's.

I know some people living under similar conditions—a lot worse, actually, since they have nobody to support them; people who have been living in a country for months without any papers or indeed anything much to eat, then are deported and have to start the whole process all over again on the far side of the border; emigrants who have been moving back and forth between Prague and Barcelona since 1933, with long intervals in prison—but those are all younger people, who can if necessary endure such an adventurous and dangerous life. For older people like Schäffer, the situation is almost hopeless. If he were a friend of mine, I could only say something along these lines: "Like so many others, you'll have to reconcile yourself to the hopelessness of your situation; just wait stoically and see what happens when your passport expires; let yourself be shoved across the border, then sent back by the police over there. Entrust your fate to states that have gone crazy, and be happy that, for the moment at least, there is a good spirit, a patron, who is keeping you from starving. Resist suicide until the situation has become absolutely unbearable; there will always be time enough for that."

Although that's an abominable thing to have to say, it's absolutely true. Somebody who has good connections with the Swiss or some other embassy in Hungary could mention Herr Schäffer to them, so that they might give him some advice and help him out in an emergency. But there is no normal, legal channel for providing help.

There are dozens of people like that living in Switzerland at the moment. Many are fellow writers, some quite famous, who have been notified that they have to leave Switzerland within a brief period. Their only crime is that they were Austrians, with good reasons for not wanting—or not being in a position—to exchange their Austrian passports for a passport of the German Reich. Our Alien Police don't need to swear an oath to Hitler; they could hardly serve his interests more diligently than they do now. I have been able to ease this particular burden for a number of people by making representations to the Alien Police and by vouching for the political and moral reliability of the endangered refugees. Unfortunately, I don't have any contacts in those countries whose laws and bureaucracy your protégé is subject to. In Vienna, for instance, there is a recent book of mine lying in a publishing house which has been expropriated by the Nazis, and so I no longer own the book. The same thing has happened to all of my German (Berlin) income from previous books; it's now in the hands of the Third Reich or some other gang of thieves. That's what government and politics amount to nowadays.

And everything one says about the Nazis and the fascists applies just as much to Stalin and his empire. Recently, I had to ask Romain Rolland to try to approach Stalin about a group of people, some are very well known, who were hauled off a year ago by the secret police. He said in a resigned tone that he himself had close friends living in Russia who had disappeared in that manner, and that he had sent Stalin numerous letters and telegrams, but never received a single reply. There are no longer any contacts between the state and the intellectuals, in every camp. [. . .]

At the moment, when not completely preoccupied with my own worries, I am trying to get some close friends of ours out of Austria; some of them are in real danger. It's slow and tough going, a bit like wading in lime, because we have to talk to one another in a roundabout way, using recondite allusions. However, we are expecting a visit from one of those people and hope to help her some more. A wonderful young woman friend of mine, whose passport is about to run out, is in Sweden looking desperately for a man willing to go through with a fictitious marriage, in exchange for a financial consideration, to enable her to become a Swede; of course, all the applicants are swindlers. What a crazy world our Christian West has become!

TO KLAUS MANN*

[*July 21, 1938*]

I was delighted to get your letter. Thank you very much.

There aren't any bombs exploding here yet, but I feel almost as absorbed in the war as I was in 1916–19 while working for the POWs. I'm worried now about the fate of the refugees and émigrés and spend most of my time working for them. I realize that all such efforts are futile, but I felt nevertheless that I had to become active again, largely because of my wife, who comes from Austria and whose close relatives and friends were all still there. There are refugees in our house, sitting at the typewriters, writing curricula vitae, petitions for entry permits, petitions to the Alien Police. In other words, I'm waging yet another paper war, and it's no prettier this time around. Last time, I set up and edited a small review for the POWs and supplied them with reading material, music, musical instruments, books for students, etc. Once, in a little package intended for a POW library in France, I enclosed a small, cheap edition of *The Golden Pot* by Hoffmann,† only to get bawled

* Son of Thomas Mann; drama critic and writer.
† E. T. A. Hoffmann.

out by the person who received it. He wrote saying that German prisoners and fighting men were not willing to waste their time on such pathetic, romantic stuff from the era of their great-grandparents. They were demanding reading matter that would keep them in touch with contemporary life in its richness and authenticity, etc.—e.g., works by Rudolf Herzog.*

The story about Hölderlin, Mörike, and Waiblinger,† which you read in Barcelona, is quite old; I wrote it circa 1913.

I hope we get to see each other again.

TO GEORG REINHART

[*February 1939*]

Dear Herr Reinhart, my dear friend,

I was so happy to get your kind letter! I have to laugh at your comments about my poem.‡ You find it pessimistic, but I have just received a long letter about the same poem from Morgenthaler, who says: "What an astonishing and unexpectedly optimistic ending! The most obvious thing would have been to hurl accusations at the heavens and curse the God who tolerates such abominations. But the image of the God that you portray is a thousand times more beautiful, comforting, and virtuous—I shall bring the poem with me when I report for duty. It should make the most difficult burden easier to bear."

Thus Morgenthaler. A poem can affect people very differently. I find that perfectly all right. Personally, I never conceived of the demiurges in either pessimistic or optimistic terms. What I had in mind was more along the lines of Indian mythology, according to which Vishnu creates the world as part of a game, or while he is asleep; then, in four stages, the young, blossoming, reverential world descends from one era to the next, until it reaches a final state of decadence; Shiva is then called upon to smash it to bits—and lying somewhere is wonderful Vishnu, all graceful and smiling; the beginnings of the new world, which he has playfully conjured up and created, once again seem charming and delightful. [. . .]

The postmark on many of my letters is deceptive. A friend of mine in Zurich handles most of my mail, buys the stamps, which I cannot afford, and, if necessary, has copies made of letters, etc.

---

* Author of patriotic novels.

† "Im Presselschen Gartenhaus" ("In the Garden House at Pressels"), a story set in Tübingen in the 1820s (*WA* 4:387ff).

‡ "Nachtgedanken" ("Night Thoughts") (*Gedichte*, pp. 665–66).

TO ROSA MUGGLI

[*ca. March 5, 1939*]

Thanks a lot for your very interesting letter and also for the commission:* I started copying the manuscript soon after the first time you mentioned it in a letter, and I think I shall be able to send it to you soon—that is, about ten days from now. [. . .]

I am pleased to see you take such loving interest in my books. But you will make sure that this doesn't degenerate into a personality cult, won't you? A certain awe for literature, and thus also for the poet, is necessary for the higher life—nowadays there are few people who recognize this and act accordingly. But beauty and the intellect form a unity, and it's well nigh impossible for a poet to express a thought that has not yet been articulated. He draws on treasures which are thousands of years old, not always intentionally, unconsciously as well. Just recently, my wife, who loves to read Greek, came across two verses by the Greek thinker Empedocles, five hundred years before Christ, which state almost verbatim something I wrote about in several verses (in the poem "All Deaths").† Since then that same idea has been expressed thousands of times, then forgotten again, and it will recur after we have departed. [. . .]

TO ERNST MORGENTHALER

[*August 1939*]

My dear friend,

Your son is quite right. Why don't we learn how to meditate?

Here is the difficulty: We Westerners have problems with the art of meditation, which is so highly developed in Indian yoga, and in China, Japan, etc., not only due to the way we are and our bad education but also because the Asian models consist of sequences of images and ideas which we cannot understand or assimilate. The psychologist C. G. Jung knows a lot about this.

The enclosed little pictures, which I am presenting to you as a gift, were inspired by the universe of Chinese meditation. They are from a recently published book, *The Great Liberation*‡ by Suzuki, but it's easier

* An illustrated manuscript version of the fairy tale "Piktor's Metamorphoses."
† "Alle Tode" (*Gedichte*, p. 457).
‡ An introduction to Zen Buddhism, with a preface by C. G. Jung (1939).

if I enclose the prospectus of the book. I would ask you to return it eventually.

I have sent Ninon away for eight days; she was so tired and worn out with worries. And, unfortunately, some construction will be going on afterward. We are getting some repairs done, and also rectifying a few mistakes made when the house was built; that will take ages.

TO OTTO BASLER

[*October 19, 1939*]

[. . .] The outbreak of war wasn't exactly unexpected. If Hitler had succeeded in capturing Danzig and the Polish Corridor without anybody saying a word, that would have been worse than war. I had half feared this might happen, and many people in Germany thought so, too.

I think I told you ages ago that I believe that a number of military catastrophes—the world war was the first in a series—will be necessary before this untenable situation collapses and is liquidated. Although it's terrible to have to live through this, it isn't at all surprising.

I am one of those elderly egotists who secretly hope they will be dead by the time the grenades start bursting in their rooms. But on second thought, if at all possible I first want to finish Josef Knecht.*

We receive a lot of letters by military post; there was a nice one the day before yesterday from Morgenthaler. My eldest son, in the home guard, is about to go on a longish furlough.

TO MAX HERRMANN-NEISSE

December 1939

Your letter with the very welcome poems arrived recently, with only a slight delay. I would like to thank you; I enjoyed reading something of yours again and discovering how you're faring.†

The last few months have been quite hectic and unsettling, because we were getting some quite necessary construction done, which took a lot out of my wife, but it's almost finished now. The war has, of course, left its mark on us too, in several ways. My wife had close relatives and

---

* *The Glass Bead Game.*

† Since September 1933, the writer Max Herrmann-Neisse had been living with his wife in voluntary exile in London.

some old friends living in Poland and hasn't heard yet whether any of them have survived; we are particularly worried about friends of hers in Prague who haven't managed to get out yet. And my three sons are in the Swiss Army and have been on active duty since the outbreak of war. I'm not all that interested in world events. Old people don't care very much anymore how the elements no longer capable of life get eliminated, even if that process is quite diabolical. I firmly believe that man is endowed with a certain sense of stability, and it seems to me that he awakes from every abomination with a bad conscience, and so each corrupt period gives rise to a new yearning for meaning and order—but I do not believe that I shall live to experience the next upward motion after this present downward slide. I'm old and tired.

Our region is very quiet and there is very little sign of the war, as opposed to the situation in German Switzerland. And finally, at the very end of a rainy year, we are having a spell of beautiful, steady weather and days of gentle sunshine. Pictorially, the colors in our landscape are most beautiful in winter, especially before the first snow has fallen. Everything is suffused in a soft, intense glow, and then at twilight, when the mountains seem to light up from within, the spectacle culminates in an intimate festival of light, which always seems like a silent, smiling protest of the friendly, enduring, motherly powers against the antics of world history.

TO ROLF SCHOTT

[*December 26, 1939*]

Thanks for your letter! Your expression of devotion to me makes me feel ashamed; I am an old and exhausted man, sitting at a table littered with mail, and I sometimes find it comforting to think that death will allow me to slip out of a role that has become merely routine and no longer suits me. Those of us who have acquired fame are recipients of much love and respect, and I have begun to realize that this show of affection is worthwhile and genuine and becomes problematic only when it degenerates into a personality cult; the love is actually intended for a far worthier object. When a person nowadays reveres a writer, poet, or musician, he is really admiring—whether consciously or not—every accomplishment of human culture which the poet has inherited and just happens to represent. Of course, as everybody knows, nowadays those cultural pursuits are controversial and imperiled. So if you have to play the role of somebody who has accidentally acquired fame, you have to act like a bishop, let people kiss your hand, and then make sure that the intended offering is forwarded to the right address.

I'm a little worried that I shan't ever finish my novel. I have spent many years weaving something which is very much a late work. I have completed the most important part, which, even as a fragment, would indicate clearly what I had in mind. But the odds of my completing the entire work are not that great. I have not been sufficiently diligent; before taking each small step, I tried to make sure that my ideas were mature enough and that I had calmed down sufficiently—but, meanwhile, old age and the onset of senility have caught up with me, and the question now is not whether I am old, intelligent, and ripe enough to complete the missing parts, but whether I have sufficient energy, drive, and willpower to tide me over the long interruptions and inevitable doldrums. I haven't touched it for months. The news of the day saps whatever I have by way of energy, receptivity, and concentration, not because of the newspapers, which I seldom read, but because of the mail spread out every day on my table, with tales of war, death, misery, homelessness, injustice, violence, the fate of all the refugees and other victims. I pass on news of families and friends, try to help find missing persons, struggle with our Alien Police, usually in vain, and then I also have worries of my own. Financially, I'm dependent on my Berlin publisher, but separating us is a frontier with barbed wire—namely, currency barriers—I have three sons serving in the Swiss Army, and so forth.

Well, today, as you can see, I am an old egotist in a foul mood and don't deserve the beautiful sunlight streaking down over my shoulder from the Generoso. I could wait, but the situation would hardly get any better tomorrow or later on; it's impossible to combat old age as an enemy or even to cause it any embarrassment; it is burying us like a landslide, choking us like a slow creeping gas. [. . .]

TO HIS SON MARTIN

[April 1940]

[. . .] I am enclosing the last version of the new poem.* Yes, it is comical. While everyone is out in the trenches and bunkers, etc., preparing to blow the world around us to smithereens, I have been spending entire days preparing a new version of this small poem. Initially, it had four verses and now it has only three; I hope it has become simpler and

---

* The last version (April 3, 1940) of "Flötenspiel" ("Flute Music") (*Gedichte*, p. 673).

better, without losing anything of substance. I was never happy with the fourth line of the first verse, and whenever I had to copy the poem out for friends, I tested every line and word in it to help me decide what was dispensable and what wasn't.

Nine-tenths of my readers wouldn't notice which version of the poem is in front of them. At best I shall get about ten francs from the newspaper that publishes it, regardless of which version I submit. This sort of pastime is quite ridiculous. It's funny, comical, a bit crazy really, and people start asking themselves: Why is the poet so worried about a couple of verses and why does he waste his time in that manner?

One possible response: In the first place, the poet's efforts are probably worthless, since it's scarcely likely that he has just written one of the very few poems that will be remembered one hundred or five hundred years from now. Nevertheless, this comical individual has just done something that is better, less harmful, and more desirable than the activities in which most people are currently engaged. He wrote some verse, threaded words together, but didn't shoot at anybody, blow up anything, spread gas, manufacture ammunition, sink ships, etc., etc.

Another possible reply: Even when surrounded by a world that may well be destroyed tomorrow, the poet continues to cull little phrases, select and arrange them; the anemones, primroses, and other flowers growing everywhere in the meadows now do exactly the same thing. In a world that may soon be covered in poison gas, they are carefully shaping their leaves and calyxes, with five or four or seven little petals, even or ridged, everything quite precise, and as pretty as can be.

TO WOLFGANG HAUSSMANN

[*1940*]

Thanks for your kind letter from Sedrun! I never received the letter you mention having written last year.

I was pleased to hear about you and your family. For me, the world you have evoked has receded into the very distant past; I don't think it's likely I shall be able to go to Stuttgart again.

It was still peacetime when I got to know your father;* we were both working on *März*. It was through him that I met the Rosenfelds,†

---

* Conrad Haussmann, a former contributor to the journal *März*.

† The family of Otto Rosenfeld, a businessman, who lived close to the Haussmanns in the Hohenzollernstrasse in Stuttgart. The correspondence between Hesse and Otto Rosenfeld was never found.

with whom I became friends; we used occasionally to play billiards there together.

My life ever since has by no means been peaceful; I feel that there has been a war in progress since 1914, and very few of my colleagues and former intellectual peers have really passed that test, with the exception of Romain Rolland, whom I first got to know in 1914, and Thomas Mann, who joined us after the war. I lived alone for about twelve years, then got married again; nowadays life isn't exactly easy—the war years count twice, so I have become an old man, and no longer travel, take vacations, socialize, etc. As for the world war, I awoke from all sorts of soft illusions in 1914 and since then I see nothing but war in the world, and so I do not attach very much importance to it, since it's wrong to assume that gunpowder, poison gases, and generals are intellectual powerhouses, even though they can get up to a lot of mischief. In a world torn apart by constant wars, it has become harder and harder to ensure that one has some tranquillity and love in one's heart and occasionally transmits some of that through one's art, yet one must keep on trying.

Greetings to your dear esteemed mother, to your brother Robert, and fond regards to you yourself

TO ERNST MORGENTHALER

Montagnola, October 25, 1940

My dear friend,

[. . .] I believe that the present erosion of moral standards in governmental and political affairs cannot be halted, but am convinced that this hell will not last forever, and that the political behavior of the people and the conduct of nations will once again become tolerably humane. I don't think any nation or constitution in the world is so secure that it cannot be overturned and taken by force. The inferno of the totalitarian state is a phase in the decline of nationalism and will not last forever, but before it disintegrates, it will almost completely destroy the things that we believe in, which make our lives worth living. At times like this it is a good idea to have some direct connection in one's own life with those who are being persecuted and are suffering, such as having a Jewish wife, so that one doesn't go blindly past the abominations, but sees them with one's own eyes; the people who survive that experience will prove useful at a later date.

A few months ago the Russians moved into my wife's homeland.*
A cousin of hers, who wanted to move into that area from Romania
because he preferred to become Russian rather than stay Romanian,
was killed by the Romanians on his way there. Although the occupation
began months ago, my wife's only sister wasn't able to send us a letter
or card until a few days ago; there is no hope of her getting a passport
so she can go abroad and see her sister again. We finally received a
card, which the Russians must have let through; the language was exceedingly diplomatic, each word chosen with great care, and every
statement was couched neutrally—like a cautious letter smuggled out
of a German concentration camp.

[. . .] In the last few weeks my wife has had an old wish fulfilled;
we came across a woman philologist, whom we invited to spend some
time with us, and for two hours a day she reads Aeschylus with Ninon
and reviews grammar. She has been here now for three or four weeks
or so, a pleasant guest.

Regards to Sasha; I often think of her when I look at the shoots of
a plant on the balcony of my studio. I remember putting some sprigs of
that plant in my purse years ago at your house; now the oldest shoot is
about two meters tall.

[January 1941]

I really have to tell you and Sasha about the plant you gave me
three years ago at Easter; I took three sprigs with me in my purse and
planted them in a pot here. Those three yielded a hundred or so little
plants, and I have given some away to acquaintances. But only one of
these plants—it's one of the oldest and probably one of the three orig-
inals—has developed fully. It grew quickly, and is now 265 centimeters
tall, without taking into account the bends and curves in its stem, which
is tied in several places to a stick. The stem, which is about the thickness
of a child's finger, is wooden, very hard, and bare until it reaches two-
thirds of its height, which is where those little branches begin, organized
around the stem. The new little blossoms are always forming at their
tips, then falling off and developing into new plants down below. Now
it has entered a new and probably final stage in its development: Over
the last few weeks, an umbel has formed at the very top, a little above
the uppermost branches; it consists of four little bundles of six to ten
pretty little calyciflorae, the majority of them are still buds, the ones
that have opened up are cup-shaped and red, a wonderfully bright red.

---

* Czernowitz in Bukovina, the easternmost tip of the former Austro-Hungarian Empire.

It may be one of those plants that blossom only once in their lives and then die; in any case, I wanted to tell you about these things, so you know how your gift has fared.

There are some strange things growing on earth. Recently I found out about the final hours of a friend of mine* whom I had been worrying about for some time and whose burdens I had often shared prior to that. He was Jewish, well off, came from the Sudetenland. He went off to war in 1914 as a fancy Austrian lieutenant, was captured, spent years in Siberia, returned to Bohemia on foot, subsequently took over his father's small factory. His workers regarded him as a comrade; some were on a first-name basis with him. He remained a bachelor for a very long time, was knowledgeable about Indian literature and the Kabbalah. We corresponded for years; he visited us here a number of times, once with a lady whom he married shortly afterward. He was hardly married when he began to see that the Germans would take over the Sudetenland, so he left his hometown and withdrew to Prague. The area did indeed become German, but he didn't get a penny for his factory. His lifestyle in Prague was elegant at first, then more and more modest, and finally he was in total poverty, and since Prague was in the hands of the Germans, he fought tenaciously, while remaining cool and patient nonetheless, to escape, to obtain an entry permit for some country. The most desirable countries were already ruled out; either they were hermetically sealed off, like ours, or they demanded huge bribes for a visa; he tried Peru, Bolivia, Shanghai, etc., etc., but to no avail. Finally, about six months ago, he boarded a ship filled with Jewish refugees, which was supposed to travel down the Danube through Romania to Palestine. I received the few last lines from him directly, asking me to do a few things, and I did whatever was possible. That was the last thing we received, and I have just heard the rest of his story. The ship arrived in Haifa all right, but the passengers were not allowed to disembark and were held in police custody. And one day they were attacked by planes, and the misery of the hundreds of half-starving people came to an end. Apparently, they identified the body of his wife, but never found that of my friend.

We were both in bed for a while with a cold, but now I can get up every day for a little.

---

* Walter Weiss (no other information available).

TO JOACHIM MAASS*

[*End of July 1941*]

I should have written to you long ago and also to our friend Bermann, but I can't hold anything in my fingers, which are swollen and so incapacitated that all sorts of things—books, garden tools, occasionally even a spoon—are constantly dropping out of my hands. You will have to be patient with me.

Ninon was anxious to find out more about my condition, and my physician wanted to cover himself, so I spent a few days in the cantonal hospital in Zurich, where they examined me for traces of the favorite terminal ailments of elderly gentlemen. They must have taken at least twenty blood samples; I had to spend whole mornings lying with a tube in my stomach. I ended up paying almost four hundred francs for those three days. Ninon was quite happy, since they hadn't found cancer or anything like that. I found those few days tough going. Contemporary medicine is not even remotely capable of detecting early signs of such fatal illnesses. It is no more reliable than we ourselves can be—that is, if a person has a delicate, potent, well-developed sensibility. I had not been at all curious or worried, and found the bustling factorylike atmosphere in the hospital miserable. I was actually ashamed that I had gritted my teeth and obeyed the doctor and Ninon. Naturally enough, the elderly Tolstoy came to mind, the way he escaped from his house, the doctor, and his wife's caresses, etc., so that rather than end his days amid the machinery of health care, he might die in the woods or on the road.

Actually, those learned experts merely came up with the following: a few irregularities in blood composition, considerable weight loss, and, finally, the excruciating rheumatism in the joints that I have had to endure for the past nine months; they had little to say about the latter, and now I'm alone again with my illness. The latest news is that I have chosen a treatment consisting of injections with the poison from bee stings, and have had four injections, no effect yet.

Suhrkamp has written to me again after months of silence. He is depressed, conditions in the business are getting worse. Readers also tell me that a number of my books aren't available anywhere.

I have not heard anything from [Martin] Beheim-Schwarzbach† for three months or so. His books are no longer available; I was able to procure a few for him, but that is no longer possible.

---

* Journalist and writer; emigrated to the United States in 1933.
† Author of novels, short stories, and poetry.

Please give my greetings to the Bermanns, and pass on the following: I received Tutti's vellum manuscript all right and immediately wrote a thank-you letter. Frau Fischer wrote to me from St. Monika, and I have also heard from Thomas Mann.

I stopped reading the news about the war quite some time ago. Ninon's sister is in Czernowitz; she and her husband* managed to survive, but they are hungry and don't have a job, money, or prospects of either.

Suhrkamp has published a very beautiful book: *Rings of Glass* by Luise Rinser.†

Unfortunately, I didn't receive the book on Schubert by Annette Kolb,‡ but I have seen some advertisements for it. My fingers are letting me down—as you can see from the mistakes. Lots of greetings from Ninon, we often think of you!

TO MAX WASSMER§

Baden, November 12, 1941

My dear friend Wassmer,

I'm writing today about an important matter and would like to ask for your help. We have been worrying for ages about my wife's only sister, whose life and liberty are currently at great risk. She is living in her homeland, Cernauti (formerly Cernowicz). She survived the Russian invasion, then the war and the recapture of that region by the Romanians, but now she is in danger every day because of the pogroms, deportation, concentration camps, etc. Finally, after much strenuous effort, we managed to get them a Cuban visa. The visas, made out for Dr. Heinz Kehlmann and Frau Lilly Kehlmann, both of Cernauti, are supposed to arrive today or tomorrow at the Cuban Consulate in Bern. When my wife receives the official written notification from the Consulate, she will forward it to you immediately. And I would entreat you, my dear friend, to help us out at this juncture. Once you have received that notification, could you bring it to the Confederate Alien Police in Bern and ask for a transit visa for the Kehlmanns? They need a permit to travel through Switzerland on the way to Cuba, and also permission to spend one month in Switzerland, for the following reason:

---

* Lilly and Heinz Kehlmann.
† Luise Rinser's first book (1941). Hesse gave copies as a present to many of his friends.
‡ *Franz Schubert: Sein Leben* (1941).
§ Cement manufacturer and patron of the arts; Hesse's close friend.

Given the present situation, they cannot travel from Cernauti to Berlin—the only Cuban Legation for Romanians is in Berlin—so they cannot pick up the visas in person. That is why we asked to have the visas sent to Bern. Moreover, my wife would like to spend a little time with her only sister and help her prepare for the long journey before she emigrates for good.

Another point: If this request is granted—as is only human and natural—the Swiss Consulate in Bucharest will have to write to the Kehlmanns in Cernauti, or better still, send them a cable (since they are in great danger of being deported), asking them to come to Bucharest to pick up the transit visa for Switzerland.

In the meantime, we shall be trying, with the help of a Ticino lawyer, to get a temporary permit from the canton so that they can come to Ticino. We know that Bern can only agree in principle and that we first have to secure permission from the canton.

Meanwhile, Ninon is also trying to procure Cuban visas for her oldest friend in Cernauti, and also her son and his wife. Although we would like to keep the two issues separate and attach a lot more importance to the first, we would nevertheless like to ask you whether there is any chance of securing permission for these three persons to travel through Switzerland; they would stay five or six days.

My wife is in Zurich, at H. C. Bodmer's, Bärengasse 22. But she is at my place in the Verenahof almost every afternoon from four o'clock onward.

Of course, I shall reimburse you right away for any costs incurred.

Addio, and God be with this letter. I hate to burden you with all of this, but have no alternative.

TO THOMAS MANN

Montagnola, April 26, 1942

Your kind letter of March 15 arrived three days ago, which is relatively quick. It was a pleasure to read, and that is saying something nowadays. I'm glad to hear that you have received my latest privately printed booklet—an enormous number have gone astray, especially in Germany. We were both delighted with the wonderful picture of you and Fridolin,* who looks very much like your wife. I happen to have one of Heiner, my son in Zurich, and his daughter, and am enclosing it.

How wonderful that you finally have a house again and a proper

---

* Thomas Mann's grandson.

study with a library, and that the climate is agreeable! I was also really delighted to hear that you're working with gusto on the fourth volume of Joseph. [. . .]

My books are not banned in Germany, but nearly were on several occasions and that could happen again anytime. The authorities frequently blocked all payments to me. Of course, they are fully aware of my Swiss and European attitude, but are on the whole happy enough to label me as an "undesirable." Most of my books are currently out of print, and, of course, in most cases there is no question of their being republished. But, after all, wars don't last forever, and even though I cannot imagine what the world will be like when this war is over, I am naïve enough to assume that our things will be brought out again, someday. A Zurich publisher, Fretz, had the idea of putting together an edition of my collected poems;* while they were assembling the material, they discovered that I have written some eleven thousand lines of verse. I felt somewhat taken aback by that figure.

The world is doing everything it can to make parting easy for us old people. It is utterly amazing how much thought, planning, and foresight it takes to perpetrate these lunacies, and the same is true of the irrationality and naïveté with which nations make virtue of necessity and ideology of slaughter. Man is so bestial and yet so naïve.

We are long accustomed here to seeing traces of the war everywhere. My three sons have been in the military for three years, with some interruptions and furloughs. The state is encroaching everywhere upon the natural, civilian life of human beings. At times it seems to me that all this warmongering since 1914 represents a gigantic, if unsuccessful, attempt by mankind to crush the excessively well-organized machinery of the state apparatus.

Fond regards to your family, and especially to your dear wife, from both of us.

TO HIS SISTER ADELE

[*October 1942*]

When celebrating the hundredth anniversary of Mother's birth,† think of me for a moment, and I shall be with you in spirit. You will no doubt be reminded of days in Octobers past on which we celebrated

---

* *Die Gedichte* (Zurich: Fretz & Wasmuth, 1942), the first collected edition, which included 608 poems.

† Marie Hesse was born on October 18, 1842, in Tellicherry, India.

Mother's birthday. I believe that Ludwig Finckh was there once, although that may have been for your birthday. We filled a basket with beautiful mushrooms from the wood. And you may also recall the pleasure Mother used to get from those events, her skill organizing parties and the like, selecting flowers for little bouquets, etc. That was her voice singing the remarkable song for our birthdays: "Is it not a great joy [to be born a human being] . . . ?" That question is still valid, and certainly not outmoded, as it once seemed.

I have always felt that our mother inherited a remarkable and mysterious combination of traits from her parents. While resembling in many ways her grandfather, whose wisdom I greatly admire, she was very much the Francophone Calvinist in her moral commitment and passionate devotion to good causes.

Our parents bequeathed us many things, including some contradictions and difficulties; the legacy is not simple or easy, but it has a certain richness and nobility. It fosters a sense of duty, and often helps one to keep one's eyes open and see things clearly and make judgments at a time when most people content themselves with slogans. Although our parents demanded quite a lot of us, they asked a lot more of themselves, and showed us through their lives something that has become rare and is unforgettable. Nowadays people always try to persuade us that our parents' faith, worldview, and judgments were primitive and antiquated; but I must say that, even though I sometimes felt that way as a youth, things have sorted themselves out over the years and now seem very different.

A pity that we have no really good pictures of Mother from the later years! But we carry her picture around inside us.

Greetings to all present!

TO ROLF CONRAD

[Baden] November 1942

My Berlin publisher* has also visited me here, and I have at least regained possession of my manuscript—it was written over the last eleven

---

* On November 25, 1942, Peter Suhrkamp brought the manuscript of *The Glass Bead Game* back to Switzerland. In 1945, he described the situation as follows: "*The Glass Bead Game* was supposed to appear in 1942. The Ministry of Propaganda prevented its publication because of one chapter, which takes place in a monastery. *The Glass Bead Game* deals with the form and history of a pedagogical province in a utopian country, in which politics and culture are administered separately. Responsibility for the culture of the country is vested exclusively in a synod consisting of the most productive minds. The work emphatically criticizes the impact of literary journalism on language and intellectual matters." Excerpt from Suhrkamp's statement to the military government when he was requesting a license for his publishing house in Berlin in 1945.

years and has just been gathering dust for seven months in Berlin. It cannot appear in Germany, and since the work of my final years could be destroyed by a fire or a bomb, I shall now have to have the book published somewhere in Switzerland, so that it will at least be preserved. Of course, its publication in Switzerland is no more meaningful than anything else taking place these days. The book is directed at those readers who are somehow expecting it and could benefit from it. It's now going to be twice as expensive, even for the few who buy it here, and will not earn me anything. But the same applies to most things we do these days—there may be some metaphysical sense to it all, perhaps.

TO THE "NATIONAL-ZEITUNG," BASEL, ON ITS HUNDREDTH ANNIVERSARY*

The *National-Zeitung* is not just the place in which many of my short pieces have been making their first appearance, but also the newspaper I read daily. There are two reasons for that. First of all, it is a Basel newspaper, with good coverage of local news, and I find that attractive and advantageous, since I like to know where what I am reading comes from, where it grew up and is at home, and am only open to ideas and opinions when they have an individual countenance, and have been molded and given a unique shape by the locality. And, moreover, Basel is the city where I first went to school. It's an old love of mine—I almost said, "an unhappy love." This is one reason why I am so fond of the *National-Zeitung*. The other reason is related to my sympathy for the newspaper's social and humanitarian point of view, for its convictions, for its special way of being Swiss, and for its interpretation of the concept of the nation-state.†

I intend to remain loyal to the *National-Zeitung* and wish it all the best on its anniversary and relocation to the new building.

---

* Printed in a special issue on March 18, 1943.

† The *National-Zeitung* was the only daily newspaper in which Hesse's critical book reviews could appear from 1920 to 1938.

TO ERNST MORGENTHALER

[*April 1943*]

Your kind letter with the two notorious sketches arrived just at the right time, when I was in need of company, or "contact," as the Bavarians put it. I have been alone for five days, Ninon is away on a trip, and I am sitting here surrounded by little bottles of medicine and Vichy water, pharmacy bills. [. . .]

You're right—if the generals could be persuaded to paint for a few hours every morning, the world would be a different place. But the generals and dictators don't like to get paint stains on their trousers, and having only one model on a chair to torment is no match for their ambitions, since they feel a need to command thousands, millions of people. The likes of us have as difficult a time trying to understand that ambition as has a general trying to comprehend our joys and our sorrows.

I just thought of a story about painting. I was in Locarno in March 1918, had just begun to paint, attempted a few watercolors; one day I asked the painter Gustav Gamper, a quick and skillful watercolorist, to take me along with him on a painting expedition. We headed off toward Gordola with our rucksacks and little chairs; I was feeling quite fearful and anxious about the tasks ahead, and as we went along, I pleaded with Gamper: "Please do me a favor—no waterfalls." I thought that was hardest of all to do. Suddenly he stopped at a fork in the path: some velvet brown foliage behind a little wall, through which one could see a gorge with a waterfall, and higher up the mountain a chapel and a couple of huts. He unpacked immediately; the scene really looked very charming, and he completely disregarded my objections. So we sat down and started painting right away. When we were almost finished, a little wagon with a horse and a local Ticino family came along, and Gamper said: "Let's paint the little carriage in quickly," and indeed within two minutes it was in his picture; I was astounded and gave up all hope.

That was back in 1918. Recently a package arrived from Gamper; he wanted to give me something, and it was the watercolor he had painted back then. I searched for a long time, and finally found mine, without the little carriage, but with bushes gone wild and a waterfall daubed in white. [. . .]

TO A YOUNG PERSON

Zurich, May 1943

I'm not capable of writing a proper letter—am being pestered again by physicians—but would nevertheless like to respond to your greetings. I can see from your letter that you're confronted by a dilemma. But since our experience can never be conveyed in words, your letter naturally only touches on the problem. The issue revolves around the word "ego." You speak of the self, as if it were a familiar, objective quantity, which, of course, it isn't. Each of us consists of two selves, and only a sage would know where the one begins and the other leaves off.

Our subjective, empirical, individual self is actually very mobile, moody, also very dependent on outward events, easily influenceable. We cannot consider it a reliable entity, nor can we allow it to serve as our standard and our voice. This ego merely teaches us something that is reiterated often enough in the Bible: we are, as a species, weak, defiant, and despondent.

But then there's another self, buried within the first; the two often mingle, but ought not be confused. This second, lofty, sacred self (the Indian Atman, which you consider an equal of Brahma) is not by any means a personal entity, but represents rather our own share of God, life, the universe, everything that is impersonal and suprapersonal. We would be better off going in pursuit of this self. However, that isn't easy: the eternal self is quiet and patient, but that other self is forward and impatient.

Religions consist in part of insights about God and self, in part of spiritual practices and methods of training that allow one to free oneself from one's moody private self and thus facilitate greater intimacy with one's own divine inner qualities.

To my mind, all religions are more or less equal in value. While any one individual religion could make a person wise, it could become degraded and get turned into a silly form of idolatry. Virtually all real knowledge, however, has been lodged in the religions, particularly in mythology. All myths are wrong unless we approach them with due reverence. Each one, however, can unlock the world's heart. Each one knows ways of transforming the idolatry of the self into the worship of God.

Enough. I regret not being a priest, although if I were, I might have to ask you for the very thing you cannot afford at this stage. And so it's preferable that I should greet you as a wanderer, one who, like you, goes about in darkness, but knows of the light and seeks it.

TO ROBERT WALSER*

[August 1943]

We are elderly people now and work is more or less out of the question. Besides, I can no longer read very much. But now and then, when I wish to read something beautiful, I take down one of your dear books and, as I read, enjoy the stroll with you through this beautiful world. I have done so again and just wished to let you know.

TO OTTO BASLER

[Bremgarten Castle, August 16, 1943]

[. . .] There once was a city that supplied me with more mail than any other; many of my friends were there, even though most of them didn't know one another. The city was called Hamburg. It no longer exists. I still don't know which friends have died. I have only heard about two of them who lost the roof over their heads along with all their belongings and are now making their way as refugees and beggars to southern Germany; one of them is my cousin Wilhelm Gundert, to whom (together with Romain Rolland) *Siddhartha* was dedicated.

Emmy Ball's daughter, who is married and had been living in Rome, has arrived in Germany as a refugee; she is completely frantic and confused, and is deathly afraid for her husband, who was not allowed to leave. And my sister, who lives near Stuttgart, writes that it is strange not knowing when one goes to bed in the evening whether one will live to see the next morning.

[. . .] People are always amazed that my very literary stories and poems, which seem so freely inventive, encompass some things that actually exist and can even be documented. Readers are often caught by surprise or laugh aloud on discovering suddenly that there is really a painter called Louis who is a friend of Hesse's,† that Castle Bremgarten, the black king,‡ the Siamese§ of the Nürnberg journey really exist! And there is a large number of other passages, known only to me, in seemingly fictional contexts that comprise a hidden memorial to real events and actual experiences.

* Walser was an inmate in an asylum at Herisau in the canton of Appenzell Ausser-Rhoden. In 1933, he had stopped writing, after having being transferred against his will from another institution at Waldau, near Bern.
† Louis Moilliet.
‡ Georg Reinhart.
§ Alice and Fritz Leuthold.

Another example: The legendary figure of Collofino (Feinhals) often appears in my stories. There is a real person called Collofino; he has written a few things: I used to be quite friendly with him, and we often exchanged greetings and presents. Most recently he appears very discreetly in the Latin quotation used as a motto for *The Glass Bead Game*. It says: "ed. Collof."—i.e., edited by Collofino—and that is correct since the Latin version of the saying, allegedly written by one Albertus Secundus but actually originally formulated in German by me, came about with assistance from Collofino. The other collaborator was Franz Schall, whom I'm also going to name in the book.* At my request Schall, an excellent Latinist, translated the motto into medieval Latin; I then showed it to Feinhals, who found some things that needed refining and so he engaged in some correspondence with Schall about the matter. All of which led to the final version of the saying, as it now stands. So, as you can see, there is more work behind some of the little details than readers might suspect.

Schall is now dead. And Collofino, a very rich man in Cologne, who owned a large business and also a large house filled with art objects, wrote to me recently from a Baden hospital: In June, his business, and a few days later his home, were so badly destroyed that there wasn't a trace left of either, nothing whatsoever. That's what is happening nowadays. Collofino is about seventy-four years old.

Addio!

TO HIS SON MARTIN

[Baden, beginning of December 1943]
Postmarked December 3, 1943

This afternoon we had a nice time. It was four o'clock; I was lying in bed, waiting for Ninon, who usually comes at this time. When she arrived she told me right away that she had met Max Wassmer, his wife, and Louis Moilliet on the train; they were traveling and wanted to pay me a quick visit. I got up, and all five of us sat together for an hour, until the guests had to catch their train. Ninon stayed until seven o'clock; she is going to a lecture in Zurich this evening. So now, after the evening meal, I have time to write you a few lines.

The motto of my fat new book, given at the beginning in Latin and German, clearly states the raison d'être and purpose of the work. It is an attempt to portray something nonexistent, but desirable and possible,

---

* *Clangor* in the Latin of the motto.

in such a way that the idea thereby moves one step closer to realization.

By the way, this motto is not what it purports to be—i.e., the aphorism of a medieval scholar (although it could well be). I wrote it in German, and it was then translated into Latin by my since deceased friend Schall.

During the more than eleven years when I was writing it, the book was far more than just an idea, a plaything; it became a protective shield against these ugly times, a magical refuge into which I could retreat for hours, whenever I was ready intellectually, and not hear a single tone from the real world.

If I made my life difficult and almost unbearable during these years—first of all, by chaining myself and my life's work to the Berlin publisher, and second, by marrying an Austrian Jewess—the many hundreds of hours that I spent on *The Glass Bead Game* enabled me to exchange all of that for a completely clean, completely free world, which I could inhabit. Some readers will derive the same kind of profit from this as I did.

It was great that I was able to finish the book—it's almost two years ago now—before my intellectual powers began to ebb. I quit at the right moment, and that makes it easier for me to accept the silly things that I have perpetrated in the course of my life.

Bruno is probably coming on Sunday. Heiner was here briefly on Monday—only for an hour and a half, but we had a nice time.

Best regards, your father

TO PROFESSOR EMIL STAIGER

Early January 1944

I really enjoyed your kind letter. My book has already had its first, unpleasant encounter with the public, in the form of feuilleton reviews—the only serious comments were those by Professor Faesi—and it's now slowly beginning to affect the kind of reader for whom it was intended. Your letter is the most beautiful such response so far. The echo was so beautiful and rich that I have been feeling very content today, even though my condition is quite wretched.

Actually, I did not intend the book as utopia (in the sense of a dogmatic program) or prophecy, but rather as an attempt to evoke what to me is one of the truly genuine, legitimate ideas. It's possible to sense the frequent occasions when that particular idea has manifested itself in world history. Your letter indicates, much to my delight, that I haven't thereby ventured into an impossible, suprahuman, theatrical realm. I had many spirits around me as I worked on this book: all the spirits who brought me up, some who had the same simple humanity and were as far removed from pathos and humbug as the Chinese sages of history and legend.

I was glad to hear that you find the fundamental attitude of my book cheerful and simple. I was also pleased by what you say about the meaning and potential impact of the book. There is a concise expression of that meaning in the motto at the very beginning of the book, which can be summed up as follows: The very evocation of an idea or the portrayal of something being realized actually brings us a step closer to its realization (*paululum appropinquant*). Here, too, I regard your judgment as a form of confirmation.

Besides thanking you for the joy you have given me, I should like to say that I got to know and like you through some pieces of yours in *Trivium*. I have occasionally had the following feeling: there are people at work who are interested in precisely the same things as myself.

I should like to meet you at some point. I'm not mobile enough to visit people, but if you happen to be in this area, you could perhaps drop in on me and my wife, who shares my burrow.

TO MARIANNE WEBER

[February 1944]

Your early-spring letter of February 2 confirms something I have often suspected. In spite of your misery over there, you people are better able to experience joy, appreciate fleeting happiness, and take what the moment has to offer than we are in this country, which has ostensibly been preserved from destruction, where everything still stands, but where there is no longer any air to breathe. There are young people here too, naturally enough, but we old people, and myself in particular, have had enough and are ready.

That is a wonderful story about the officer who recited my verses during nighttime maneuvers! But there were also more than enough officers who washed their hands after shooting ten or a hundred hostages or burning down a village, then lay down to read Rilke or Goethe for an hour. I would rather hear about an officer who never read Rilke or Hesse, but taught his soldiers to shoot their own leaders rather than the Russians and the Jews. In Germany around 1919 some of the young people had grown tired of war, and were fervent pacifists and internationalists, especially among the students. They read Rolland and Hesse and seemed a kind of yeast, but not long afterward Hitler had an army of 100,000 youngsters, which the *Volk* had supplied of its own accord, even paying for the brown uniforms. Oh, in Germany they only believe in the Janus face, the "Faustian" disposition, which can burn down villages today and play Mozart so wonderfully tomorrow. And we have certainly had enough of that for all time. Well, forgive me for having written to you in such a mood. But that cannot be helped, since my mood hasn't really changed in years.

TO ROLF V. HOERSCHELMANN

February 22, 1944

Many thanks for your letter. One ought to keep in mind that Castalia doesn't consist primarily of utopia, dreams, the future; it also embraces reality, since such things as orders, Platonic academies, schools of yoga have been around for a long time. And as regards women: the poet Bhartrihari, for instance, was a Buddhist monk, who was always running away because he felt he couldn't survive without women, but each time he returned, feeling repentant, and was welcomed back with great warmth.

Your other question: The Glass Bead Game is a language, a complete system; it can be played in every manner conceivable, by one person improvising, by several people in a structured way, competitively and also hieratically.

My friend Christoph Schrempf, who was well over eighty, has died in Stuttgart. Among the people I have known, he most resembled Socrates (and had written some marvelous things about him).

Well, you had one further question: Knecht's death can naturally be interpreted in many different ways. To me, the most significant meaning attaches to the sacrifice that he makes in such a courageous and joyous manner. In my view, he hasn't at all interrupted his education of the youth, but brought it to fulfillment.

TO A READER

Montagnola, Peter and Paul's Day [1944]

Thanks for your birthday letter, which I enjoyed. As for the litter of kittens, which you mentioned, it now consists of the following: Our dear dwarf (Zwinkeler) died about a year ago; Ninon grieved as much

(*Above*) Am Erlenloh, the house with Hesse built in Gaienhofen in 1907

(*Below*) The house on Melchenbühlweg, formerly the residence of his friend Albert Welti, the painter. Hesse lived in this house, "a neglected old aristocratic country estate," until April 1919. The first work completed there was the novel *Rosshalde*

(*Above*) Casa Camuzzi in Montagnola, where Hesse lived from May 1919 to
August 1931

(*Below*) The house in Montagnola which H. C. Bodmer had built for Hesse
in 1931. Hesse moved in in August 1931

for him as for the Architect, and I mourned him no less than I mourned our unforgettable Lion. Shortly afterward we adopted a very young kitten from Frau Geroe's litter.* It's called Snow White, or Snow, and looks the part. We wanted to get another tomcat, so that he wouldn't be lonesome, and ordered one from Zurich: a small, very beautiful, tigerlike animal with a pedigree teeming with Siamese, Angoras, etc. Ninon knew the people. We called this tomcat "the Zurich one," which is still its name, even though it has turned out to be a tabby cat, and had kittens three days ago; we only let her keep one. There are constant pilgrimages in this household to the childbed with the Zurich baby.

Radio Basel is giving me a "Hesse hour" for my birthday, but that won't be until July 3. Moreover, my Zurich printer is presenting me with a small private edition,† an old, short piece of mine—one of the ones I still like—which will be forwarded to friends and well-wishers. [. . .]

TO PROFESSOR EUGEN ZELLER

July 17, 1944

I enjoyed your letter of June 29, and would like to thank you for it.

My youngest son‡ is getting married next week, but I shall not be present; I seem to have a knack for avoiding such occasions. For instance, on July 3, Radio Basel devoted an evening to me, produced in collaboration with the author, and on the evening of July 3, I was sitting in Montagnola with my wife, listening just as reverently and curiously to the Hesse evening as any other Swiss citizen. I heard myself reciting a few poems—which had been recorded a few weeks beforehand at my house.

There were quite a few responses to the evening. My eldest granddaughter wrote to me delightedly, saying that I was a great writer, and Elisabeth wrote too, the Elisabeth of *Camenzind* and of the early poems.§ There were many other letters, two of which I found interesting.

One was from a woman who was once our cook in Bern. She was intelligent, decent, attractive, a remarkable girl, we liked her, and she was fond of the children, but then she became unpleasant, and ended

---

* The carpet weaver Maria Geroe-Tobler. Hesse wrote a contemplative piece about a carpet of hers depicting a pair of lovers, "Über einen Teppich" ("On a Carpet") (*Die Kunst des Müssiggangs*, pp. 340ff).

† *Zwischen Sommer und Herbst* (Zurich: Fretz & Wasmuth, 1944).

‡ The marriage of Martin and Isabelle Hesse took place on July 22, 1944.

§ Elisabeth La Roche, teacher of dance and choreographer.

up causing us a lot of vexation. In the letter she said that she had been intending for decades to apologize for what had taken place, and now, having heard my voice on the radio after thirty years, she wanted to go ahead and do so.

A pastor in Thurgau* wrote saying he owned a manuscript of mine, a portfolio containing many poems, which I wrote in 1892 (in other words, when I was fifteen); I had dedicated it to his aunt Eugenie Kolb.† The name is certainly right. I wrote to him and attempted to acquire this rarity, but the man would not agree to give me the portfolio permanently. However, I was able to persuade him to loan it to me for fourteen days. It has been lying around here for the past four days, so I am rereading the little verses that I wrote there while still virtually a child:

> *The power, you know, of the child with the bow*
> *Who arises in May like fragrance from roses*
> *And strikes the heart, a blow so sweet, so sharp.*

or

> *I sang a little song,*
> *Poured out my very heart,*
> *Now it has faded away,*
> *And she has heard it not.*

I was glad to read what you said about *The Glass Bead Game*.

TO PASTOR W. FINK

March 21, 1945

Yesterday I received your kind letter of January 16, in which you try to cheer me up by telling me the story about the evening in Maulbronn. I enjoyed that. You are right, I have always perceived things intensely, and tasted fully all the joys and sorrows of life; at times this has seemed a boon and a blessing, at others merely a curse.

A dear friend of mine‡ is severely ill; the doctor thinks that he will not survive. He had a stroke a year ago. It is strange. This man, who was brought up along strictly Catholic, clerical lines by some priests, kept in monastic seclusion and inadequately fed, has retained the stigma that was inflicted on him in two rather infantile ways. First of all, he

---

* Pastor G. Schläpfer of Sirnach.

† The portfolio consisted of twenty-three poems, which Hesse wrote while in the mental clinic at Stetten. They are dedicated to Hesse's early "love" in Cannstatt, Eugenie Kolb, whose acquaintance he had made through his brother Theo.

‡ The psychoanalyst Josef B. Lang.

has remained hungry physically, and can never get enough; he used to get up at night occasionally and eat pounds of sugar or bread, etc. Second, throughout his life he retained the spiteful pose of the atheist and rebel, and as an old man wrote a very scholarly book directed against his personal enemy, Yahweh.* Now, close to death, he gratefully permits the Catholic prayers to be spoken, not by the priest, but by a woman who is helping care for him, and he says his *ora pro me* or *ora pro nobis* like a believer.

Spring is always very difficult for me, especially the gout in my hands and feet, and yet it can still be very beautiful. May it also bring you some warm, beautiful days!

TO OTTO BASLER

Easter 1945

Thanks for your last letter. I hope that this is really your last stint of military service.

Unfortunately, that Easter poem† does not merit your enthusiastic response. Of course, the sentiments are all fine and good, but the how lacks the true blossom or intangible quality that alone makes a poem worthwhile. It is well meant, but nothing more.

Since I have occasionally mentioned my poor friend and publisher Suhrkamp, I have copied the latest news about him for you.‡ It's doubtful he is still alive. Those apes in England have suddenly become furious at all of Germany, as if the German people had really perpetrated the abominations in the camps, but nobody is saying a word about the thousands of quiet stoics and heroes who, like Suhrkamp, repeatedly confronted a superior force, thereby risking life and liberty, and nobly represented the German people in its most difficult hour. The English have only just discovered the abominations in the camps, even though magazines in Prague were already describing them in 1934, sufficient grounds, one would think, for the English diplomats in Berlin to distance themselves from Hitler and stop genuflecting, such apes! Nobody says a word about that nowadays. And in Italy the Allies have to this day kept many people imprisoned who were persecuted by the Germans and fascists and are commonly regarded as courageous anti-fascists.

---

* J. B. Lang, *"Hat ein Gott die Welt erschaffen?" Zur Theologie und Anthropologie von Genesis I–II, 4a; ein exegetischer Versuch* (1942).

† "Dem Frieden entgegen," ("Toward Peace") (*Gedichte*, p. 695).

‡ At the end of January 1945, Peter Suhrkamp was released from the Sachsenhausen concentration camp in a virtually moribund condition.

TO GÜNTHER FRIEDRICH

Montagnola, June 18, 1945

Thank you for your letter, which arrived the day before yesterday. I am sorry I cannot send you anything apart from these lines.* Until recently, I could at least send an occasional present of books to German émigré friends in England, but since the so-called end of the war that has also ceased; the post office will not accept anything apart from letters. And we have had no contact at all with Germany since the capitulation: I haven't heard anything about my sisters and friends or about my poor, faithful publisher, who was incarcerated for a long time in Gestapo prisons—I don't even know whether he is still alive. So I can't tell you anything about your people, but there is no cause for worry, although there will most likely be food shortages in Germany soon and they will probably be better off if they don't happen to live in one of the larger cities.

In your letter you say that it would have been better if Hitler had died in that assassination attempt. That is correct, since Germany would indeed be in a slightly better situation were that so. But Germany accepted Hitler, and invaded and plundered Bohemia, Austria, Poland, Norway, and, finally, half the world, slaughtering millions of people and plundering one country after another; those sad facts would still be true if Hitler had died earlier. Germany's misfortunes and disgrace are rooted not in its current suffering and defeat, but in the continual abominations that it perpetrated for years. Even prior to 1939, we used to grit our teeth in anger when we heard your recruits striking up the song: "Today Germany is ours, tomorrow the whole world," and we are now saddened by the thought that your people has only a limited awareness of what it has wrought.

Enough of that. It's just that I didn't want to gloss over this issue in my first letter to you.

May your fate be tolerable and may you yet live to witness some of the reconstruction.

---

* Günther Friedrich, a relative of Hesse's, was a POW in England at the time.

TO MARIANNE WEBER

[ca. August 1945]

Your letter and one from the Engels reached me at Rigi, where I have been trying to make sure my wife gets some rest. Today I can only acknowledge having received it. I shall soon be back home, but am not doing well, have no energy. My wife was ill and completely run-down; at least she is recuperating now.

You take C. G. Jung, etc., far too seriously. Since the end of the First World War, Germany has been behaving suspiciously and making itself hated in the eyes of the whole world, and has ended up destroying half the world in an almost diabolical manner; so the entire world naturally hates the Germans, and does not stop to ask each and every individual whether he might not have been an opponent of Hitler's. And, ultimately, there is a small kernel of truth underlying this comprehensive hatred and guilt. Why, for instance, in all those years since 1923, did a nation of eighty million people not produce a single individual with the courage to shoot the huge beast?

You ought not to expect a world that has been robbed, besmirched, and destroyed by the Germans to display much interest in the sufferings of the more decent Germans. There are gaping wounds everywhere, over here as well. I have some too.

I would add: While your anger at professors such as Jung is understandable, it's also rather pointless. You people need to learn how to stop taking those admonitory sermons personally; any other kind of response betrays a vestige of nationalism.

TO CARL GEMPERLE

August 22, 1945

Thanks for your letter. I do not have sufficient energy to respond adequately. I agree wholeheartedly with the sentiments expressed by H. Bischoff, and would just like to add that I have never complained about a dearth of readers in Germany, and never had any occasion to do so. Hitler (or rather Goebbels and Rosenberg) wiped me out over there, and even he needed some help from American bombs.

The average Swiss takes pride in his democratic virtue, even though almost half the governing National Council was still pro-fascist only yesterday. When he sees one of those horror films about German camps, he often forgets that it is not just the Satans and chief devils who are

Germans, but also the majority of their victims. And these Germans, who have suffered for years, not just since 1939 but also for years beforehand under Hitler, lost everything, their positions, honor, freedom, and the chance to have any impact; they suffered and starved in prisons and camps, and today they are perhaps the wisest and most mature people in Europe. I have many friends among them.

TO HIS COUSIN FRITZ GUNDERT

October 23, 1945

You wrote some time ago saying that a poem of mine, "Toward Peace," had been printed in a Stuttgart newspaper and that the final two lines, which were also the most important ones, had been omitted.* I protested to the press office of the American Army, more as a matter of principle than with any real hope of receiving an answer. I complained about the unauthorized use of the poem and also about its having been mangled. I have just received a less than beautiful reply. I'm enclosing a copy for your information.† I have not yet decided how (or whether) to respond. I don't feel I should have to answer in any way to a man capable of writing such a stupid and nasty letter; I am not a vanquished Germanic slave in the occupied area and am not inclined to explain my actions to some little officer. If there is no possibility of a diplomatic approach, our authorities could perhaps lodge a complaint at the American Embasssy, but it's not clear that they will actually do so, and I may have to respond publicly. In any case, you now know why you will never again come across anything of mine in those newspapers. This affair hasn't done me any harm; I don't believe that I shall ever get another penny from Germany. But we heard some good news yesterday, not firsthand, but from a reliable source: Suhrkamp is still alive, and

---

* Written for Radio Basel on the occasion of the cessation of hostilities, the poem ends with the verses: "Wish. Hope. Love. / And the earth will again be yours."

† A letter from the "Press and Publications Section of the Twelfth U.S. Army Group." The writer Hans Habe, then chief editor of the German newspapers appearing in the American zone of occupation and entrusted by the Americans with the task of reconstituting the German press, had accused Hesse in a letter of October 8, 1945, of failing to "scream to the heavens" in protest against the Nazi regime as Thomas Mann, Stefan Zweig, and Franz Werfel had done, and of having chosen instead "to remain elegantly isolated in Ticino." Hesse called the mutilation of his poem "a barbaric act," whereupon Habe seized on that phrase and lectured Hesse on the barbarism of recent history, concluding as follows: "But we believe that Hermann Hesse has forfeited any right to speak in Germany, ever again." Habe referred to this incident on several other occasions, but his position varied and it was also contradictory. For the Habe letter, see appendix to Hesse, *Gesammelte Briefe*, Vol. 3, p. 533.

people are trying to get him into Switzerland (I have also tried to be of some help).

There was a nice letter from Wilhelm Schussen* in Tübingen. Mergenthalerstrasse, where he used live, is now proudly called Ebertstrasse. That would be fine if the entire German "Republic" had not voted so unanimously for old Hindenburg!

How often I think of you!

TO BISHOP THEOPHIL WURM

Montagnola, November 3, 1945

Thank you for your letter, which I received the day before yesterday.† I was extremely sorry to hear that they have not yet given you permission to travel. My experience corroborates what you say about the disinclination of powerful people to think in differentiated terms, etc. As a result of Hitler and Goebbels, I was deprived of the proceeds and resonance of my life's work, and now the person entrusted by the occupying forces with the task of reconstituting the German press informs me that I belong to a group of people who will never again be allowed to speak out in Germany. The man may be malicious, but it is more probable that he is just not well enough informed and too complacent to remedy that deficiency. This whole thing is certainly disgusting, yet we are glad that Germany has been defeated and that the daily killing and torturing of thousands of people has finally come to an end. My wife is Jewish and comes from Bukovina; she hasn't had any news of her only sister for a year, and has lost almost all her relatives and close friends in the gas ovens at Auschwitz, etc. It is certainly true that we are still very much shaken by these events.

I had no difficulty adopting Swiss citizenship after seeing virtually all of Germany sabotaging its own republic in the early years after the first war and thus showing clearly that the country hadn't learned anything at all from the war. I hadn't managed to take that step during the war, in spite of my denunciations of the aggressive tactics of the Germans. As a kind of warning, in one of my books I anxiously sketched the

---

* A writer and poet and friend of Hesse's.

† In a letter of November 2, 1945, to Franz Xaver Münzel, Hesse had observed: "The (Protestant) Diocesan Bishop Wurm wrote to me yesterday saying that he had read my essays from the period around 1918 and must admit that he would have rejected them out of hand at that time, but that he found them utterly convincing today. And in twenty-five years some people will understand my current ideas and approve of them."

specter of the coming second war, but people just laughed that off politely. So I bade farewell to political Germany. Nowadays I receive many letters from Germans who were still young in 1918; they say that the tone of my essays from those years still rings in their ears, and they wished they, and everybody else, had taken those warnings more seriously at the time.

Well, it was easier for me than for others not to be a nationalist. Our family was very international, which, of course, accorded well with the mission to the pagans, and I came under the influence early on not just of Luther and Bengel but also of the Indian world. People like my grandfather Gundert and my father had no reason to be nationalists, but another generation needed to emerge before that position was completely clarified. And now we are confronted with such terrifying new situations and tasks! I agree with you that penal measures and the principle of revenge will be of no great use, and that those who are suffering the most at present are precisely the ones who must free themselves from that way of thinking. I often feel glad that I am so old and rickety. But I cannot abandon hope when I think of all that thoughtfulness, goodwill, and insight acquired by dint of suffering; I find traces of that in some of the letters from German friends and readers, especially those in POW camps in England, America, Italy, France, Egypt, etc.

TO FRANZ GHISLER

January [ca. 15] 1946

My wife has just been reading me some selected letters from the heap of still unread mail; she read out a long, moving letter from Dr. Hans Huber in Heidelberg, and I immediately began thinking about my reply. Your letter, which was next because of the postmark, brought very painful tidings of the termination of our forwarding arrangement.* That will really impede many of my efforts, and it is also happening at a sad moment, since my elder sister† is hopelessly ill in Korntal.

The other question, about the street name in Constance,‡ fits in with everything else one hears about the concerns and actions of the victors. Let them go ahead and name that little street after Eisenhower, Truman, or somebody else! I really couldn't care less.

* Franz Ghisler, the Swiss Consul in Constance, relayed Hesse's letters to and from southern Germany.

† Adele Gundert.

‡ The former Hermann-Hesse-Way in Constance, which in the Nazi period had been renamed the Ludwig-Finckh-Way, was given back its old name.

I'm reluctantly enclosing the Rigi Journal for that officer of yours. If you had not recommended this course, I would never even have made a token gesture indicating any degree of compliance with the victors. But let's go ahead now.

I found it odd that one of my crimes, according to America (or rather Herr Bekessy), is that I wasn't delighted when the German cities were destroyed. The people who come up with ideas like that! Actually, it's a great exaggeration to call them "ideas." I have never criticized the way the Americans conducted the war, either in private or in public, but have always fully supported it, even though I was not sufficiently blind to miss the fact that American's entry into the war was, to some extent, a good economic move. No, I welcomed every Allied victory. But this is the first time anybody has ever demanded that I should be delighted by the by-products of these victories: the destruction of so many cities and cathedrals, libraries and publishing houses (including my entire life's work).

No, I shall not get involved, and if America insists, it can go ahead and ban me for the next fifty or a hundred years. The intellect cannot prevail against force, just as quality cannot compete witn quantity. We want to die without ever having made even the slightest concession to those surface currents in world history.

So I shall keep sending you some printed matter occasionally; I would like to send a lot of people a copy of the New Year speech.

TO THE AMERICAN EMBASSY
[*never sent*]

Montagnola, January 25, 1946

As you know, in the fall of 1945 a certain Captain Habe, who was at the time managing editor of several newspapers published by the American Army, wrote to me stating that I didn't deserve to be heard and shouldn't be allowed to play any literary role whatsoever in present-day Germany. I never answered that strange letter; Herr Habe's tone was so arrogant and hostile that I couldn't possibly have responded, especially since he apparently knows nothing of my work, political convictions, and public impact. Moreover, I have no particular ambition to write for the current German press.

Some references to this ridiculous affair have appeared in a portion of the Swiss press—due to the efforts of some friends to whom I had mentioned Habe's letter—to the effect that America has placed me on a "blacklist" or forbidden my works in Germany. At that point I wrote to the newspapers that had insisted on leaping to my defense, saying that they should let the matter rest at that, and through a few telephone calls, I was able to prevent several papers, the *Neue Zürcher Zeitung* in particular, from running a story about this incident.

I received another letter recently from Herr Habe, and I am enclosing a copy. He takes it for granted that I "launched" those press commentaries, and then proceeds to engage in further invectives against me.

In any case, I wish to insist that I had nothing to do with the decision certain Swiss papers made to speak out on this matter. I have never regarded the attacks of this Herr Habe, whom I have never answered, as official American pronouncements, and merely see them as an expression of that gentleman's impertinence.

I sent my friend Thomas Mann a copy of Habe's first letter, in which he accused me of not having bombarded Hitler with articles and radio talks the way Thomas Mann did, and enclose Mann's answer, but would like to add that this letter is purely for your information and should not be passed on or publicized in any way.

I am not expecting an answer or statement from you; I merely wished to inform you about this matter.

Respectfully

TO ERNST MORGENTHALER

Montagnola, February 1, 1946

[. . .] As regards Richard Strauss,* I fear that your hunch will turn out to be true: no matter what you do, you will end up regretting your decision. That is one of the disgusting things about the present situation. All the fronts overlap, and so just after having done the right thing, one keeps on asking oneself: Have I made the wrong decision? That happens to me too.

Strauss was in Baden when I was there, and I carefully avoided making his acquaintance, even though I felt he was a fine old gentleman, very much to my liking. Once, after I had arranged one evening to see the Markwalders at a certain time, they told me that would be fine, since Strauss was going to be there at the same time and was looking forward to meeting me. I withdrew, saying that I did not wish to get to know Strauss. Naturally, he was not told in quite that way; they came up with some sort of excuse for my absence.

---

* Morgenthaler was supposed to do a portrait of Richard Strauss.

The fact that Strauss has Jewish relatives is, of course, neither a recommendation nor an excuse. The existence of those relatives should have prevented him from accepting any advantages and homages from the Nazis, especially since he already had more than his fill of riches. He was at an age when he could have withdrawn and kept his distance. His inability to do so may conceivably be a product of his vitality. For him "life" means success, homages, a huge income, banquets, festival performances, etc., etc. He could not live without that—and wouldn't have wanted to—and so he wasn't wily enough to resist the devil. We don't have any right to reproach him in any substantive way. But I think we have a right to keep our distance.

That's all I can say. Ultimately, Strauss will always win, since he will never pull out his hair or allow himself any pangs of conscience. Even though he adapted to the Nazis, he was one of the very few Germans whom the victors immediately permitted to travel to Switzerland. It's been six months since several others, just as old as he, who suffered and were imprisoned under Hitler, received an invitation from Switzerland to spend time convalescing here, but the victorious powers have not yet let them out. The very thought is enough to give one heartburn.

TO WALTHER MEIER

[*Early March 1946*]

Many thanks for the welcome books and letter.

Naturally enough, the beautiful offprints* came not from the Zurich newspaper—a nice idea like that would never have occurred to them— but from a friend of mine, who had it printed for me at his expense, since the issue in which the letter appeared was immediately sold out.

On Friday, Bishop Wurm of Württemberg spent half a day here with me. He has had an invitation to visit Switzerland since last summer, but the Americans have only let him out now, obviously because they did not want to be responsible for the nonappearance of an important participant at the ecumenical church conference. Whereas they had no problem giving an exit visa to that darling of the Nazis, Richard Strauss. And Hitler's favorite artist, the sculptor who produced that ultra-life-size, monumental kitsch for him,† thereby earning himself millions, is just as popular now with the Americans, and his income is almost back

---

* Of the "Letter to Adele," which had appeared in the *Neue Zürcher Zeitung* of February 10, 1946.

† Josef Thorak.

to its previous level. Similarly, at the University of Milan, virtually all the old fascist professors are still thriving. Everything has been in vain.

I have naturally given up hope of seeing my work brought together, not to mention the prospect of ever living from the proceeds again. If only Suhrkamp at least could get something out of it! But I fear his share will not amount to much either.

It's almost ideal for us old people that one gets sick of the world after a certain amount of time, and this makes parting easy.

TO JOACHIM MAASS

Montagnola, March 23, 1946

Dear Herr Maass,

Thanks for your letter. I accept my lack of fertility and increasing inability to work in much the same spirit as you do; in old age, when one's physical powers go on strike, one immediately needs to think in terms of years rather than weeks and months. The work on *The Glass Bead Game*, the stay in Castalia, and my belief in the meaningfulness of that absorbing task helped me to survive the Hitler years and the war up to the spring of 1942, when I wrote those final few pages about Knecht's death. That is now exactly four years ago, and ever since then I have been without any refuge, comfort, and meaning. So as to give myself a chance to experience that kind of thing again, at least for a few hours, I wrote the Rigi booklet or "The Stolen Suitcase"* and two or three other trifles. The mail is consuming my time and energy, and has become extremely cumbersome; I no longer have a publisher, and Ninon is only able to help in a limited way (as a housewife, correspondent, courier for letters, etc., for émigrés in every country, she is more harried than I). My friends and relatives in Germany are starving; I sell privately printed pieces in exchange for contributions; the rich refuse, the poor donate. Since December I was able to send off packets worth 1,000 francs, and have invited four people to come and recuperate over here, and that requires a lot of correspondence, etc., with the authorities—two are sisters of mine. I shall not go into cases in my own circle, similar to that of your dear Lampe;† we have been up to our necks for years in that sort of misery and absurdity. Here in Europe life has lost the substance it once had. Well, in a way that is good, since the world

---

* "Der gestohlene Koffer" (*WA*, 8:393ff).
† The writer Friedo Lampe.

always elicits a sense of wonder; it always thrills young people and makes parting easier for those who are seasoned.

Spring is here for the time being, and at least the blue, white, and yellow flowers in the meadow and forest are still the same as ever.

Fond regards from Ninon and myself. We shall keep our fingers crossed for you and your book,* and we're very fond of the magical year.

The January edition of the *Rundschau*† arrived recently.

TO GEORG REINHART

June 1946

I was glad to get your letter. It's enviable that you receive only a limited quantity of personal mail and can answer almost all of it by hand. Having a famous name is often a nuisance, and, moreover, I live in Switzerland. Half my family and friends are in Germany, the other half are émigrés abroad, so I have had a heavy burden ever since 1933 doing the correspondence, passing on news, etc., etc. And there is a big disappointment at the close of my life: my work has been destroyed, a wall the height of a tower has been erected between me and my real sphere of influence, and all of this is plaguing me in strange ways. People in Germany are always asking me to see to it that my books are again made available or simply requesting the books as presents.

Some of them scold me very naïvely and accuse me of reneging on my obligations toward my readers, etc. Those impatient readers don't seem to realize that the elimination of my books, of my ability to communicate, and of my material income creates far greater difficulties for me than for them. And that only represents a small, insignificant portion of my mail. Another portion deals with hunger; then there are the very numerous letters about the POWs, of whom there are hundreds of thousands, cut off for years and half crazy by now, sitting behind barbed wire in Egypt, Morocco, Syria, etc. The letters about hunger and the POWs are not at all intellectual or literary; it's a question of providing immediate material help, and unfortunately the machinery of the Red Cross, etc., has been of no great use. So I have had to assume personal responsibility for these matters. I have taken over the task of supplying the prisoners with as much good reading, etc., as possible, and have sent hundreds of volumes to selected addresses; the response has been

---

* *The Weeping and the Laughter* (1947).

† Maass edited the Stockholm *Neue Rundschau* from 1945 to 1952.

extremely gratifying. And on top of that, I have taken it upon myself to ensure that a small number of worthwhile people in Germany, whom I regard highly, do not go hungry, more than a dozen. That in itself calls for considerable effort and an unbelievable amount of work, since on each such occasion I have to raise the necessary funds in small amounts, through the sale of privately printed pieces or manuscripts, and the pillaging of my library, etc. But that's enough. I just wanted to suggest the situation that gave rise to such pieces as the "Letter to Germany." By the way, it was originally addressed to an individual who, like my publisher, had been imprisoned for a long time and could have faced death. [. . .]

Two months ago I invited my two sisters in Swabia to visit, and I have been waiting in vain for weeks and months for these two seventy-year-old sick women, who are now seriously malnourished, even with our few packages of foodstuffs. The Americans and French are introducing a system of harassment that is eliminating every vestige of humanity and rationality and may even be somewhat worse than the one under Hitler. A pity, because these victors, who a year ago were still being regarded as the champions of an idea dear to the whole world, have slipped into a disastrous role, not because there may be many rascals and gangsters among them but simply because they lack qualities like alertness, imagination, love, empathy, and the capacity for serious work, conscious of nuances.* The English have long seemed the only ones who are behaving in a noble, humane manner, for which one can be grateful.

It is sunny and hot today. The cuckoo has been calling all morning close by the house, and the drenched roses are beginning to release their fragrance.

---

* At the end of May, Hesse had written as follows to his son Bruno: "Just recently everything seemed to have been arranged so that our guests could enter the country, but the bestial American and French authorities are continually producing additional requirements and harassments and thereby preventing two ill and starving old women from undertaking a convalescent journey. I derive a certain amount of bitter satisfaction from this age-old spectacle: the victors are becoming more and more like beasts and are transforming their natural right into an injustice. That is one of the most uncanny laws of world history."

TO JOHANNA ATTENHOFER

[*July 1946*]

Thank you very much for your welcome gift and kind letter.

You ask: What's the point in being sad? Along the same lines, one could ask a dying person: What's the point in suffering from pneumonia? There's no answer to that. [. . .]

I have had few positive experiences with large welfare machines such as the Red Cross, etc.; every initiative is crushed by the organization, which is too large and, to some extent, also badly managed. As for my two welfare areas, the hungry and the POWs, I'm taking care of them entirely on my own, and am constantly having to raise funds by selling special editions, manuscripts, etc., etc. It's a lot of work and only partly successful. Nevertheless, I have been able to help a small number of splendid people whose lives are at risk keep their heads above water, and shall keep on doing so. I see the extremity of the hunger most clearly in those letters that try very hard to keep a lid on the matter rather than in those voicing complaints. And as for the POWs, since God has given you the gift of imagination, imagine a highly educated person who was drafted in 1939 or 1940, arrived in Africa, was captured there, has been kept two, three, four years in the desert in Egypt or Morocco, without knowing whether he will ever get back again and not knowing who is still alive at home, etc., etc. Well, I have to support quite a number of people like that with letters, books, etc., etc. I'm holding a rope, as on a mountain-climbing expedition, and a number of people who are at risk are hanging from it, and I know that, should everything become too much for me and I let go, they will all perish.

But enough of that. After receiving your gift, I felt that I ought to let you know about this.

TO H. C. BODMER

[*August 16, 1946*]
Bremgarten, on the day of the trip home

[. . .] I have had to read a lot of derogatory letters from Germany again, because a Munich newspaper has printed the "Letter to Germany" (without ever asking or receiving permission).

I was asked at the same time whether I would accept the Goethe

Prize,* for which I had been unanimously proposed. I was very opposed to the idea, but was persuaded to the contrary; I asked some extremely precise questions and ascertained that the Prize Committee had acted courageously and irreproachably under Goebbels. By the way, the whole affair is a mere formality, since I shall, of course, not receive one cent of the prize money.

For the past fourteen days, I have been trying to get some rest here, but without much success. I have the same daily work load as I have at home, and also the same frustrations and disappointments. I am tired and am not getting much fun out of life, literature, or the entire works, which I now find quite meaningless. The end is nigh.

I wanted to let you know first about the prize. I would like to take this opportunity to assure you once again of my gratitude.

TO WALTER KOLB, MAYOR OF FRANKFURT

Montagnola near Lugano, September 30, 1946

I received your letter of September 16 yesterday, and I wish to thank both the city of Frankfurt and you for the Goethe Prize. For several reasons, which I have described for myself and my friends in the enclosed thank-you note, I had to overcome some inner resistance and objections before accepting this prize, even though I certainly appreciate the honor. The fact that the prize is being awarded by the city of Frankfurt, which I knew well in the period before 1914, has greatly influenced my decision, since my ties to your city† used to be very friendly and cordial, and I regarded Frankfurt as one of my favorite German cities. I think with great sadness of everything it has had to endure.

As regards the material part of the prize, I would like to divide it up and present it to friends and relatives of mine in Germany.‡ As soon as I hear that you are ready to distribute the funds, I shall send you the addresses and amounts.

---

* On August 28, 1946, the city of Frankfurt am Main awarded Hesse the Goethe Prize, the first official honor he had ever received from Germany.

† Described in "Recollections of Some Physicians" (1960).

‡ One of the related surviving documents is a letter from the mayor of Calw of November 28, 1946, in which he says: "We wish to convey our sincere thanks for your donation of 3,000 RM from the Goethe Prize you were awarded; the city of Frankfurt has forwarded us that amount. The sum will be distributed among the poor in Calw, according to your specifications, and will be received with great joy as a Christmas present from you."

I would have liked to write at greater length, but have been over-burdened for a long time; my exhaustion is such that I am going to close my house three weeks from now and spend some time in a sanatorium.

TO FELIX LÜTZKENDORF*

[*October 25, 1946*]

I'm heading off tomorrow for a sanatorium, and my house will remain empty for several months at least. First, I want to thank you for your letter of October 10. It arrived at the same time as a letter from Thomas Mann, in which he says in his own way much the same things about the German mentality as I have been saying in mine, and your comments about your former colleagues in Germanistics provide further confirmation.

No, on the whole I don't expect anything good to come out of Germany, and never have. The rest of the world, which it had wanted to rape and dominate, is now finding Germany thoroughly indigestible, in intellectual terms as well. But I feel that the world is comprised not of nations but of people, and as far as people go, there are still many worthwhile individuals in your country. Even though I have been living outside Germany for thirty-four years now, I know a few dozen of them, and would rank them among the best anywhere. They are the ones who matter, it seems to me, especially their ability to work on the masses like salt and leaven and keep them under control. Here I am thinking far more of intellectual and moral life than actual political action.

I have been less taken up with the denunciatory letters that have come my way over the past months than with the various honors. Hesse evenings are being held in a series of cities and towns, talks as well; I receive copies of the formal addresses. Then there was the Goethe Prize, and Calw, my hometown, is producing a Hesse selection in two volumes, just those writings dealing with Calw and Swabia. Almost all of this is a burden, I find, what with the new letters, questions, misunderstandings, often also respectful letters from people who just yesterday still believed in the opposite. And I regard my utter inability to relate to this whole business as a sign that I have lived differently from most people, and relied almost entirely on my own resources, had no fatherland, no like-minded souls around me, no sense of community. I had roots in a homeland, but it was not close by, or even in the present era; my

* Author of a dissertation on Hesse, Romanticism, and the Orient (1932).

fatherland was called Castalia, and I discerned my saints and kings in the old Indians and Chinese, etc.

I shall feel disappointed and somewhat bitter as I die, but only in regard to my person, my private sphere, and the way I was embedded in the world. I have had to work for a people that reacts either with sentimentality and reverence or with animal-like brutality. Because of the language into which I was born, I have had to entrust my life's work to that people, and now feel disappointed and cheated. But taken as a whole and in a higher sense, my life and work have certainly been meaningful, and whatever is left of my work will survive. So, to that extent, I am not ending in bankruptcy.

My present relationship to the Germans is subject to all sorts of strange overlappings and sudden changes. For instance, some political friends of mine, who were proven martyrs under Hitler, have drifted away from me and I have been disappointed in them, whereas several former fellow travelers under Hitler have already won me over by means of a pure confession and repentance.

My next address is: c/o Dr. O. Riggenbach in Marin near Neuchâtel. If possible, pass this on to Suhrkamp as well.

Enough. I haven't written this long a letter for months, and shall not be able to do so again for some time.

NOTE TO HIS WIFE, NINON

[Early November 1946]

Monday morning

I have just got up, and wish to add a greeting. I have not seen today's mail yet; it's lying in wait; my eyes are completely exhausted.

Having this Stockholm thing* hanging over my head is all I needed. If it comes about, then I would ask you to call Fretz right away and ask him if he would print something I could use to answer the new flood of letters, perhaps something on the lines of a postcard, with a picture of me on one side and a few words of thanks on the other. I would select the picture and write the text. To hell with the whole thing! Just in case,

---

* Hesse had hardly arrived in the Préfargier Sanatorium when the news came that he had been awarded the Nobel Prize for Literature. Hesse himself did not attend the award ceremony. The Swiss Ambassador to Sweden, Minister Valloton, accepted the award on December 10, 1946, and Hesse's greetings were read at "the banquet on the occasion of the Nobel ceremony." (*WA* 10:102f).

I shall write to the postal authorities today, saying that any telegrams which arrive should only be forwarded as letters. [. . .]

TO ISA, HIS DAUGHTER-IN-LAW

[*November 1946*]

Thanks for your letter with the two wonderful drawings. I am in Marin near Neuchâtel, but don't give anybody my address. The Nobel Prize has been quite a burden, and, of course, the peace I had been seeking here has been utterly shattered. There are still a few hundred letters from many countries lying around unopened, even though I have been working on the mail for fourteen days, and we must have spent some 200 francs on telegrams and phone calls. The Swiss Ambassador will represent me at the Nobel ceremony in Stockholm, but I still had to compose a little speech for the occasion.

There was something funny in the *Gazette de Lausanne*. They published a nice, humorous little essay about me, and there was a funny typo in it. They meant to say that I had grown up in a family of missionaries, but misspelled the word as "millionaires."

Ninon is here again for a few days and can be of some help. But the crazy, continuous pain in my eyes and the headaches, which often go on all night, force me to keep to myself most of the time.

Fond regards to you and the children, your father, Hesse

TO THOMAS MANN

Marin près Neuchâtel, November 19, 1946

I wish to thank you very heartfeltly for your congratulations and also for your role in bringing about the Stockholm decision;* I wish I could do so in a letter worthy of you and the occasion. But for some time now, my little flame has been flickering, and often seems to have gone out completely, and so you will have to content yourself with this. This year has brought me several fine gifts I had been hoping for: In the summer my two sisters spent a few weeks with us, and we were able to feed, clothe, and comfort them until they had to go back to dark

---

* Since 1929, when he himself was awarded the Nobel Prize, Thomas Mann had continually suggested to the Prize Committee that Hesse was a worthy recipient.

Germania. I was awarded the Goethe Prize. Then they hanged the most horrible and evil enemy I have ever had, Rosenberg by name, in Nürnberg. November saw the award of the Nobel Prize. The first of these events, the visit of my sisters, was truly wonderful, the only one that seemed truly real to me. The others have not penetrated through to me yet. I have always perceived and digested the setbacks more quickly than the successes, and it was almost a shock the way I was besieged by journalists from Sweden and elsewhere, who were skulking about like real detectives—they had not been given my address. But, of course, I am gradually seeing the positive elements in this piece of good fortune, and my friends, and especially my wife, have taken a really childlike pleasure in the whole thing, which they have celebrated with champagne.* My old friend Basler† is also delighted, and many old readers of mine are perhaps glad to find out that their weak spot for me was more than just a vice. If my health eventually improves, all this will seem quite funny. I shake your hand, and think of the day long ago when I first met you in Munich, at the hotel where the Fischers were staying, in about 1904.

I hope you have received the little book with my essays.‡ They are harmless enough, but at least my point of view and attitude have always been the same.

DUPLICATED TYPESCRIPT, ENCLOSED WITH SOME LETTERS TO FRIENDS

On the 10th of December, the anniversary of Nobel's death, the Nobel Prizes were awarded in Stockholm. We ought to have been in Stockholm, and Ninon decided that she definitely wanted to spend the day with me and celebrate it in some way or other. So we invited Dr. Riggenbach and his wife to a festive evening meal, either in Neuenburg or at some nice guesthouse in the area, whichever they preferred. They accepted, but on the eve of the occasion made a counterproposal, which

---

* Hesse had recently written the following to Max Wassmer: "It's a pity that the external fulfillments take place mostly at a time when they are no longer any fun. At least, Ninon is delighted like a child about it, and my friend Bodmer and his wife spent a highly enjoyable evening with her, drinking the best champagne. As for myself, I have been completely abstemious for the first time in several decades, for three weeks now.

† Their mutual friend Otto Basler, a teacher and publicist in Burg/Aargau.

‡ *Krieg und Frieden* (Zurich: Fretz & Wasmuth, 1946), which bore the dedication: "For Thomas von der Trave from Josef Knecht, Waldzell, October 1946"; English translation: *If the War Goes On . . .* (1971), with more or less the same contents.

involved postponing the meal we had planned and spending the evening of December 10 at their place. I agreed without suspecting anything; I thought the Riggenbachs were simply not keen on going out to celebrate. We arrived at their place, Ninon and I, on the evening of the 10th, and from the outset everything looked a little different and more festive than usual. They didn't show us into the living room, as they usually do before dinner, but into one of the large, formal, tall-ceilinged rooms belonging to the management. There was a large fire burning in the fireplace, and we were seated on a sofa beside it, then Frau Doktor disappeared. We sat there on our own, and a small choir of about five women and girls and three men appeared, including the doctor and Trautwein, who had trained the choir. They sang the song "Often in the circle of beloved ones" in three parts. I sat there and was a little embarrassed, then I went over and shook hands with each singer and thanked them. We were barely seated again when one of the high doors at the other end of the room opened, and a four-year-old blond girl with red cheeks came in, behind her a second, somewhat bigger, and so on, each one a little bigger than the one before, six children, then two bigger ones at the end of the line, Monika and Christoph, the doctor's children.

Each one gave me a present and recited a verse composed by Frau Doktor. The smallest one brought a small basket of fir cones for my oven, the next, the chef's child, a plate with baked goods, which her father had baked, then a little jar of jam, made from the oranges from the little orange trees in front of the director's apartment. Finally, Christoph presented a huge sheet of beautiful drawing paper, and in a little verse he apologized because the sheet was not quite as big as the Spalen-Tor in Basel.* I praised the children and thanked them and they got some of the cookies; then Dr. Riggenbach came with Christoph and played in two parts (two violins) "How beautiful shines the morning star" and something from *Figaro*.

Whereupon we all sat down to eat, and the singers and children, except for the doctor's, took their leave. We had a lavish meal in the beautiful dining room on beautiful old porcelain. The table was covered with flowers, red primroses, trout, chicken, beautiful wine, etc. During the second course the old servant Léon came with a tray and said that some more telegrams had arrived for me. The doctor opened and read them—he and his wife had devised every one—some were funny, some

---

* "In Hours at the Desk," Hesse had written: "As a small child, I always wanted a present of paper for Christmas and my birthday, and when I was about eight years old, I requested the following on a wish list: 'A sheet of paper as big as the Spalen-Tor' " (city gate in Basel; the Hesse family lived close by from 1881 to 1886).

serious, some very beautiful. One, with pictures, was supposed to have come from King Gustav of Sweden. One came from heaven and was signed by Knulp, another arrived from the arch at Mount Sinai and was penned by the last European,* one came from Baden and brought tidings and greetings from the Dutchman,† etc., and there was a beautiful one from Turu, the rainmaker's son.‡

These wonderful people showered us with gifts and feted us, and I was more moved than I could ever have been by the Stockholm ceremony.

RESPONSE TO LETTERS REQUESTING HELP§

[*1947*]

I am receiving so many hundreds of letters asking for help that I shall have to use these printed lines to reply, especially since I am no longer capable of doing much work and am also continually overburdened.

There is no way I can consider the countless pleas for foodstuffs and other gifts of that nature from people whom I don't know. I have great difficulty meeting the obligations that I have already undertaken in this regard—for the past two years I have been supporting a number of people in Germany whom I cherish, by sending them packages regularly. It costs several hundred francs a month to support these people, and I cannot expand that circle.

None of these supplicants realizes that, as the author of books in the German language, I am also very much affected by the massive German bankruptcy. I entrusted my entire life's work to Germany and was cheated out of it. I have not received a penny from my German publishers for many years, and have little hope that the situation will change during my lifetime.

During the period of German megalomania, my books were partly banned, partly suppressed in other ways. And the remainder—all the inventory and composed type, etc.—has been completely destroyed by bombs together with the publishers, Fischer-Suhrkamp.

It's true that I have brought out a series of my books in new Swiss

---

* See Hesse's story "Der Europäer" (*WA*, 6: 423ff).
† A figure from Hesse's "Kurgast" ("Guest at the Spa") (*WA*, 7: 5–113).
‡ A figure from *The Glass Bead Game*.
§ Printed matter which Hesse enclosed with many individual replies.

editions over the last few years. But Switzerland is small, an absolutely tiny market; it is only possible to do small printings here, and the books cannot be exported either to Germany or to Austria.

In Berlin my devoted publisher Peter Suhrkamp is doing everything he can to republish some of my books. I am doing what I can to help him direct these books to really serious readers; otherwise people would just buy them as a speculative investment.

Many of the requests, quite apart from those for food and books, show a complete lack of understanding of my real situation: requests for entry visas to Switzerland and work permits, even for immediate citizenship, for jobs and positions. It is painful to have to read all of these often very fanciful requests, none of which can be met.

My friends know that I'm doing whatever I can and have been devoting most of my work and resources to the situation in Germany since war's end. They also realize what an astonishing amount of assistance tiny Switzerland is constantly giving large, starving Germany, even though other countries with whom we are on friendly terms are no better off, and even though there are still very many Swiss who for understandable reasons are not particularly fond of Germany. It is sad that for every case in which we can be of some help, there are hundreds of requests that just cannot be met. We cannot help that.

TO GERHARD (?) BAUER

Marin près Neuchâtel, February 1, 1947

In the last few months I have hardly been able to write a single real letter, and I fear the situation is not going to improve as long as I am here. To get through the correspondence, I would have to have one, or rather two secretaries, and my life isn't set up that way: I have always done everything myself, except for proofreading, which my wife has frequently taken over, and at present she is swamped with business letters (translations, etc.) [. . .]

You need not bother letting me know what your newspapers say about me and my book. That just doesn't interest me. As far as I can see, the press hasn't improved. The tone is democratic now, and rather servile vis-à-vis the victors; the contents are as devoid of substance as ever. But I follow your own thoughts with great interest and sympathy, and am usually delighted with them. And I regard your descriptions, for instance in the passage about your mother, as a true gift.

As regards the attitude people have toward politics, in my opinion the state official who "doesn't want to have anything to do with politics" is merely a parasite, and the soldier who lays waste an entire country and shoots at people every day, always thinking about heroism and a soldier's honor and never about the spilled blood and the destroyed cities, is dangerously simpleminded. The mentality of the officials and soldiers in most nations is similar, and so they cannot point a finger at one another unless the coarse behavior and brutal slaughter so oversteps all customary boundaries that the entire world is aghast. The fact that this has happened in Germany is the fate or "guilt" that has to be assumed and reconciled with life.

Enough. I have often expressed my insignificant ideas on this issue better than I can manage in such a hasty letter.

TO MARGARETE KREBS*

[February 1947]

I can only answer your letter briefly since I have been months in the sanatorium, suffering from great exhaustion. I see from your letter that you became acquainted with somebody who was pretending to be me. I myself have never lived in Berlin, was there only once for a few days, and am now sixty-nine years old. But, unfortunately, I have come across that man who pretended to be me and to have written my books, even though I have never seen him in person. He incurred debts in my name and got up to other mischief of that kind. For instance, in the period you mention in your letter, I asked several Berlin newspapers and also my Berlin publisher to issue warnings about him. By the way, he also turned up in Munich, where he made friends with women, introduced himself as a well-known writer to certain families, and carried out all sorts of mischief. I am sorry that a man with my name, or who had at least assumed my name, has apparently harmed you as well. May you never meet him again!

* The situation described in this letter is typical of the frauds perpetrated in Hesse's name during the period of his greatest fame.

TO LUDWIG FINCKH

Baden, March 6, 1947

I am writing this letter because I think you might be able to use it in court. It is not possible for me to appeal directly to the court or to any other German or Allied authority.

You know my attitude toward your political convictions and passions since about 1915. I have always found your form of patriotism repellent, and you have always stood on the opposite side from me, with your name, talent, and authority as an author. You were and remain a typical German nationalist; they are the ones who brought us Hitler and his diabolic antics. It is sad and unforgivable that you should have regarded Hitler and his party as a purely patriotic and idealistic movement; ninety percent of German intellectuals committed the same sin, and the ordinary people and the whole world have had to pay dearly for this biggest German sin.

But this guilt or sin or idiocy, whatever one wants to call it, is shared by thousands of colleagues on whom nobody has laid a finger. People like Gerhart Hauptmann also committed this sin, yet his work and memory are still being commemorated today.

Morally and in human terms, the most decisive factor in your case is the following: You were silly and inflicted real harm, but you were pure at heart, acted in good faith, and had no ulterior motives. You are as guilty as all those other Germans who tried to sabotage the young German Republic from 1919 onward and thus helped Hitlerism come into being; that behavior had already begun with the election of Hindenburg, even much earlier, and it would be totally perverse to exact punishment for it now. The important thing now is not that you believed in Hitler and the entire swindle, but that your motives were utterly sincere and not just egoistical. Again, the important thing is not that you may, say, have once intervened on behalf of a Jew, contrary to party doctrine, or tried to do so for me (something I would certainly never have asked of you), but that you never avoided conflicts with the representatives and power brokers of the Hitler regime and risked unpopularity whenever your conscience prompted you to take a stand. Morally, that is what is crucial. You were blinded, but you weren't a coward or just out for your own good. You wanted to serve your people and safeguard your ideals, even when this put you in danger and did you some harm. You are thus less guilty than tens of thousands of people who are running around with impunity.

By the way, my books have suffered the same fate as yours. They were destroyed along with my publishers, and for several years the only benefit I have been receiving from all my work has come from tiny Switzerland. That will remain the case, since I have never felt that I would ever get anything more than worthless bulk goods from Germany in exchange for the pieces of mine it is republishing. The Nobel Prize was welcome for that reason, also because I have a few dozen people to feed in your part of the world, but I'm quite indifferent to it otherwise. I gave away the Goethe Prize immediately to people inside Germany.

TO FANNY SCHILER

April 26, 1947

Many thanks for your kind letter and the gift of that etching of the chapel on the bridge;* I was very pleased with both of them. Standing there on that bridge for hours, rod in hand, watching the river, fish, neighborhood, and traffic on the bridge, etc., was one of the best preparations for my career; God knows what gave me the idea.

Toward the middle of May, Ninon wants to bring me to Lausanne for a few days; they are supposed to do some tests, which may suggest a new form of treatment. I am no longer all that interested in this sort of thing, but since they tell me that the professor there is a decent, fine person who is particularly interested in me, I shall risk it, although I am a little afraid of the arduous journey.

A famous and honored guest appeared unexpectedly at our door recently: André Gide. He is my favorite among my generation in France. The seventy-seven-year-old was very alert and lively, he brought along his beautiful daughter† and her husband,‡ and this young man is thinking of translating *The Journey to the East*.

I am glad that you received *War and Peace*; I only rarely get an opportunity to send people books, yours had been on order for months. [. . .]

---

* The Nicholas Chapel on the Nagold Bridge in Calw.

† Gide's twenty-four-year-old daughter Catherine from his relationship with Elisabeth van Rysselberghes.

‡ Jean Lambert; his translation of the novel was published by Calmann-Lévy in 1948. Later editions included a preface by André Gide and notes by Jean Lambert.

TO OSKAR BLESSING, MAYOR OF CALW

Montagnola, July 6, 1947

Although my condition makes correspondence virtually impossible, I wish to convey my thanks right away. Your beautiful package* arrived in good condition, and when we came back from the Bern area, it was ceremoniously opened and admired by everyone, including my sister Adele, who was also present.

I was deeply pleased and touched by the honor that my hometown has thus bestowed on me, even to the extent of making me an honorary citizen. I would like to express my deeply felt gratitude to the town, to the council, and to you, esteemed Herr Bürgermeister, for that and also for not forgetting my sister Marulla at the ceremony.

Beautiful old Calw is still my home, even though I may seem to have moved far afield through my kind of world citizenship and by having become a Swiss citizen. I never regarded home as a political concept and have always seen it in purely human terms. Home is the place where we were children and received our first impressions of the world and of life itself, and learned to see, speak, and think, and I have always gratefully cherished mine.

TO H. C. BODMER

Montagnola, July 8, 1947

Thanks for your kind, beautiful present;† we shall both have great fun with it. It's a bit late, since we have had to postpone the birthday celebration in Montagnola. We celebrated July 2 in Bremgarten Castle, and sorely missed you and Frau Elsy. Present, aside from my sons and their wives, were Morgenthaler and Louis the Cruel, my eldest granddaughter, and Herr and Frau Leuthold, and so together with our friend Wassmer, the circle was almost the same as ten years ago on the Brestenberg. We dined in the splendid rococo salon, and in the afternoon there was a large celebration, which was very strenuous, yet also pretty and dignified. A few musicians appeared, a pianist and five woodwinds, and played some Danzi and Mozart. After that came two delegations, one consisting of three professors, the other of three students. They

---

* The scroll bearing the honorary citizenship of his hometown, Calw.

† Elsy and H. C. Bodmer had given Hesse a record player for his seventieth birthday.

handed me the honorary doctorate, and the students brought a ceremonial scroll.

We returned home on the 3rd, opened gifts, and invited a few friends: Böhmer and his wife, the painter Purrmann,* and Frau Emmy Ball. My sister Adele was present; she was in Bremgarten as well. In the morning Ninon showed me the table with the presents. Then she led me up to her studio, where the radio set is, and there was your splendid present. It was inaugurated, dear friends, with a Handel concerto in your honor.

Then we heard accounts of several festivals and lectures in Germany. Hesse has suddenly become fashionable, and I very much hope that I shall never again have to encounter this kind of thing; I have had more than enough of it. I sometimes felt like an ape decked out as a general. There was a special ceremony in Calw, where they made me an honorary citizen and named a square after me.

Now we are sitting around and have to open, read, and answer a massive quantity of mail.†

I wish you more beautiful days over there and a safe journey home. We are looking forward to seeing you again.

TO HANS FRETZ

Montagnola, August 27, 1947

Thanks for your kind letter of August 25. I have no wish to disregard your sensibility as a publisher or insult you in any way. If you look at my earlier letters to you, you will find that I have often expressed sincere appreciation for your work, especially as regards actual book production. But I must nevertheless turn to you if the contact between publisher and author seems deficient, and the indignant tone which I may perhaps adopt on such occasions reflects the general condition of an ill man who has been overburdened for years with work and worries and has absolutely no secretarial support for his work, which includes a massive amount of correspondence.

One of the issues I became sensitive about was the long delay in reissuing *The Glass Bead Game*. It was almost two years out of print, we made insistent inquiries about it, and I constantly had to put up with

---

* Hans Purrmann, who lived in Montagnola.

† Hesse was still busy reading mail on July 20, when he wrote to Max Wassmer: "We have read more than ten thousand pages of letters."

letters from readers and booksellers who accused me of neglecting my work and found it scandalous that this book in particular should be out of print for so long and wouldn't even appear now in time for my seventieth birthday. I feel everything would have been fine and good again if, after the interminable wait for *The Glass Bead Game*, my publisher had sent me two lines informing me of its appearance. But I have only just found out about that, accidentally, by means of the letter that my recent demand has enticed from you. And here I am touching on the crux of our relationship: There is nobody in your publishing house who keeps in touch with me on a regular basis. So I often get postcards or letters from your office simply acknowledging the receipt of addresses for complimentary copies, etc.; that sort of thing is quite superfluous, as far as I'm concerned. But if I had never inquired myself, I would, for instance, have only heard later on or never at all that a new edition of *The Blossom Branch** appeared months ago or that the long-awaited *Glass Bead Game* is finally available. And that is just not right. This has nothing at all to do with your accomplishments as a publisher, for which I have never withheld my grateful acknowledgment, but is connected with the deficiency mentioned above, the lack of a literary director or adviser who would maintain contact with the author. You yourself, dear Herr Fretz, are extremely overworked; Herr Köpfli† is doing a great job as publisher and businessman, but is not really a colleague of mine when there are literary issues at stake, and your literary adviser, Herr Doktor Korrodi, has never written to me on any matter related to publishing.

A word or two about Herr Basler. He wrote a piece commissioned by you,‡ and I feel I should start worrying about his honorarium, since he himself would never dream of making any demands, even if ten years from now he still hadn't received anything. So I felt I had to intervene on his behalf. He told me that he hadn't heard anything from you since sending you his piece. If that is not so, as you seem to suggest, then I'm very sorry. I had to take him at his word.

I hope that I have managed to suggest the way I see our relationship. There are great benefits in it for me, but also some disadvantages— especially the fact that, as I mentioned above, there is nobody at the publishers with whom I can keep in touch in both literary and human terms. So as to avoid my having to wait around nervously for months in vain, a person like that could, for instance, have let me know right away

---

* *Der Blütenzweig* (Zurich, 1945), a selection of poetry.
† Ernst Köpfli, editor at Fretz & Wasmuth, Zurich.
‡ Afterword to the new edition of Hugo Ball's biography of Hesse.

that for such and such a reason the publisher would have to delay publication of the Ball book, for which we have been waiting since May. And if I had come knocking on the door because there was no reply or a postcard hadn't been sent, he wouldn't have taken it as a criticism of the publishing enterprise.

Thank you again for your letter; it provided me with some important information. We need to support each other by cooperating and occasionally plaguing each other with demands. Life is imperfect, especially in this crazy era, and to hold our own against it, we must be not only industrious but also psychologically acute. Fondly

P.S. We have just received news that Suhrkamp will be coming soon with his wife. For the final step, a document is required, and I would ask you to provide the following:

A statement, certified by a notary, that the Verlag Fretz (or better still, Herr Fretz personally) will guarantee payment of the expenses for a convalescent stay by Peter Suhrkamp and his wife from Berlin.

May I ask you for a note along those lines?

If this turns out to be true and Suhrkamp actually comes, there will be many things for us to talk over and sort out.* I can imagine that he will first discuss with you all matters relating to me, and then, if necessary, the three of us can meet in person.

TO A READER OF "THE GLASS BEAD GAME"

September 1947

You will find in the motto prefacing the first volume a precise answer to the question of how the Glass Bead Game is constituted, the extent to which it actually exists, has existed, or is utopian, the degree to which the author believes in it, etc.

As the author of the biography of Josef Knecht and the inventor of Albertus Secundus, I have contributed somewhat to the *paululum appropinquant*†—as have those who gained access to the essence of music and developed the musicology of the past few decades, or those philologists who tried to establish ways of measuring the melodies in a prose style, as well as a few others. My nephew and friend Carlo Isenberg,

---

* Hesse did not get to see Suhrkamp at that time, as he had hoped. Their first meeting after the war did not take place until January 1948 in Montagnola.

† Latin, "brings them a step closer," from the *The Glass Bead Game*'s motto.

the Ferromonte of my book, was one of those pioneers in *non ens*, one of those individuals who brought that condition closer to a *facultas nascendi*. He conducted musical research, played the harpsichord and clavichord, was in charge of an organ and directed a choir, searched throughout southern and southeastern Europe for fragments of the most ancient music. He has been missing since the end of the war, and, if still alive, is imprisoned somewhere in Russia.

As for myself, I have never lived in Castalia, am a hermit, have never joined a community, with the exception of the Travelers to the East, a league of believers whose way of life is very similar to that of Castalia. But in the course of the past dozen years, ever since portions of my book about Josef Knecht have become known, I have not infrequently been glad to receive greetings from people working away quietly somewhere who like to engage in speculation and for whom the concept that I called the Glass Bead Game has long been as real as it has been for me. They know in their very souls that it exists; they had known of it, or intuitively sensed it, for years before the appearance of my book; they regarded it as an intellectual and ethical challenge, and are beginning to recognize it, increasingly, as a force capable of forging a community. They are further developing the approach suggested in my book: *paululum appropinquant*. And it seems to me that you are one of them and thus live closer to Castalia than you had imagined.

TO PETER SUHRKAMP

October 2, 1947

I already asked you months ago why you occasionally insist on giving unpublished pieces of mine to the press, even though you don't own the rights to them, and I protested against this practice of yours. But you never replied.

And now along comes another surprise. Two poems* have appeared in Volume 4 of the *Deutsche Beiträge*, which you offered to the editors

---

* The poems were "Josef Knechts Berufung" and "Verlieren sich im Sand," which the editors had presumably received from the Munich Hesse collector and bibliographer Horst Kliemann. On November 21, Hesse wrote to Kliemann: ". . . I had finally hoped to find out who it was who had arbitrarily ascribed two poems by somebody else to me . . . What I discover instead is that you have, unfortunately, a large number of poems of mine, of which any number may, of course, not be by me but might nevertheless appear one day under my name." A statement underneath the poems read as follows: "We would like to thank the Suhrkamp Verlag, Berlin, for permission to publish the two poems by Hermann Hesse for the first time."

without my knowledge or authorization. Actually, neither of the poems was by me! They are poems enclosed by readers with their letters, which I would occasionally copy for a friend, and now the editors of that journal have published those pieces, passing them off, rather grotesquely, as my work. I'm more than accustomed to seeing you dispose of my property without my prior knowledge, and I'm also accustomed to strange practices in the present-day German press, but this is the most ludicrous, vulgar such occurrence to date. I simply cannot avoid making the following reproach: You had no right to allow them to print unpublished pieces of mine, and if this should happen again with any frequency, I shall break off our relationship. I know what friendship is all about, but that sort of behavior has nothing to do with it. And so, for the umpteenth time, I repeat my request: Instead of disposing of manuscript pages behind my back, have a little respect for my wishes, which I have repeated often enough, and do everything you can to prevent such use of the material, and cease promoting it, as if to spite me.

I'm sorry, but our relationship has to be based on something resembling trust and order.

TO ERNST PENZOLDT*

[October 1947]

My drawings certainly aren't as beautiful and accurate as yours, but in the last few days I have been dabbling in my own way with a quill and a small brush. Somebody ordered a manuscript of a poem with illustrations, so I have been playing around with paper, watercolors, and paint for two hours or so a day, filling in a few inlets with some villages and mountains. I have left some space in the sky for a few white clouds, and I still need three days' worth of leisure time to write the texts for the poems, which I am selecting from virtually every period in my life. After I have transformed the sheet into an illuminated manuscript, I shall send it off to the person who commissioned it. The payment will arrive a few days later, and it in turn will be transformed into a dozen packets for needy friends across the border. You may gladly have one, if you need coffee, tea, sugar, or lard. But there is a long interval between the initial order for the packet and the day it actually arrives— usually six to eight weeks.

Well, let me know at some point how I should address it.† [. . .]

* Sculptor and writer.
† Penzoldt was staying in Peter Suhrkamp's vacation home in Kampen on Sylt.

I'm starting to give up wine, haven't smoked in the last four or five years. It's good that Suhrkamp is back in Frankfurt!* And good you told me. Otherwise I wouldn't have found out about it for weeks. Have a good time on your island!

TO SALOME WILHELM

Montagnola, January 11, 1948

I felt very unhappy after reading your kind December letter. Obviously, you never—or haven't yet—received the two letters in which I gave some hints about my situation and also explained why I cannot read that novel by your acquaintance. The situation is as follows. For the past two years my daily mail has been so voluminous that the task of reading it once would exhaust a healthy young man: anywhere between a hundred and five hundred pages of letters a day, a continuous stream of dull and corrosive water seeping into my eyes, my mind, and my heart, day after day; the world it portrays is full of misery, complaints, desperation, also some stupidity and coarseness. Those letters ask me to help, issue statements, send things, and give advice; the tone ranges from straightforward requests to actual threats. Moreover, I have to feed some two dozen people in Germany; working on the side, I earn several hundred francs a month to keep my sisters and friends alive. My eyes have been damaged for years. All that time I have not known a day without some eye pain; my only help comes from my wife, and she is already heavily overburdened with household chores, guests, volunteer work for the émigrés, etc. She is gradually wilting, consumed, like me, by this awful treadmill.

Even three or four years ago almost nothing would have pleased me as much as hearing that somebody had written a biography of Wilhelm† and that I might be of some use. But, things being the way they are, I have had to take another pill and work overtime another hour to get this miserable letter written. Here is the only advice I can think of: Mentioning those old ties, ask Dr. C. G. Jung, who lives in Küsnacht near Zurich, to do something for your manuscript. He himself will hardly be able to do anything; he has been very ill and is probably just as overworked as I. But he has something I lack, lots of help from secre-

---

* In the fall of 1947, Peter Suhrkamp, who had been granted a license to operate as a publisher in the American occupation zone, was able to set up the Suhrkamp Verlag, formerly the S. Fischer Verlag, in Frankfurt.

† Salome Wilhelm's *Richard Wilhelm: Mittler zwischen China und Europa* was not published until 1956.

taries, students, etc., and it might possibly suffice if he persuaded his Zurich publisher, Rascher, to have a look at the manuscript. It could be a suitable addition to his list.

Well, enough of that. We're living in a period of transition; we don't know what the future will bring, but the current outlook is unfavorable. Although it seems as though I myself haven't inhaled any air or eaten any bread in years, I have to enjoy the following task: I scrape resources together to prevent a group of righteous citizens from starving, even though they voted for Hindenburg and, to some extent, for Hitler as well. By the way, on the positive side, some former Nazis have really converted, and become alert, honorable-minded people, but people with nobility have always been in a small minority, everywhere. Farewell, and don't be angry with me—you aren't, of course—you realize that, despite everything, I have faithful memories of you and Wilhelm and feel grateful to you.

TO HIS SON HEINER

[End of February 1948]

There is something on the way to you for your birthday, along with my best wishes.

We had Frau Geroe here for a few weeks—she was ill—and my poor Berlin publisher and his wife spent a few days with us. Then, two weeks ago, after months of senseless worries and excitement, our Romanian refugees finally arrived—Ninon's only sister and her husband. They have lost their homeland and have not yet found a country willing to issue them an immigration visa. They were only allowed into Switzerland as my guests for a brief period of "recuperation"; they couldn't take a single penny along. Even in Bucharest they weren't allowed to buy the tickets; we had to send money for the journey, etc., by messenger to the Hungarian border. At least they are out of Romania, having narrowly escaped a frightful end, since they are not only undesirable intellectuals but also Jews, and Romania prides itself on not being any less anti-Semitic now that it is Communist and loyal to Stalin than it was under Hitler or Antonescu.* They are systematically "liquidating" the entire section of the population to which Ninon's people belong. Naturally, we are going to harbor both of them at our place, with or without the consent of the Alien Police, until they can get a visa for

---

* Ion Antonescu, authoritarian Romanian politician, ally of Hitler.

some country where they could eke out a living. They have experienced unmentionable horrors, which only get talked about incidentally or by chance, and one feels ashamed again to be part of this infernal world, in which a person's life—ten thousand lives even—is worth less than a pound of flour.

TO A PATRON

Montagnola, March 1948

Thanks for your kind letter. Your guess is right: I'm continuing my activities on behalf of Germany. They have consumed most of my time for almost three years, and I shall possibly die serving this cause, since no serious change can be expected in the foreseeable future. Only yesterday a cousin of mine was here. He is head of a Stuttgart clinic, a brilliant doctor, passionately committed to his profession. He works in a half-destroyed building; there is a huge crowd of patients every day, and they do not have enough rooms, beds, or anything else. The treatment of severely ill patients has to be constantly interrupted, since they are always running out of the necessary medicine, etc., etc., and cannot acquire any more.

I devote about a third of my activities to the task of supplying food to almost two dozen friends of mine in Germany; for this I need some five hundred francs each month, and that easily amounts to a third of my income. In addition, I supply them with books, and the third part has to do with the provision of reading matter, advice, instruction, etc., to the POWs. Some of them have been living behind barbed wire in camps in Africa or Syria for three to four years, and even the shortest good book can virtually save their lives. In the last three years I have sent the prisoners almost 2,000 books. Incidentally, that is a service I performed once before, for over three years, during the First World War. [. . .]

But enough of that. It's a crazy age, since one cannot even write anybody a letter without inundating them with miseries, of which they no doubt already have more than enough themselves.

I'm sending you copies of all my privately printed works. If you can and so wish, you may send me whatever amount you think fitting, to help support my army of problem children.

TO MAX BROD*

Montagnola, May 25, 1948

Almost every day I receive a small handful of supplicatory letters, mostly from Germany. A person is ill and ought to get into a sanatorium with good food. Another is a literary person, researcher, or artist, has been living in a single room with three or four other people for years, doesn't even have a table; he should get some space, relaxation, and a job. One writes: "All it takes is a nod from you, then the recognized welfare agencies will do everything they can to help." Another: "A word from you to the federal agencies would be enough to secure for the poor man an entrance visa and work permit, perhaps citizenship as well." Whereupon I always have to reply that not a single authority, agency, sanatorium, or baker's shop in this country would give a meal to anybody merely on the basis of a nod or whisper from me. What is so amazing and painful about these requests is the petitioners' faith in the existence of a fairy-tale magician who has only to lift a finger and misery will yield to happiness, war to peace.

And now even you, a close friend of Kafka's, the profound trage-dian, are addressing me with that sort of request, and this time I am not just being asked to support an individual or two, but to assist an entire people and also "restore peace"! I'm frightened at the very thought, since I must confess that I cannot believe in the ability of "intellectuals" to unite or in the noble intentions of the "civilized world." In matters of the intellect, quantity is irrelevant, and it doesn't matter whether ten or a hundred "prominent people" are petitioning the holders of power for some change in policy, since the cause is in any case quite hopeless. If, years ago, you had turned to the new groups in your own country that had terrorist training and had appealed to them to be humane, God-fearing, and nonviolent, you would have heard in no uncertain terms what activists and people under arms think of those ideals.

No, no matter how noble your intentions, I cannot share your view. On the contrary, I believe that all the "intellectual" pseudo-protests, endless petitions, demands, sermons, or even warnings directed by in-tellectuals at those who control the world are wrong and merely damage and degrade the cause of the intellect, and all such efforts should definitely cease. Dear Max Brod, our realm is certainly "not of this world." Our role is not to preach or give orders or make demands, but to remain steadfast amid the infernos and the devils and to refuse to put

---

* Austrian writer and Zionist; best known as biographer and editor of Franz Kafka.

much hope in the effectiveness of our fame or in the impact of large numbers of people like us. In the long term, for sure, we shall certainly prevail, since people will remember some of our work long after the ministers or generals of today have fallen into oblivion. But as for the short term, the here and now, it is we who are the poor fellows, and the world has absolutely no intention of letting us play its game. We poets and thinkers only amount to something because we are human beings who, whatever our faults, have a heart and a head and some fellow feeling for everything natural and organic. The ministers and other political operators base their temporary power, not on the heart and mind, but on the masses, of whom they are the "exponents"! We should avoid the things with which they operate: numbers and quantity. We have to leave this area to them. It's not easy for them either, and that is something we ought not forget: They often find things even more difficult than we do. They don't have a life or mind of their own, and cannot be tranquil or worried, or have a sense of equilibrium, since they are carried along, pushed about, and swept aside by millions of voters. It is not that they are entirely unmoved by the abominations which occur under their very eyes and for which they themselves share some responsibility; they are just at a loss. They have their own ground rules, which provide some cover and can make their responsibility more tolerable. As custodians of the intellectual heritage, servants of the word and of truth itself, we feel as much compassion as horror. But we think our ground rules are more than ground rules, that they are real commandments, real laws, eternal, divine. Our duty is to preserve them, and every compromise and concession we make to those other "ground rules" puts them at risk, even if our intentions are most noble.

I realize that, by stating all of this so bluntly, I may cause superficial observers to conclude that I am by nature one of those artistic dreamers who believe that art bears no relation to politics and that the artist should remain ensconced in his ivory-towered, aesthetic existence, and shouldn't have any contact with harsh realities that would spoil his mood or make him dirty his hands. I know that in this regard I don't have to defend myself in your eyes. Ever since the First World War relentlessly opened my eyes to reality, I have raised my voice often; indeed the sense of responsibility thus awakened in me has consumed a large portion of my life. But I have carefully remained within certain bounds; as an artist and man of letters, I have tried to remind my readers continually of the sacred, basic commandments that we ought to obey as human beings, but I have never tried to influence politics myself, in the style of the hundreds of petitions, protests, and warnings that intellectuals are constantly issuing, with great ceremony, but to no avail; those activities merely damage the reputation of our humanitarian cause. And my position is not about to change.

Although I was not able to grant your wish, as you can see, I have at least tried to make your concern known to others, by publishing your letter and my response.*

TO A STUDENT†

[*ca. July 1948*]

Dear Herr Z.,

I am an old, sick man; for the past three years, I have been utterly consumed and exhausted by the tasks of the day, which are fundamentally alien to me—caring for a large number of starving people, having to contend with volumes of daily mail that would defeat the youngest, healthiest person—so I cannot respond adequately.

In your letter, which I find admirably serious-minded, you equate yourself right away with the "poets and thinkers" I mention in my letter to Brod. You are a student, and as a student you have a right to register a solemn protest against any injustice taking place in the world by getting together with your fellow students and organizing meetings and processions, and then, having done your bit, you can quietly resume your studies. But the situation is very different when an old man such as myself, who is considered a poet and thinker and has done more for other people in the course of his life than most of you will ever do, asks himself whether it really makes much sense to take part in pathetic and completely ineffective protests that only serve to devalue the intellectual cause and further undermine whatever weak authority it has. You cannot understand me because you do not have my life and work behind you.

Just conceive for a moment of President Truman, Stalin, the King of Jordan, and the leaders of the Jewish and Arab terror groups reading a protest written by me, Thomas Mann, Einstein, and fifty other well-known intellectuals. Imagine the kind of face that each one of these politicians would make were somebody to remind them that the literary remains of Novalis or a valuable collection of paintings could be de-

---

* Published as "An Attempt at Self-Justification" in the June 1948 issue of the *Neue Schweizer Rundschau*, Zurich.

† The addressee had read Hesse's letter to Max Brod in the *Neue Schweizer Rundschau* of June 1948 and had been shocked by the notion that it is no longer possible for intellectuals to cooperate directly with politicians.

stroyed tomorrow. Do you seriously believe that any one of these brokers of world power would spend a single second worrying about such matters?

No, there are many tasks facing the intellect, but one stands out above all others: caring for the truth and making sure that people can see and understand reality. Ninety-nine percent of the population keeps ignoring reality, because it simply cannot tolerate it. What I said in the letter to Brod about the intellect and its opportunities for action forms a part of that reality.

If you want to find other intellectual witnesses, you should at some point read the talk that Paul Valéry gave in 1932 at the Sorbonne in commemoration of Goethe. It would suffice to read the first few sentences of that speech.* He describes the present relationship between intellectuals and power more clearly than it has probably ever been enunciated in our time.

That will have to do. I have many other tasks ahead of me today, and if I spent as much time and energy on each of them as on this letter to you, the day would have to last a month.

Immerse yourself in life. If you find that you cannot stand the thought of things I said that have shocked you, then forget about them. Your tasks in life are probably different from mine. You have to be alert to other aspects of life, and nobody demands of you what Max Brod or you yourself ask of me. Then you will leave the futile protests up to those who have the right to engage in them, young people without any responsibilities yet, and you will follow your conscience in your true sphere of influence.

TO HORST KLIEMANN

[*1948*]

I should have thanked you long ago for your essay about my ties to Munich,† but I couldn't do so in a few words. And even today I don't have the time and energy to write the kind of letter that would be necessary. Your essay is fine, friendly in tone, but there is one big omission. It describes a few of my friendships there. But there isn't a word about what Munich increasingly came to represent for us for-

* The passage highlighted by Hesse begins: "The intellect detests all groups; it prefers not to engage in party politics; it feels compromised when unanimity is reached; it considers that it has something to gain from mutual disagreement."

† "Hermann Hesse und München," in *Münchner Tagebuch*, Vol. 3 (1948).

eigners—i.e., non-Nazi Germans. It was the bastion of the "Pan-Germans." We didn't take them very seriously at the time, but nonetheless hated them bitterly. It was the bastion of an arrogant intelligentsia, which was well versed in every conceivable subject, with the exception of politics, knew everything better always, mocked all things; Stefan George also turned us against that group. And it was also the bastion of the entire reactionary clique, the place where Landauer was killed and Hitler got his education, the city of Hitlerism par excellence. I have no doubt that a good number of former Nazi luminaries are back in business again at the university and elsewhere.

Thomas Mann has said enough in *Faustus* about this wonderful, hospitable city, to which we owe half of Hitler; he knew the city better than I. So it is really strange to see you describe my relationship to Munich as innocuous and peaceful.

I have now said the most important thing. You meant well, and I bear you no grudge, but I felt I had to correct that perception.

TO ELISABETH FELLER

February 7, 1949

I don't have sufficient energy for a letter, and shan't manage to hear the *St. Matthew Passion* either—unless it's broadcast on the radio, in which case I shall certainly listen. This reminds me of something in early childhood. The only work of Bach's I knew was the *St. Matthew Passion*, which I had heard once or twice, as well as many rehearsals. I heard a man who knew a lot about music saying that he preferred the *St. John Passion*, but when my uncle began rehearsing the *St. John* with his little choir in Calw, I was extremely disappointed, because it sounded less dramatic than the *St. Matthew*. Then there was a time, much later, when I too far preferred the *St. John*. Today I like both equally, and that preference is unlikely to change.

I'm sending you what I could find by way of privately printed works and bibliophile editions. These pieces aren't sold; they're printed in editions of two hundred to eight hundred, and virtually all of the copies are given away as presents. But the desperate hunger in Germany (the currency reform hasn't improved matters in intellectual and artistic circles), which has become more severe in many places, is such that I occasionally let collectors have some copies. I still need to come up with between 500 and 700 francs a month to prevent the people dependent on me from going hungry, and that is very difficult to do. If you would like to give me 100 or 120 francs for the prints, you would certainly be helping out.

TO EDMUND NATTER

[*February 22, 1949*]

I read your recent letter with pleasure, and my wife also enjoyed it. Your sister and her husband have been our guests here for a year; they're leaving for France tomorrow, on a trial basis. I used to know wine lovers like your friends in the Rhineland; they can be found wherever wine is grown, especially in France and on the Rhine. As for me, over the years I have turned from heavier to lighter wines, and have discovered that "small" and by no means renowned wines can have their own distinctive qualities. By the way, I have never particularly liked Rhenish wines and tend to favor certain Mosels; here in Switzerland I prefer the Fendant wines of Vaud and Wallis. Goodbye, somebody is calling. More anon!

TO OTTO BASLER

April 1949

Thanks for your pleasant letter. I find Thomas Mann's expression of sympathy and comradeship rather moving. He once said in the course of a conversation with us: "In the intellectual sphere there is no such thing as unhappy love," and that certainly applies to the relationship between the two of us. I have occasionally discovered to my great surprise that several contemporaries knew of my writings and loved them; the two most surprising such names were André Gide, who wrote me a note many years ago, and Franz Kafka. Many years after Kafka's death, Brod told me that his friend Kafka had read all my work and greatly liked it. I, in turn, had similar feelings of sympathy and admiration for them.

I don't read any newspapers, so I have no idea what the Zurich newspaper said about Mann's attitude toward communism. But I would be surprised if his ideas on that score were different from mine. From the very outset I have rejected both communism and fascism—with the distinction that I consider communism a necessary experiment, whereas fascism merely seems a useless attempt at regression. But unless communism sets itself the task of bringing about an equitable distribution of wealth and property rather than a "dictatorship of the proletariat," it constitutes a regression vis-à-vis Marx, and if a small clique of party bosses continue to profit from it rather than the people as a whole, there is no point discussing it any further.

I'm sure Th. Mann has very similar ideas in that regard.

One further thing: Kindly give my best regards to Mann, and let him know I have finally managed to place the wonderful lecture on Mann by my friend Dr. Amstein. It will be appearing in the May issue of the *Neue Schweizer Rundschau*, probably alongside a little prose piece of mine.

TO OTHMAR SCHOECK

[*May 1949*]

Your letter was like a visit from a friend. I had wanted to hear you talk about your trip to Swabia, and my hopes were more than fulfilled, since I had imagined your experience there more or less as you describe it, the way you scoured the once cheerful countryside with the Mörike poems in your suitcase, hoping to find traces of the old magic. And you did find that; how wonderful to have received such a fraternal welcome from the kind spirits of Swabia.*

We have visitors here at the moment from Swabia, my sister Adele and her husband. The three of us look quite ancient, I'm the youngest at seventy-two, but I enjoy hearing Swabian again occasionally and talking about the people and places of our childhood. I rarely get that kind of opportunity. My days are full, and I seldom feel sufficiently comfortable and free from pain to wish to engage in much conversation.

The chestnut wood is in bloom, the cuckoo can still be heard, but the roses are finished. Let's hope we can get together in the fall. Ninon also sends fond regards to Hilde and yourself.

TO THOMAS MANN

Montagnola, May 26, 1949

Like all your friends and acquaintances, we were shocked and deeply saddened on receiving your sad news.† We old people are accustomed to seeing our friends and companions disappearing, but there

---

* The premiere of the first part of Othmar Schoeck's Mörike Song Cycle, "Das holde Bescheiden," 1949.

† Klaus Mann, Thomas Mann's eldest son, committed suicide in Cannes on May 21, 1949.

is something terrifying about losing somebody who is close to us and belongs to the generation meant to replace us after our departure and then shield us somewhat from the icy silence of eternity. That is hard to accept.

I don't know much about how things stood between you and Klaus. I myself followed his early work closely and sympathetically. Later on I was irritated on your account by certain flaws in his literary efforts, and find it consoling to think that these efforts ultimately culminated in a wonderful, fine, valuable work, the book about André Gide,* which has won over the hearts of both his friends and yours. That book will survive its author by many years.

We shake hands in heartfelt sympathy with you and your wife, who is very much on our minds.

TO LUISE RINSER†

Bremgarten near Bern, August 1949

Since my wife cannot tolerate the heat, we spent the hottest period in the Engadine, then came here to our friends' for a brief visit; two of my sons live nearby. I received your letter here, pleasant reading apart from the news of Suhrkamp's condition; I had already heard some disquieting reports about that.

This time I didn't meet Thomas Mann.‡ I had assumed that his German trip was going to take place later on, so we missed each other. But we have both promised to get together next year. It's always refreshing and comforting to talk to him, since his worldly demeanor and disciplined manner mask the imaginative range and artistic youthfulness of the artist, qualities which are accessible, if one knows how to address them.

I'm glad to hear that you're diligently finishing a new novel.§ As for me, I have abandoned the complexities of the literary trade and have gone back to the beginnings; whatever writing I have done over the last few years has been restricted to the narrowest framework: the attempt to capture a morsel of truth, a mouthful of experience or observation. In the process I have rediscovered things that I had once known, but

---

* *André Gide: Die Geschichte eines Europäers* (1948).

† German Catholic writer and critic.

‡ Mann had returned to the United States on August 5, 1949, at the end of his second postwar visit to Europe.

§ *Mitte des Lebens* (1950).

since forgotten—for example, the illusory nature of all such striving for truth. Well, that's what discoveries are all about.

I'm expecting my younger sister, who will be staying for a few weeks; the elder spent the early part of the summer here.

Farewell, regards to Suhrkamp, and keep chewing away at the novel.

TO ISA, BARONESS VON BERNUS

[August 18, 1949]

Thanks for your letter, which reaches me at the house of some friends in the Bern area.

I cannot understand why the experience of Germany since 1933 should make the entire world seem incomprehensible and render the very notion of humanity questionable. All those Germans who endorsed the First World War and supported the war effort with enthusiasm, subsequently helped sabotage the young German Republic, or voted for Hindenburg's election as President, have in effect worked for Hitler and aided his cause. When I hear or read about a crime, I very rarely feel that I wouldn't be capable of something similar or couldn't be seduced into it. Man is neither good nor evil, but has the inner potential for both, and if his consciousness and will are inclined to good, that already means a lot. But even in such a case, man's primeval impulses are all still very much alive under the surface, and could lead him in unexpected directions. It's hardly a coincidence that these absolutely diabolic events occurred in Germany, a country known for its excessively wonderful idealism and verbose intellectuality.

Enough. I didn't want to argue, that's not my style. I'm just making sure your kind greetings don't go unanswered.

TO SIEGFRIED UNSELD

1949/50

I ought to feel embarrassed by your aesthetic question concerning Josef Knecht, since I'm not as fortunate as you, and cannot devote myself to such wonderful, Castalian studies. I have not had an opportunity to reread *The Glass Bead Game* since its appearance seven years ago, and indeed have more work on my plate each day than I can possibly manage.

But I feel that I owe you an answer. The questions readers are constantly asking me about Castalia and Knecht are often shockingly mediocre; yours stands out because it is wonderfully perceptive and precise, and for a moment it even gave me some pause.

I shall have to rely on my memory here, even though I have managed, with the help of my wife, to check out the passages that you are calling into question.

You believe that Josef Knecht's biographer was trying to "portray life through Knecht's perspective, in other words to describe only those things that are visible from the perceptual and experiential vantage point of Knecht himself." And you think that this perspective has been violated in those passages you mentioned, since they refer to facts, words, or other people's thoughts that Knecht couldn't possibly have known about.

The writing of the book stretched out over eleven years (and what years!). In spite of the concentration and care I put into the work, it may contain such structural flaws. But I have never used the perspective that you think the book is built around. Indeed, in the course of the first three years, my perspective changed somewhat. At first, I merely wanted to make Castalia visible, as a scholarly state, an ideal secular monastery, an idea, or, as my critics think, an idle dream, that has existed and been effective since the age of the Platonic academy, one of the ideals that have served as effectual "guiding images" throughout intellectual history. Then it dawned on me that if I really wanted to show the inner reality of Castalia in a convincing way, I would have to create a dominant character, a spiritual hero, a figure who knows how to endure. Knecht thus became the focus of the story, an exemplary and unique character, not so much because he is an ideal, perfect Castalian, since he is not alone in that regard, but rather because, ultimately, he cannot remain satisfied with Castalia and its perfect isolation.

But the biographer whom I envisioned is an advanced pupil or tutor in Waldzell; out of love for the great renegade, he has begun writing the novel of Knecht's life for a group of Knecht's friends and admirers. This biographer has access to everything that Castalia possesses: the oral and written tradition, the archives, and, of course, his own imagination and powers of empathy. He draws on these sources, and I don't think anything in his account would be improbable in terms of that framework. In the final portion of his biography, he stresses that the individual details and milieu, for which no corroboration can be found in Castalia, constitute the "legend" of the missing Magister Ludi, as it has been handed down among his pupils and in Waldzell lore.

I derived the individual traits of some figures in the book from real people; some of these models have been recognized by perceptive readers, others are still known only to me. Father Jacobus was the figure most readily recognized; he represents my homage to Jacob Burckhardt, whom I dearly loved. I even took the liberty of putting one of Burckhardt's sayings into the mouth of my priest. His resigned realism makes him one of the opponents of the Castalian intellect.

There is only one figure in my story drawn almost entirely from life. That is Carlo Ferromonte. This Carlo Ferromonte, or rather the original on whom he is based, was an extremely dear friend and close relative of mine, a generation younger than I, a musician and musical expert. All of Monteport would have been delighted with him. An organist, choral director, harpsichord player, and passionate collector of the remaining traces of living folk music, he followed the faint trail of that vanishing tradition on his travels, especially in the Balkans. Then my dear Carlo had to serve as a medical orderly in this senseless war, was ultimately stationed at military hospitals in Poland, and ever since the end of the war, he has been missing without a trace.

TO GEORG WERNER

January 16, 1950

Thanks for your letter. Yes, artists can occasionally wield power, at least to the extent of being able to prevent truly powerful people from committing crimes. Romain Rolland was that kind of individual. He came to the aid of many who were doomed and secured their release. I don't think the Russians ever understood or appreciated his utterly Western mentality. He did, however, join the Communist party, since in those days an idealist could still hope that communism would yield a new humanity of some kind. Above all, he was a friend of Gorki's, who thought a lot of him, and Gorki was very powerful indeed. Whenever Rolland heard of somebody with a decent reputation having vanished into the prisons of the Russian Gestapo, he usually managed through Gorki to have the sentence revoked and the person freed. But Gorki's death put an end to that.

I hope your children's magazine is successful, both for yourself and for the cause.

I feel rather depressed as I emerge slowly from the flood of letters I receive every year from mid-December until early January; there's still an unopened heap lying around.

I'm sending you a new piece separately, as printed matter. The Baden experience described therein has affected me very deeply—I was weaker at the time than I had imagined.*

* "Aufzeichnung bei einer Kur in Baden" ("Notes from a Spa in Baden") (*WA*, 8:508ff).

I'm enclosing two small samples of my day-to-day existence, copies of two letters.

TO A STATE COUNSELOR

[February 1950]

Life is really too short for such long letters. In the meantime, your wife has resolved the matter that she herself instigated through some utterly incomprehensible niggling about Thomas Mann,* and has written to me. And since I have sent her a publication and my regards, she ought to realize that I'm no longer angry with her. You have recounted all those fateful blows that befell your wife. Well, most of my close relatives—the relatively few descendants of my Baltic grandfather—lost their homes and possessions, and fourteen perished in the war. And the relatives and friends of my wife are Bukovina Jews. You in Germany, a country where people never stop bewailing their woes, haven't an inkling of what those people had to endure.

As a result of this German compulsion to complain and beg for pity, I—an old man saddled with eye problems—have to read thousands and thousands of letters in which completely unknown people describe in great detail what they and their families have been through. There are several women who believe that they must not only inform me about the food prices in their area but also give detailed descriptions of the illnesses affecting every single family member, their operations, etc. But if one even so much as mentions the fate of the Jews or the guilt of the Germans, their response makes one blush with shame.

You will have to realize that I'm human too and that there are limits to my tolerance. You won't hold this against me.

TO HANS CAROSSA

End of February 1950

Ninon and I enjoyed your letter; we were glad to hear that we can hope for a new book of yours† in the fall, and perhaps another visit.

---

* Hesse had recently refuted a similar criticism of Mann's "Letter to Vienna": "On the whole, the German excitement about Thomas Mann says something about the nature of their preoccupations and indicates once again how unwilling they are to tackle serious matters. Ultimately, what harm has Mann done with any of his 'political' attitudes and activities since losing his citizenship? None!"

† Possibly the memoirs *Ungleiche Welten* (1951).

Things have been quite hectic here recently; there were always visitors around—pleasant ones, fortunately. But I often considered that a nuisance, since the spring has been my worst season for many years. I begin feeling unwell in January and remain in that condition until the beginning of summer. In the meantime, in spite of gout and dizzy spells, I have had some joyful experiences, and was able to greet the returning flowers and butterflies as fervently as ever.

As regards the joys of old age, I had a good laugh at myself yesterday. A childhood friend of mine published some innocuous reminiscences of Calw during the 1870s and 1880s.* Just hearing again the names of forgotten people and alleyways was wonderful, and when I heard that a giant pipe, taller than a man, which used to hang above the workshop of a turner,† and was very old even then, hasn't disappeared, I was as delighted as if my gout had healed or something significant had happened.

I want to let my friends know what I'm doing with myself these days by means of an "Epistolary Mosaic,"‡ which I shall also send you. A thank-you and salutation will have to suffice for today.

TO HERBERT SCHULZ

[April 1950]

Your informative letter must have crossed my last two publications. They aren't as personal as real letters, but are all I can manage given my condition. They have no doubt told you more about me than I could have said in a letter.

I first became acquainted with psychoanalysis in 1916, when my private life and the pressure of the war had become excessively burdensome. The doctor§ wasn't at all overbearing—he was far too young and too respectful of celebrity for that—but he went about it seriously, and became a very dear friend of mine, even decades afterward when there was no longer any question of our conducting an analysis. I only realized at a very late stage, long after the analysis (primarily Jungian) was over, that, for all his enthusiasm about art, my friend had no real understanding of it. And I gradually realized that none of the psychoanalysts I have encountered, above all Jung, ever regarded art as anything

---

* August Rentschler, *Erinnerungen eine alten Calwers*, in the *Calwer Zeitung*.

† A turner's workshop at 22 Lederstrasse in Calw, next door to the house inhabited by the Hesse family from 1889 to 1893.

‡ "Briefmosaik (1)" appeared in the *Neue Schweizer Rundschau*, Zurich, in March 1950.

§ Dr. Josef B. Lang.

more than an expression of the unconscious; they felt that the neurotic dream of any patient was just as valuable as, and far more interesting than, all of Goethe. It was ultimately this insight that allowed me to extricate myself totally from the climate of analysis. But, on the whole, the treatment had a positive effect on me, as did my reading of some of Freud's main works.

It's a pity that you couldn't accept Knecht's* sacrificial death. Do you think his story would be more valuable if it had lasted another ten or twenty years? The call that draws him away from Castalia and into the world is a call from his conscience, but it's also a call from death. And how great for him, to have encountered such a short, beautiful death so soon after his breakthrough. [. . .]

TO FELIX LÜTZKENDORF

May 1950

Your letter has been lying around here unanswered for over a month. It would be easy to find some excuse for this delay, but I feel I should respond with something other than a polite formality. Twenty or twenty-five years ago, you wrote a dissertation about me, the best one at that time, in which you paid particular attention to the origins and affiliations of my religious and Asian concerns. Your grasp of the issues was well above average, and when the stormy period beginning in 1933 was over, you often contacted me; we exchanged letters, and I, like an old child, was still living under the blithe illusion that you understood me and took me seriously.

Your letter partly destroyed this illusion, and moreover—I'm just realizing this right now—also created the inner resistance that made it so difficult for me to respond.

You wanted my permission to film one of my books. I was disappointed by the way you responded when I had to say no.

You write that I'm "utterly unwilling to get involved in any way in such a diabolic activity as film," as if I were some old pastor or ascetic type who is convinced that the film would jeopardize "the morality of the people."

By now you may have had second thoughts about this, but I would nevertheless like to correct your rather naïve understanding of my ideas about film.

I do not regard film as a "diabolic activity," and have no objection

---

* Josef Knecht, the main character in Hesse's *The Glass Bead Game*.

to its competing against literature and books. I admire and treasure certain films that reflect a high level of artistic taste and are imbued with worthwhile convictions. And I have no qualms when I see productive, talented people with a literary background, such as yourself, turning to film. Indeed, I think film can create opportunities for strong talents and allow them to be truly creative, and thus ensure they don't end up in some other art form as mere dilettantes. There are more than enough talented people who would make the most of the opportunity to invest their energy in creating suspense, awakening interest and empathy in all of life's peaks and depths, bringing about interesting and typical situations and combinations—talented people with an intense imagination who are admirably curious about the utter variousness of life and, in some cases, possess an acute moral sensibility—i.e., a strong sense of responsibility for the tens of thousands of souls whom they affect. Besides, it's not merely possible. There are enough real cases to prove that the author of a good script can also be a genuine artist.

But there is a big difference between a film conceived by a writer and a film that appropriates and exploits an existing work of literature for its own ends. The former is a genuine, legitimate achievement; the latter is a theft or, somewhat euphemistically, a borrowing. A work of literature relies on literary effects, in other words on language alone, and ought never be regarded merely as "material" to be exploited through the techniques of another art form. That's degrading, barbarous.

You're certainly right about the potential impact of film. It can reach, satisfy, influence countless thousands of hungry souls who are avid for art, without being open to literature in print. But if you make a film out of *Crime and Punishment, Madame Bovary, Green Henry*, or any other work of literature, even if you go about the task with a lot of taste, skill, and even an extremely strong sense of moral responsibility, you merely destroy its utterly unique, most intimate meaning, and replace it with the equivalent of an Esperanto translation. We are left with a sentimental memory or a moral. The heart of the work is gone, and so is its inimitable otherness.

What has vanished is the old but still vibrant element of culture that is inherent in every verbal work of art.

One could compare somebody filming a literary work with a literary illustrator, and argue that some illustrators are more brilliant than the works they illustrate. Maybe, but that only makes the second-rate illustrations seem all the more disturbing.

It is certainly possible, probable even, that life in the near future will be such that film will acquire almost all the tasks once assumed by literature. There may well come a time when virtually nobody will be capable of reading books. Even in that case, I would still oppose the filming of my books, and wouldn't have any difficulty resisting the lure of fame or money. The more endangered literature and language become, the more I cherish and value them.

Oh, what long letters! I'm really tired now. This shall have to suffice.

TO HIS SON BRUNO

May 1950

I enjoyed your letter, thanks. But I'm sorry to hear you're copying out *Krisis*.* If it weren't so occasional, a piece limited to a specific phase in life, I would gladly have given it to you, but this was something I wanted to spare you. It was only published once, in a small edition. The *Collected Poems* contains only verse that transcends confessional horizons and seems to me worth preserving.

I would like a watercolor of yours for Marulla's birthday in November; it can cost 200 francs, which I'm enclosing right away, since I'm getting rather forgetful. You, of course, have time enough until the fall. [. . .]

The most important event here recently was a session eight days ago with the heirs of my old publisher, S. Fischer: Dr. Bermann and his wife (Fischer's daughter). Since the newspapers often report on these matters in a distorted manner, I would like to give you a brief account of the story.

My friend Suhrkamp joined the publishers shortly before the beginning of the Hitler period, while dear Papa S. Fischer was still alive, first as editor of *Die Neue Rundschau* and then increasingly as a member of the managerial team at the publishers. Fischer père died shortly after Hitler appeared on the scene; his son-in-law then took over the press, which was owned by his wife. That only worked out for a few years. The Bermanns were Jews and had to emigrate. Suhrkamp subsequently took over as director of the press, with the idea of keeping it going, perhaps until the day when Hitlerism was finally over. From that point on, Suhrkamp ran the press. The owners lived at first in Vienna, then in Stockholm, and finally in America. They published a number of books abroad that were banned in Hitler Germany, especially those of Thomas Mann, but the overseas firm never really flourished. Around 1938, Suhr-

---

* H. Hesse, *Krisis: Ein Stück Tagebuch* (Berlin: S. Fischer, 1928); 1,150 copies were printed.

kamp, in Berlin, was forced to buy the firm, since the Nazis would no longer tolerate the existence of such a large enterprise with Jewish owners. He contacted the Bermanns, who requested the normal price for the firm, and since nobody wanted to pay that much for it under the prevailing circumstances, Suhrkamp, who had no fortune of his own, tried to round up two or three rich investors willing to take the risk, and he did indeed find them. They bought and paid for the press in the normal manner, and Suhrkamp stayed on as director. Around 1939, Suhrkamp was forced to drop S. Fischer from the firm's name; it subsequently became the Suhrkamp Verlag, formerly S. Fischer. Suhrkamp, who had been very fond of the elder Fischer and utterly loathed the Nazis, fought continuously from then on to save the firm from the Nazis, always with the intention of returning it to the Fischer family after the fall of Hitler. Although he succeeded in preserving the firm, he had to endure some cruel suffering: prison, concentration camp and severe mistreatment, a death sentence (by chance, never carried out). And it became clear, after Hitler was finished and the Bermanns returned, that they had gone on living in style all those years and still were, in fact. When they eventually discovered they weren't getting along with Suhrkamp, they tried to get rid of him under conditions I considered indecent and intolerable. So a decision was made to separate the two firms: Bermann changes the name of his press back to S. Fischer Verlag, and Suhrkamp, after he leaves, sets up his own press. Chief among the older and famous authors remaining with Fischer were Thomas Mann, Werfel, Stefan Zweig, etc.; Suhrkamp retains the authors he himself had brought in.

Then there were some authors—such as myself—who belonged to the house under the old Fischer but had worked exclusively with Suhrkamp for many years, and the Bermanns struggled to get me to return to their Fischer press. But I felt that this tough battle, in which Suhrkamp revealed his decency and chivalrousness,* was demeaning, and have announced that I plan to continue with Suhrkamp rather than Bermann-Fischer.

That's the situation. We have reached a decision, but for the past six months the whole affair has been a great source of worry and torment. And, of course, Suhrkamp has no money and is experiencing great difficulties because of the critical condition of the entire German book trade. [. . .]

* In another letter to Ernst Rheinwald, Hesse wrote: "Suhrkamp's exaggerated and idiosyncratic notions of chivalry caused him to forfeit many options that could have been retained." To Felix Braun: "Suhrkamp thought it wasn't right for a German to make any demands on Jews."

TO THOMAS MANN
[*On the occasion of his 75th birthday*]

June 1950

It is quite a while since I first got to know you. We met in a hotel in Munich, at the invitation of our publisher, S. Fischer. Your first novellas and *Buddenbrooks* had already appeared, as had my *Peter Camenzind*; both of us were still bachelors then, and people were expecting great things from us. Of course, we weren't all that similar in other respects; one could tell this by our clothes and footwear, and our first meeting—in the course of which I asked you whether you weren't by any chance related to the author of the three novels about the Duchess of Assy*—came about by chance or literary curiosity and hardly seemed to prefigure our future friendship and comradeship.

But before we could become friends and comrades—one of the most agreeable and unproblematic friendships of my later years—many things had to happen, of which we hadn't an inkling during that pleasant hour in Munich; each of us had to follow a difficult and often dark path, from the illusory comfort of a national community through isolation and ostracization into the clean and rather cold air of world citizenship, which looks quite different in your case from mine, but nonetheless binds us a lot more solidly and reliably than the things we had in common in those days, when we were moral and political innocents.

We are old-timers now, and few of our associates from those days are still living. And you are celebrating your seventy-fifth birthday, and I am celebrating along with you: I'm grateful for everything that you have written, for everything that you have thought and endured, grateful also for your prose, which is as intelligent as it is enchanting, as uncompromising as it is playful, grateful also for the wellspring of your life's work, the great fund of love, warmth and the dedication, all of which your former compatriots shamefully failed to acknowledge. I am grateful, too, for your fidelity toward your language, your honesty and warmth of conviction, and I hope these qualities will endure as a legacy beyond our lifetime and constitute part of a new morality in world politics, a world conscience, which we are now watching with concern and hope, as it makes its first childlike attempts to walk.

Dear Thomas Mann, stay with us for a long time. I speak gratefully to you, not as the emissary of a nation, but as a loner whose real fatherland, like yours, is still being created.

---

* Written by Mann's brother, Heinrich.

TO PROFESSOR KARL SCHMID

[Sils Maria, August 3, 1950]

[. . .] I don't attach terribly much importance to the decision by the Swabians to reclaim me as one of their own. In the town council of Calw, my little hometown, in 1914 or 1915, somebody proposed naming a street after me or making some such gesture of recognition. But the majority voted against the motion, and when a newspaper campaign was unleashed against me for having made a few statements, which were quite innocuous, if less than wildly enthusiastic about the war, people started to see me as a reptile reared at Germany's bosom, and the people of Calw were very glad they had averted a terrible disgrace. The situation in Constance was even more comical. They named some new street Hesse-Way, because I had lived there by the lake for some seven years, and the name remained on the sign until 1933. By then it had become intolerable, so they repainted the sign, replacing my name with that of my erstwhile friend Finckh. And then in 1945, when Hitler was gone, they scratched out Finckh's name and painted mine back on there. Who but the devil could take these namings and unnamings seriously!

I would have liked Switzerland to accept me as one of her own; as a child, I was a Swiss citizen, had lived there again, uninterruptedly, since 1912, reacquiring citizenship in 1924, and my opposition to the dictatorships in the neighboring countries was more vigorous than that of a thousand native Swiss. But over the years I have realized that I'm not Swiss either and do not fit into any fatherland. [. . .]

TO KARL DETTINGER

Sils Maria [August 8, 1950]

Your kind letter has had to wait a few days. I was ill, but it was read to me on a good day, the first time I was allowed up for a bit. I was lying on a chaise longue on the sunny terrace by my room, had just eaten breakfast and listened to a small quantity of mail, so I was attentive to your letter and grateful for it. I greatly enjoyed your special gift, the lines by the missionary brother from that little hut of yours on the Hohenstaufen.*

Although you say your question (the nature of the "faith" that I find in Thomas Mann and myself) is purely rhetorical, it does call for a short

---

* "He who likes it fine / Should write along this line. / He who likes it not / Had better mosey off."

answer. In spite of a considerable degree of resignation and skepticism, he and I share certain beliefs, which have, of course, no bearing on theology. Neither of us believes that there are sovereign and "higher" powers, independent of the human will, capable of intervening in human affairs, but we do believe most people possess a fund of decency, which is impossible to quantify. We also believe, to some extent, that it's possible to awaken and strengthen these modest virtues in our readers. We're not alone in this. Mann's eldest daughter, Erika, has written a wonderful essay on the moral aspect of the contemporary global situation.* His youngest daughter—the one who experienced the "early" sorrow in the famous novella†—is married to Borgese,‡ the anti-fascist writer and scholar, who wrote the classic account of Mussolini and his huge swindle. She herself is president of an international federation set up to prepare for a future world government. It's not a question of how much they can achieve in practical terms. These are very talented and determined people who have emancipated themselves completely from all nationalist feeling, have also experienced emigration and homelessness, and are now devoting their lives to the cause of peace and rationality. They actively resist all temptations and programs proposed by parties and fronts, as I myself once did in a different environment, after having been awakened and enlightened by the first war.

Unfortunately, I have to say goodbye tomorrow to Thomas, his wife, and Erika. They're continuing on their travels. But we have seen each other often up here in the Engadine and have deepened our friendship and the "faith" you were asking about.

The scene at our comfortable Grand Hotel is the familiar one at such places: an elite group of rich, well-dressed, and moderately polite guests, comprising different nationalities, who are busy recuperating, eating well, displaying their attire, and, within certain bounds, allowing themselves to feel edified by the alpine splendor. There is no problem with the youngsters, who look like the usual American type: good, nice-looking boys, very knowledgeable about sports, which they follow keenly, generally unintellectual, unless appearances are misleading.

But the older and elderly people, up to seventy-five, either seem entirely unaffected by the state of the world and the new horrors on the horizon or are utterly determined to close their eyes and ears to it. They can be seen dancing three times a week in the bar, where in any case

---

* "Der Fall John Peet." The article, with a short foreword by Hesse, was rejected by the media.

† *Disorder and Early Sorrow* (1926), a novella about a childhood experience of Thomas Mann's daughter Elisabeth.

‡ The Italian Germanist and writer Giuseppe Antonio Borgese.

they spend each evening consuming expensive drinks in large quantities. They dance until midnight, until two o'clock. One sees seventy-year-olds with impressive snow-white heads dancing and drinking for many hours on end. At a late hour, after the pianist has slipped away, an elderly person sits down at the piano, and one of the ladies takes over the percussion instruments. All this cheerful humming and buzzing would be delightful if these people were young or if some exceptional occasion were being celebrated. But these actually rather innocent orgies of the upper orders occur as regularly as eating and sleeping. It's certainly none of my business. I have no wish to begin preaching about morals, but at times, after having been taken up all day with letters from Germany exuding anxiety and lamentation, or when I have been thinking somewhat more intently than usual about the stories in the newspapers, the ghostly nature of this artificially induced upper-class good cheer leaves me feeling shocked and constrained, and I ask myself whether many of them really understand the bitter state of affairs, for which they are partly responsible, and the fragility of the floor on which they are dancing.

But I have digressed, and am tired and rather sad. Goodbye, old friend, my regards

TO TRAUGOTT VOGEL

October 22, 1950

I would like to say a quick thank-you and add that my first impression of *Der Bogen** is very favorable. I'm particularly pleased that you have also included Walser.† His fatherland let him down on every count: it failed to recognize his great talent for language, showed no understanding of his idiosyncratic work and life, and never even gave him the crumbs it doles out to every pensioned ape of a state official. I hope you can get some more Walser for *Der Bogen*. In any case, it will prove difficult to keep up the standard once the dilettantes and ambitious incompetents begin showing up in droves.

As for Mühlestein,‡ I'm sure you'll take into account that it was not he but Michelangelo who wrote those extraordinary, anguished poems.

* *Der Bogen*, a series of short literary texts, edited by Traugott Vogel (1950–64).
† Robert Walser, "Die Schlacht bei Sempach." Cf. Robert Walser, *Masquerade and Other Stories*, trans. Susan Bernofsky (1990).
‡ Hans Mühlestein, *Dichtungen des Michelangelo Buonarota* (1950).

TO THOMAS MANN

Montagnola, November 8, 1950

The mail hasn't been very pleasant of late. Even my tame, cautiously written article on the fear of war has reawakened the anger and hostility against me in Germany. Still, that caution has enabled me to smuggle the article into the *National-Zeitung* and the Munich *Neue Zeitung* as well. They both treated the piece as a feuilleton, and failed to detect the smidgeon of political spice in it. On the other hand, somebody in America growled right away at the *Neue Zeitung*, which, a few days later, printed a sad and rather shabby reply. But that doesn't matter; a lot of people saw the article, and many of them got the point.

And now—amidst this idiotic daily mail—a letter arrives from you, a fine, really delightful letter, which also bears the glad tidings that you have completed Gregorius.* That is a joyous event, and although you may miss your daily conversations with Gregorius, we congratulate you heartily nonetheless, and look forward to the reappearance of this fabled, legendary creature. A great many people will welcome it. Most readers will be astute enough to appreciate the ironies in this magnificent work, but I'm not so sure they will all recognize the hidden seriousness and piety that lend those ironies such sublime good cheer.

The only troubling thing in your letter was the news about Frau Erika. Your diagnosis is correct, and I can easily imagine how frustrating it must be in such a deadening atmosphere for so richly talented and energetic a person. I received a lovely letter recently from your daughter; my friendship with her is one of the few good, pure experiences to have come my way in the course of this strange year.†

We have been very busy; otherwise I would have written to you long ago. And we intend to go to Baden again a week from now. There are other attractions aside from the baths: the Zurich library for Ninon, and some friends close by for both of us. Martin Buber will be in Switzerland by then, and will no doubt visit me in Baden.‡

---

* *The Holy Sinner.* At Sils Maria, Mann had read Hesse excerpts from the book, which was first published in 1951. In April 1951, Hesse wrote to Max Silber: "On two separate occasions in the Engadine last summer, Th. Mann read us a few chapters from Gregorius. It was pleasant and fun. Everything transpired behind a mask of objectivity in an endlessly cheerful, soothingly ironic mode. I wouldn't wish for any changes."

† Erika Mann corresponded regularly with Hesse until his death. Twenty-eight extensive letters from Erika Mann, written between 1950 and 1962, were discovered among Hesse's papers.

‡ Buber visited Hesse in Baden in early December. Hesse's friendship with Buber reaches back almost as far as his friendship with Mann. Between 1909 and 1950 he reviewed thirteen books by Buber, and in 1950 proposed him for the Nobel Prize.

We shall hold a day of rejoicing when Gregorius arrives in his handsome binding, and I hope we get to see each other before long.

We're thinking of you three and wish you all the best.

TO THE CITY OF BRUNSWICK

November 1950

As you know, I felt the award of the Wilhelm Raabe Prize was not just an honor but also a joyous and touching occasion, because of my fond and long-lasting ties to the city of Wilhelm Raabe, where the estimable Ricarda Huch was born, as well as to Raabe himself.

All of this comes alive again as I contemplate the beautiful honorary scroll, with its splendid Brunswick lion. As a half-Swiss southern German, I have always regarded Lower Saxony as my favorite region in northern Germany, in terms of both the people and the culture. And within that region my favorite city was Brunswick; I also loved Wilhelm Raabe and regarded him as the bearer and representative of those traditions.

So, for me the echo that my old love has evoked in your venerable city counts among the most valuable experiences life has to offer: the discovery that the love and honor we accord intellectual, suprapersonal values are not lost in a void, never go unanswered, but are reflected back to us.

I wish to convey my gratitude and heartfelt wishes to the city of Brunswick. After the terrible events it has endured, may it be granted a period of peaceful and productive work.

TO KARL VOTTELER

[Baden, December 17, 1950]

Thanks for your letter. I'm almost completely in agreement with you. I'm also well aware of what has happened to the cultural scene and even life itself in the communist countries. I not only get letters from several hundred people in the East, but have put up a series of émigrés or refugees from Eastern countries in my house, including my wife's sisters, who had endured the bitter terror of Hitler, Antonescu, and the Russians in Romania and stayed here for a year as my guests, after we had finally succeeded in getting them released.

Naturally enough, my article on the fear of war was exploited by the Eastern press; they picked out two or three sentences and praised me, to the beat of a tom-tom, for espousing the Soviets. One has to swallow that sort of thing, without taking it all that seriously.

In the twenties I wrote a political statement in verse, which remained incomplete. It began:

> *Better to be killed by the fascists*
> *Than be a fascist oneself.*
> *Better to be killed by the*
> *Communists*
> *Than be a communist oneself . . .**

I'm still of that opinion.

I wasn't able to comment in public on the shameless treatment to which I have been subjected by the Eastern press. The East would not have allowed a single word of protest to be aired, let alone printed; the Western press isn't exactly renowned for its tact and fidelity to the truth.

Another matter: I would ask you not to send me your text on Bach. I haven't been able to read any personal material for years, since my daily mail would tax a healthy young person.

TO MARCEL OCHSENBEIN

[*End of 1950*]

Thanks for your letter, which I enjoyed.

I cannot write you a long letter. I'm old, have too much to do each day; my fingers are crippled with gout, they're reluctant to tackle the burdensome chore that writing has become for me.

In reply to your question: As a young man I would definitely not have wanted any religious ceremony or secular ratification; I would have felt that the question of marriage ought to be a matter of individual conscience. But over the years I have noticed that not everybody has a conscience (or willingness to make use of it). And living together affects not just the lovers but also those who suffer from their mistakes and sins. In some cases, the children who arrive need better protection than that afforded by the consciences of their progenitors. I now realize it's better not to leave the issue of marriage or separation entirely up to the whim of the particular couple.

I'm enclosing a few trifles to amuse you in the sanatorium.

* "Absage" (1933) (*Gedichte*, p. 778).

TO A STUDENT
who has read Beneath the Wheel *and occasionally has suicidal
thoughts*

January 1951

Thanks for your letter; I was as taken with the cheerful, literary
part as with the more serious thoughts. I first sent you a printed letter
pertaining to your problem, just so as not to keep you waiting, and should
now like to respond as personally as I can.

You have two questions. First of all: "What should we do?" I have
no answer to that. I have been a defender of individuality and personality
all my life, and don't believe in the existence of general laws that would
be of any use to the individual. On the contrary, laws and prescriptions
were created not for individuals, but for the many, the herds, peoples,
and collectives. For real personalities, life is certainly tougher, but it
is also more beautiful. Personalities like that cannot bask in the shelter
of the herd, but take pleasure in their own imaginations; if they survive
their adolescent years, they have to shoulder a great deal of responsibility.

Your second question: "How come I never hanged myself as a
seminarian, even though I sometimes longed to do so." I cannot explain
my inactivity; although I had many reasons for going ahead, my throat
simply balked at the rope. Unbeknownst to me, my inner will to live
was stronger than my will to die. Even though I felt hemmed in and
tormented at boarding school and thought my future looked very doubtful,
I was endowed with senses and a soul, was capable of seeing, tasting,
and feeling the sheer beauty and delight of all things, of the stars and
the seasons, the first green in spring, the first golds and reds in the fall,
the taste of an apple, the thought of beautiful girls. Moreover, I wasn't
just a sensuous being, I was also an artist. I could reproduce in my
memory the pictures and experiences made available to me by life, could
play around with them and attempt to turn them into something new of
my own by drawing sketches, humming melodies, writing poems. That
artistic joy and curiosity may have been responsible for my choice of
life over death.

That was my particular case. I'm not sure whether yours is identical,
or even similar. I don't know you and can only hope that your soul also
harbors talents and forces that will come to your aid.

As for hanging oneself, the author of that book about transitoriness
and vanity didn't avail himself of that option, but found so much delight
and secret joy in discerning and describing the fragility of the phenom-

enal world that he was able to go on living and writing. He was no longer a youth, and by the time he wrote the book, he had already thought rationally about the idea of suicide, emptied it of its sentimental content, and told himself dispassionately that suicide would always remain an option for him and everybody else. He could always wait and see whether a rope around his neck would ever seem more appealing than the life ahead of him.

TO ERIKA MANN

May 1951

Because of my gout—*quella puttana maledetta*,* as an old neighbor once called it—I can only use something like two and a half to three fingers, so this scrawl will just have to suffice.

I was glad to get your nice letter, but disturbed by the bad tidings, especially concerning you and your condition.† As for the other atmospheric ills affecting your entire household, although I would give up a lot to see them taken care of, they aren't exactly unexpected, and are offset, to some extent, by the reception now being accorded *The Holy Sinner*. The delighted praise one hears from German readers often sounds like a belated form of compensation for earlier iniquities. We had quite a feast here while Ninon was reading the book to me in the evening; those three pairs of ears in your household must have been buzzing.

Our friend Suhrkamp was here for a week recently, partly to recuperate, partly for some necessary discussions. We talked fondly about your book of reminiscences in memory of Klaus.‡

Otherwise we have been leading a quiet life, often feeling somewhat depressed. My increasing ricketiness and never-ending pains aren't exactly making me any more pleasant, but we both still greatly enjoy reading, listening to music. And we had a festive occasion recently: Our friend Adolf Busch, traveling to Rome with his quartet, interrupted his journey in Lugano, brought the group here, and spent two hours performing quartets by Mozart and Beethoven.

We have visitors again. The wife of our house patron§ is here for

---

* Italian: this damn whore.

† Erika Mann had informed Hesse on April 26, 1951, about her tumor operation and the American "political witch hunt against Thomas Mann, which the Nazis couldn't have waged with greater infamy in 1933."

‡ *Klaus Mann zum Gedächtnis*, with a foreword by Thomas Mann (1950).

§ Elsy Bodmer, the wife of Hesse's patron Dr. Hans Conrad Bodmer.

a week's rest; she is Ninon's best friend, and also a friend of mine, since the days when she was the most beautiful girl in Zurich. Her husband is the patron who had the house in Montagnola built for us.

The response to my article last fall on war psychosis was exactly as you suspected. Some touching responses from people who agreed with me, but they were far outnumbered by the letters of denunciation. That kind of thing hardly affects me anymore, but I am a little hurt by what is happening to the "Glass Bead Game," once my nice, exclusive little property. The extreme nationalists in West Germany are employing it as a term of abuse in their pamphlets and announcements. But this is just something else to be endured and forgotten.

My book of letters, which should have appeared around Easter, is coming out late through my own fault, but it will be here by early summer and a copy will also reach you in Pacific Palisades.

TO OSKAR JANCKE

Montagnola, early June 1951

I'm distressed that you have once again placed me in the unpleasant position of having to decline an invitation.* I have already informed you in some detail about my attitude toward the Academy. That shall have to suffice.

Meanwhile, another matter has underlined my reservations about the Academy.

A few months ago, after I was awarded the Raabe Prize, the journal of the Academy published a protest by Herr von Schulenburg. I don't know what the exact wording was, but I have been able to gauge its import and tone from several letters about the issue which I subsequently received from Germany.

I believe that the protest was raised on the grounds that the Raabe Prize had been awarded to a Swiss. I understand that objection, which has something to be said for it, even though Herr von Schulenburg, who has lived a number of years in Switzerland, may not be the right person to raise the issue.

Apparently, he justified his criticism of the award by attributing to me a statement he had actually fabricated. That is repulsive behavior, which the editors of your periodical ought not to have tolerated.

Moreover, it never seems to have occurred to anybody in the Acad-

---

* Jancke was the founder and director of the Darmstadt Academy.

emy or on the editorial staff of your journal that they should at least have alerted me to the attack. They printed Schulenburg's libelous words, but I only heard about the matter long afterward, from a third party.

As for the German prizes I have received, I never used a single penny of the Goethe or Raabe Prize, and gave the money away as presents to people in Germany. Should I be offered another German prize, I shall turn it down, citing your journal.

You will no doubt understand why this ridiculous Schulenburg affair has further strengthened my prior resolve, which I announced a long time ago, to decline the offer of membership in the Academy.

Thank you very much for the invitation to the Bürgenstock. But I haven't attended any official social occasions in years.

TO PETER SUHRKAMP

June 25 [1951]

My dear friend,
I have been having an odd time with the volume of letters.* I found out from the first review, in the *Neue Zürcher Zeitung*, that the letter on the fear of war does appear in the book, even though I told you and Ninon that you should definitely not include it. Ninon denies vehemently that I ever said anything of the sort; she finds it hard to understand why I feel so embarrassed, but now, in Weber's review and the lines he appended to my reply, this letter has been singled out by the *Neue Zürcher Zeitung* and used as an argument in favor of armaments. Never again, for as long as I have my wits about me, shall I allow my name on any book I haven't edited myself. And while somebody in Zurich is using me to promote rearmament, a section of the Swiss press is conducting a small witch hunt against me, unfortunately in Ticino as well, as though I were a communist, or a fellow traveler at least.

Since winter, since I got back from Baden, my condition has been declining a little every month; life tastes of bile.

Thanks for letting me know about your move!† My doctor has finally given his approval for the Engadine, so we shall travel to Sils during the second part of July, stay there until mid-August, and then go to Bremgarten for ten to fourteen days.

---

* Hesse resisted any publication of his letters for many years. The first selection was published at Ninon's particular initiative, and she selected letters only of a general, not personal nature.
† The Suhrkamp Verlag had moved into new quarters at 53 Schaumainkai in Frankfurt.

PS: I received a letter from a pious old lady, a faithful reader, who commented on my letter to Dr. Weber in the *Neue Zürcher Zeitung* of June 23: "When the person who has broken loose kills his defenseless brother, who shall ensure the continued existence of the divine plan?"

I responded as follows: Ideas like that call for systematic thought rather than a few plausible phrases. What if Abel had surprised Cain and killed him in self-defense, would that in any way salvage the divine plan?

TO HANS CONRAD BODMER

Montagnola, July 2, 1951

My dear friend Bodmer,

Of late, whenever I have gone down to the cellar to fetch a bottle of wine, I have felt depressed, because of various worries and ailments, and also somewhat anxious, because we were running out of wine. But now I'm wealthy again and, thanks to your kind gift, no longer have to feel any trepidation when entering the cellar. I wish to thank you for this present on my seventy-fourth birthday, as well as for the countless others over the years.

Fame, the most acute of my old-age ailments, has become wondrously complex of late; it's assailing me in a novel manner. At the very moment when I was under attack from a section of the daily press, due to certain political misunderstandings—in Ticino as well, unfortunately—I was being deluged with honors. I couldn't accept them, and my refusal may well attract further salvos.

Even though I had already rejected an offer of membership, the West German Academy wanted to make me and some other Swiss corresponding foreign members, and I found it rather difficult to decline the invitation politely. Then the East German press came up with the alarming suggestion that I should be awarded the National Prize. At first, there was no need to say anything.

But in the past few days the East has begun breathing down my neck. The two key figures in East German literature, the president of the East German Academy* and the president of the Cultural Federation,† came to Switzerland for the PEN Club meeting, and called by

* Arnold Zweig, novelist and essayist.
† Johannes R. Becher, Expressionist poet who became Minister of Culture in the German Democratic Republic.

phone to say they would come by to offer me honorary membership in their Academy. Ninon did what she could to ward off the ceremonious double visit and that ominous honor, and acquitted herself very well. Of course, these "honors" from the East don't mean that they hold me in high regard over there.

Then I finally received an agreeable, touching offer: The International Union for Cultural Cooperation wanted to enroll me alongside Albert Schweitzer and Nobel Peace laureate Lord Boyd Orr.* That would certainly have been great company.

So there I was, an old shark swimming in the dull waters of contemporary events, surrounded by bait from East and West, and still refusing to bite.

Goodbye, our fond regards also to your dear wife, Elsy.

TO ERNST MORGENTHALER

[*January 1952*]

My dear friend,

I enjoyed your welcome letter, as I always do, and felt almost vain reading what you wrote about Normalia.† Jean Paul and Kafka are good— better than good—company, and I only feel worthy of them at very rarefied moments.

We greatly enjoyed your account of Thomas Mann and his lecture. As for his appearance and clothing, although I always found him utterly soigné and elegant, I never felt that he was "virtually a fop." He is, besides many other things, the offspring of a Hanseatic patrician household, and either considers a certain decorum a necessity of life or, having been surrounded by it since early childhood, just regards it as self-evident. Wonderful, the way the first words of his lecture canceled the natty impression he had made on you. I never heard him lecture in public, but have heard him addressing a very small group here on a few occasions, and also twice when we met in the Engadine. He speaks exactly as he reads, always pronouncing words extremely carefully, with some mimicry and considerable distance and irony, and his manner is always so jocose and roguish that we would be captivated right away if we hadn't already fallen for him for other reasons. [. . .]

---

* Albert Schweitzer was a candidate for the next Nobel Peace Prize, which he received in 1952; John Orr, Lord Boyd Orr of Brechin, director of the Food and Agriculture Organization of the United Nations, had received the Nobel Peace Prize in 1949.

† Narrative fragment, "A Report from Normalia" (1951; *WA* 8:531ff).

PS: From my answer to a lady in Weddingen (District of Goslar) who finds modern art, especially music, too cold and rational:

". . . Art shouldn't be subject to constraints. The lover of art who doesn't feel at ease when confronted with contemporary art ought not attack it, nor should he force himself to take pleasure in it. Since there are works from approximately three centuries available for our enjoyment, we ought not ask contemporary musicians to renounce their experiments and novel directions, which enrich rather than impoverish art. And if contemporary music occasionally sounds cool and calculated, we ought to keep in mind that it is a reaction against a half century of music that may have been rather too sweet and sensual. (Wagner, Tchaikovsky, Strauss, to name but a few)."

A CIRCULAR LETTER*

July 1952

Dear friends,

A circular letter was never more called for than now; it will have to answer a large portion of the roughly 1,200 letters that I received on the occasion of my seventy-fifth birthday. And I have never had such difficulty sitting down to write. That may be due to old age, the incredible heat wave, all the mail with which I have to contend. In any case, you ought not expect too much from this letter; it's only intended as a thank-you note and brief account of the occasion.

"What one wishes for in youth, one receives in excess as an old man," says Goethe, and it's happening to me too. Some, not all, of my most intense dreams as a boy and adolescent have been fulfilled, some in such "excess" that I now find them embarrassing and distressing. My wildest fantasies as a child never encompassed these presents and honors: a marketplace in my charming little hometown adorned with flags, a concert by the town's musicians, a ceremonial speech, the unveiling of a plaque on the house where I was born (it's often confused with the other childhood house mentioned in many of my stories, which is on the far side of Nagold Bridge), and also congratulations from the mayors of many cities, including ones that named a street after me, congratulations from school classes in Germany and Switzerland, the awarding of honorary titles, festivals—with or without music—in theaters, town halls, schools, speeches by federal presidents, famous writers, professors.

* Published as "Birthday," a circular letter, in the *Neue Zürcher Zeitung* of July 15, 1952.

(*Above*) Ninon Dolbin shortly after first meeting Hesse

(*Below*) With his wife, Ninon

(Above) "*I divide my days between the study and garden work, the latter is intended for meditation and spiritual digestion and thus is usually undertaken in solitude*" —*Letter, 1934*

(Below) Hesse, about 1951

That's not what I had expected or wanted, and whenever I was in a good mood the following thought would occur to me: "All that is missing now is a stone pedestal two meters high and a little ladder; then I could get up there and begin my new life as a monument."

But not all the presents, acclamations, and honors called for such embarrassed jokes on my part. I found the following events delightfully soothing: My eldest granddaughter recited some poems during the largest and most ceremonial birthday celebration; Rudolf Alexander Schröder, a wonderful, greatly esteemed person, delivered the ceremonial address and presented me with a most beautiful watercolor, which he had painted himself; the beautiful edition of the *Complete Works*, put together with great care by my friend Suhrkamp, sold out immediately; I was presented with a few letters written by my grandfather Gundert; many of my friends offered to come here on July 2 to ward off possible intruders; not to mention all those kind, beautiful, and, occasionally, funny letters.

But the whole thing was a bit much. Too many things had arrived from heaven in a downpour; these bountiful blessings overwhelmed my heart and mind. Their very excess proved somewhat burdensome, even frightening, enough to induce a fear of envious gods. And on the morning of my birthday, after the postmen had already come several times, we were somewhat overawed and depressed just standing there in the house, which seemed to have shrunk, since every table and sideboard was laden with flowers and piles of letters, and there were books all over the studio, library, and corridor. We didn't think we could handle the situation and felt we didn't deserve all these presents. At several points we were ready to turn down all the other gifts on their way to us. Then we tore ourselves away from this excess of good fortune, just broke loose, leaving everything lying there, got into the car and drove away, through sweltering Lugano, sweltering Bellinzona, up to sweltering Misox, which I was seeing for the first time. We glanced up at the powerful waterfalls, the castles, and the churches, and although we didn't feel any lessening of the sweltering heat, not even in Mesocco, it was good to see a growing distance between us and that roomful of gifts, which old age bestows in such excess. Two overburdened, exhausted people were transformed into a couple out celebrating a birthday. The car exerted itself, and almost got us as far as the inn, recommended by somebody in Mesocco, before it broke down; the repairs allowed us time for a snack, and the opportunity to begin celebrating the real, private festivity, which we had planned ahead of time. Even though we had rather dishonorably abandoned that menacing excess, a portion of it was with us all along: an elite batch of letters, carefully selected by Ninon. We began reading them after the meal. Oh, such splendid, wonderful, beautiful letters, from Peter the Faithful, Frau Elsy, the lord of the manor in Bremgarten, Alice,* E. Korrodi, and Fritz Strich, and so many others! There was also a letter from a worker in the canton of Solothurn, which read:

> *An open journal*
> *Before my eyes.*
> *I see it says*
> *Your birthday is here.*
>
> *Best wishes for many years*
> *And a sunny life still*
> *From a very ordinary man*
> *With nothing else to give.*

It was quite a while before the convalescent car pulled up outside, and by then we were very much looking forward to the things we had promised ourselves from this trip: a little mountain air, shade, a cool spot. Ninon was undaunted and drove with gusto up the many steep curves; a splendid, fresh breeze was already blowing in our direction from San Giacomo, and soon we were lying in the shade under fir trees. We read as much of that anthology of letters† as we desired, and I would have liked to respond immediately to each of these friends, to thank them, say something nice, and give them an account of our day. This circular letter will have to act as a substitute.

Goodbye, friends, thank you and best regards, yours

TO INA SEIDEL‡

[*Summer 1953*]

It's nice to be able to exchange a few presents from time to time. I felt that your kind letter, the two fine, contemplative poems, and the fine, sad picture addressed me clearly, as a colleague, and I wish to thank you for them. I have also been reading some of H. W. Seidel's letters.§ And I intend to read more.

---

* List: Peter Suhrkamp, Elsy Bodmer, Tilly and Max Wassmer, and Alice Leuthold.

† A special issue of the *Neue Schweizer Rundschau*, Zurich, on the occasion of the seventy-fifth birthday of Hermann Hesse, which consisted largely of letters from Rudolf Alexander Schröder, Thomas Mann, Othmar Schoeck, Ernst Morgenthaler, Otto Basler, and contributions by, among others, Martin Buber, R. J. Humm, Hermann Kasack, Karl Kerényi, Ernst Penzoldt, and Werner Weber.

‡ Poet, novelist, and essayist.

§ *Briefe: 1934–1944.* Seidel was Ina Seidel's cousin; she married him in 1907.

Oh no, so you too are having problems with your hands! I have an advanced form of arthritis, and even though Irgapyrin and vitamins are keeping it in check, it's often unbearable.

This hasn't been a great year for us so far. My wife got back from her third, very strenuous, trip to Hellas in the fall of 1952, but she hasn't fully recovered yet; our household and daily existence are in a bit of a shambles. There are some distractions to lessen our discomfort for a while. A very young fellow from America was here recently; he works in a factory, took a year off to study and learn German, has read many of my things in German, and told us that he translated *Siddhartha* into English. We were taken aback and informed him that an English edition had appeared long ago, but he just laughed and said it didn't matter, he had translated it for his own amusement.

We want to go to the Engadine as soon as possible, even if we have to freeze. But my wife has always recuperated best in the mountains, the higher the better.

Goodbye. I hope the summer brings some fine, delightful experiences your way. That is just what we need, since conditions are as you describe them in your poem "Das Gedicht."*

TO A FRIEND†

End of September 1953

Thanks for your letter and Lehmann's new poem.

Those are certainly two characteristic models of new and old-fashioned poems. Now, that contrast would be all very natural if Lehmann were forty years younger than I, but he's only five or six years my junior.

Your comments about the poem‡ touch on the central issue: Why do we allow an old-fashioned and rather senile poem to take liberties that wouldn't be acceptable in the poem of a younger person? Why aren't the words of this poem marked, to any appreciable extent, by the devaluation that has afflicted poetic language of this kind over the last two generations?

None of us—neither you, I, nor our friends—can resolve that ques-

---

* From the final stanza of the poem: "Long after I have flowed into the vast circulation of oceans / a drop of bitter tears / floods flushing the bottled mail strandward— / Someday a person reading and interpreting these lines."

† Excerpts from the letter appeared as "Correspondence about a poem by Hermann Hesse" in the *Neue Zürcher Zeitung*, January 17, 1954.

‡ "Licht der Frühe" (*Gedichte*, p. 706).

tion. We wouldn't be capable of reading my verse as though I hadn't penned it, as if there weren't a long life and a sizable body of work behind it. But I fear and suspect the following: If we were capable of that, or handed my verse to some reader who is receptive to poetry but never came across my work, then he would judge the poems to be well intentioned, but reactionary and ineffective. They really fail to live up to what is demanded of poetry nowadays, and for a person without any parti pris my words would seem more like inflated money than gold.

Well, we don't have to resolve the issue. What would happen to us, and indeed to philosophy, if instead of striving for truth, we were actually in possession of it?

Writing the last line, I realized that I wasn't saying anything new or original, but simply varying a classical saying of Lessing's. It seems as if I can never escape from the hallowed values and sayings. We just have to accept that . . .

TO H. SADECKI

[Fall 1953]

I cannot say much by way of response, even though I read your letter with the utmost care and sympathy. Thinking of my own experience, I feel that readers have a right to appropriate—or indeed reject—a book as they see fit, a case in point being the varied reactions to *Goldmund*. I received more letters about it than about any other book of mine, with the possible exception of *The Glass Bead Game*. The letters ranged all the way from extreme irritation and annoyance to utterly uncritical enthusiasm. I hadn't looked at the book in some twenty years, but read it recently for a new edition. I describe this renewed acquaintance in a little piece, "Events in the Engadine," which I'm sending to you. It starts on page 31. So, as you can see, my impression upon rereading it was very different from yours. I very much agreed with it. Your opinion differs from mine in one crucial respect: You're a Christian in the sense that, for you, Christianity is unique and represents the only path to salvation. You feel that those who believe in other religions ought to be pitied, since they do not have a Savior and Redeemer. But, in my opinion at least, and judging from what I have seen, this certainly isn't true. The life and death of a Japanese Buddhist monk or of a Hindu who believes in Krishna are as pious, trustful, and confident as those of a Christian. And, moreover, those Eastern religions have something else in their favor: They never produced any Crusades, burnings of heretics, or pogroms against the Jews; that was a specialty of Christianity and Islam. Even a Hitler or a Stalin couldn't surpass the brutality and murderous self-righteousness of certain lines Luther wrote about the Jews. Of course, Jesus isn't to blame for that. But one can love Jesus, yet acknowledge nevertheless that the other paths to salvation, which God has shown to man, are perfectly valid. Enough. I can rarely afford to devote so much time and energy to a single letter.

TO WERNER HASSENPFLUG*

October 1953

Thanks for your letter, which I enjoyed. I'm not "accusing" most Germans—actually, I find their behavior incomprehensible—because certain youthful circles displayed such enthusiasm for an inherently rather good idea promulgated by young National Socialism, but because of what subsequently happened to that idea. One should no longer have to remind Germany that it murdered, raped, and destroyed as a result of the young generation's decision to cast its lot with the Nazis. Even with all the goodwill in the world, one would still have to fault the young generation for failing to see through the diabolic and porcine antics of Hitler, Goebbels, Rosenberg, Streicher, etc., and for tolerating Hitler's stupid, flat speeches and hysterical screeching. After seeing Hitler once and listening to a portion of one of his radio speeches, I figured out what was happening. Obviously, I find nationalism, the hubris of any artificially aroused patriotism, just as silly and dangerous when nations other than the Germans engage in it. But my home is in the German world and the German language, the only place where I could ever have had any impact, since I wasn't allotted the task of preaching to the Americans or Argentinians. Those events haven't been as totally discarded as you seem to think. The ruling class in Bavaria—the ones who raised Hitler and spoiled him—are as cheekily anti-Semitic as ever. Nationalism is certainly "over," which also applies, for instance, to capitalism, but these observations are based on the philosophy of history rather than on history itself—i.e., naked reality. The Nazis still control Bavaria, and the communist nations have to work and starve to feed their bloated commissars, even though capitalism is "over."

I have no desire to start a conflict or become self-righteous; I'm just jotting down the ideas that occurred to me as I read your letter. The letter was worthwhile, I enjoyed it, thank you.

* With a written comment: "Please treat this letter very confidentially. It is intended only for you and isn't adequately formulated for publication."

TO ELSY AND HANS CONRAD BODMER

December 25, 1953

My dear friends,

We celebrated Christmas yesterday with our guest, Frau Anni Carlsson;* it's morning now and soon our midday guests will be arriving: Emmy Ball's daughter with two big children. We're going to serve them goose and a glass of Girsberger '47, and we shall be thinking fondly and gratefully of you, as we did yesterday evening. I thank you heartfeltly for your good, kind presents, for the good wine and the delightful surprise, that anonymous little book by Jacob Burckhardt,† which also deeply impressed Frau Carlsson.

A messenger arrived yesterday evening bearing carnations from a flower shop and a letter from the donor, a Munich reader previously unknown to me. We read it today and, among other things, learned of a grotesque incident: Her first, unhappy marriage was to a lecturer in philosophy. In 1922, she arrived in Lugano with him, as a very young woman, and found out that the writer H. lived in the vicinity. She asked her husband to accompany her to Montagnola. He came along, but then insisted that he had to visit the poet alone, since Hesse obviously couldn't be expected to receive a young woman. And so the silly philosopher sat at my place for half an hour trying to be clever, while his poor wife waited outside, feeling bitter. There are still many professors like that. But now I have to fetch the wine and prepare things for the guests. Regards and thanks from an old and yet ever new friend

TO THE EDITORS OF "DAS VOLK," OLTEN

January 13, 1954

Dear Herr Kräuchli,

I received your package and the letter. There isn't much I can say. If I had answered every attack and insult to which I have ever been subjected by the right and the left, I wouldn't be here now. Moreover, I don't see any way I could possibly respond to the tone adopted by these belligerent Christians of various persuasions. The poem‡ was writ-

---

* A publicist friend of Hesse's, who expanded Hugo Ball's biography of Hesse and edited Hesse's correspondence with Thomas Mann (1968).

† *Ferien: Eine Herbstgabe* (1849).

‡ "Jesus und die Armen" ("Jesus and the Poor") (*Gedichte*, p. 587).

ten in 1929 and has been included in each printing of the collected edition. That should show you the extent to which I stand behind the poem, even though I wouldn't write it today as an old man.

What all my attackers fail to recognize, partly out of stupidity and partly for tactical reasons, is that I myself don't speak in the poem, but lend my voice to the poor and oppressed, for whom I have always had great sympathy and love.

But I have to say a word about your printing of the poem. You know just as well as I do that there is such a thing as intellectual property, which is internationally recognized and protected by law. You printed my poem, the work of a still living author, whom you could easily have contacted, without securing permission or even indicating the source, and have thus committed an offense in both legal and moral terms. If you had asked me for permission to print it—only the price of a post-card—I would have refused permission, since I am aware of the way Catholics and Protestants react to this kind of poetry, and have no desire for scandal and polemics.

TO A GERMAN STUDENT

Excerpt from a letter by a German student to Hesse:
    . . . And now I'm coming to the basic reason for writing to you. The first time I read a book of yours (it was Demian*), I came across many things that I had already experienced myself, more or less unconsciously . . . Naturally, I became more and more interested in your works and read everything I could lay my hands on. I liked* The Glass Bead Game *most of all. Recently, I discussed your works with a good acquaintance of mine, a professor of theology. Naturally, being a representative of the Catholic Church, he took exception to your insistence that one's conscience affords the only guideline for individual behavior. He singled out* Demian *for special condemnation. You write as follows: "One ought not rule out or feel anxious about anything our soul desires. Everybody has to find out for himself what is permissible and what is forbidden—forbidden for him . . ."* The theologian considered this a very dangerous approach, since it *"would justify a form of self-idolatry." Of course, I sprang enthusiastically to your defense, but was unable to convince him. Finally, he said—and I don't know whether he was trying to calm me down or excuse you in his own eyes—that he loves your work nonetheless, and, besides, that you yourself had once stated quite clearly that*

you didn't stand behind your figures (and their opinions), that you had never agreed with these ideas, and, just like Gertrud von Le Fort,* had only wished to create a merciless likeness of modern man while remaining mockingly aloof yourself. Naturally, I didn't believe a word of this, but my acquaintance kept on reiterating that you had once said so yourself.

Dear Herr Hesse, I just cannot—and don't want to—believe that! If your works are not a product of your own inner experience, then that must be even more true in the case of other writers. I entreat you—unless my letter happens to end up in your wastepaper basket— to confirm my convictions . . . I am very confident that I shall hear from you . . .

March 1954

Dear Fräulein,

Well, you have answered your own question, and I must agree with you. If your acquaintance were right, you would be better off laying my books aside for good. I have no reason to doubt his honesty; it's quite possible that I was objecting in some letter or essay to being pegged for the rest of my life to a single utterance of mine. The professor may have come across a passage like that and drawn false conclusions from it. As a representative of his church, he is certainly entitled to reject my ideas and fight against them. I admit that these ideas could be dangerous under certain circumstances. I know it's possible that they might occasionally mislead some weak persons and even lead them to suicide. But the harm caused by my writings and those in a similar vein pales when compared with the impact of the harsh regime in conventional schools, which has caused so many weak young people to fail.

My books were composed without any set goals or agenda. But when I look for a common denominator now, I realize the following: my works, from *Camenzind* to *Steppenwolf* and Josef Knecht† can all be described as a defense (and at times as a cry for help) of personality, of the individual. Each unique individual, with his heredity and possibilities, talents and inclinations, is a gentle, fragile creature; he could certainly do with an advocate. After all, the great, powerful forces are all ranged against him: the state, schools, churches, organizations of every kind, patriots, the orthodox and Catholics in every camp, not to speak of the communists or fascists. My books and I have always had to face all of

---

* Distinguished Catholic novelist.
† *The Glass Bead Game.*

these forces and contend with their methods of combat, which were decent, coarse, or downright brutal. I have repeatedly observed the dangers and hostility that nonconformist individuals have to confront, and realize how much protection, encouragement, and love they really need. It also became apparent in the course of my experiences that there are countless numbers of Christians, communists, and fascists who, regardless of the material advantages and comforts that they enjoy, find that kind of orthodoxy spiritually unsatisfying. And so, in addition to blanket condemnations and attacks by all those groups, I get to hear thousands of questions and confessions from individuals who are more or less baffled, and who get some warmth, comfort, and consolation from my books (and also those of others, of course). They don't always consider those books a source of strength and encouragement, and often feel misled and confused by them. They're accustomed to the language used by the church and state, the language of orthodoxies, catechisms, programs—a language that never acknowledges any doubts and demands only credulity and obedience. I have lots of young readers who get excited for a short while about *Demian, Steppenwolf*, or *Goldmund* but then return gladly to their catechism or their Marx, Lenin, or Hitler. And then there are those who, after reading my books, invoke my name to justify their decision to withdraw from all communal activities and obligations. But I trust that there are also very many others who can take from our work as much as their nature allows. Those readers allow me to act as an advocate for the individual, the soul, the conscience, yet don't treat what I say as if it were some form of catechism, orthodoxy, marching order, and don't jettison the lofty values of community and togetherness. These readers realize that I have no wish to destroy the sense of order and mutual obligations that makes it possible for human beings to live together and that I have no intention of deifying the individual. They sense that I'm actually advocating a form of life in which love, beauty, and order can prevail, a togetherness that does not reduce man to a beast in the herd, but allows him to retain the beauty, dignity, and tragedy of his unique nature. I realize that I have occasionally erred and gone astray, or been excessively passionate, with the result that some words of mine have left a number of young readers confused and endangered. But if you think of the forces nowadays that make it so difficult for individuals to develop a personality of their own and become fully human, when you look at the unimaginative, weak-souled, completely assimilated, purely obedient and co-opted type of person idolized by the large organizations and, above all, by the state, you will find it easier to understand the militant gestures of little Don

Quixote against those large windmills. The battle seems hopeless and nonsensical. A lot of people consider it ridiculous. And yet the struggle must be waged; after all, Don Quixote is as much in the right as the windmills.

TO THEODOR HEUSS*

Pentecost [June 6] 1954

Thank you for your letter of June 3 with the two enclosures, the memorandum about the Pour le Mérite and your 1942 essay "An Areopagus of the Mind."

I was embarrassed at first by your offer of the order,† but have decided to accept it with gratitude, since it signifies both honor and friendship.

I need to let you know briefly how I arrived at this positive decision, which runs counter to my instinctive response.

A very dear guest, my "Japanese" cousin, W. Gundert, left here the morning your letter arrived. I hadn't seen him in twenty-four years, and had invited him so that I could once again meet a relative who has been a friend of mine since childhood. We were comrades as well; my long-standing affection for East Asia had forged a special bond between us. We spent the few days he was here exchanging memories and discussing the literature and wisdom of the East.

When your query about the order arrived, I was still full of Zen Buddhist-like disdain for the goods and honors this world has to offer, and if the letter hadn't come from you personally, I would have responded immediately with a polite no. But I felt that both of us were entitled to a thorough investigation of the issue, which I construed as follows: "Which is more stupid and vain, to accept an honor of this kind or reject it, from the heights of one's esoteric wisdom?"

The question was never resolved. According to the Zen masters, there is no distinction between the vanity of somebody entering the hierarchy and the vanity of a frondeur. So, for an answer, I turned to the Chinese book of oracles, the I Ching. The verdict came to me through the character T'ai; it was clear-cut and, incidentally, also very flattering

---

* Writer, liberal politician, and first president (1949–59) of the Federal Republic.

† Pour le Mérite (Peace category, awarded to foreigners). "A nice thing about it," Hesse wrote at the end of June to his cousin Wilhelm Gundert, "is that the previous recipients include people like Jacob Grimm."

for you, Herr Dr. Heuss. It says such things as: "Heaven and earth unite. . . . The ruler divides and orders the course of heaven and earth, rules and orders the gifts of heaven and earth . . . and thereby assists the people."

I have accepted the judgment of the I Ching and thus accepted your invitation.

My wife also sends her regards. We think of you often here.

TO B.G.

Sils Maria, end of June/early August 1954

Thank you for your letter with the clipping about the poor American on death row. Your letter took a long time to reach me in the Graubünden mountains, and I wouldn't have had time to seek additional information and maybe launch an appeal for help.

But even if it had arrived a little earlier, I might very well have decided against pursuing that course. Your appeal for help is based on the belief that people like me have some say in the raw world of reality. Actually, the opposite is true. Neither European nor American judges like being told what to do by literati and scholars. The most striking recent case was that of Rosenberg, who was executed in America, together with his wife, despite protests from all over the world. Even Eisenhower didn't dare take advantage of his right to grant clemency. So there is always a danger that protests by intellectuals can actually worsen the predicament of those at risk, and the frequency of such protests further diminishes whatever value they may have. Enough. I have said the main thing. By now, Chessman may have atoned for his crime through his death. If so, he has evaded the numerous lifelong torments to which he would have been subjected because of his sad fame and the ravenous sensationalism of the press. May he rest in peace.

TO PETER SUHRKAMP

[End of October 1954]

My dear friend Peter,

When I imagine you sitting there in Frankfurt in your bee's nest,* I realize that I can only partly understand the life in which you're

---

* The publishing house.

enmeshed. Now that I know you're in Oberstdorf,* I often think of you during the day, and can more or less imagine the course of your day.

Nonetheless, I'm only writing to you now: I have been having increasing difficulties writing, and we have also had many visitors, and so much mail each day that my personal affairs have suffered. Then we received notification one day from the forestry office, and a young ranger arrived to inspect our little patch of woods; the chestnuts everywhere are coming down with a fatal illness, and some of our trees are ill. After some negotiations and correspondence, I agreed to cut down virtually all the tall old trees, which—quite apart from the loss—will be worrisome, a lot of bother. And we had barely digested that (they will probably be working away in the woods for weeks) when we had another scare: A neighbor below us has sold his land to a businessman who intends to build four new houses. And since the story wouldn't end there, we're trying to buy the plot of land that would be most harmful to us if it were developed. In short, by our standards, there was a lot going on. Fortunately, old age has made me increasingly indifferent, and the whole thing no longer seems all that real to me. But I feel the encroachment of the city, and all the noise, the cars, the increasing scarcity of breathing room, even in what was, until quite recently, a peaceful rural haven, are part of a general pattern in the world at large; those are the waves, and we old folk just have to succumb; there's no point fighting for those last few breaths of air. The world is right, the old people will doubtlessly have to go, the gardens will be turned into sports stadiums and highways, the air will be ruined by planes and blaring radios. And so on. Pack up, my dear child, and let yourself be buried; your time is long over. And I realize that it isn't even all that easy to get buried. We have been wanting for years to buy ourselves a plot in the cemetery of Sant' Abbondio, but haven't got around to it, and never shall.

Enough now of these tones, O friend . . .

The Frisch, Penzoldt, and Monique† have just arrived, so we have lots of pleasurable reading ahead.

A number of readers have written to me about *Piktor*; some have ascertained the deeper meaning behind the fairy tale and realize it's something else in addition to a fairy tale.‡

---

* In October–November, 1954, Peter Suhrkamp had to undergo treatment again in the Allgäu for his heart and lung complaints.

† New publications by Max Frisch (the novel *Stiller*), Ernst Penzoldt (the story "Squirrel"), and Monique Saint-Hélier (the novel *Der Eisvogel*).

‡ In 1954 Suhrkamp published a facsimile edition of Hesse's tale *Piktor's Metamorphoses* in his own handwriting and with his watercolor illustrations.

I'm not going to inquire about your condition and the cure. There's no need to write from there; I'm glad you're at least being cared for by people who have your best interests at heart and want to prevent you from destroying yourself. I can imagine that you feel dejected occasionally and have macabre thoughts, as is only to be expected. But I hope that you sense that other force, life, in the quiet Konrad and are able to heed the delicate birdsong.

TO MAX RASCHER*

[Early] January 1955

You sent me a large package of books over the holidays, and it's a pleasure to be able to thank you. You have been very kind, and I'm always delighted when you think of me in this way.

They include some splendid and attractive works; purely externally, the covers of some of them look valuable and attractive, especially the study of the painter Bodmer,† and I shall take a good look at them.

But my favorite this time is a modest little book which somehow managed to attract my attention right away. It will be in my hands often. It's the new edition of the Bhagavad-Gita in Ilse Krämer's translation. Whenever I leaf through it, I recall my first serious encounters with the world of India. There was no such thing at that time as a branch of modern scholarship devoted to India, and none of the Upanishads, etc., etc., had been translated. Of course, there was always Oldenberg's book about Buddha,‡ but in the main one had to rely on somewhat suspect sources, such as theosophist publications (Steiner was still with them). They were small booklets, a little like the propagandistic tracts of Pietism, written mostly in bad German, translated from the English. A lot of it was insipid and watered down, but the few great, fundamental Indian ideas nonetheless managed to shimmer through. By far the most beautiful of these tracts was a translation of the Bhagavad-Gita by Franz Hartmann. It was the first genuine Indian work I had come across, and I was greatly impressed.

Leafing through my various German renderings of this noble work, I notice that, although I no longer own that early edition of Hartmann's

* This letter to Hesse's Swiss publisher was printed in *Die Weltwoche*, Zurich, January 7, 1955.
† The Zurich painter Paul Bodmer.
‡ Hermann Oldenberg, *Buddha* (1906).

translation—some truth seeker failed to return it—in its place I have your 1946 edition, along with some other versions. And I realize once again the extent of your firm's efforts over several decades to propagate Indian wisdom. For me, that, together with your furtherance of C. G. Jung's work, ranks as the most important accomplishment among your varied activities as a publisher.

TO RUDOLF PANNWITZ*

January 1955

I rarely receive letters like the one you wrote after reading *The Glass Bead Game*. I was delighted with it, and shall treasure it like a belated and unexpected gift. As an old man I have been inundated with recognition and success—much to my own surprise—but the understanding and praise have come mostly from ordinary readers, whom I couldn't really consider entirely competent, since they were only able to fathom half the complexities in the work. Moreover, they often seized on the work because they felt that it could help them resolve practical issues, and this further diminished the value of any such recognition.

And now your letter brings me the understanding of a superior mind. I know that your mind is superior to mine as regards critical ability and educational breadth, and I also respect you as a poet.

For an old man who basically doesn't wish for anything any longer, this is a noble gift indeed, and I shall remain grateful to you. I'm ashamed that I cannot produce a better reply, but I'm no longer able to do all that much reading and correspondence. I'm satisfied if my hands and eyes manage to do a modest amount of work each day, even though for a long time now none of that work has been devoted to my own production.

Perhaps, as a counter-offering, I can sketch a few memories from the period when the book was conceived, since your letter has brought back vivid recollections of those days.

I had the first glimmerings when I began to think of reincarnation as a manifestation of stability amidst flux, of continuity in tradition, even of intellectual life *tout court*. One day, several years before I began trying to write anything down, I suddenly envisioned an individual life that transcended time: I imagined a person who lives through the great epochs of human history in several reincarnations. As you can see, the series of biographies of Knecht—three historical and one Castalian—is

* Poet and cultural philosopher.

all that remains of that intention. The original plan had also foreseen another biography, transposed into the eighteenth century when there was a blossoming in music. I worked on this piece for almost a year and researched it more thoroughly than all the other biographies of Knecht, but it never worked out, and has remained a fragment.* That eighteenth-century world is exceedingly well known and thoroughly documented, and couldn't be integrated into the more legendary world of Knecht's other vitae.

In the years between that first sketch and the time when I sat down to work in earnest—I was busy with two other projects—the book, which subsequently became *The Glass Bead Game*, hovered before me in ever-changing shapes, now solemn, now cheerful. I had come through a serious crisis in my life and was only tolerably well. Germany and Europe were recuperating from wartime fatigue and were discovering a new joie de vivre. Politically, I was alert and skeptical. I didn't put much stock in the German Republic and the pacific intentions of the Germans, but the prevailing atmosphere of optimism and even contentment helped improve my spirits. I was living in Switzerland, only rarely visited Germany, and for quite some time found it hard to take the Hitler movement seriously. But that sense of contentment vanished when I found out more about the movement and the dangers it posed, after the appearance of the so-called Boxheim document and then when the movement actually came to power. The speeches of Hitler and his ministers, their newspapers and pamphlets, had risen up like poison gas, a wave of dirty tricks, lies, unbridled ambition—the atmosphere was putrid. Faced with all that poison gas, the desecration of the language, and the lack of respect for truth, I realized that I was confronted with an abyss similar to the one I had confronted during the war years; news of the massive atrocities only emerged years later. The atmosphere had again become poisonous; again life itself was at stake. I had to summon up all the positive forces in me; I also had to subject all my convictions to some scrutiny and strengthen them wherever necessary. This new phenomenon was a lot worse than the spectacle of the vain Kaiser and his semi-divine generals. It would presumably result in something worse than the kind of war to which we had grown accustomed. Amidst all these threats and dangers, which jeopardized the physical and intellectual existence of a German-language writer, I resorted to the artist's favored method of escape: I became productive, and returned to that rather old plan, which underwent radical change under the pressure of the circumstances. Two

---

* See "The Fourth Life" in *Tales of Student Life.*

things were important to me: first of all, I had to create an intellectual space, a refuge and a fortress, where I would be able to draw breath, and remain alive, no matter how poisonous the world had become; second, that space would have to convey the intellect's resistance against those barbaric forces and strengthen the resistance and powers of endurance of my friends in Germany.

To create that space, where I hoped to find shelter, strength, and endurance, I would have to do more than just conjure up some past era or other and describe it lovingly, as my earlier plan had more or less anticipated. I would have to defy the unpropitious present circumstances by making that intellectual realm extremely visible and unmistakable. My work could thus become a utopia, the picture was projected into the future, the evil present was relegated to a past that had been overcome. And, to my surprise, the world of Castalia came about as if of its own accord. It did not have to be thought out and constructed. It had taken shape within me, without my knowing it. And so the breathing space I sought was available to me.

I also gave vent to my need to protest against the barbarity. In my first manuscript there were some passages, especially in the section dealing with the pre-history of Castalia, which passionately opposed the dictators and the rape of both life and mind. These combative statements, which were deleted for the most part in the final version, were secretly copied and distributed to others by my German friends. The work first appeared in Switzerland while the war was still on. In an attempt to get permission to publish it in Germany, my publisher there submitted to the German censors a copy in which the most glaring anti-Hitler passages had been deleted, but naturally his request was rejected. Later on, I lost interest in the combative-protest function of my book.

Enough of that! I've simply been dwelling on some memories of the period when I wrote the book, which your letter resuscitated. Look kindly on them.

TO HANS BAYER

[*July 1955*]

[. . .] My relationship to death hasn't changed: I neither hate nor fear it. A closer look at the people I prefer to be around—aside from my wife and sons—would indicate that they're all dead: dead musicians, writers, painters from many centuries. Their essence, condensed in their works, is more present and real to me than that of most of my contemporaries. And the same is true of those whom I have known, loved, and "lost": my parents, sisters, the friends of my youth—they belong as much to me now as they did when alive; I think of them, dream of them, and feel they're part of my everyday life.

My relationship to death isn't just a whim, a nice fantasy; it's real and completely integral to my life. I fully understand the grief that the transience of life can arouse, and am often saddened by the sight of a wilting flower. But it's a sadness without despair. That's all I can say.

TO THOMAS MANN

Hotel Waldhaus, Sils Maria, the Engadine [*August 2, 1955*]
Permit me a short visit to your sickbed. We have often been reminded of you up here, and were really shocked to learn of your illness. Your wife kindly gave us some detailed, reassuring information. I wish you a quick recovery and then a period of well-being, the kind that ensures that one hardly even regrets the attack from which one has recovered so completely.

For us here, the last two days have been overshadowed by a death. Georg Reinhart* in Winterthur and I were close friends; I loved him and prized him, for I knew him not just as a grand seigneur and a man of the world with splendid principles, but also intimately in his private, domestic life, when he was in his prime. He was a man with very unusual gifts, interests, and habits.

So far my holiday reading here at Sils has consisted of the *Letters* of Lessing,† a book I hadn't looked at in decades. What a mind and what a poor, hard life! Just two years before his death, after the appearance of *Nathan*, he writes: "It's possible that *Nathan* wouldn't be very successful, even if somebody were to stage it, but that will probably never happen. It would be sufficient if it gets read with interest and if it causes even one person, among thousands of readers, to doubt the evidence of his religion."

This makes one ashamed of one's spoiled condition, and yet I do not feel that we are living in a better age.

---

* Hesse described his relationship with his patron and friend Georg Reinhart in his memoir "Der schwarze König," in *Gedenkblätter* (Frankfurt, 1984), pp. 234ff.

† Gotthold Ephraim Lessing, author of the play *Nathan the Wise* (1779).

TO FANNY SCHILER

Sils Maria [August 10, 1955]

Thanks for your letter, which reached me in Sils at the same time as a letter from my cousin Wilhelm Gundert in the Black Forest, at Kappel. Ninon set off at a very early hour this morning on a short but arduous journey. A relative of hers, a member of the Romanian delegation at a conference of atomic physicists being held in Geneva, had asked her to meet him there. He never received her letter; the people from Eastern countries are kept under constant surveillance; she had to spend half the night on the telephone, etc., then left today at seven, will get to Geneva around five in the afternoon, be two hours there, then start the return trip immediately, spend the night in Zurich, and be back here with me tomorrow afternoon. I hope everything goes well. The trip will be a nervous strain for her; she has, of late, become very susceptible to stress.

It's very cold here, but occasionally quite beautiful. We've been to some festival-week concerts. And one of the performances was possibly among the best I have ever heard. The Collegium Musicum of Rome (chamber orchestra, very small, with harpsichord) played Vivaldi all evening, including some unknown pieces. Vivaldi is always splendid, but this performance was unbelievably flawless. I have never heard the likes of it from a string ensemble; compared to them that vain fellow in Stuttgart, Münchinger,* is just a beginner. The first solo violin part was played by a different musician each time, so the composition of the group kept on changing somewhat. They were all first-class soloists; every instrument was splendid; the little orchestra was so exact, sensitive, and discriminating that it almost sounded like a single soloist.

Enough. I'm having a difficult time, have a lot of mail, also the proofs of a book;† there are also some acquaintances of ours in the hotel and surrounding area. One of them would interest your husband: a mathematician, Professor Weyl, who was for many years a close colleague and friend of A. Einstein's. Adorno,‡ too, is here—the musicologist who advised Thomas Mann on *Faustus*.

---

* Karl Münchinger, who had been director of the Stuttgart Chamber Orchestra since 1954.
† Proofs of the collection *Beschwörungen: Späte Prosa* (Frankfurt, 1955).
‡ Theodor W. Adorno, philosopher, musicologist, critic.

TO KATIA MANN

Sils Maria, August 1955

Since receiving the terrible news,* I have been thinking, wishing, and worrying about you and our dear, irreplaceable departed. On hearing the news of his death, I felt as empty and lonely as I did when the last of my sisters† died a few years ago. I haven't yet fully registered this loss; I never thought seriously that I would outlive him.

My heart grieves to think of you. In my circles I have never encountered any lifelong companionship as intensive, faithful, and productive as yours.

Everybody who loves him realizes with gratitude and sympathy that, without you, our loyal friend couldn't have lived such an incredibly rich, courageous, great life to an advanced age.

TO H.S.

[Postmarked August 15, 1955]

Thanks for your letter. Life is too short, however, for such disputes.‡ Like many of my readers, you have often acknowledged my need for honesty, but as soon as that honesty begins to affect my readers personally, no matter how remotely, they take offense and become agitated.

I never doubted your convictions or goodwill. But you failed to take kindly to my attempt to correct your rather clumsy expression. You momentarily confused quantity and quality—maybe it was just the actual phrasing; I wanted to rectify the error, but now regret having done so, since I have put you in a bad mood and can no longer express myself with any frankness.

Apparently, you thought I didn't know about the circulation, impact, print runs, etc., of my writings in Germany, and felt bound to enlighten me on such matters. But my information is far more precise than yours, and I am able to assess the print runs and newspaper headlines far more precisely than you can. You still think that quantity is a relevant issue. I'm telling you for the last time that this is not so. The booksellers in Germany may well recommend and promote me, so a lot of people buy

* Thomas Mann, who had just turned eighty, died in the Zurich Cantonal Hospital on August 12, 1955.

† Marulla, Hesse's youngest sister, died at the age of seventy-three on March 17, 1953.

‡ In an earlier letter of August 1955 Hesse had responded to Frau H.S.'s observation that he was currently the "most widely read" writer in Germany.

my books, which accounts for the impressive statistics. But those figures say little about the actual impact of my writing. I have become famous, received prizes, honorary titles, and orders; such labels prove virtually irresistible to the public and the booksellers. It is ten times easier for the latter to sell a book by a Nobel and Goethe Prize winner than a possibly more talented work by a beginner who hasn't yet acquired any such titles or orders.

You're utterly mistaken to assume that my works truly reached these numerous thousands of book buyers and readers, awakened their hearts and consciences, etc. In actual reality, only a very tiny minority of German readers are even remotely inclined to wake up and scrutinize themselves, etc., etc., and I'm in contact with a portion of this minority, through personal or open letters, privately printed material such as the "Letters from Readers,"* etc. I'm trying to preserve and strengthen this tiny minority of truly awakened and affected readers, often at considerable cost to myself. The other readership, reflected in the figures you try to console me with, means absolutely nothing, either to me or objectively speaking; those people devour my books the way they devour best-sellers.

I no longer have the time and energy for a correspondence of this kind. But I made the effort because I knew this would have to be my last letter to you.

TO HANS OPRECHT

End of May 1956

There is no such thing as a "Hesse Foundation for East German Students Fleeing to the West." I have only assisted a small number of people—a few deserving individuals with convictions I consider decent; they have all been victimized by war or terror. Naturally, they include some intellectuals who have fled from the East. Over the past few years, there were four East German teachers and an East German student. The latter still gets 150 marks a month from me; he is in his final semesters. The same amount goes to a West German woman; she is studying Romance languages, is the highly talented daughter of a war widow without means, has studied in Tübingen, Paris, and Munich, and passed all her exams with distinction. So I always have some protégés.

---

* A privately printed piece, "Ein Paar Leserbriefe an H.H.," which had appeared recently (Montagnola, 1955).

TO PETER SUHRKAMP

[*End of August 1956*]

My dear friend,

When I heard the news of Brecht's death,* I thought of you right away. I realize what Brecht has meant to you. I didn't know him, or rather only met him once, in 1933, at the beginning of his period in exile. He and several other refugees from Germany spent an afternoon here;† we talked, among other things, about the book burnings. As a writer, he wasn't as close to me as he was to you, since I have hardly any affinity for drama. But I always loved and admired his poems and stories, from the very beginning until today, and so his death is also a painful loss for me. He was the only real poet among the German Communists, the only one who still had a thorough grounding in literature. [. . .]

TO ERNST MORGENTHALER

[*December 12, 1956*]

My dear friend,

I was surprised and rather depressed to hear of the death of your Bern friend. I never met him, although we did exchange a few letters recently. Of course, I have often heard his wife singing.

Saying goodbye to people and then burying them, part of the burden of old age, gradually increases our intimacy with death. Your note arrived during a week when we have with us the widow of a dear friend; he died suddenly at the age of fifty, was robust and in bloom. But the death of Hans Bodmer was the worst loss of all in this year full of losses.‡ It was strange. We had known each other for decades; it was he who built this house, and I have only lived here as his guest, but we never became intimate friends. He was hampered by a certain awkwardness toward the older, famous person and, in spite of his cordiality, I felt somewhat constrained by his lordly manner and considerable wealth. Then, during our last get-together in the summer of 1955, those constraints vanished

---

* Bertolt Brecht died in East Berlin on August 14, 1956, at the age of fifty-eight.

† The writer Kurt Kläber, editor of the journal *Die Linkskurve*, lived in neighboring Carona. On March 19, 1933, he took his friends Brecht and Bernard von Brentano to visit Hesse in Montagnola.

‡ Hesse's friend and patron Dr. H. C. Bodmer had died on May 28, 1956. See the poem "Nachruf" (*Gedichte*, p. 710).

completely. I was a guest for three days at his country house, and we became such good friends that I even suggested we call each other *Du*. I haven't celebrated friendship in such a fashion for decades. At the time Ninon was about to go to Frankfurt to accept the Peace Prize on my behalf. Since I was somewhat anxious about her, I asked my friend whether he would like to accompany her, and he accepted right away, with obvious delight. So he and his wife assisted Ninon in the Paulskirche and at the receptions, etc. They enjoyed the festivities and were still beaming when they returned, even though my friend was already beginning to feel sick at nighttime. Soon thereafter, the illness took a turn for the worse, and he had to endure months of intense suffering. He died at the end of May.

I'm glad you came across my story in a recent *Zürcher Zeitung*.* It's something completely new, the only worthwhile piece I have done this year. Apart from that—insofar as I'm at all capable of working— I'm being worn out by the daily bustle with which the world honors and devours its famous people.

We're having warm, springlike days, a light foehn is blowing, and a brimstone butterfly occasionally hovers brightly amidst the muted pink and violet of the landscape.

TO CARL SEELIG

[*January 1957*]

I'm finding it increasingly difficult to wield a pen, otherwise I would have written to you immediately after hearing about the death of dear Robert Walser.† I would at least like to take this opportunity to say that you have been on my mind frequently these past few days. All who loved Walser have cause to be grateful to you, but not all will say so. I'm grateful to you for having lit up his solitary life over the course of many years with joy and a glimmer of companionship, for taking care of his work, and for helping to preserve his memory. I'm also grateful for the obituary in the *National-Zeitung*.‡

---

* "Der Trauermarsch," first published in the *Neue Zürcher Zeitung*, December 2, 1956; reprinted in *Gedenkblätter* (Frankfurt, 1984).

† Walser died of a heart attack during a solitary walk in the snow on December 25, 1956.

‡ Carl Seelig, "Am Grab von Robert Walser," in *National-Zeitung*, Basel, January 6, 1957.

POSTCARD TO J. J. SCH.

January 30/31, 1957

I dislike the useless dissection of poetry in the schools. If I haven't managed to express myself adequately in my poem, how could I possibly do any better in countless letters to students and teachers?

Let me say the following about "Steps:"* The poem is part of *The Glass Bead Game*, a book in which the religions and philosophies of India and China play a certain role. In that part of the world, people generally believe in the reincarnation of all beings rather than in the Christian hereafter, with its paradise, purgatory, and hell. I'm quite conversant with that idea, and so is Josef Knecht, the fictive author of the poem. I was indeed thinking of an afterlife or new beginning after death, even though I do not believe in reincarnation in a crude, material form. The religions and mythologies represent an attempt on the part of mankind to convey those inimitable truths in pictures, and your attempt to translate the poem into flat, rational terms will be futile.

TO PETER SUHRKAMP

Sunday [July 11, 1957]

My dear friend,

Your kind, lengthy letter-cum-report arrived yesterday.† I'm utterly amazed by everything you have undertaken and accomplished in the past few days. *Quod Deus bene vertat!*‡

We celebrated July 2 way up on the Gotthard, with sons, daughters-in-law, and grandchildren; we had hired a taxi for the day and were back home shortly after 8 p.m. Our wonderful secretary§ had already sorted out the newly arrived packages and letters, opened some and glanced at them, and all the rooms were full of flowers. We've been battling through the piles of presents and letters ever since; a week later there are still more than 1,000 letters waiting to be read.

* One of Hesse's best-known poems.

† Suhrkamp's letter of July 6, 1957, described the ceremonies in the Liederhalle in Stuttgart celebrating Hesse's eightieth birthday and in Calw and Baden-Baden during the award of the first Hermann Hesse Prize to Martin Walser. In *H. Hesse–Peter Suhrkamp Briefwechsel* (Frankfurt: Suhrkamp, 1967).

‡ Latin: "May God make things turn out well."

§ Carl J. Burckhardt had allowed Hesse to avail himself of his secretary, Frau Henriette Speiser, for a few days.

As happens every summer, Ninon has finally broken down in the great heat and fallen ill; tomorrow is the secretary's last day here. The uncanny saga of the runoff water* around the house continues unabated; we have had earth walls built in front of the house. The architect is finally supposed to arrive on Thursday from Zurich. No doubt there will be a lot of construction going on for weeks, and that will mean having to dig up our driveway, which will be unusable. So you see, the atmosphere isn't particularly festive, many of the flowers are already wilting. [. . .]

Enough. Must get back to the drudgery. But many of the gifts were kind and touching.

TO MAX WASSMER

[*1957*]

A few readers wrote expressing anger at the pamphlet of a young writer who has attacked me for producing romantic kitsch.† They asked how I'm going to respond, and I replied:

A boy on the street sticks out his tongue at an old man and throws a handful of dirt at him.

Will the old man pursue the boy, who can probably run much faster? Or will he contact a lawyer and file a suit against the boy's parents?

He adopts neither course, unless he is uncommonly stupid, and simply says to himself that the left wing of the avant-garde has always greatly enjoyed sticking out its tongue and throwing mud about. He will go home, get his coat cleaned, and resume his activities.

TO MAX BREITHAUPT, DIRECTOR OF STUDIES

January 30, 1958

Thanks for your letter about the talk by Thornton Wilder.‡

I don't agree with everything in the talk either. But my response isn't as negative and passionate as yours. I love Wilder's work and have

---

* "Besides, all hell had broken loose in the house. The cellar was constantly under water, and it became evident that the entire drainage system, which is about 160 meters long, is broken or clogged. They have dug up half the property by now, and the road as well, as much as two meters deep." (From a letter to Otto Engel.)

† Karlheinz Deschner, *Kitsch, Konvention und Kunst: Eine literarische Streitschrift* (1957).

‡ Thornton Wilder was awarded the German book trade's Peace Prize.

a high regard for him, and don't find anything wrong with his decision to avoid voicing the idealistic sentiments that would be pleasing to church and state, and to focus instead on his personal convictions. If contenders for the Frankfurt Peace Prize had to be unobjectionable, believing Christians, Albert Schweitzer and Reinhold Schneider would be the only previous recipients worthy of the award.

No, I approve of Wilder's right to entertain and express those convictions, even though I don't share his touching, childlike belief in the ideals of democracy. The thing I didn't like about his speech was no more than a minor blemish. I felt that, as a representative of the cultural and intellectual life of America, he shouldn't have given the Germans yet another lecture on democracy.

TO HIS SON HEINER ON HIS FIFTIETH BIRTHDAY

[February 1959]

Well, on my fiftieth birthday, Max Wassmer arrived, and we had a festive meal at a small inn in Sorengo. After dinner we climbed up to the Casa Camuzzi, where we continued celebrating; Ninon was there for the first time. That very same day my best friend at the time, Hugo Ball, had an operation in Zurich. They opened him up, saw how hopeless things were, and stitched him together again. It was two months before he died. But on July 2 we hadn't yet grasped the gravity of the situation, and celebrated with chicken, risotto, and lots of wine, then had coffee and cake at my place; Natalina* was there too. Among the presents from Ninon was a Japanese dwarf tree, which looked tiny and comical in its pot; a few years later I planted the little tree in the garden of the new house, where it grew to be immensely strong and stout. That's what comes to mind when I think of you celebrating your fiftieth birthday. I'm sending you my presents together with a thousand good wishes for you and your family. Ciao, my dear!

TO HIS FORMER WIFE, RUTH (HAUSSMANN)

Sils Maria [End of July 1959]

Your letter catches me in the Engadine; I have been here a few days, am staying three to four weeks. I took along Peter Suhrkamp's essays, radio talks, etc., and am supposed to make a selection. It wasn't

---

* Hesse's former housekeeper.

my idea in the first place; Peter's successor at the publishers talked me into it.* I have become completely indifferent to literary matters since the death of Suhrkamp; I just don't feel like being involved anymore.

I understand why you can't look at the pictures of Ticino in Dresden† without becoming nostalgic. But you have to realize that more or less the same thing is happening to me. The fairy-tale Ticino of our good times together exists no longer. Although the prominent features of the landscape have remained the same, and the mountains and valleys are still covered in forests, the villages have turned into small suburbs. Montagnola has three to four times as many houses and inhabitants as it had then; the vineyards and meadows have given way to new houses with little fenced-in gardens and broad cement highways; factories are sprouting in the valleys, etc., etc. Well, that no longer upsets us old people so much, but corruption has naturally also surfaced in this "booming" new era. The farmers around Montagnola have hiked the price of their land to between thirty-five and forty francs a meter; the speculators purchase it, subdivide it, and construct entire developments; the village has an ultramodern post office, two cafés, a newspaper kiosk, etc.

Enough of that. I was delighted to get your kind letter and the wonderful picture of Charles VII, thank you.

TO KURT KARL ROHBRA

[*1960*]

Thanks for your greetings from the mountains.

My first taste of a mountain winter was in Grindelwald in 1902— one of the first winters the Swiss mountain hotels remained open. The book contains the poems I wrote there.‡ Very few skiers were to be seen yet; we enjoyed walking, skating, and tobogganing. I had been sent there on doctor's orders to recuperate after an appendicitis.

In Munich around 1909, my friend Olaf Gulbransson supplied me with my first pair of skis. They were made of ash wood and lasted until around 1928, when one of the skis broke, and I bought new ones in St. Moritz, made of hickory. Until 1931, I used to spend a few weeks every winter skiing in the mountains, but not since then.

* Preparatory work on a little volume of writings by Peter Suhrkamp, which Siegfried Unseld had proposed, and which Hermann Kasack subsequently edited: *Der Leser: Aufsätze und Reden* (1960).

† Ruth and her husband, the actor Erich Haussmann, were living in Dresden.

‡ *Die Gedichte.*

I hope you felt rested when you got home.

I have just thought of something. A good photo of me* was used without my knowledge in a picture postcard series, "The Portrait"; I just happened to come across a copy. If you can find them anywhere, I would be grateful if you could send me some (A. Egger, Publishers, Cologne 10). Things aren't going especially well, but I'm managing somehow.

TO ADOLF GEPRÄGS

January 1960

I read your letter with some astonishment. So you want to set up a Hesse room,† and expect me to fund it, donate the furniture, pictures, etc., etc. You want all this from a person who has never liked personality cults and has only tolerated that kind of thing in his old age, out of a mixture of exhaustion and good-naturedness.

Now that you have described your request in detail—in your first letter you unfortunately neglected to do so—I would advise you that it would be better to abandon your plans for the room. You certainly have no right to expect me to assume this burden; it's absolutely out of the question. As regards the furniture: I don't have a single piece from my parents' house. When there were legacies, etc., I gave everything to my sisters, including money, furniture, pictures, etc. All my sisters are deceased. As far as I know, any material, such as documents, correspondence, etc., in their possession has gone to Marbach, where the Schiller Museum is carefully collecting everything concerning me and my family. But there are also other Hesse collections, which have been around for many years. The Swiss State Library has the largest collection of letters; the library of the Zurich Polytechnic has another large collection.‡ Recently, Herr Kliemann of Munich sold somebody in America§ a large collection of newspaper and privately printed pieces, which he had spent many years collecting, with some assistance from me. There was also a teacher named Weiss in Cologne who established

---

* A picture taken by Martin Hesse.

† Calw, Hesse's birthplace, was planning to transform the Vischers' courtly house in Bischofstrasse into a local museum that would include a Hesse room. This plan, which was subsequently implemented, led to the creation of the present-day Hermann Hesse Museum, the only permanent exhibition in Europe devoted to Hesse.

‡ The collection of Hesse's friends Alice and Fritz Leuthold.

§ In 1959 Professor Joseph Mileck acquired the collection of Horst Kliemann for the University of California, Berkeley.

a Hesse Archive there, entirely on his own initiative; it lasted for many years. Without informing me, he visited all my relatives, friends, and correspondents, soliciting money, books, manuscripts, photos, etc., and then, finally, sold his entire archive to Marbach for 14,000 Deutsche-marks. So, as you can see, you're too late in the day with your plans, and will no doubt understand how utterly disillusioned I am after all these experiences. I regret having to cause you such disappointment.

TO G. WALLIS FIELD*

[*February 10, 1960*]

H. Hesse, who is ill and overworked, dictates the following answer for you:

You can find something on older English literature in my booklet *Library of World Literature*, published by Reclam.

I have the same high esteem for English literature as I have for that of Germany and France. In my younger days I used often to read French. I never understood English well enough to read good literature in the original. My parents and sisters spoke English fluently; we often had English and American visitors in our home. But I only practiced reading a little easy literature, some Mark Twain, some Kipling. I read a considerable amount of English literature in translation; I have loved recent authors such as Hardy, Meredith, Virginia Woolf, Forster, some others.

That's all I can say in reply to your questions.

TO A MUSICIAN†

[*March 1960*]

Some time ago, you sent me a handsome little book by Erich Valentin, *Musica Domestica*.‡ I wish to thank you and the author for the hours of stimulation it has afforded me. What captivated me at once in the first chapter were those often delightfully baroque titles adorning seventeenth-century musical publications. And that brought to mind a classical saying of Anatole France's: No book could interest him more

---

* Professor at the University of Toronto; author of an introductory volume to Hermann Hesse (1970).

† Published in the *Neue Zürcher Zeitung*, April 8, 1960.

‡ E. Valentin, *Musica Domestica: Von Geschichte und Wesen der Hausmusik* (1959).

or give him greater pleasure than the catalogue of a secondhand book-seller. By weaving together scholarship and folksiness, by compressing an enormous mass of knowledge and research into a tight space, while nonetheless managing to get through it, he informs readers with a halfway decent musical education about the history and semantic metamorphoses of such terms as "musica domestica"; he also kindly takes us along on a stroll through the imposing fields of music history and musical inter-pretation; he refers en passant to virtually everything we ever came across in books of that sort. Of course, I was amused and a little flattered by his attempt to highlight and upgrade the role of listener vis-à-vis that of musician: the musically incompetent amateur lying on the sofa lis-tening to the radio or record player is ennobled as a collaborator and connoisseur. Some people will be pleased to hear this—with varying degrees of justification. Encouraged by my enhanced status, I shall attempt, at a later point, to describe something beautiful I heard on the radio.

Of course, it was only in old age that I began listening to the radio, and when I think back on my musical experiences, I see that the plea-sures of broadcast or canned music are not all that significant; they didn't make me a music lover or, in some areas, even a demi-connoisseur. No, before I began lapping up music all alone in my room, I spent decades attending hundreds of public concerts, operas, festivals, and solemn performances of church music in the "proper," venerable places—that is, concert halls, theaters, and churches—amid a congre-gation of like-minded and similarly receptive souls, whose faces were attentive yet lost in contemplation, full of reverent devotion, illuminated from within, in a manner that reflects the beauty of their perceptions, and, for several measures, I paid them as much attention as the music. For decades I haven't been able to listen to the final chorus of *St. John's Passion* without recalling a performance in the Zurich Concert Hall under the direction of Andreä.* Sitting on the chair in front of me was an elderly lady whom I had hardly noticed during the concert. The last chorus had died away, and the congregation was beginning to leave, Volkmar was laying down his baton, and I, too, was taking my leave and preparing to return to the secular world, with feelings of reluctance and regret—something that happens frequently to me on such occa-sions—when the old lady in front arose slowly, stood there for a moment before leaving, and when she turned her head a little to one side, I could see tear after tear coursing across her cheeks.

* Hesse's friend Volkmar Andreä, composer and director of the Zurich Conservatory.

My eyes and ears did more than glance at, and feast on, my neighboring worshippers: my eyes witnessed the solemn, sprightly, or tempestuous motions of the strings, the energetic parallel motions of the violin bows, the heavy sawing of the basses. I observed the director and the soloists, who were often close friends of mine. Those friendships and encounters with composers, directors, virtuosi, male and female singers were an indispensable part of my musical life and musical education, and whenever I recall particularly striking concerts in the festival hall or church, I not only hear the music again and sense the special atmosphere and temperature of those houses, but also see the touching apparition of Dinu Lipatti, and elegant Paderewski, versatile Sarasate, also the blazing eyes of Schoeck, the casual, lordly manner of Richard Strauss, the fanatical style of Toscanini, the nervous style of Furtwängler; I see Busoni's wonderful face sunk in raptures over the keys, see Philippi in a vestal oratorio pose, Durigo with her eyes wide open at the conclusion of the "Lied von der Erde," Edwin Fischer's sturdy childlike head, Hans Huber's sharp, gypsylike profile, Fritz Brun's beautiful, wide arm movements executing a movement in andante, and twenty or a hundred other noble and wonderful figures, faces, and gestures. None of this comes across on the radio, and I only know about television from hearsay.

I would like to jot down some brief notes on two passages in Valentin's book, so you can pass them along to the author. In one passage he quotes Mörike as hearing "Strauss" sing. The Strauss in question was undoubtedly the famous opera singer Agnese Schebest, who was unhappily married to D. F. Strauss, the even more famous author of *The Life of Jesus*. The correspondence between Strauss and Fr. Th. Vischer tells that heartrending tale, with greater accuracy than one might find desirable.

The other passage I would like to comment on, and correct as well, concerns my friend and patron H. C. Bodmer. Valentin states: "The Zurich physician H. C. Bodmer was a Beethoven specialist." That's inadequate and somewhat incorrect. My friend Bodmer wasn't a physician nor was he a specialist of any kind. It's true that he started studying medicine at the age of thirty-six, and took all the tests including the doctoral exam, but he never practiced. He had studied music in his youth and would probably have most liked to be a director; he was friends all his life with a great many significant musicians and became a musical Maecenas on a grand scale. Over the decades he built up one of the largest and most valuable Beethoven collections, which, in keeping with his characteristically regal generosity, he donated to the Beethoven Archive in Bonn. But his horizons were far broader than those of a specialist, and even though he reserved his greatest love and enthusiasm for Beethoven, he also had a thorough grasp of later music history, and loved several contemporaries deeply, Mahler in particular.

But I promised to tell you about my wonderful radio experience.

It was an evening of Chopin, performed by a Chinese named Fou Tsong. I had never heard his name before and still know nothing about his age, schooling, or other personal data. The program was beautiful, and I was naturally enthralled by the wondrous prospect of hearing the great love of my youth, Chopin, performed by none other than a Chinese. I have heard the elder Paderewski, the child prodigy Raoul Koschalski, Edwin Fischer, Lipatti, Cortot, and many other great pianists playing Chopin. The style varied considerably: cool but correct, melodious, animated, or moody and idiosyncratic, some emphasizing the rich timbre, others the rhythm, pious here, frivolous there, some anxious, others cheerful; although the performances were often extremely beautiful, they seldom corresponded to my notion of how Chopin ought to be played. Of course, I was convinced, naturally, that this ideal method corresponded to Chopin's own style as a performer. And I would have given a lot to hear A. Gide playing one of the ballades. As a pianist, Gide had worked intensively on Chopin all his life.

Well, the unknown Chinese gained my respect in the first few minutes, and acquired my love soon thereafter; he was utterly equal to the challenge. I had unwittingly expected the highest degree of technical perfection—one takes that for granted in view of Chinese perseverance and ingenuity. His virtuoso, technical perfection couldn't have been surpassed by Cortot or Rubinstein. But that wasn't all. I wasn't just hearing a masterly performance, but rather Chopin, the real Chopin. It brought to mind Warsaw and Paris, the Paris of Heinrich Heine and the young Liszt. There was a fragrance of violets, rain in Mallorca, and exclusive salons; the sound was both melancholic and courtly, and the rhythmic differentiation and dynamics were of equal sensitivity. It was a miracle.

But I would have liked to see that highly talented Chinese with my own eyes. Perhaps his bearing, gestures, and face would have answered a question that had occurred to me after the program: Has this highly gifted individual arrived at an inner understanding of this European, Polish, Parisian music, with all its melancholia and skepticism, or is there a teacher, colleague, master, or model whose music he has learned by heart and is now imitating down to the last detail? I would like to hear him playing the same program again repeatedly, on several different days. If everything was genuine and priceless, if Fou Tsong was truly the musician I felt inclined to see in him, then each new performance would constitute something new, unique, and individual—even if only noticeable in small details—and wouldn't merely replay an extremely beautiful record.

Well, maybe an answer will be forthcoming someday. The thought hadn't disturbed me during the concert, only afterward. And as I listened to him, I almost glimpsed for a few moments the man from the East, not the real Fou Tsong, of course, but a creature I myself had imagined, created, and conjured up. He resembled a figure from Chuang-tze or the Kin Ku Ki Kwan, and I felt that, as it played, his hand became the same kind of eerily sovereign, utterly relaxed, and devout instrument, under the guidance of the Tao, that allowed the painters of ancient China to get their brushes close to what in a happy moment can be intuitively apprehended as the meaning of the world and of life itself.

TO OTTO ENGEL

[*October 1960*]

You deserve a lot of credit for having written this good and, ultimately, consoling letter while still in the throes of severe suffering.

I tend to shrug off the abuse and mockery that the young literary roughnecks occasionally fling at me. People are more cruel as youngsters than they are later in life, and in the past I myself have poked fun mercilessly at several venerable figures, although not in public. In such cases, Meng Hsiä* says: "Child throws dirt at old fellow. Old fellow brushes off his coat." And, of course, there is some truth in the avant-garde's critique: I have always tried to find a decent form for my work, and have also employed artistic practices that merely heed a spirit of play, but on the whole I considered the what as important as the how, a horrific notion to any pure artist, whether he swears by Mallarmé, George, or the Surrealists. In addition to a love of play and the usual artistic ambition, I have always had other concerns, which could be called religious, psychoanalytic, whatever—and at an early stage I sensed the atmosphere of decline in the West, and since I didn't always manage to keep my head stuck in the sand, I often felt drawn toward the wisdom and doctrines that we inherited from the ancients and the Orient.

---

* A kind of pseudonym or Chinese mask Hesse assumed in his latter years when he wanted to convey a special message. Meng Hsiä means "dream writer."

Your letter is the fruit of a severe illness, from which you haven't yet recovered, and this lends weight to the courageous statement of your beliefs. Like all who are enlightened, you accept the Buddha's doctrine that suffering is a central part of life, but what you find lacking in him is any reference to the delicate effect of beauty and joy on the fabric of existence. Indian scholars of Buddhism would laugh at that idea, but I couldn't agree with you more, since I'm of the same opinion myself: "One shouldn't reject anything in life, even its delightful blessings." We children like to hear that.

May you persevere, and may life shine on you again!

Ninon is spending fourteen days in Paris, and will be seeing Carlo Isenberg's daughter, who is now a fine scholar in Romance languages.

GREETINGS TO A HESSE FESTIVAL IN PRETORIA*

[*June 1961*]

I haven't been able to accede to Herr Etzel's† request for tape-recorded greetings addressed to the participants and audience at the Hesse Festival. One of the scourges afflicting me in old age is having to contend with a certain impediment in my voice and speaking ability. But I would certainly like to convey my heartfelt greetings to those present. What I find especially pleasing about the honor accorded me is the honor conferred thereby on the German language. The dear German language has been my fond comrade and solace in life, my greatest treasure, together with its great works, which range from the *Song of the Nibelungs* through Luther and Goethe to the present. As a language, it is rich, elastic, powerful, playful, moody, and frequently irregular; strongly musical, animated, and humorous. At any celebrations in honor of works or writers in this language, the language itself should get most of the credit. We writers are indeed helping to build up and refine the language, but even the contributions made by the greatest writers are as nothing when compared to what the language gives us and means to us. These words are intended as a reminder of this.

---

* Under the honorary chairmanship of Theodor Heuss on October 20, 1961.

† Tilbert Etzel, chairman of the German Club in Pretoria, South Africa.

TO HIS SONS

June 1961

We had to renew my contract with Suhrkamp, which had expired, and have inserted a few minor changes. The following provision is important for you: After my death, Ninon will assume responsibility for negotiating with the publishers. She understands my thoughts and wishes regarding the future of my works, and will advise the publishers on such matters. My sons need only concern themselves with these matters after Ninon's death. Since there are three of you and the publishers cannot discuss whatever controversial issues arise with each of you separately, you should assign the power of attorney to one of you for negotiations with the publishers.

Ninon will carry out my wishes as long as she is still alive. Rather than making any provision beyond that point, I wish to leave any eventual decisions up to you. For instance, I have never allowed any of my books to be turned into a film. If this question should ever arise again, you're free to arrive at your own decision. Thus if somebody should come with a film offer when you're experiencing financial difficulties, there isn't any prohibition on my part. In that case, just do what you think is right; you can have total confidence in Dr. Unseld, Suhrkamp's successor.

TO RUDOLF KAYSER

Sils Maria [August 12, 1961]

Thanks for your letter. I have had a lot of contact and correspondence with Israel, also with Buber. My relationship to Germany is similar to yours. In my case the "emigration" occurred before the first war, in 1912, and ever since then I have been living in Switzerland, which was my homeland as a child. I was last in Germany about twenty-six years ago. I would have liked to revisit the haunts of my childhood, but first the Nazis came along, and then bombs demolished almost everything that I cherished. I found Germany after 1945 far more alien and unappealing than the Germany of 1912, even with its Kaiser, generals, and gleaming weaponry.

TO ERIKA MANN

[*October 4, 1961*]

It's been a few weeks since your kind letter, and I was reminded of this by Klaus's anniversary* and Kantorovicz's radio program (Heinrich and Thomas).† Many things came to mind as I was reading your father's letters to Heinrich,‡ especially those from his youth. I believe your father's first visit to Florence coincided with mine; we must have strolled through the same Gothic alleys without having any idea of each other. I lived on the third floor above the Piazza Signoria, and could see the Loggia dei Lanzi§ and the place where Savonarola's funeral pile had stood. I went carousing in Lapi's tavern.

Kantorovicz seems a nice man; his account of the "brotherly row" speaks highly in his favor. He would like to call on me sometime, and I shall indeed see him, whereas I don't regret not having received Becher,‖ etc.

Tomorrow I'm expecting my Japanese cousin, whom you know from my circular letters. I am looking forward to a few evenings suffused with an Eastern atmosphere, Zen Buddhist discussions; that to me is like a bath or fresh air. My condition is seriously out of whack, but I have more of a right to be that way than you have, at merely fifty years of age. I'm greatly saddened to hear that you aren't feeling well, but I have much faith in your nature; my wishes are with you.

December 1961

You already know what this letter is about: Volume One of the letters,** of course, which I received a few days ago. I have been dipping into it several times a day, initially in a rather unsystematic manner. First I read your good, fine foreword, and thought about what you said. Had you devoted your eventful life solely to the cultivation of his memory, the world—and indeed posterity—would have reason to feel grateful to you.

I shall spend a lot more time with the book, and am glad to have lived to witness its appearance.

This first glance has confirmed many things that I have previously

---

* Klaus Mann would have been fifty-five years old on November 18, 1961.
† Alfred Kantorovicz, *Heinrich und Thomas Mann* (1956).
‡ *Thomas Mann, Briefe 1889–1936*, ed. by Erika Mann (1961).
§ Fourteenth-century arched hall used for public meetings and festivities.
‖ Johannes R. Becher, Minister of Cultural Affairs of the German Democratic Republic.
** *Thomas Mann, Briefe 1889–1936*, ed. Erika Mann (1961).

noted when comparing Th.M. and myself. The differences, indeed utter contrasts, are clear enough: northern and southern German, the urbanite and the man from the country, etc., etc. But, at present, I'm more conscious of the similarities and affinities, especially the gentleness, sensitivity, and feeling of being exposed to danger—those tendencies are present in both of us, but the evidence suggests that they diminished and eventually disappeared as we got older.

I discover with delight the sovereign, at times ceremonial, at times hidden, mocking politeness which served as his armor against the coarseness and crudity of the world. He is splendid at that, often very much the Royal Highness, often a rascal-like mocker, with his soul always covered and protected by means of roles and masks.

I am concerned about your well-being. Please convey best regards from both of us to your family, especially to your esteemed dear mother.

TO WERNER WEBER

December 19, 1961, at night

I'm fighting the flu, and am having some difficulty shaking it off, because something else is depriving me of my sleep. I'm referring to the review of Thomas Mann's letters, which doesn't reflect well on the newspaper or the reviewer.* It isn't all that difficult to ascertain what a fine, significant book it is and then do it justice. And the reviewer did just that. But then, instead of saying a word or two to thank the person without whom this book—which was assembled with uncommon devotion—wouldn't even exist, he nags, abuses, even spits at the editor out of sheer personal animosity. It's sad to see him mimick a sadistic teacher grilling a hated student and then come up with numerous farfetched reasons for his criticism, carping, and downgrading of the book. He even welcomes each missing comma—actually the responsibility of the publishers and editors—because that allows him to give the author's daughter yet another slap in the face. His hatred is transparent, and the piece will prove more damaging to him than to the editor. Besides, it's easy to disprove nine-tenths of his allegations against Erika Mann. Not a single accusation is truly significant.

It's no secret that Erika Mann has a talent for behaving in a passionate, embattled manner that leaves her exposed to the enemies she

* Carl Helbling's review of *Thomas Mann, Briefe 1889–1936*, in the *Neue Zürcher Zeitung*, December 17, 1961.

creates so easily. But there is no trace of that in this work of devotion. And people in Zurich realize that, during the Pfeffermühle* era, there was another very active opposing party,† of which the reviewer was a loyal adherent. He hasn't felt bound to revise his views over the decades nor has he learned how to control his hatred.

TO KURT KARL ROHBRA

[July 1962]

My dear assistant in Lübeck,

I owe you a short report on the festivities before sitting down with my wife to tackle the nine thousand or so letters and cables that my birthday has elicited.

Something else was going on besides my birthday: Montagnola made me an honorary citizen; two receptions were held, complete with music, speeches, food service, etc., which made us somewhat apprehensive, since we were both ill and accustomed to our peace and quiet. But the whole thing was very cheerful and went off nicely; the doctor assisted me with some shots, and my wife had a relative here for a few days to help out.

The musicians turned up on Saturday evening, a brass band of some twenty-two men; they stood in front of the house and played for about an hour, with a few interruptions for wine. The music was naïve, but the performance itself was impeccable. I listened to about half of it, spoke to some of the musicians, gave a little speech in Italian expressing my gratitude, and withdrew. There was a bench in the garage covered with glasses, which we had borrowed from the hotel, and many bottles of wine, though they barely sufficed. On Sunday morning the atmosphere was more formal: presentation of the scroll before the mayor, town council, representatives of various agencies, clubs, etc.; there were speeches, wine, and bread rolls in the library. Then, in the evening, the whole thing was repeated on the radio. And still missing is an account of July 2, which we celebrated in Faido with an opulent and festive meal provided by the proprietor of the castle, Max, but paper and time are running out—more anon!

---

* A cabaret opposing National Socialism, founded in Munich in 1933 by Klaus Mann, Erika Mann, and Therese Giehse.

† The National Front, adherents of Hitler.

TO GERTRUD VON LE FORT

[July/August 1962]

Very few of the almost one thousand letters in honor of this festive occasion were as delightful as yours. I listened with grateful pleasure as my wife read it aloud, and now I'm reading it myself.

It didn't find me in the "good health" you had wished for; I was quite ill all winter, and have been very weak and anemic ever since, but usually in good spirits; I enjoy reading and music, and my eighty-fifth birthday party was a very wonderful, cheerful affair: a festive meal in Faido, with my two sons and their wives, the mistress of the hilltop, my doctor, and, above all, the proprietor of the castle, Max von Bremgarten, who hosted and organized the occasion, which included a Mozart performance by a good string quartet from Bern. We spent about five hours together, and then I drove home with Ninon and the other guests, northward over the Gotthard.

Since then, of course, I have had three blood transfusions, and spent as many hours as I could clearing away the mail; we aren't yet done. There were many kind, wonderful letters, including two from maids in my first household, who were sending regards after fifty, sixty years.

I hope your condition has since improved. Brother Body can pester us like an irksome relative. Of course, "overcoming the world" is not a state, but a process, or struggle, and one doesn't always emerge on top.

SELECTED BIBLIOGRAPHY
OF HERMANN HESSE'S WORKS
IN AMERICAN TRANSLATION

(Unless otherwise indicated, published in New York by Farrar, Straus and Giroux.

Most translations have been frequently reprinted and reissued in paperback.)

Autobiographical Writings. Ed., and with an introduction, by Theodore Ziolkowski. Trans. Denver Lindley. 1972.

Beneath the Wheel. Trans. Michael Roloff. 1968.

Crisis: Pages from a Diary. Trans. Ralph Manheim. 1975.

Demian. Trans. Michael Roloff and Michael Lebeck. New York: Harper & Row, 1965.

Gertrude. Trans. Hilda Rosner. 1969.

The Glass Bead Game. Trans. Richard and Clara Winston. New York: Holt, Rinehart & Winston, 1969.

The Hesse-Mann Letters: The Correspondence of Hermann Hesse and Thomas Mann. Trans. Ralph Manheim. New York: Harper & Row, 1975.

Hours in the Garden and Other Poems. Trans. Rika Lesser. 1979.

If the War Goes On . . . Reflections on War and Politics. Trans. Ralph Manheim. 1971.

The Journey to the East. Trans. Hilda Rosner. 1968.

Knulp. Trans. Ralph Manheim. 1971.

Klingsor's Last Summer. Trans. Richard and Clara Winston. 1970.

My Belief: Essays on Life and Art. Ed., and with an introduction, by Theodore Ziolkowski. Trans. Denver Lindley and Ralph Manheim. 1974.

Narcissus and Goldmund. Trans. Ursule Molinaro. 1968.

Peter Camenzind. Trans. Michael Roloff. 1969.

Pictor's Metamorphoses and Other Fantasies. Ed., and with an introduction, by Theodore Ziolkowski. Trans. Rika Lesser. 1982.

Poems. Trans. James Wright. 1970.

Reflections. Selected from Hesse's books and letters by Volker Michels. Trans. Ralph Manheim. 1974.

Rosshalde. Trans. Ralph Manheim. 1970.

Siddhartha. Trans. Hilda Rosner. New York: New Directions, 1951.

Steppenwolf. Trans. Basil Creighton (1929); rev. Joseph Mileck and Horst Frenz. New York: Holt, Rinehart & Winston, 1963.

Stories of Five Decades. Ed., and with an introduction, by Theodore

Ziolkowski. Trans. Ralph Manheim and Denver Lindley. 1972.
Strange News from Another Star and Other Tales. Trans. Denver Lindley. 1972.
Tales of Student Life. Ed., and with an introduction, by Theodore Ziolkowski. Trans. Ralph Manheim. 1976.
Wandering: Notes and Sketches. Trans. James Wright. 1972.

All references to Hesse's works in German by volume and page refer to the twelve-volume *Werkausgabe*: Hermann Hesse, *Gesammelte Werke in zwölf Bänden*, Frankfurt am Main: Suhrkamp Verlag, 1970.

INDEX